The Apprentice Tattoo

Guardians of the Circles: Book One

D J Eastwood

Copyright © 2020 by D J Eastwood

All rights reserved. This book or any portion thereof
may not be reproduced or used in any manner whatsoever
without the express written permission of the publisher
except for the use of brief quotations in a book review.

First Printing, 2020

ISBN: 979 - 8577153496

www.apprenticetattoo.co.uk

Map created by Dewi Hargreaves

Cover photo: Andrew Bennett

This book is dedicated to all those who have believed in me and my story. You are the reason this book exists.

THE GREAT ISLAND

The Long Islands
- CLASSAC
- Cheel People
- SHORE CLAN
- *Atay Clans*
- *Doran Clans*
- *Canna People*
- The Great Forested Isle
- Manu's Isle
- *Uru Tribe*
- Outlaws
- RIVER CLAN
- CAVE OF THE EARTH SPIRIT
- *Cambay Clans*
- TWISTING WINDS
- *Poan Lands*
- *Ammen Tribe*
- *Yofa People*
- *Danna Tribe*
- STANNA
- BAY CLAN
- BEACH CLAN
- *Lands of the Frass*

Prologue.

The old man was wheezing by the time he got to the top of the hill. Once he'd caught his breath, he reached into the crevice in the great rock and pulled out the faded red bundle. He unwrapped the cloth and pulled a necklace from the crumbling birch bark wrapping. The dawn light reflected through the yellow beads, illuminating an insect within, caught forever in its death throes.

He reached to place the cord around his neck, then paused. The sun breached the horizon, and the distant hills blazed with fire. With a shake of his head, he wrapped the beads again, placed them in his pouch, and hurried back to the village.

Chapter 1

The stench of the deer hide seared Col's nose as he entered. He'd have to finish curing it that day. He kicked it outside, liberating a cloud of flies. Pushing the roundhouse door closed, he hung the filled waterskin on its peg.

At the hearth, he took a half-burned stick to stir the grey ashes. Red showed, and he smiled. Now he wouldn't have to get the fire-bow to start it anew.

He piled dried moss on the embers and lay down to blow into the faint glow. He added wood chips as flames climbed, then twigs. The sweet smell of birch sap filled the air as the charred remains of yesterday's firewood caught alight.

The reedy voice from behind him made him jump.

"Fetch me water."

Albyn, the old spirit messenger, was struggling to sit up in bed, fingers pushing the hair from his face. Col ran to the water skin, filling a wooden cup. He returned to his master.

"Good morning, Spirit Messenger," he said, bowing his head.

"Good morning, boy," the old man said, sipping the water. He set the cup down and stretched his arms, joints cracking.

"Shoes, shoes," he called. Col fetched the worn moccasins from beside the fire.

Taking the arm he offered, the old man pulled himself to his feet.

"Tea," he said, "Meadowsweet tea," as he hobbled outside to relieve himself. Col smiled at the terse commands as he pulled stones from the fire to heat water.

* * *

Col wandered along the riverbank, gathering Coltsfoot leaves, dropping them into the basket. Good for sore throats, he remembered.

"Well, well, it's the Messenger's pet." Col spun around. Art, the son of the Clan leader, and Sil, his perpetual companion, stood blocking the path.

"I'm his apprentice," Col said, as he cast about for an escape route.

"You're a cripple, the old man keeps you out of pity," Art said.

Col glanced down at his leg, the scar was no longer red and raised; the bone knitted back together, so Albyn said.

"I am gathering healing herbs, for Messenger Albyn."

"Really?" said Art, shoving Col, "Then perhaps you're his slave?"

"Yeah, his slave," added Sil, shoving him too.

Col's left leg gave way, and he staggered back. "Leave me alone."

Art leant towards him. "Or what?"

Col grabbed the open basket and ran. Cries of *cripple* echoed in his ears as he limped along the pebbled riverside, up the bank to the village. Their laughter still in his head as he slammed the roundhouse door.

"Why are you running?" Albyn asked.

Col wiped a tear from his cheek and rubbed his aching thigh. "Just exercising my leg."

"Let me see," the old man said. Col moved closer, untying his leggings. Albyn's warm fingers traced the scar, his eyes closed, concentrating.

Col had been with his father, collecting gulls' eggs on the cliffs. Father liked to do these things. He'd take them back to the village, distributing them to everyone, always starting with the widows, the old.

He had reached too far and fallen. Col had watched his body tumble down the steep cliff, bouncing at the base, a halo of blood flowering against the black rock. He was trying to reach his father, tears clouding his eyes, when he lost his balance, falling onto a narrow ledge. He'd woken up in the Messenger's roundhouse, his leg in agony. He still carried the hollow in his chest, from when they'd told him his father was dead.

"Exercise is good," Albyn said, startling him from his memory, "The bone and skin are healed." Col reached for the basket. "What have you got?" Albyn asked.

"Coltsfoot."

The spirit messenger peered inside. "Is this what you've spent the entire morning gathering? Hang it to dry, we'll need that and more come the winter."

* * *

Col had just finished hanging the herbs high in the roof timbers when there was a disturbance outside.

"What's that?" Albyn asked.

From the door, Col could peer down through the village. Six figures were walking along the path, their clothing dark and plain. "Visitors," he said, turning back towards Albyn.

"Who?"

Col shrugged. "I don't know."

"Find out, boy!" the old man said.

Outside he found Geth, the old song keeper. She laid down the basket she was weaving, craning her neck to see the small group entering the village. Col watched as each one bowed and touched the ancient bull's skull that hung from a post beside the track.

"Who are they?" Col asked.

"Tribe of the South, it looks like," she said, "Tell the old man their spirit messenger is with them."

Col almost ran into Albyn as he entered the house.

"Fetch my swan feather cloak," he said, fastening on a necklace.

"You knew?"

"The spirits told me. Get my staff and my remedy bag, Boy!"

Col had seen these meetings before, they weren't about greeting the visitors; they were about status. Albyn stood, his face impassive. The intricate tattoos around his right eye told of his power, his wisdom. He looked down his beak-like nose as a couple detached themselves from the group and approached.

The leading figure was short, his dark hair thinning. His clothes were plain compared to the Hill Clan, his cape decorated with only a few swan feathers. A lean dog trailed at his heel.

The second figure wore a dark cloak, head lost in the hood.

"I am Harag, Spirit Messenger of the Island Clan of the Tribe of the South. Plant Keeper and Lore Keeper of my people," the man said, holding his hands out, palms up, in greeting. Col studied the visitor's face. Two simple zigzag lines on the forehead and an eye on his cheek were the only tattoos.

The old man nodded. "I am Albyn, Spirit Messenger of the Hill Clan of the Tribe of the West, guardian of the great stones of Classac, Plant Master, Lore Master and Healer of my people. I welcome you, Harag."

The visitor bowed his head, then sat at the feet of the older man, a sign of his lower status. He lashed out at the figure beside him. "Sit. Idiot." The second figure sat, hands folded in their lap—small, pale hands.

Col waited for the old man to invite the visitors into the house, but Albyn extended no such welcome. He sat opposite Harag, gave a shrill whistle, and turned his head as a wren alighted on his shoulder.

Harag stared, recovering to drag the reluctant dog to his side, pushing it into a sitting position.

"Fetch water for our guests," the old man said. Col ran to retrieve the water skin and wooden cups. He handed a cup to Harag, filling it, then moving to the hooded figure. A white hand reached up, pulling the hood back. Col gasped, almost dropping the water. The girl before him could only be a spirit. Her hair was long and straight, white as milk. Her skin was almost translucent in the sunlight. But it was her eyes that transfixed him. Staring from beneath the hoar frost lashes, they were the colour of dog violets. Her pale fingers reached for the cup.

"Sorry," he said, filling her cup before moving to serve his master.

The two men talked trading herbs, most of which Col knew the old man didn't need. Albyn turned to the girl.

"Is this your apprentice?" he asked Harag.

"Slave," he said, without looking up from his cache of goods.

"Is she for sale?" Col's head turned. Albyn disliked the practice of keeping slaves.

Harag pushed his fingers through his thin hair. "Maybe."

"Her price?"

The visitor smiled, rubbing a hand across his thin lips. "They say your necklace has great power," he said.

"That is true. Where did you hear of it?"

"I don't remember, idle gossip I expect. May I see it?"

Albyn untied the leather thong around his neck, producing a threaded row of boar tusks and antler points. Harag examined them.

"Great power," he whispered. "The necklace, then... and the bird."

Albyn looked at the tiny wren on his shoulder. "You ask a high price for her," he said, drawing Harag's gaze at last.

"Look at her colouring, she comes from the very southernmost island."

Albyn stared at the visitor until he blinked and looked away. "Very well. Col, fetch a basket," he said.

* * *

The wren fluttered against the sides of the small basket as Albyn tied the top shut. He rose, bowing his head to the visitor who also stood. Harag fastened the necklace around his throat, picking up the basket and trade goods.

"Messenger," he said, then bowed before turning to walk away.

The pale girl stood, facing Albyn, lowering her eyes at his gaze.

"Your name, child?"

"My name is Talla," she said, glancing up, "I have sixteen summers."

"Go with Col," Albyn said, turning away, "He will show you your bed and give you food. Go."

* * *

Geth smiled as Albyn shuffled over to her. She was close to his age, over fifty years lived. She showed him little deference unless they were in company.

"Your necklace has great power," she mimicked. She'd been eavesdropping, as usual.

"Yes, it has," Albyn said, smiling.

"Not the one you gave him," she laughed. "How long will he have the bird?"

"She'll be back by tonight," Albyn said. "He won't be able to resist taking her from the basket. She'll be out of his hand in a flash."

"And the girl?" she asked.

"I have a use for the girl," he said.

* * *

Col cleared the clutter from a sleeping platform, piling it onto a vacant bed. They seldom had visitors, and the old man had no mate. Col's mother had died giving birth to him and, since his father's fall from the cliff, Col was alone.

"Here?" the girl asked, meeting his gaze for the first time.

"Yes, unless you want the other bed. The old man snores, this one is further away."

"In the house?"

"Were you not in Harag's house?" Col asked.

"I haven't slept in a house since my father sold me," she said. Col looked up, but she was staring at her feet again. He readily understood her speech, but her accent was... different.

"Here," he said, patting the dusty frame. He rummaged underneath, coming out with a thick cowhide and two sleeping furs. His nose wrinkled at the smell. "Take these out and shake the dust off them. They will be yours."

The girl took the bedding and walked outside. When she returned, Col was pulling a hot stone from the fire, dropping it into a pot of liquid. The broth bubbled, and he removed the stone. He set the bowl on a low table with a hunk of hardened barley bread. "Eat," he said.

The girl sat on the floor, dipping the bread into the meaty broth, shovelling it into her mouth. The bread gone, she tipped the bowl, drinking the last of the warm soup.

"More?" he asked. She looked surprised, but nodded, passing the bowl to him.

"You may take off your cloak, if you wish," he said, filling the bowl and pulling another heated stone from the fire. The girl hesitated and glanced at Col before standing, unfastening the tie at her neck, and removing the cloak. She was tall for a girl but so thin. Her legs, visible under the grey linen shift, were spindly, her bare arms wasted. The dress showed the top of her chest, collar bones protruding. Col set the broth on the table and reached for another hunk of bread.

"Do you always eat this well?" she mumbled, sitting and packing another lump of the broth-soaked loaf in her mouth.

"It's leftovers," Col said, still staring at her. "We eat our main meal later."

She looked at him unbelieving. "We'll eat again? Today?" He nodded.

She smiled and ate in silence, apart from the wet slurping of her food.

"You're staring," she said.

"I... I've seen no one with your colouring before," he stuttered. He'd only ever seen people like himself, dark hair and brown eyes, skin that tanned in the summer.

"No one has," she said, sitting on her bed.

"Are you a spirit... enchanted?"

"No." Talla paused, "I was born this way. Different. That's why I have been a slave for nine years."

"With Harag?" he asked.

She laughed, "No, with him for only four seasons." She peeled back her fingers from a fist, then held up an open palm, fingers straight. "Five," she said, satisfied. "I have had five masters. The old man will be..."

"Six?" said Col.

"Yes, six."

They sat, eyeing each other. "I don't mind you staring," she said, "I'm used to it."

Col shifted in his seat. He wanted to ask so much, but not even the Tribe legends spoke of one such as her.

"Is the work hard?" she asked.

"What?"

"The work, is it hard?"

"I don't know," Col said, "The old man objects to the keeping of slaves, he's never had one."

She scowled. "Will he expect me to share his bed?"

"No... I don't think so. He's so old..."

Her smile returned. "Perhaps it will be good here for a while," she said, lifting her bare foot, picking something from the sole.

"For a while?" Col asked.

"Oh, they never keep me long," she said, pushing back her hair, "I'm cursed."

Chapter 2

Rain pattered on the roof, the drip of leaking water rousing Talla from her sleep. She crept around the room, looking, never touching. The waterskin was almost empty. The ashes in the hearth still felt warm. She studied Col for a moment. He was wiry with a ready smile. She liked his soft, brown eyes and the way he kept his long hair tied back like a horse's tail. She squatted on the floor beside his bed.

"What is it, Talla?" he asked.

She jumped. "You're awake! I don't know what to do; don't know my tasks. The old man will beat me."

Col pulled back the furs. "He won't beat you, he has no reason."

"Why does he need a reason? Beatings don't need a reason," she whispered, glancing at Albyn's slumbering form.

Col pushed himself up from the bed, straightening his clothing. "Come," he said. "A fire needs lighting, the water skin needs filling from the river. Bring firewood in too."

There was a rustle behind them, and the old man stirred. "If she were a slave," Albyn said, sitting up, "she would be my slave, not yours. Do your own tasks as always."

Col bowed, blushing. "Good morning, Spirit Messenger," he said. Talla copied him, keeping her head bent.

"Girl." She looked up, hoping Albyn was not angry. "You are not a slave any longer. I do not keep slaves. You may stay or go. Stay, and I will make sure you are cared for and fed. Become an apprentice, the same as Col, if you wish. Given your colouring, I suggest you stay, people will forgive much of the apprentice of a spirit messenger."

"But you paid for me, I am yours," she said.

"What did I pay?"

"Your necklace of power."

Reaching for the table, Albyn picked up a small bundle. He unwrapped the red cloth, lifting a string of polished amber beads and tying them around his neck. "I have my necklace of power," he said.

"The bird," Talla said. "Your wren." The old man whistled, and the small bird settled on his shoulder.

"You fooled him," Talla said.

"It's easy to fool the greedy, remember that both of you. So I paid next to nothing for you... a trinket. Harag has sold you, but I do not own you. You must belong to yourself."

Talla threw herself on her knees before Albyn. "Thank you," she whispered.

"Stand!" he said, "And help me up too." Talla saw Col grin at the return of the old man's grumpy demeanour as he fetched water for their master.

* * *

"There's not enough here," Talla said, walking beside the river.

Col peered at the patch of coltsfoot. "There's plenty."

"No, if we take all this, the plants will die, there'll be none next year," she said.

"So?"

Talla stood, shading her eyes. "There. Those gravel banks by the bend, there's bound to be coltsfoot there."

They set off, Talla leading. "Why do you care, Talla?" Col asked.

"Because you may need those next year, if they're gone, you must walk further."

"I'm fine," he said, rubbing his thigh, "I can walk as far as I need to. My leg is healed."

Talla stopped. "No, I meant, pretend you're me. You need to get coltsfoot, or you'll get a beating. You never strip all the plants closest to home."

"Oh," he said, looking ashamed. "I'm sorry."

"It's all right," she said.

Col reached to take her hand. She smiled, squeezing his fingers, then let go.

"Come on," she said, letting Col lead the way along the bank. She was still unsure if she was free, but Col told her that the spirit messenger was trustworthy. With his soft, brown eyes and shy smile, she was almost ready to believe Col, now.

* * *

When they'd filled the basket, they turned for home.

"Oh, look Sil, a ghost," said a voice.

Col flinched at Art's leering smile. "Leave her alone," he said.

"Has the messenger's pet got a slave friend?" said Art, standing beside Talla, touching her hair. "Give me a kiss, Slave." Talla spat in his face. "Filthy sow," he screamed, his hand raised to strike.

Col charged; head lowered, knocking Art off his feet. He pummelled Art with clenched fists, until Sil dragged him off, pinning him to the ground. Art recovered, falling on Col, punching him repeatedly. Talla leapt at Sil with a scream, freeing Col. She dragged him to his feet, pulling him along the river.

"I will kill you, cripple!" Art shouted.

* * *

Talla was washing the blood from Col's face when Albyn entered the roundhouse.

"What happened?" he asked, shuffling toward the fire.

"I fell," said Col.

The Messenger looked at Talla. "He fell at the river, hit his head and his cheek," she said, dabbing at crusting blood.

"And his arm?" Albyn asked.

"He tried to save himself from falling," said Talla, turning redder with each lie.

"Hmm," the old man said, pointing to a shelf on the far wall. "Third basket from the left, make an infusion to bathe the wounds." Talla nodded, pushing stones into the fire to heat, before walking to the shelf.

* * *

"You lied for me," Col said.

"You tried to save me," she replied. "Why are you here with the old man?"

Col closed his eyes and sighed. "My mother died giving birth to me. My father brought me up. Two years ago, my father fell from a cliff and died. I was with him. I fell too, breaking my leg." He untied the side of his leggings, showing the long scar on his outer thigh. Talla reached out, concerned, as her finger traced the jagged white line. "I was filled with bad spirits, sweating and talking to the ancestors. Albyn said it destined me to serve the spirits. He took me in and made me his apprentice."

"And you will stay?" Talla asked.

"It is not a bad life," Col said. "One day, I may become the clan messenger."

Talla watched him for a moment. "Like you, my mother died when I was born. My father blamed me. He kept me until I was old enough to work, then he sold me."

"Your own father?" Col asked.

Talla nodded. "The first master treated me well. He let me sleep in the barn, he fed me. His mate was barren, they blamed me and soon sold me. The next master whipped me. He enjoyed it. I had to be a worthless slave just to get him to sell me. Then I was the slave of a Clan leader. A boar injured his son, again, it was my fault."

"Why?" said Col.

"Look at me," she said, running pale fingers through her white hair, "I'm not the same as you, not like anyone else. I'm the odd one, the cursed one, the one to blame." Talla sat for a moment. "An old man was next. He wanted a cook... and a bedmate."

"A bedmate?" Col asked.

"He died..." She looked at her fingers, fidgeting in her lap. "He was old. They sold me on to Harag."

"So now you're free," said Col.

"Yes. If Albyn is true to his word," she said.

"He will be. He is a good man," Col said.

* * *

"Take the ceremonial things to the stones," Albyn said, waving at the pile beside the wall. "There will be a drum journey and a feast."

"What's the occasion?" Col asked.

"Do you pay no attention?" Albyn said, shaking his head, "It's the full moon. Talla, help him."

They dragged skins and furs, drums and herbs, firewood and kindling to the sacred site on the hilltop and piled them near the huge stones. "What will happen?" asked Talla.

"A ceremony," Col said. "In the past, I have drummed for Albyn while he travels to the world below. He communicates with the ancestors."

"How?" Talla asked, running her fingers across a seam of crystals in one of the standing stones.

"I don't know, I've never travelled with him. When he returns, he speaks to the people, giving prophecies. After that, there will be feasting."

"Will we get to eat?" she asked.

"Of course," he smiled, punching her arm. Talla stiffened at the blow, eyes narrowing, then a grin crept across her face.

"Just asking," she said, shoving him back.

* * *

People gathered outside the ring of stones. A fire close by illuminated the avenue to the north. Albyn walked up the centre, Col beating the frame drum in time with his steps. They reached the fire, and Talla handed the old man his drum. He sat near to the blaze, Col to one side, Talla to the other. He closed his eyes and began a fast beat, his two apprentices accompanying him.

Col heard Talla gasp, then felt a physical pull into the earth as he too closed his eyes.

* * *

This world was dark, like dusk, or dawn. The colours were missing, only black and grey. The old man walked ahead. They reached a river, forming a line along the bank, facing the far side. Col shuddered as he looked across the death river for the first time.

Shadow people gathered opposite them. Albyn raised his hands, calling out a verse to those across the water. A young woman appeared, and he talked to her as if in conversation. Nodding, moving his hands and arms. Col stared as Talla stepped into the water.

"No!" Albyn shouted, "You can't do that." Talla turned and smiled, stepping out of the stream on the far side. She walked up to the dark figure of a woman and hugged her. Col could hear her sobs from across the water. Talla pulled away and stepped back into the current.

The old man shied away from her as she stepped from the water. "Fool. How did you do that? How did you return?"

"It was my mother," she said.
"Back," Albyn said.

* * *

Col opened his eyes, wondering if it was a dream. He'd been at these ceremonies many times but never travelled below with the old man. Albyn stopped his rhythm, and Col helped him to his feet as he turned to the crowd.

"I have spoken with the ancestors," he called in his reedy voice. "They wish us well but warn of troubled times ahead. Poor weather and poor crops will blight us soon. We must prepare for this." There was mumbling from the people at the premonition. Tan, the Clan leader, pushed to the front.

"Are the ancestors angry with us? Have we offended them?"

"No," the old man said, holding up his hands to quiet the crowd. "There are greater powers at work here."

"Greater powers than the ancestors?" Tan asked.

"Yes, the spirits of the elements themselves. I can tell you no more. Now, let us celebrate this full moon together." The crowd dispersed into uneasy groups as the food was spread on the wooden platform.

"Col," Albyn called, "Take the ancestors' share."

Col knew of this, though Albyn had always performed this part himself. He took a platter and went to the feast. He selected the best piece of meat, the biggest portion of barley bread, the choicest vegetables and fruit, then took the platter to Albyn.

The old man held his hands over the food, muttering an incantation under his breath. He nodded to Col, who walked to the centre of the circle, placing the platter on the ground.

"Begin," Albyn called, bowing to the Clan leader.

Tan walked to the table, taking food for his family, stepping back and dividing it up between his mate, his son and his daughter before eating himself.

"Col, fetch our food," Albyn said.

He felt the eyes of the Clan on him. This was different, this was for himself, Albyn and Talla. He selected enough for three, taking good pieces but not too much. Then returned to the old man and set down the platter.

"Well? Divide the food up," Albyn said. Col filled the old man's plate, glancing up every so often. "Enough, now the girl," he said.

Col placed some of each food onto Talla's platter, looking at what he'd left himself. He gauged it to be even, but then put an extra piece of meat on hers, passing it to her. She smiled and started eating. Col sat with his own meal.

Later, the old man recounted the creation tale, and Geth sang songs of love and loss, battles and heroes, in her sweet high voice. It was late when they returned home that night.

"Tomorrow, we must talk about the journey to the river," Albyn said, as they prepared to sleep.

* * *

The old man was up when Col returned from the river with the waterskin. He was working his way along the shelves, checking the neat baskets of herbs and medicines, muttering, "Headaches… Fever… Coughs… Pain..." He turned, hearing Col enter. "Get the fire going," he said. "Make tea."

Col hung the waterskin, then raked through the ashes, bringing the fire to life and setting stones to heat. Albyn was waiting for Talla to wake. Col wondered why he didn't shake her as he did if he overslept. Finally, the girl stirred. Spotting the old man hovering near her bed, she leapt to her feet.

"Sorry, master," she whimpered, cowering.

"You are no longer a slave, Talla. I am not your master," he said, "Now sit."

Col brought cups of meadowsweet tea, and they sat near the fire.

"We need to talk about the drum journey, yesterday," Albyn said. "Why did you cross the river, Talla?"

"I saw my mother," she said.

"Your mother is dead?"

"She died giving birth to me, yes," Talla said.

"Yet you recognised her."

"Yes, I don't know how."

"How did you return?"

"I came back to you, Messenger," she said.

"Do you understand what that river is?" Talla shook her head. "It is the river that separates the living from the dead. You entered the land of the dead. No one returns from that place, yet you did," he said, pacing the floor.

"I'm sorry, Messenger," Talla sobbed. "I needed to touch her, to feel someone who loved me once."

"You did nothing wrong," the old man said, "just something unexpected... something that should not be possible." Talla shuffled to Col's side, feeling for his hand. Col squeezed her fingers.

"Fetch me raspberry leaves and feverfew," Albyn said as his hand stroked his belly, then touched his brow, indicating their uses. "Don't return before noon, I need time to consult the ancestors."

Col grabbed two collecting baskets and led Talla outside, heading off towards the woods. "Will he send me away?" Talla asked.

They stopped, sitting on a log.

"I don't know," Col said. "You realise what you did, don't you?"

"I crossed the river, in the 'dream'," she said.

Col drew a deep breath. "It wasn't a dream. When you cross that river, you are dead. You belong in the land of the dead, you can't return."

"So why was I able to come back?" she asked.

"That is what's bothering the Messenger," Col said.

They walked further, finding raspberry plants and collecting the leaves.

"I told you I was cursed," Talla said, placing a handful of leaves in Col's basket.

"No, if you were cursed, you would have died, wouldn't you?"

Talla sighed. "I don't know."

They spotted feverfew plants a little way off and set out to harvest them.

* * *

It was past noon when they tied Talla's basket closed and headed back towards the village.

"Well, if it's not the cripple and the slave," Art said. Sil was a step behind him. "I still haven't had that kiss, slave," he said, grabbing Talla's hair.

"Leave her alone," Col shouted. He was about to go for Art when Sil grabbed his arms. "Let me go," he said. Sil laughed as he struggled, and Art pushed Talla against a tree.

"Now, that kiss, slave." Talla tried to push him away, but her slight frame was no match for Art's muscles. Her face lost all expression, and she closed her eyes, resigned to her fate.

"Leave her alone!" Col shouted, "She's the Messenger's apprentice now, she journeyed with us last night."

Art slowed, turning towards Col, his hand on Talla's throat. "Any fool can bang a drum."

"Yes, but she travelled to the world below and crossed the death river, so you'd better let her go. She has the power to return from the land of the dead," Col said.

Art's pulled his hand from Talla's throat as if it had burned him. "That's not possible." He turned to Talla. "He's lying."

"I crossed the river," she said, "to be with my mother."

"Your mother is dead?" Art said, backing away.

"Yes."

"You touched an ancestor spirit?" he whispered.

"Yes."

"Sil, come on, leave them," he said, turning. His face a mask of horror.

"But..." said Sil, releasing Col.

"Come on," Art called, heading towards the village. Sil followed him.

"Are you all right?" Col asked when they'd gone.

Talla lifted her hand to her throat, rubbing the reddened skin. "I'm fine."

"Did he hurt you?" Col said, worried.

"No."

"The marks on your throat, Talla..."

"Are nothing!" she snapped. "Sorry," she said. She turned away from him, pulling her dress from one shoulder, displaying her bare back. Col gasped, reaching out his hand to trace the network of fading white welts covering her shoulders.

"Don't," she said, pulling away. "That hurt me. He didn't."

"How?" Col whispered. "Who?"

Talla straightened her dress and turned towards him. "The second master," she said, looking at the ground, her eyes blinking. "I told you he liked to hurt me."

Col pulled her into a hug. She stiffened, then buried her face in his chest.

"I'm sorry," he whispered.

Talla shook her head, pulling away and scrubbing the tears from her eyes.

"Come on," she said. "We'd better get back."

Chapter 3

Col sat watching the raven's nest. Albyn had shown it to him half a moon ago, and the young birds were almost fledged. Raven was his spirit animal, and practically every spirit messenger had the physical representation of their totem as a companion. Col had asked about his animal, how it represented him.

"The raven seldom hunts," Albyn had said. "It lives off the carrion of others. It is a bird that likes the company of its kind and is fiercely protective." Col had spent many hours thinking about that.

He saw the enormous black bird circling, bringing food to the chicks. As soon as it flew off again, Col ran up the hill, scaling the rocks. As he'd thought, there were four chicks, fully feathered. They cowered in the nest as he reached in, picking up the largest bird and tucking it into his tunic as it squawked. He heard the distant cawing of the parent returning and slipped down the rocks, breaking into a run. The gathering and foraging he'd done with Talla over the last two moons had strengthened his leg far more than the rest that Albyn had advised.

Col rushed into the roundhouse, red-faced, with a smile on his lips. Talla grinned at him.

"You have it?" Albyn asked. Col pulled the struggling bird from his tunic, clasping it in both hands.

"It knows only its parents," Albyn said. "You must feed him now, become his mother. If you connect with him, then you can release him, but he will always return to you when you call."

"How will I keep him?" Col asked.

"A basket for now. Later a perch, with his leg tied until you tame him."

"What is my animal, Spirit Messenger?" Talla asked, looking up from the mat she was weaving. He beckoned her to him.

"Sit," he said, then took her hands once she'd settled. He looked at her, then closed his eyes. Talla felt as if the messenger was peering into her mind.

"Slim and agile," he said, "vicious if cornered. Brave and intelligent." He opened his eyes. "Stoat," he said, "Your animal is the stoat, and in winter, he even has your colouring."

Talla smiled, turning to Col. Then her face fell. "Messenger, how will I find my animal? They're so elusive."

"He will find you, Talla." Albyn struggled to his feet, "Now, make me tea. An old man could die of thirst."

* * *

Talla reached the top of the small hill first, collapsing in the heather, panting.

"Come on, snail," she called as Col sprawled on the ground beside her. They'd been collecting moss which, when dried, they used for lighting the fire.

The weather had confined the two youngsters to the house for the last four days, weaving baskets and crumbling herbs while the grey skies rained non-stop. Albyn had almost thrown them out when the morning dawned bright, sick of their bickering.

Small clouds raced across the blue, casting alternating light and shade over the landscape as they lay recovering from their race.

"Do you enjoy living here?" Col asked, turning towards Talla.

"Yes," her face fell, "but it can't last."

Col looked over at her. "I'll miss you if you leave."

Talla toyed with the hem of her dress. "Something bad will happen. It always does," she said.

* * *

Driving rain blew through the gaps in the door as the wind screamed in the thatch. Col only just heard the knock over the shriek and lash of the weather.

"Is the Messenger here?" asked a lad of about ten. Col pulled him inside, slamming the door as the boy dripped onto the threshold flagstones.

"Messenger Albyn," Col called, rousing the slumbering elder. He turned to the boy. "Who are you, and where are you from?" Talla brought a fur to wrap around his shoulders.

"I am Shan," he said as Talla shepherded him towards the hearth, "I am the son of Terrat of the Cove Clan of the Tribe of the West."

"The Cove Clan?" asked Albyn, walking over to the drenched boy. "The new community along the coast?"

Shan bowed. "Yes, Messenger. Just two families and no healer. My uncle cut his arm a few days back, and it's not healing. Mother sent me to ask for your help."

Albyn turned to Col. "Gather your tools and medicines. Go with the boy and treat the wound," he said.

Col's mouth opened and closed a few times before his voice emerged. "Spirit Messenger, I do not have the experience to do this."

"Oh, and how do you hope to gain experience?" Albyn asked, reaching for an oiled leather bag, placing a basket of herbs into it.

Col looked at his feet. Talla took his hand and squeezed it as he answered.

"I will do my best, Messenger," he said.

* * *

Shan led the way south, skipping along the cliff path. Col kept well back from the sheer drop to his right, placing his feet with care.

It was dusk before they arrived at the Cove Clan; just two houses with a third framed nearby. Shan showed Col into the larger building, and he went straight to the man laying on the bed. The wound, in his forearm, was a finger-length long. The edges were red and angry, and the smell of bad spirits was coming from it.

Col turned to the woman helping Shan from his wet clothing. "Bring me boiling water," he said, "and bread if you have it to spare." The woman stared for a moment, and Col raised his voice. "Do it now! The bad spirits are at work in this. He could die."

She nodded and pulled stones from the fire while Col pressed around the wound. The man shouted in pain and pulled the arm back.

"What is your name?" Col asked, taking tools and herbs from the waterproof bag.

"Ulan," the man groaned, "Treya is my sister." He nodded towards the woman heating water.

"Ulan, you should have cleaned this wound. You have allowed the bad spirits into it. I'll do my best to help you, but the treatment will hurt." Ulan nodded. "Treya, I'm sorry I shouted, this is worse than it looks. Is the water ready?"

"Here, Messenger," she said, setting the bowl beside him.

"I am an apprentice, but Messenger Albyn has entrusted me to treat your brother," Col said, crumbling the stale bread into the water. He took a strip of thick leather and offered it to Ulan. "Bite on this," he said, placing it in the injured man's mouth.

Col scooped the scalding bread paste onto the wound, wincing at Ulan's scream. He placed damp moss over the poultice and wrapped the arm in a bandage.

Ulan pulled the leather gag from his mouth and moaned.

"I'm sorry, Ulan," Col said. "This is the only way to remove the bad spirits. Now rest awhile."

Later, Col replaced the poultice with a mixture of honey and comfrey, packing it again with moss. Treya served a tasty stew, and the family ate, while Col instructed Treya on how to treat wounds.

He waited until the third morning before satisfying himself that the bad spirits were no longer in the wound, and it was healing. He left the honey and herbs with Treya, before setting off through the rain for Classac.

* * *

Col traipsed through the sodden field, heading into his village. The barley should have been knee high by now, but it was drowned in the mud. He was soaked and chilled. He'd given up on his shoes soon after he set out, the wet leather sliding off his feet with every step.

Treya had fed him hot barley porridge before he started the day's walk home, but now he was hungry, and his teeth chattered. He clattered in the roundhouse door, shaking his head to drive wet hair out of his eyes.

Talla flew at him, hugging him. The old man looked up, and Col was sure he saw the trace of a smile. "Well?" he asked.

Talla turned to him. "Spirit Messenger," she said, bowing her head, "Col is wet and, I'm sure, hungry. Can your questions wait until I get him dry clothing and a drink of tea?" There was a glint in his eye this time as he waved her away as if to say 'do as you please'.

Col stripped out of the dripping clothes and squeezed the water from his hair. Talla passed dry leggings and a tunic to him and sat him by the fire. Once he had a cup of hot tea in his hand, Albyn spoke.

"Tell me what happened," he said.

Col described the wound on the man's arm and how it was showing signs of bad spirits. He told Albyn about the poultice and the dressing, adding that he'd taught one woman how to treat wounds.

"You did the right things, and passed on knowledge," Albyn said, "Do they have crops?"

"Yes, rotting in the ground, like our own," Col said, grimacing at the black mud still clinging to his feet. The old man nodded.

Talla sat beside Col, chopping beef for a stew. Col smiled and held out his arm, giving a loud cry. "Kaaark!"

The almost fully grown raven dropped from its perch in the roof timbers, landing on his wrist. Col sneaked a piece of meat from the platter on Talla's lap, getting a slap on the hand, before feeding it to his bird.

Albyn made sure neither was looking before giving a wry grin. He stood from his seat, muttering, "Blessed animals are better fed than I am," and wandered outside.

* * *

"The stew was good," Col said, rubbing his belly, warm at last. Talla's face glowed at the praise.

"I don't suppose I'll starve while you're here," Albyn said.

"No, I don't suppose you will, Messenger," she said, stopping to give the old man a hug.

He stiffened, pushing at her. "Stop that nonsense, girl."

Col made up the fire against the damp air, still cold despite it being late spring, and they prepared for bed.

* * *

The roundhouse door slammed open, wakening Talla from a restless sleep. She tried to sit up, but rough hands pushed her down and turned her over. She shouted as they bound her hands behind her back.

What was crime her this time, she wondered? What excuse would they use to be rid of her? She'd grown fond of Col, and the grumpy messenger, Albyn, in her time at the Hill Clan.

They pulled Talla to her feet as Tan, the clan leader, came in the door with a torch. The light illuminated Col, standing like herself, hands tied.

"What do you mean by this?" Albyn said, struggling from his bed.

Tan strode across the floor, his finger wagging in Albyn's face.

"*You* cannot appease the spirits, so *I* will do it," he said. "Our crops are rotting. The sun hasn't shown its face in over a moon, yet you do nothing."

"The ancestors warned us of this," Albyn said. "How will you change the will of the spirits of the elements?"

"I will sacrifice these cursed ones," he said, turning to Talla. Spittle flew, and his pointing finger shook as he ranted. "This... creature is evil incarnate. No human has white hair like that, no human has pink eyes. My son tells me she even crossed the death river. She is a curse on our clan."

He wheeled around, looming over Col. "And this abomination, dragged back from the jaws of death. He should have died with his father, but you brought back his spirit and healed a mortal wound. A wound that would have killed anyone else."

Tan turned to his two warriors. "Take them to the old house. Guard them."

Talla stumbled as they pushed her outside, just keeping her balance as her guard shoved her toward a disused house at the edge of the village. She was thrown onto a pile of stinking furs atop a rickety bed platform, and the door banged closed.

"Are you hurt?" Col asked, his voice trembling.

"No. You?"

"No." He was quiet for a moment. "They mean to kill us, Talla. I'm frightened."

Talla stood, unsteady with her hands bound, and followed his voice to the bed opposite. She sat beside him, hearing his panicked breathing in the dark.

"Albyn won't let that happen," she said.

"How can he stop Tan?" Col asked.

Talla turned her back to him, wriggling her fingers. "See if you can untie my hands," she said.

* * *

Geth ran into Albyn's house as he was pulling stones from the fire to heat water.

"What was the commotion?" she said, looking around. "Where are Talla and Col?"

"Tan means to sacrifice them to appease the spirits," he said, sprinkling several herbs into the pot of hot water.

"And you're making tea? Do something!"

"Sit," Albyn ordered. "When this has infused, I want you to take it to the warrior guarding the old house, it's where they're holding Col and Talla."

"You're aiding him in this madness? Do you want them killed?"

"I want you to take the guard a drink, then watch from a distance," he said. "Let me know when he falls asleep."

"Is that…" Geth began.

Albyn tipped some of the brew into a cup, passing it to Geth. "A little nightshade, a little spirit mushroom. Rosehip to hide the flavour," he said. "Take it now."

* * *

The scrabbling at the back of the house roused Col. He nudged Talla, who'd fallen asleep beside him.

"What is it?" she said, fear in her voice.

"Listen."

"Col. Talla. Can you hear me?" It was Albyn's voice. They crawled to the back wall.

"Quiet. You'll alert the guard," Col whispered.

Part of the mud plaster dropped away, and he could see Albyn's face by the moonlight.

"The guard is asleep," he said. "Help me."

Col and Talla tore at the damp, rotting laths, hoping the warrior outside would not hear them. Soon there was a hole big enough to crawl through. Talla squeezed out first, then Col.

"He may wake up any time," Col said. "We must get away."

"He will not wake for a long while," Albyn said. "Come with me."

Albyn led them to his house. Geth was sitting by the door, wrapped in furs, watching the front of the old house.

"What did you do to the guard?" Col asked as they entered.

"Geth took him some hot tea," he said. "Come on, there's no time to waste."

"We must leave," said Talla, tears streaming now, "If I am free, we can leave."

"You are free," Albyn said, taking Talla's hand. "There is one thing I can do for you, though."

Col watched as he took a scallop shell, holding it above the smoking lamp. He inspected the black residue, then set it on the table.

"Get the leather pouch, with my tools," he said, pointing to the shelf. Talla got the decorated bundle and passed it to him. "Sit at my feet," he told her, opening the roll and selecting a small flint blade. He closed his eyes, muttering a prayer, then reached for Talla's forehead.

"This will hurt," he said, cutting fine lines in a zigzag pattern above her left eye. Talla took a breath but remained silent. Satisfied with the lines, Albyn dabbed away the blood with soft leather, then filled his fingertip with the lamp-black. He rubbed the oily deposit into the wounds as Talla hissed.

"One more," he said. He carved the shape of an eye into the pale skin of her cheek. Col saw Talla clamp her quivering lip with her teeth, as Albyn applied the black dye, determined not to show her pain.

"Done!" he said, straightening his back. "Col."

Col replaced Talla, flinching when the old man held his head. The cuts over his right eye were bearable, but the black colouring burned like coals.

"Ah!" he cried, twisting away.

"Hold still!" Albyn said, pulling him back. "This may be all I can do to help you."

When Albyn had finished, Col filled the shallow bowl the spirit messenger handed him with water, then went back to packing.

Albyn crouched over the bowl, gazing into the reflection. His mind searched for his helpers, spirits of ancestors who loved him, drawing them to him.

"Why do you treat these young people so?" he asked.

"They are the key, messenger," the image in the water hissed.

"To what?"

"To the rift between man and nature, they can heal this," the voice said.

"How?"

"The spirits of the four directions, earth, air, fire and water, have lost their love for humans. Only these apprentices can set this right."

"They are little more than children," Albyn said.

"Their souls are old. They will find their way south; they will learn what they must do."

"I..." Albyn began.

"Do it!" the spirit voice commanded. "It is their destiny."

The spirit's presence faded. The old man dipped his fingers into the water, swirling it around the bowl, dispersing the images.

* * *

Albyn looked at the two young people before him, their eyes wide. Blood still seeped from Talla's tattoo. She wiped it away.

"Where will we go? Why the tattoos?" she said.

The old man eased himself onto his bed. "I have marked you as spirit apprentices, herb apprentices and lore apprentices," he said. "The tattoos will give you protection. Your knowledge is not complete, but Col has more lore knowledge, and Talla more plant learning. Between you, no one will question your skills."

"Where will we go, Spirit Messenger?" Col asked.

"South. I am charging you with finding why the spirits of the elements have turned against us. The ancestors say it's your destiny, that only you can heal this."

"South, to the end of the island?" Talla asked.

Albyn shook his head. "You must cross the water to the Great Island," he said. "Travel south from there. Follow where the spirits lead you."

"How many days must we travel, Messenger?" Col said.

"Not days, moons, perhaps even a whole turn of the seasons."

"May we ever return?" Talla asked, a blood-tinged tear dripping from her eye.

"When you have fulfilled your destiny, yes, then you may return."

Col reached for his damp cloak hanging near the door.

"Wait," Albyn said, struggling to reach under his bed and pulling out a cloth bundle. He unfolded it and handed a new travelling cape to each of them. Sewn to the shoulders of each one were five swan feathers.

"These were to be your gifts when you earned your tattoos; when you were fully apprenticed. That day has arrived. Now go, it will soon be sunrise. The future of our tribe, perhaps all the tribes, rests with you. I am sorry it has to be this way, but the ancestors have chosen you. Travel well."

It surprised Col when Albyn clasped him to his spindly frame, hugging with a fierceness that Col didn't know he still possessed. Talla received a similar farewell, though she clutched the old man back.

"Go!" Albyn said, turning back towards his bed. He screwed his eyes shut and swallowed his sobs until the door closed.

* * *

It was a rare, cloudless morning in a year of rain. Col took Talla's hand for comfort; his or hers, he wasn't sure. They followed the coast south, their feet squelching on the soft ground as the sky lightened and turned red gold.

They walked in silence, then Col heard the swish of wings. "Here, Kark!" he called, holding up his arm. The bird swooped, unbalancing Col as he landed. He stroked the glossy head and moved him to his shoulder. Col felt his crop; it was full, he'd eaten well somewhere.

"Will they chase us... hunt us?" Talla asked.

Col squeezed her hand, "I hope not. There's no sign," he said, looking behind them.

"I'm worried for Alb..."

They both jumped as an agonised scream carried through the still morning air.

"What was that?" Talla asked.

"Albyn!" Col said, turning around. "We must go back."

Talla took his hand. "We can't return until we have completed our quest."

"But, Albyn..." Col began.

"If we go back, Tan will kill us," Talla said, dragging him away.

There was a howl, followed by frenzied barking.

"Tan's hunting dogs," Col said.

He'd been on deer hunts, seen the huge hounds tear the throat out of a wounded stag before it could hit the ground. He turned to Talla, eyes wide.

"Run," he said, "Run, and don't stop."

Chapter 4

Talla's breath was catching in her throat, and Col's leg was aching by the time they slowed to a walk. They kept the sun to their left but moved inland, avoiding the hills. Albyn had given them food, stale barley bread and the last of the stew. Talla and Col sat when the sun reached its height, eating half of their provisions and drinking from a stream.

"What do you know of the south people," Col asked, looking back the way they'd come, scanning the skyline.

"They are poorer than the Hill Clan. Food is hard to grow on their thin soils," Talla said. "They consider Harag their most senior spirit messenger, though the old man told me his knowledge is basic."

Col nodded. "We must keep you away from him. Can we avoid his Clan?"

"Yes, they're on the west side of the island," she said.

"We'll need a boat," Col said, as they set off again, weaving through the hills, making south.

* * *

They hid in a copse of hazel trees that night. Unwilling to pitch their shelter, they pulled it over their heads instead. Col sat most of the night, watching the north, hoping not to see the flare of torches or hear the baying of Tan's hounds.

Talla shook him awake.

"Mmmh?"

"Get up, it's light enough to see now, we should go."

Col climbed to his feet, easing weight onto the stiff, left leg. "I fell asleep."

"It's alright, they didn't come. Help me pack the shelter," she said.

* * *

The next day dawned grey. They'd tied their shelter alongside a massive rock, piling bracken inside. Talla lay at his back, her breathing even, as Col heard spots of rain on the shelter and turned to shake her.

"Wake up. We need to move, I don't want to be carrying the shelter wet."

She grumbled and stretched, but was soon outside, helping him roll up the hide. They'd finished the food, but they drank from their water skin and set off.

Rain followed them the entire day, and they could not see any distance ahead. Kark flapped off sometime after noon, settling nearby, feeding. He and Talla ran over, finding a deer carcass, the belly ripped out, and the front end gnawed away. Col inspected the marks on the dead animal.

"Wolves?" Talla asked.

"Yes. It looks fresh, killed last night."

"Shall we take some?" she asked. Their Clan considered it wrong to take carrion meat, but they seldom hunted, having pigs and cattle of their own. This meat was fresh, though.

"Let's take a leg. The wolves haven't touched this one," Col said, taking a flint knife from his pouch. He cut into the skin, knowing from experience where to sever the leg. Talla joined in, hacking off the chewed foot.

They stowed the meat in Col's pack, and he returned the blade to his pouch. He felt a piece of cloth in the pouch and pulled out a red wrapped bundle. He looked at Talla, but she shook her head. Col tipped the contents into his hand.

"Col!" Talla gasped when she saw the amber beads. "Did you take them?"

"No, I wouldn't dare," he said, "Albyn must have slipped them in. But why?"

"He must have thought we'd need them," she said, reaching to take the beads. She held them up to the light, twisting them this way and that. "Beautiful!" she whispered.

* * *

They stopped early that day, needing to light a fire to cook. Talla fetched wood while Col got out the kindling and the fire bow. He set the stick into the scorched hole in the board and wrapped the bow-string around it, pulling the bow back and forth until it formed a tiny glowing coal. He piled on dry moss, then small twigs, blowing onto it the whole time.

A small flame burst to life, and Talla arrived with more wood. They cut slivers off the joint, grilling the meat on sticks. Kark had fed himself, gorging on the carcass before catching up with them.

They had just settled after their meal when there was an angry scream from across the valley. An eagle was diving at the rocks on the opposite hilltop, its talons raking at an unseen target.

"What's it doing?" Talla asked.

"I don't know," Col said, climbing to his feet. "Come on!"

They ran down the hillside, Col's leg supporting him well now with barely a limp. They jumped the stream in the valley, scaling the steep slope to the next peak. The eagle had gone, and they searched amongst the rocks for the cause of the struggle.

"There," said Col, spotting the bloodied hare, tufts of fur blowing around the carcass.

"Look," Talla said. Beside it was the mangled remains of a stoat.

"Perhaps it was after the eagle's kill," Col said.

"Maybe." Talla sat in silence.

"What's wrong?" Col asked.

"Albyn said the stoat would find me," she said, rubbing her thumb across her eyes, "But it's dead." Col picked up the stoat, taking a flake of flint from his pouch, cutting into the animal's belly. "What are you doing?" Talla asked.

"Taking the pelt for you. It's better than nothing." Col cut up the belly, peeling back the skin. "Talla, look," he said, holding out the bloodied body.

"What?"

"She has milk. There are young somewhere."

"I'll search for them," Talla said.

"Wait. Listen first."

They sat in silence, Col stripping the skin from the dead stoat. Hearing a faint squealing in a nearby pile of stones, Talla scrambled over, putting her head to the ground. "Here," she said, pulling at the loose rocks. A moment later she'd uncovered a matted ball of dried grass. She prised it open to find five red-brown kits squirming in a heap.

"They're young," Col said, "Perhaps too young to survive."

"No," said Talla, "I'll care for them."

She fed them tiny slivers of raw meat and dripped water into their little mouths every few hours, staying up much of the night while Col slept.

Despite her efforts, two of the tiny animals were dead by morning. She tucked the nest into her pack to keep the others warm.

* * *

They packed up in the rain the following morning, pulling the wet hide over their heads as they walked side by side through the downpour. It was past noon when they spotted the smoke rising from a cluster of huts on the coast.

"What now?" Talla asked.

"We have to hope they're friendly," Col said. "Come on."

They walked downhill, keeping out in the open so they would be seen. Dogs barked and ran out to meet them, as a small cluster of people formed.

"Greetings," Col called, "May we approach?"

"Yes," called a voice. Col pulled back his hood, holding out his hands in the recognised greeting, showing himself unarmed. A man stepped forward.

"Greetings. Who are your people? I don't recognise you."

"I am Col, Spirit Apprentice of the Hill Clan of the Tribe of the West," he said, using his official title for the first time.

"I am Sarn, leader of the Boat Clan of the Tribe of the South, welcome Col." He looked at Talla, and his mouth gaped. Col smiled, Sarn had spotted her white hair.

"I am Talla, Spirit Apprentice of the Hill Clan of the Tribe of the West," she said, holding out her hands.

"Y... y... your colour," stuttered the leader, "Are you a spirit?"

Talla smiled. "No, I was born this way." She turned her head, displaying the fresh scars of her tattoo. "Would our master have tattooed a spirit?"

"There was talk of a slave with your colouring on the west coast," he said.

"That was me," Talla said. "They sold me to Albyn, but he freed me, made me his apprentice."

"Albyn lives still?" Sarn asked. "I met him ten years ago, he was old then."

"Still alive," Col said, "And still grumpy."

Sarn laughed, breaking the tension. "Yes, I never once saw him smile," he said.

"We lived in his house, and neither did we," Talla replied.

"Come," he said, turning, "You must be hungry and thirsty." They walked into a village of ten houses, and Sarn took them to a central hut, larger than the rest. "Forgive me," he said, "we have no spirit messenger to greet you. She was old and died a moon ago. We hope to find someone soon. She had no apprentice."

"We have healing skills if you need them," Col said.

"Thank you, we are all well." He looked at Col, then Talla. "Our spirit messenger treated Harag of the Island Clan before she died. You'd have known him."

Talla glanced at Col. "Yes, I knew him. Is he recovered now?"

"He had some new amulet he'd traded for," Sarn said. "Tried to do some kind of fire magic with it. He got badly burnt."

"But your messenger treated him?"

"Mmm," Sarn said. "She said he took five days to die."

Talla shuddered and reached for Col's hand.

"Do you have the tribe lore?" Sarn asked.

"Yes," Col said.

Sarn smiled. "Join us for a meal and stay the night. But if you're willing, our young ones would love to hear the creation story."

They ate well, talking of the poor weather. The Boat Clan's crops had fared better than the Hill Clan's, but the yield would be low. Col and Talla sat beside the fire, a dozen children gathered around them, the adults to the rear.

"This is the story of Tarren, the first warrior," Col began, telling them the adventures of the hero in the dark land of creation. He recounted his first hunt, by moonlight, his battle with the clouds and the lightning. He told of Tarren stealing fire from the lightning spirit.

Talla took over the tale, telling of Tarren's need for light. How he'd set fire to his spear, holding it high to discover his world. He tried to get higher still, flinging his flaming spear up to the stars, where it burst into a ball of fire—the sun.

The little ones gasped, clapping their hands as the adults murmured their thanks and took the children to bed.

"You are born story-tellers," Sarn said, smiling at them as his mate brought tea. Talla thanked her, sipping the hot drink.

"Chamomile?" she asked. Sarn's mate nodded.

"Where are you heading," Sarn said, sitting next to Col by the fire's glow.

"We need to go to the far shore," Col said. "Is this a journey you make?"

Sarn nodded. "Yes, we trade across the water, for flint and grain. They like our soft leather and pottery."

"Could you take us?" Talla said.

Sarn looked doubtful. "More people means fewer goods," he said. "It would be a poor trading journey."

Col's hand went to his pouch on his belt. He glanced at Talla. She nodded.

"Would these make it worth your while to take us," he said, pulling out the red cloth and tipping the necklace into his palm.

Sarn gasped. "Amber?"

"Yes, Albyn gave them to us before we left. Will you accept them as a trade?"

Sarn reached for the beads, glancing into Col's eyes before inspecting them. He shuddered, handing them straight back to Col.

"They have great trade value, Col, but I cannot take them," he said.

"We hope to return sometime," Col said, "Would they be enough for both journeys?"

"Yes, but please keep them and pay me on your return," he said, moving a little further from the necklace. "We have a boat leaving as soon as the weather clears."

Col reached out his hand, clasping Sarn's. "Thank you. May we stay here until you sail?"

"If you will tell our young ones the tribe stories, you are both welcome. Do you have spirit animals?" he asked.

Talla pulled the nest of grass from its pouch, opening it to reveal the three kits.

"Stoats? They are young," he said.

"I only found them yesterday. I'm hoping at least one will survive."

"And you, Col?" Sarn asked.

He lifted his arm. "Kark!" he called. There was a cawing and the huge bird flapped into the evening air. A few of the remaining tribes-people made warding signs as Kark skimmed between them, swooping to land on Col's arm.

"Our own spirit messenger had a blackbird," Sarn said, "It died the day she did."

They talked as the day faded, then Sarn took them to the empty messenger's house. A fire had been lit for them, and they hung up their wet things before climbing into their bed.

* * *

In the two days that followed, they became friendly with Sarn and his Clan, telling many of the tribe stories, to their delight. The third day dawned bright, and Sarn said they would sail that day. They helped load the wooden boat with supplies and stowed their own bags.

"My son and daughter, Bek and Solla will take you," Sarn said as they stood by the shore. He hugged them both. "Travel well," he said.

"Thank you for your hospitality. We hope to see you again someday," Col said.

"Thank you," Talla added as they climbed aboard and shoved off from the beach.

* * *

Bek rowed the boat out from the shore, then Solla set a small sail. The wooden vessel creaked as the wind caught it and carried them east.

The brother and sister kept turning the boat, zigzagging across the blue water, the mountains of the far shore looming ever larger. They were making good headway when the wind dropped. Col went to sit beside Bek, taking one oar as he showed him how to propel the boat. Then the fog came.

"Curse it!" Bek said, stopping rowing.

"Can't we keep going?" Col asked.

"We can't tell if we're going in the right direction," Bek said, "We may come ashore on rocks." They sat in the eerie silence, the mist blocking out the sun, not letting them see twenty paces.

"What can we do?" Talla asked.
"Wait," said Solla, "And hope we don't drift too far."

Chapter 5

The four travellers sat in the fog-bound boat. They were still too far from the shore to hear the surf, even in the becalmed silence. They ate their packed food and drank from the waterskin.

"This is not good," Solla said, "We could drift on the currents, end up anywhere."

"If we knew which way to go, I'd chance rowing," Bek said, looking around for any hint of direction.

"Let me try something," Col said, putting his hand up and grabbing Kark's feet. The bird cawed, unused to the rough handling. Col grasped him, holding him up to his face. "I think you know which way to go," he said, smoothing the glossy feathers, "Why don't you show us."

Col tossed him up into the air, his wings spreading, flapping to gain height. "Kaark, kaark!" he complained, circling the small boat. They watched him flap around, his head turning, before he flew off in a straight line, disappearing into the gloom.

"That way," Col said.

"You're sure?" Bek asked, grabbing his oar.

"He can't land on water," Col said, "If he didn't know which way land was, he'd have come back."

They pulled hard on the oars, trying to keep a straight line, following the raven's flight. Col's shoulders were aching when Solla held up a hand. "Wait," she said, "Listen."

They sat for a moment, then heard it—the lap of waves on a beach ahead of them. "Gently," warned Bek, as they put their oars back into the water.

"Stop," Solla said, "I can see waves forming."

Col glanced to the side. Little crests were rolling past the boat. He'd just got his oar out of the water when there was a soft crunch, and they lurched to a stop.

"Thank the spirits," Bek said, "a beach." He jumped out of the boat, waist-deep in the water, as Solla leapt off the other side. Each had a rope in their hands, pulling the craft higher onto the sand. Talla and Col joined them.

"I'm glad you had your raven," Bek smiled.

Col stood and called. "Kark." There was a swish of wings and the bird streaked out of the mist, settling on his outstretched arm. "So you have a use, apart from eating," Col told him. Kark warbled in his throat, a repeated purring sound.

"I think he's pleased with himself," Talla said.

"He should be," said Bek.

They collected driftwood for a fire, lighting it high on the beach. Bek and Col hauled the boat up every so often until the tide turned and the light faded. They made shelters for the night and slept.

* * *

"Hello!" called a voice. Col rubbed at his eyes, trying to remember where he was. He heard the sea, and it came back to him. They'd pitched their skin shelter beside the boat, sleeping on the soft sand. Col crawled out of the shelter, as a tall man approached, spear in hand.

"Who are you?" he demanded.

Col held out his hands, palms forward, showing he was unarmed. "I am Col, Spirit Apprentice of the Hill Clan of the Tribe of the West," he said. The spear bearer glanced at the fresh tattoo marks on Col's face, then looked at the shelter as Talla emerged. His hand gripped the spear tighter.

"Hello," she said, standing. "I am Talla, Spirit Apprentice of the Hill Clan of the Tribe of the West."

"You... you're..."

"I'm different," she said, smiling and brushing the hair from her left eye, exposing her tattoos.

"Gan!" shouted Bek, emerging from his shelter, "Good to see you." He embraced the visitor. "These are our friends," he said, turning to Talla and Col. "They are on a journey. You have nothing to fear from Talla, she is human."

Solla came out, running to the young man. She hugged him, and he wrapped his arms around her.

"Hello Solla," he said. He turned to Talla and Col. "I apologise, I recognised the boat, but not you." he said.

"We are pleased to meet you. Gan, was it?" Col asked.

"My manners are poor," Gan said, laying down the spear. He held out his hands, standing tall. "I am Gan, son of the leader of the Shore Clan of the Atay Tribe. Please, let me take you to our village and get you some food and drink."

They pulled the boat further up the beach, each carrying trade goods as they followed Gan back to his village. Most of the attention fell on Talla, and she kept close to Col as Gan introduced them to his father, then took them to the spirit messenger. The older woman eyed Talla until she spotted the tattoos.

"Greetings," she said. "I am Genna, Spirit Messenger of the Shore Clan of the Atay Tribe, Plant Master, Lore Master, and healer." Col recited his status, followed by Talla. Then they both sat at her feet. "Stand, stand," she said, beckoning them towards her roundhouse. "It's good to see you have manners, but sitting is unnecessary. We bow to more experienced messengers."

They followed her. "Are our ways old-fashioned?" Talla asked.

"Different," she said, "Come in."

They settled around her fire, and a young girl of maybe eight summers made them tea and brought bread and cooked meat.

"This is Yella," the messenger said as the girl served them. "She will be my apprentice if she stays with me."

"If, messenger?" the girl asked, grinning.

"Yes, if I continue to put up with your insolence," the older woman smiled, ruffling the girl's hair. Col noticed Yella's arm was a mass of scars. Genna saw him looking.

"Yella, fill the water skin," she said.

"It's... oh, yes Messenger," the girl said, realising she was being dismissed.

"She was six summers," Genna said, when she'd gone, "Her parents' house burned down, she was the only survivor. The burns on her arm and body took many moons to heal. She was in great pain for so long."

"Many of the protected-of-spirit are wounded," Talla said. "Col lost his parents and had a broken leg, Yella is an orphan too."

"Disease orphaned me," Genna said, her face losing its smile for the first time. "It is common for spirit apprentices to have lost parents or to have had long or difficult illnesses. It is often the challenge the ancestors use to choose them for this path. What about you, Talla?"

Talla looked down, her fingers tracing the pattern on her leggings. "I was a slave," she said. "Our master bought me, but freed me to become an apprentice."

"He does not agree with slavery?" Genna asked.

"Albyn is against it," Col said.

"Albyn?" Genna gasped, "I met him. I was only a child, Yella's age. He is your master?"

"Yes," Col said.

She nodded, "Then I am not surprised he freed you," she smiled.

She walked to the back of the roundhouse, "Tarna, are you awake?" she called.

"Yes," said a brittle voice.

"We have visitors. Apprentices of Albyn."

There was a groan, then the voice came again. "Albyn? Albyn? Why do I know that name? Help me up, girl."

Col turned to Talla, grinning. Genna must be well past her thirtieth year and was no girl. A cloaked figure shuffled from the back of the dwelling, one hand held a stick, the other grasped Genna's arm. Genna seated her on a stool beside the fire.

"This is Tarna, Spirit Master of the Shore Clan of the Atay Tribe and my teacher," Genna told them.

"I can introduce myself," the old woman said.

"Yes, but I am here, and it hurts you to stand, Tarna," said Genna.

Talla and Col stood, bowing to the old master and reciting their status.

"Albyn? Albyn?" Tarna muttered. "The handsome young man," she gasped as her mind recalled something.

"He *was* a handsome young man," giggled Genna, "That was over twenty-five summers ago, Tarna."

"Hmm, yes, I forget," Tarna said. She closed her eyes and rubbed at her swollen knees.

"Do you treat the swelling-joint disease?" Talla asked, pointing to Tarna's legs

"Oh, yes, nettles," Genna said.

"Does nightshade grow here?" Talla said.

"Nightshade? That's a poison, we don't harvest it," Genna gasped.

"If eaten, yes," Col said, "But applied to the skin it will treat swelling-joints."

"You've tried this?" Genna asked.

"Albyn uses it," Talla said. She reached into her pack, rummaging. "Ah. Here it is." She pulled out a small pouch, checking the knots on the cord. "Do you have animal fat?" she asked.

Genna turned to Yella. The small girl had been sitting by the door since her return. "Fetch pig fat, Yella," she said. The girl jumped up, smiling, and ran off again.

Talla asked for a small bowl and tipped the dried herb into it. She added the fat Yella brought and crushed them together with a smooth pebble. Once satisfied with the mix, she knelt at Tarna's feet and rubbed it into her knees and ankles. "She may feel better by tomorrow," Col said, "It can take a short while to work."

They ate together that evening, talking about lore and plant knowledge. They impressed Genna with their skills, and she questioned why Albyn had not given them their keeper's tattoos. "We are young," Col said, "We only just got our apprentice tattoos."

Talla and Col settled later, onto a large bed platform, back to back. Sleep soon took them.

* * *

Yella was starting the fire in the roundhouse when they woke. The girl flashed her cheeky grin at Col and Talla, offering them tea. They sat outside, Yella at their side, sipping their drinks. Talla fed tiny slivers of raw meat to the last surviving stoat. It looked as though he'd live now, as he bolted the strips of beef.

"What will you call it?" Col asked.

"Raf," Talla said, stroking the soft fur.

"That's a boy's name," Col said, laughing.

Talla turned the small creature over, inspecting its belly. "He's a boy," she said. Col shook his head.

"Are you two bonded?" Yella asked.

"Spirits, no!" Col laughed.

"Not yet," Talla said.

He had just opened his mouth to speak when the house door opened, and Genna came out.

"Look," she said. They turned, and Tarna followed her from the building. She was still shuffling but was walking without her stick, and without holding on to her protégé.

"Thank you," the old woman said. She walked to Talla, taking her face in her hands, peering at the tattoos above her left eye. Crossing to Col, she scrutinised the marks over his right eye. "Finish their tattoos, Genna," she said. "They are both entitled to wear plant keeper marks now. Yella," she called.

The child ran out of the house, standing close to the old woman. Col realised Tarna had very poor eyesight.

"Yes, Spirit Master?"

"Are you ready to commit to being an apprentice?"

"Yes, Master Tarna!"

"Then Genna will give you your apprentice marks too." She turned to shuffle back into the house. "Come and put more of the nightshade on my joints first," she called over her shoulder.

* * *

Col tensed as Genna cut the intricate spirals into his forehead, finishing the marks made by Albyn. The lamp-black stung.

"There, Plant keeper," Genna said. Talla sat as Genna finished her tattoos in the same way, then took Yella on her lap.

"Are you ready, little one?" Genna asked. Yella nodded and closed her eyes.

Col watched as Genna cut the zigzags. The child's face betrayed no pain, even when Genna rubbed the black colour into the cuts. Genna moved on to the intricate spirit apprentice mark, but Yella sat still.

"You were very brave," Col said, as Genna finished.

"It didn't hurt much," the child said, glancing at her scarred arm, and he realised that she'd experienced pain far worse than the simple cuts of the tattoo.

* * *

Col and Talla stayed two more nights, leaving with food for three or four days. They said their goodbyes to the Clan, and to Bek, and to Solla, who was planning to become bonded to Gan soon. Genna told them about the people to the south, sending a gift for their spirit messenger. So it continued.

The Atay lands ended, and they encountered the Canna people. Often settlements were close together, and they passed through three in a day. Sometimes there were days between villages.

They carried gifts and greetings, messages, and warnings as they journeyed. They'd been travelling for half a moon, the weather still cold and wet every day, when they came to a halt. The village they'd stopped at was poor. Their crops were failing, their cattle and pigs thin and few. They could give Col and Talla no information about people to their south, except to tell them not to go that way.

"Why can we not travel south?" Col asked their spirit messenger, Gerik.

"There are outlaws," he said.

The words were familiar, but their meaning was not. "Outlaw?" Col asked.

"Yes, people who have done terrible things, murder, rape, theft, and their tribes have banished them."

Col looked to Talla, who was shaking her head. "We don't have this on our island," she said.

"You are lucky," Gerik replied, "There are, perhaps, twenty of them. They live by raiding and stealing. We don't have the means to stop them."

* * *

They stayed two days with Gerik, trading herbs, and treatments with the young messenger, then, despite Gerik's protestations, they set off south.

The mountainous country made for slow travelling, but after two days they stopped and made camp to try their luck at hunting and fishing. They set up the shelter between large rocks, and Col showed Talla how to catch trout in the stream using just his hands, a skill his father had taught him. They found signs of hare, tracks, and droppings, so he set rawhide snares. A feast of fish and fruit meant they went to bed with their bellies full.

Col wasn't sure what had woken him, but he'd no sooner opened his eyes when he felt something cold and sharp at his throat. Two men stood over them, each of them holding a flint-tipped spear.

Chapter 6

The first thing Talla noticed was the smell. Unwashed bodies and carrion. The spear-point at her throat made her gasp.

"Talla!" Col whispered.

"I'm awake," she said, her voice quavering.

"Silence," shouted the man with the spear, "Get up."

His accent was unusual, difficult to understand. Talla climbed to her feet; Col did the same.

"Food," the man said, the spear levelled at her throat.

"We have none," Col said. "We caught fish last night, we ate it."

"Search the bags," he said to his companion. Talla could make out their features now, in the early dawn light. Bushy beards, straggly hair, and each had a thick black line tattooed under their right eye. The talker looked at her face, pulling her around to the light. "Spirit apprentices," he said. "How do we get rid of these?"

His companion spoke for the first time. "Brev will know. Let's get them back to camp."

The men made them carry their own bags, abandoning the shelter, and prodded them up the hill. They walked for a long while, and it was daylight when they arrived at a large, low cave in the hillside. A woman in a filthy linen shift was starting a fire, while two emaciated, naked children played in a puddle.

"In there," said one of their captors, forcing them under a low overhang at the far edge of the cave mouth. The second man bound their hands before going inside.

"Damn!" said Col. "We should have listened to Gerik."

"You couldn't have known," Talla said. "They haven't killed us… yet. What do you think they'll do with us?"

"I don't know," Col said, watching a man approach. This one was taller and tidier.

"I am Brev. Who are you?" he asked.

"I am Col, Spirit Apprentice of the Hill Clan of the Tribe of the West."

"Where?"

"The Tribe of the West."

"Never heard of it. Where were you going?"

"South," said Col.

He turned. "Give them water," he called to the woman, walking away. She approached, a water skin in her hand.

"Where are we?" Talla asked.

She looked around, making sure no one was near. "The mountains."

"Does this place have a name?" Col said.

She shook her head. "Just the camp," she said, holding the cup to Talla's mouth.

"Are you an outlaw?" Talla asked.

"No, slave to them. I am Vinna, I was of the Poan Tribe."

"What will they do with us, Vinna," Talla asked, smiling when Vinna lifted her downcast eyes.

"Take you south, sell you as slaves," she said. "I have to go, they will beat me for talking."

Talla sighed. "A slave. It is my curse again."

* * *

They spent the day in the cave. Someone gave them water a few times, but there was no food, nor did they smell any cooking. Talla asked to relieve herself, and Vinna led her to a stand of trees. They must have been using it for a long time, and the stench was nauseating. Vinna freed Talla's hands, then pointed a spear at her.

"Don't run," she said. "I will kill you. If I don't, they will kill me."

Talla nodded. She had been in that position, made to do something on pain of death.

"I will not to run," she said, unfastening her clothes. Vinna watched the whole time, never lowering the spear. She gasped as Tall hitched up her tunic.

"Your back!" Vinna said, spotting the tangle of scars.

"I was a slave too," Talla said.

* * *

The next morning two men dragged them out of the shelter, and they began a journey south. They had bound their hands with enough movement to balance themselves, but not enough to be any danger to their captors. Brev led the way, and two other men followed them. One man who'd captured them, and another much older man; the only one without the broad tattoo under his eye. They travelled for two days, soaked by the rain. Col and Talla huddled together, shivering, each night.

On the third day they saw, in the distance, a settlement beside a river. It must have been over four times the size of any they'd seen so far. Brev and his men left them sitting by a tree while they talked nearby.

"What do you think will happen?" Col asked.

"I expect they'll take us to the village and sell us," Talla said.

The men returned at that point, and Brev threw the empty waterskin at Talla. "Fill it," he said.

She reached for the skin, but her tied hands would come no further forward than her waist. "I can't," she said. He untied her bonds, tying them again at the front of her body.

"Go."

Talla struggled to her feet and took the empty skin to the stream, one man following her with a spear. She crouched, dipping the open neck of the vessel into the fast-flowing water. She checked behind her. The guard was urinating into a bush. Talla slipped a hand into her pouch, taking out a small bag. She tipped the contents into the water skin. "Come on," the man shouted, beckoning with his spear. She stood and followed him, eyes downcast, though a smile played on her lips.

Once they'd returned, Brev took a leather strap and tied one end around each of their necks, tethering them together. Talla stiffened as he tightened the collar, but caught Col's eye as he shook his head. The old man took them aside, pouring water onto the ground, then spreading handfuls of the mud over their exposed skin. He covered their faces, arms and lower legs then rubbed the goo into Talla's hair too. He bade farewell to Brev and the other man, then led them towards the settlement.

Col followed Talla, seeing her straighten her back and hold her head up, as they were taken to be sold.

* * *

They garnered little attention as they entered the village. People passed, but no one spoke. It was like they were invisible. The old man took them to a house, knocking. A thin, rodent-faced man appeared, glancing at Col and Talla before turning to the old man.

"Drav," he said, his face emotionless. "What have you brought me?"

"Strong young slaves, Adra. Not a day over fifteen summers."

Adra pushed back Talla's cloak, feeling her arm. "This one's thin," he said.

"Just needs feeding, that's all. A pig carcass and a bag of meal, that's all I'm asking," Drav said, a false smile creasing his face.

"Come in," Adra said. They entered the smoky house. "Sit there," he ordered Col and Talla, pointing to the floor behind the door. "Why are they so filthy?" he asked Drav.

"Got caught in a mudslide, you know how the weather is." The men walked over to a table, sitting haggling over the captives.

"What are we going to do?" Talla asked.

"Wait," Col said. "The mud is to hide our tattoos. I'm guessing spirit apprentices are not sold as slaves."

"Shall we tell him?" Talla asked.

"Not until the old man's gone."

Finally, they reached a deal, though Drav was complaining even as he left the house.

"Give him half the carcass we killed last night, and a bag of meal," Adra shouted to someone from the door. He turned to Col and Talla. "Come and get washed," he said. "I can't sell you looking like that."

They struggled to their feet and followed him. He led them to the river, nodding to the water. "Get in, get clean," he ordered, untying them. Col slipped into the shallow water at the edge, taking Talla's hand as she followed him. He scooped water as she bent over, sluicing the dried mud from her hair.

"Your hair. It's white!" Adra gasped.

Col scooped water to his own face, washing the dirt from his skin, revealing the tattoos around his eye. Adra blinked, staring at what his eyes didn't want to believe.

"That thieving old crook! Stay there," he said, running back towards his house. There was a great deal of commotion, Adra trying to send someone to find Drav before he got too far. Col and Talla continued to wash, then waded out of the water and sat on the bank. Soon a woman came to them.

"Adra asked me to take you to the spirit master," she said.

"Thank you," said Col, taking Talla's hand.

* * *

The tall man stood at the door. He had, maybe, forty summers. His hair was ash grey, and his clothing was clean and well decorated. A swan-feather cloak hung from his shoulders. He held out his hands in greeting.

"I am Garav, Spirit Master of the River Clan of the Uru Tribe. Lore Master, Plant Master, Fire Keeper, and Healer of my people," he recited.

Col bowed his head, then looked up at Garav. "I am Col, Spirit Apprentice of the Hill Clan of the Tribe of the West. Lore Keeper, Plant Keeper, and healing apprentice."

"I am Talla," she said. She shivered, and her voice trembled as she gave her own status.

"Should we sit, or bow?" Col asked. "We do not know your customs."

Garav smiled. "You have been polite, Col, Talla, please come in and get out of your wet clothes." He called for a young man with apprentice tattoos to fetch furs for them. Talla stripped off her dripping leggings and tunic, gripping Col's hand as soon as they were seated at the edge of the hearth.

"I do not know your Tribe," Garav said. "Forgive my ignorance."

"We come from the Islands to the West, some call them the Long Islands," Talla said. "Our messenger has charged us with travelling to find the cause of nature's anger with our people."

"Nature seems angry with all of our kind," Garav said, "It is a task I do not envy you."

Col smiled. "We had little choice."

They told him of their journey, working their way south until the outlaws captured them. Garav asked about the outlaws, where they might find them, who had brought them to the village.

"The old man called Drav brought us," Talla said.

"He works with the outlaws?" Garav asked. "He has no outlaw tattoo."

"The black lines, under the eyes?" Talla asked. He nodded.

"They will have gone by now," Col said.

"No," Talla said, smiling, "Maybe not." She stood and went outside, the warm fur clutched tight around her. Garav and Col followed. She looked up to the hill behind the settlement, finding the stream they'd followed.

"There," she said, pointing, "The bend in the stream." Garav nodded. "The dip beyond is where they were waiting," Talla said.

"Why would they still be there?" Col asked.

"Because I put nightshade in their waterskin," she said.

* * *

It was evening when Adra and his men returned to the village. They were dragging the two younger men, while the old man stumbled along with a rope around his neck.

"What will happen to them?" Talla asked Garav.

"Adra will sell them as slaves if they survive," he said. "Why do you carry poisonous plants?"

"Mixed with fat, and rubbed into the skin, it treats the swelling-joint disease," she explained.

Garav put a hand on each of their shoulders, guiding them to his house. "Come and sit," he said, "We have healing remedies to exchange."

They talked long into the night, discussing treatments and cures. Garav's apprentice, Ban, served them food, then sat and listened to their talk, occasionally asking a question.

Talla yawned, and Garav grinned at them. "Time to sleep," he said. "Ban, make up a bed for our guests."

Ban showed them to a sleeping platform with thick furs, wishing them a good night. Talla pulled off her clothing and crawled into bed, Col followed.

He rolled onto his side and Talla snuggled up behind him. "They think we're bonded," he whispered.

"Do you mind?" she said.

"No," he said. He turned to face her. "Do you?"

Talla shook her head. "No, but you haven't asked me to be your mate."

He rolled back, facing away from her again. "No, I haven't, have I?" he said.

* * *

The activity in the roundhouse woke Talla. Col was sitting on the edge of the bed, pulling on his leggings and shirt. He turned when he heard her move, smiling and tossing over her clothes. Ban made them barley porridge and tea.

Talla sniffed the hot drink. "Mint?" she asked.

He nodded. "And?" he said grinning.

She sipped the tea, swilling it around her mouth. "Rosehip."

"Yes, you're good, you know that?" he said.

"Years of practice," Talla said, "Where's Garav?"

"Checking the outlaws you poisoned," he said.

"Will they live?" she asked, her voice betraying her fear.

Garav walked in the door as she spoke. "They'll live," he said, ruffling the morning rat's nest that was Talla's hair.

"Thank the spirits," she said.

"They'd have killed you as soon as blink."

"I know," she said, combing her unruly hair with her fingers.

"There's a raven on the roof," Garav said. "Does it belong to one of you?"

Col smiled. "Mine," he said, "Can he come in?" Garav nodded, and Col called to his bird. The glossy black form of Kark appeared in the doorway, peering in at the strangers with his keeper.

"Come on, lazy bird," Col said, holding out an arm. Kark flapped up, scrabbling at his sleeve before balancing himself.

"And you, Talla?" Garav asked.

A whistle brought Raf from the furs on their bed. He crawled to the edge and waited. Talla smiled and allowed him to run up her arm to his preferred nest in her hood.

Garav whistled a series of notes they recognised, so neither was surprised when a speckled thrush flew in to sit on his shoulder. "The Beaver has chosen Ban," Garav said, "We have hopes of finding a young one yet this summer."

"You called yourself a Fire Keeper, when you introduced yourself," Col said, "What does that mean?"

"You don't have Fire Keepers?" Garav asked.

"No, anyone can make a fire," Col said.

"Of course, but you align yourself with the plants to become a Plant Keeper, don't you?"

"Yes."

"Well, a Fire Keeper aligns themselves with fire," said Garav. "They learn to build and control fire, to preserve it, to tame it. They learn how to make hotter fires, or cooler. How to command the fire spirits themselves."

"Could you teach us?" Talla asked.

"If you stay for a moon, I'll teach you what I can," he said.

She glanced at Col. He nodded, his eyes wide with excitement.

"We'll work for our keep," Talla said. "We can labour in the fields."

"Help me here," he said. "Treat the sick, help Ban gather herbs, teach him the ones he doesn't yet know, help him tie them for drying. That will be work enough."

So their time as fire apprentices began. They lit the hearth fire each day, Ban showing them the proper way, and how to recite an incantation to the fire spirits. Garav taught them about different woods, and how they burned, how to keep the fire small or make it grow bigger. They learned to harness the wind to make the fire hotter. Garav showed them compounds, herbs and powdered rock, each for a different purpose, each giving its own colour or scent to the flames.

* * *

It was late, sunset, and Talla found Garav sitting on a rock near to the river, watching the horizon.

"What are you doing?" she asked, sitting beside him. He pointed to the setting sun.

"See where the sun sets?" he asked, "At the join of those hills?"

"Yes."

"It is mid-summer," he said. "In a few days, the sun will set a little further south. It is time for our celebration."

"A feast?" she asked.

"Like none you've ever seen," he said, smiling.

* * *

Excitement spread through the village after Garav announced the mid-summer festival. Col and Talla worked with Ban to build the two large fires for roasting the meat; a whole pig and a quarter of beef.

The day of the festival dawned dry. Garav had introduced them to the village as journeying apprentices, and each had a role in the ceremony to mark the season. Col held the place of fire in the south, while Talla took the east and air. Ban stood in the west, for water, while Garav led the proceedings from the north, representing earth. Later they chatted with the villagers, learning the similarities and differences of these people.

Garav had them build a small fire at the centre of the village, and he walked around it, chanting and invoking the spirits. He flung his arms across the blaze, yellow sparks erupting from the flames. He shouted another invocation, this time raising a flash of white, then another with bright blue flames. Talla grasped Col's arm, eyes wide at the spectacle, her excitement contagious. The people cheered his mastery as he slowed his circling and finally sat beside the fire with his drum. Ban, Col, and Talla joined him, each with a frame drum, and the journey began.

First, there was a soft heartbeat of drumming, getting faster and faster until it was a frenzied rhythm. Garav had taught them each their part, and as the drumming settled to a steady rate, they closed their eyes and let the beat take them below.

* * *

They were back to the twilight of the lower world. Garav walked ahead, striding across the dusty land, followed by Ban, Col, and Talla. Four figures appeared, stepping out of the gloom, blocking the way forward.

"Who are you, and what is your quest?" said the character to the left, his face painted jet black.

"I am Garav, of the Uru Tribe, and we seek knowledge, Spirit," Garav said.

"What do you seek?" said the second figure. His face was blue with the plant dye of warriors.

Ban stuttered at being addressed by the spirit. "I... I... I am an apprentice," he said. "I seek to learn."

The third figure's face was as white as the foam on waves. "What do you journey for?" he asked Talla.

She stood tall, looking into the spirit's eyes. "I seek to placate the nature spirits that ruin the crops of our people," she said.

The fourth figure stepped forward, standing only a pace from Col. Its face was red, and shimmered like hot coals. "You, who journey with her, what is your quest?"

Col's eyes flicked to Talla, then back to the spirit standing before him. "I seek to heal the rift between man and nature, Spirit."

The spirit nodded and stepped back. They called their names, starting with the first to speak.

"I am the Spirit of Earth."

"I am the Spirit of Water."

"I am the Spirit of Air."

"I am the Spirit of Fire. You who travel will do battle with each of us before you have finished your journey. If you beat us, you will succeed; if you fail, you will die." With that, the four spirits seemed to melt away.

Garav continued towards the river, just as they'd seen Albyn doing. He called across the water to the ancestor spirits, conversing with them. Talla looked amongst the spirits of the dead, spotting her again; her mother. Col took her hand, and she looked away.

Garav turned and smiled at them. "We must return," he said.

* * *

Talla opened her eyes, her hand still beating the drum cradled in her lap as Garav raised his arm to stop them.

"Let the feast begin!" he called as the people cheered. He turned to Col and Talla. "Did you understand the elemental spirits?" he asked.

"They wish us to battle with them?" Talla asked.

"Yes. They will each challenge you on your journey. Not in the form you saw, but in their natural forms as earth and air, water, and fire."

"And we may die?" Col said.

"If you fail their tests, yes. Are you prepared for that?"

Talla turned to Col, taking both his hands. Her gaze was steady, her face calm. "We'll face them together, Col."

Col turned to Garav. "Yes, we're ready."

They joined the feast, along with Ban, while Garav went to talk to the clan elders about the messages from the ancestors. They ate well, roasted meats and barley bread, and beer, an unfamiliar experience for them. With the feast finished, Ban asked them to help him with the fires. They'd no idea what they were doing as they raked the hot coals into a long bed of embers, just a pace wide.

Garav re-appeared. "It's time to amaze people," he said, slipping off his sandals.

He walked to the end of the line of coals and spread his arms. Col and Talla gasped as he set one foot on the glowing embers, then paced the length of the fire. He circled, coming back to them. "Ban?" he said. The lad nodded and took off his shoes. They watched open-mouthed as he strolled over the hot coals.

Garav stood between them, an arm over each of their shoulders. "Now you two," he said.

Talla stared at the red-hot embers. "B... but we can't!" she said, turning to Col.

"We have not trained for this, Garav," Col said.

"You have studied to align yourselves with the fire spirits," Garav told them. "I will go with you. Take my hands. Place your foot firmly, and flat, do not twist your foot or roll off of your toes. Repeat the incantation with me."

They repeated the verse they'd learned to call the fire spirits. Then Garav stepped forward. Col stepped onto the coals, his foot feeling the heat yet not hurting. He lifted the other foot, placing flat on the bed of embers.

"Look ahead, not at your feet," Garav whispered. "Keep moving, and smile for the people, they think you're a magician now." They reached the end of the fire and stepped onto the cool grass again.

"Success?" Garav asked. Talla reached over and hugged him, then turned and hugged Col.

"We did it Col. We walked across fire!"

Col held her close as she bounced on her toes. Her joy was infectious. "Can we go again?" he asked Garav, "The two of us?"

"Go ahead," the spirit master said.

Col took Talla's hand as they stepped onto the coals. They smiled and watched the crowd as they walked until their feet touched the grass again.

"Well, my little fire keepers," Garav said, throwing an arm over each of their shoulders, "Tomorrow you get new tattoos."

Chapter 7

Col's head throbbed. Talla was sprawled across the bed, an arm and a leg draped across him.

"Talla."

"Mmmph."

"Talla!"

"Mmmh? What? Oh, sorry," she said, removing the stray limbs. "Ooh. My head."

"Yes, me too," Col said, "I think it must be the beer we had."

"I need water," Talla muttered, climbing over him and reaching for the waterskin.

"Pour some for me," Col said.

They dressed, finding that Ban was suffering that morning too. Garav was his usual self.

"So, tattoos today?" he asked them.

"Yes," Col said, peering at Garav's right eye. "Which is the Fire Keeper tattoo?" Garav pointed to the intricate scroll-work beside his eye. "If you're agreeable, I'll let Ban do them, he needs the practice."

* * *

They sat for Ban as he cut the designs into their skin. Col went first, wincing at the sting of the black dye. Talla followed, as always the braver.

"How does it look?" Talla asked when Ban had finished.

"The black looks good against your white hair and pale skin," Col said.

"Thank you, Ban," she said, hugging him.

"Yes, thanks Ban," Col added.

Garav stopped to inspect the new marks they wore. "Hmm, better than mine," he said. "Ban, you got yourself a new job." The young apprentice blushed.

They stayed another seven days with the River Clan, learning of the lands to the south. Col looked around the settlement, realising how fast he had slipped back into village life.

"We will miss you," Garav said. Ban nodded as Col and Talla lifted their packs. "We will welcome you on your return."

"If we return," Col said, remembering the fire spirit's message.

"You'll return," he said. "Travel well." They waved and took the path leading south.

* * *

It took a few days to get used to travelling again, calling at settlements on the way, meeting spirit messengers or masters. Some places they passed through, others invited them to stay overnight, or a few days. Not half a moon after mid-summer, there was snow. Talla and Col huddled in a cave mouth out of the unseasonal, driving sleet.

"We need to sit this out, Talla," Col said. "I'll explore inside the cave."

He walked back into the dark interior, his eyes adjusting. There was a hearth; a circle of stones and a blackened rock floor. Someone had sheltered or lived here long ago. He checked around the cave, finding a pile of dry wood.

"Talla, we can light a fire," he called. She joined him beside the old fireplace, smiling at the thought of warmth. Col got out the fire bow and kindling from his pack while Talla brought wood. He chanted the incantation to the fire spirits and soon they were sitting by a warm blaze. They ate their food and, when the fire was hot enough, heated stones to make tea.

"I need to pee," Talla said, "but it's so cold and wet outside."

"Take a torch and use the back of the cave," Col told her. She grinned, took a burning branch, and set off back into the darkness. Col was warming his hands when there was a scream.

"Col, come quick," she shouted. He grabbed another brand from the fire and ran towards the back of the cave. Talla was staring, mouth open. Following her gaze, Col saw a crude sleeping platform with the remains of animal furs. Lying amongst the rotting hides were the white bones of a human, dressed in the remains of a man's tunic and leggings. "He must have lived here," Talla whispered.

"And died here," Col added.

"He's had no funeral rites," she said, clasping her fist to her chest. "No one has ever sent him to the next world."

"His spirit is trapped," Col said. "We have to send him onwards."

"Do you remember how to conduct the ceremony?" Talla asked.

"I think so. We must place the bones too, they should be in a tomb. I suppose this cave will do."

"When will you do it?" she asked.

"Now. I don't want to sleep here until he's sent across the river of death. Do you?"

Talla shook her head. "We don't have a drum," she said.

"Get two solid sticks from the woodpile," he said. "Will you drum for me with them?"

She nodded, fetching two thick sticks that made a satisfying clunk when banged together. Col inspected the skeleton, bare of any flesh, and began the death chant. Albyn had used it many times, and the words were simple; an invitation to the ancestor spirits to come and greet one of their own and take him home across the river.

Talla drummed with her makeshift instrument as he repeated the invocation five times and laid his hands, one on the skull, one where the heart would have been. Col realised he knew neither the man's name nor his tribe, so he improvised. "Your kin are here to take you, brother of an unknown tribe. We free your spirit from your body so you may go with them. Travel well."

Col sat beside Talla as she continued a steady beat. "Journey with me," he said.

"You're sure?"

"Yes," he said, "But no crossing the river."

She smiled. "No, not this time." They closed their eyes.

* * *

They emerged in the barren landscape once more. Talla's spirit took the hand of Col's, walking forward to the river.

"There," she said, pointing across the fast-flowing water.

A man of perhaps forty summers stood opposite, six or seven other vague outlines beyond him. "Thank you, Spirit Apprentice," he called.

Talla waved and shouted, "Travel well, brother."

His shape became indistinct and drew back from the water, disappearing. "Let's go back," Col said.

* * *

Col opened his eyes and turned to Talla as she stopped the rhythm.

"Thank you. Let's take his bones to that alcove," Col said, pointing. They carried the remains to the niche in the cave wall, piling them neatly.

"I'm so glad we could do that," Talla said.

"Me too," Col said, "It's getting dark, let's find a spot to sleep."

They found a place across from the old bed, flat, dry, and away from the cave mouth and its draughts. They laid out their spare clothing and cloaks, making a place to sleep.

Col pulled the furs over them. "Goodnight, Talla."

"Goodnight, Col."

* * *

A terrible roar wakened Col. Talla clung to him in the dark.

"What was that?" she asked, her body trembling.

"I don't know. Perhaps an earth-shaking, I remember that from when I was a child."

"Yes, me too," Talla said. "It was before my father sold me. Two of the houses in our village collapsed."

Col opened his mouth to speak, tasting the gritty dust before his throat tightened and he coughed. Talla was spluttering beside him. He pulled the cloak over his mouth, pushing a corner towards Talla. "Breathe through this," he gasped.

It took a while for them to recover as the air cleared. Col noticed the glow towards the cave mouth. "We need to rescue the fire," he said, standing. They felt their way toward the faint glimmer, and Col raked the coals together, blowing onto them as he laid half-burnt twigs onto the embers. He heard Talla recite the chant for the fire spirits, as the flame flickered to life and he fed in larger sticks.

A thick layer of dust covered everything. Col turned towards the cave mouth as Talla gasped. The entrance to the cave was no longer there. A pile of rock and mud filled the space, the odd piece still tumbling and settling as they watched. "We're trapped," she whispered.

Col pulled her into his arms, hugging her thin body. "It's alright. We'll find a way. Maybe we can shift the rocks enough to climb out," he said.

"I'll build up the fire," she said, wiping her eyes with dirty fists.

They drank water to wash the dust from their throats, and Col took a stick from the fire, holding it high to see the rockfall. The rocks were huge; the size of his body or bigger. He could never move them. He climbed onto the lower boulders, holding the light higher to check right across the cave mouth.

"Col. The flame," Talla said.

"It's all right, it won't go out," he reassured her.

"No, watch," she said. Col studied the blazing brand for a moment. The flame was being pulled towards the fallen rocks, and he felt a draught on his face.

"Do you think there's a way out through this?" he said.

"No, but the smoke is finding its way out," she said. "If it's blowing the smoke out, there must be air coming in somewhere."

"You think there's another entrance?" Col asked.

"Let's see," she said, a smile crossing her face.

They packed their belongings and selected two good torches from the fire, along with another two to light later. Col took the lead, with Talla holding his hand. The roof of the cave got lower as they moved back until it forced them to crawl, but they kept going, deeper and deeper into the hillside. They had to crawl single file to fit through one narrow gap. The draught, funnelling through the opening, almost blew out the burning brands they carried.

Then the walls and ceiling were no longer visible. Col held up the torch, finding he could stand. Talla joined him, and they gazed into the darkness. "See anything?" she asked.

"No. Hold the torches behind us so we can see." Their eyes accustomed to the dark, then they could see the walls and the roof stretching away from them until they disappeared into the gloom. "We'd better follow a wall," Col said, "We don't know what we'll find if we go straight into the dark."

"Which way?" Talla asked.

Col shook his head. Talla wet her finger and held it up, trying to trace the draught in the vast cavern. "This way," she said, pointing left. Col stooped, finding small rocks on the floor, piling them into a cairn.

"What's that for?" Talla asked.

"In case we end up back here," he said. "We'll find this, and we'll know we've walked in a circle."

"Clever man," she said, kissing him on the cheek.

"I'm not the one that spotted the draught," he said, setting off along the cave wall.

They walked for ages, not knowing if it was day or night or how long they'd been trapped. Both were tired as they sat for a break, draining the last of the water. Col heard the trickling; a small stream of water flowing off an overhang. Talla held the water skin under it to fill it, then held up a wet finger.

"Still ahead of us," she said.

They moved on, not daring to stop. The torches were burning low, and they put one out to save their light, then walked on.

"Look," said Talla. The roof of the cavern was visible for the first time since they'd entered. It got lower until they were crawling again. The flame of the torch flickered, and Col held the light up, finding another tight opening to their left.

"It looks too small," he said.

"Let me go first," Talla said, "I'm thinner." She wriggled along the cave floor, pushing with her toes, pulling with her fingers as she disappeared into the narrow slot. Her voice came back to him, echoing around the chamber.

"I'm through. Come on."

"I won't fit, I'm bigger than you," he said.

"It's alright, the floor is sand, you can push it out of the way."

Col slid forward, the torch held in front, blinding him.

"Keep going, not much further," Talla called. "I can almost reach you."

The rock scraped his back now as his ribs pressed into the sand. He couldn't raise his head at all, so he kept wriggling forward. Col stopped, what if the rock shifted as it had at the cave mouth? It would crush him. Squash the breath out of him.

"Col. What's wrong?" Talla said.

"N... nothing," he said, his breath coming in gasps now.

"A little further," she said, "Come on." He wriggled on a pace. "More."

Another wriggle, then he felt it, Talla's hand gripping his, pulling him forward out of the jaws of rock. He stumbled to his feet as Talla's arms found him and wrapped him in warm security. "You're safe now," she said, her breath hot on his neck.

They sat and took a drink. The space they were in was a passage, high enough to stand, wide enough to just touch both walls. The breeze was stronger now, blowing past Col, cooling the sweat that had formed on his face.

"Col, I can see daylight!" Talla said.

Far ahead was a bright circle on the floor. They ran forward, finding the end of the passage and a narrow shaft above them.

"How do we get out?" Talla asked. The gap was wide enough, but over twenty paces high and dripping with water.

"We must climb," Col said.

They fixed their packs and Talla set off first, gripping on to the wet rock, pulling with her thin arms as her feet sought purchase to take her weight. Col followed.

They'd got a quarter of the way up when Talla cursed. He looked up as a rock struck his head. Col's vision blurred for a moment, then he was falling. Pain pierced the back of his head as the air was driven out of his lungs. Then everything went black.

Chapter 8

Col lay sprawled on the floor of the cave below. Talla screamed his name and scrambled down the slippery wall as fast as possible, jumping the last part to land beside him. She rolled him onto his back, placing a hand on his chest, her ear beside his mouth. Talla whispered a prayer of thanks as she felt his warm breath on her cheek.

Checking his head, she found a cut where the rock must have hit him. There was a bigger lump on the back of his skull. She worked her way along his arms and his legs, but there was no noticeable damage. Talla sat beside him, watching the rise and fall of his chest, and waited.

* * *

His voice woke her.

"Talla. Talla." She must have drifted off to sleep.

"Col. How do you feel, is anything broken?" she asked as he tried to sit up. She pulled him to her, holding him close. He was everything she had.

"My head," he said, reaching back to the lump.

"You banged it. I'm so sorry, Col. I knocked a rock loose, and it hit you."

"It's all right, Talla. Not your fault," he said, closing his eyes. "Help me up, will you?"

Talla took his hands, pulling him to his feet. He wobbled for a heartbeat, putting his hand on her shoulder, leaning on her to steady himself.

"All right now?" she asked.

"Yes, just unsteady," he said, smiling.

"Sit for a while," Talla said, "I'll climb up and see where we are."

"What do you mean?"

"We could come out halfway up a cliff. Stay there, I'll be back soon."

She left her pack, clambering up the rock wall of the narrow shaft. She soon realised that she could lean back, bracing her shoulders against the wall, giving her time to rest or look for the next hand or foothold. "Col, look," she shouted. He looked up, seeing her lying against the wall behind her.

"Is that easier?" he asked.

"Yes. I'll go to the top now." She climbed the last part faster, the rock being rougher, giving more grip. She hauled herself over the lip and lay panting on the bare rock at the top.

"What can you see?" Col called. She looked around at the landscape.

"It's all right. We can get down from here," she said. "It's a simple walk."

"I'll come up."

"No," Talla shouted. "I'll come back. I need my pack." She slipped back over the edge, finding her first foothold, and clambered down to him. "Col, we should wait before we go up again," she said.

"Why?"

"You've hit your head, I don't want you to climb yet. The sun will set soon, and it's very exposed up there. I think we should sleep in the tunnel tonight, see how you're feeling tomorrow."

"I don't know," he said.

Talla took his face in her hands. "If I'd fallen, would you let me climb now?" she said.

"No," he said.

"It's settled then. We climb out in the morning."

They made their bed a few paces back from the shaft in case there was rain. Talla cuddled beside Col as the last of the daylight faded, and his arm wrapped around her waist.

"This was the test of the earth spirit, wasn't it?" she said.

"Yes."

"We won."

"Yes, barely," he whispered.

"I don't know what I'd do if I lost you, Col," Talla said.

"You didn't." It was quiet for a moment, and she wondered if he'd drifted off to sleep. The arm at her waist tightened. His body pressed to her back in the dark.

"I never want to lose you either, Talla," he said.

* * *

They were up with the first light the next morning. They ate dry bread and cold meat, then packed their bags. Talla started up the shaft again, leaning her back against the side every so often to rest. She pointed out the better handholds to Col as he followed her up, then slipped over the lip at the top.

Talla lay flat. "Give me your hand," she said, reaching down to haul him up.

"Thanks, Talla," he gasped as he lay back beside her. Raf peeked out of Talla's hood and crawled along her arm, looking in each of her hands; his way of asking for food. She smiled and gave him a piece of meat from her pack.

"Kark!" Col called. There was no reply for a moment, then the raven glided from the rocks above them. Col set him on his shoulder as he bobbed his head and warbled. "You can hunt for yourself, lazy bird," he chuckled.

They stood and secured their packs before setting off south again. They made it to a village by nightfall, finding a friendly community and being invited to stay a day or two. Col needed the rest to get over his fall, so they agreed. They chatted late into the night with the spirit messenger. He'd travelled as a young apprentice and talked of a great circular earthwork, far to the south, where he'd seen their winter solstice celebration.

They spent the next day with him, foraging for herbs and remedies. He showed them a few new plants and their uses, and they pointed out things they used that were strange to him. At first light they set off again, waving a farewell. His Clan had given them food, as he said there were no settlements to the south for some day's travel.

They were into heather-covered uplands now, the bleak landscape stretching ahead. They walked holding hands often, and Talla wondered if there was a future for them after this journey; if they both survived. He'd never mentioned becoming bonded again, and she wouldn't ask. It was usual for the man to ask.

She'd have said yes.

"We'll need a fire tonight," Col said, bringing her back from her daydream.

"Yes, it's cold." She thought for a moment. "Why do you think nature has turned against us?" she asked.

"It's not just us," Col said. "It's all the tribes, every place we've visited has had poor crops, many clans will be hungry this winter. I guess we'll find out why wherever our journey ends. It has something to do with the spirits of the elements."

"Look," she said, pointing, "We could camp there." There was a rocky outcrop ahead; they could pitch the shelter on the lee-side.

They put up the shelter, pulling in heather to make their bed comfortable. A copse of trees provided wood for a small fire, and Talla lit it while Col fetched fuel. They skewered cold meat on sticks and warmed it over the flames, eating half a loaf along with it. The day had been chilly but dry, and they were glad to crawl into their shelter, buried under their cloaks for the night.

"Do you miss home, Col?" she asked him, as she snuggled beside him.

"Yes. I know Albyn was grumpy, but he cared for us."

"I miss him too," she said. "Do you think we'll ever see him again?"

"We have to hope so. We have to believe we can meet the challenges of the spirits, Talla. You and me together."

She reached back for his arm, pulling it around her waist. He chuckled. "Goodnight, Talla."

"Goodnight, Col."

* * *

They lay in their bed longer than planned the next morning. There was a bitter wind from the east, and their little nest was so cosy.

"We'd better move," said Col.

"If we must," Talla said, throwing off the bedding and pulling on her leggings and cloak. Col followed her, and they were soon packing. It was dry for a second day, unusual this summer, which had been the wettest in memory.

They set off south again, the strong winds keeping them off balance on the uneven ground. Talla grabbed for Col's hand, trying to stay upright.

"We need to find shelter," she shouted above the roar of the blast.

Col looked around; open moorland stretched in every direction. "There's nowhere to go," he said into her ear. "We must keep going."

They struggled on, leaning into the buffeting gusts. Talla caught movement out of the corner of her eye and looked to her left. A massive column of black cloud was moving towards them, wide at the base with a waist, then spreading again at the top. "Col. What is that?" she shouted, grasping his arm.

He turned, eyes wide. "I don't know. It's coming this way, though."

"What do we do?" she said.

"Get on the ground," he said, dragging her down beside him, "I think it's some kind of storm."

They lay side by side in the deep heather. Talla clung to his hand, her body shaking now, as the roaring of the wind got louder. She opened her eyes for a moment, seeing clumps of earth and heather flying past them.

"Col, I'm scared!" she screamed. His hand tightened as Talla felt herself being lifted as if she was floating. Col's hand pulled on hers, then was dragged from her grip as she flew into the air, tossed over and over as the terrifying winds pushed and slapped at her body. She tried to scream but breathed in nothing but wet earth. Coughing, she struggled to spit the foul mess out. She reached for her mouth, but the wind whipped away her hands; she wasn't strong enough to fight it.

When the buffeting stopped, Talla knew she was falling. She opened her eyes, watching, terrified, as the ground rushed up to meet her.

* * *

There was a pain. Talla tried to breathe, and it hurt. She moved, that hurt too. Her mouth was still full of the gritty soil, and she spat out as much as she could, coughing up some she'd almost swallowed. She moved her legs a little. They seemed to work. She lifted her left arm. That was working too.

She was lying face down on her right arm, so she rolled to her right. Pain shot through her forearm and chest, and she gave a cry. She got onto her back, running her hand across her chest, wincing as she worked over the ribs below her right breast. There was no blood, but she guessed she had broken them. She'd seen these injuries before. It was only a matter of time for it to heal. She moved her right arm. The forearm was sore, so she lifted her head to peer at it. The skin wasn't broken, but she was sure she'd damaged it. She lay back, panting as the fear coursed through her. Where was Col?

Talla lay still until she got her breath back, then struggled to her feet using her good arm. She looked around in disbelief. The wind had torn a swathe, maybe thirty or forty paces across, through the land. It had ripped up heather and turf, leaving a band of bare earth across the flat moorland.

She tried to draw a deep breath to shout Col's name, but pain lanced through her chest. The winds were still strong, but gradually lessening. She didn't even know where to look for him, so she walked back towards the east, following the trail of destruction left by the storm.

She'd been walking for a long while. In this open country, there were no landmarks to know where they'd come from, or where she'd landed. It was the fluttering of a white feather she saw first. She wondered if it was an unfortunate bird, then she spotted the brown fabric of Col's cloak. She ran over, pulling on the garment to find him lying beneath it.

"Col!" she squeaked, holding her side. He had to be alright. "Col!"

"Mmmh?"

"Oh, Col, you're alive."

"Mm, yeah," he muttered. Talla rolled him onto his back. There was a bruise on his face, and the cheek was swelling.

"Are you hurt?" she said, checking him with her left hand.

"No... no... I don't think so. My face..."

"It's a bruise, Col. Anywhere else?" she said.

He sat up, rubbing at his cheek, blood smearing his face as he felt his bruises.

"Your hands," she said.

He looked at them, inspecting the parallel cuts. "I tried to hold on to the heather," he explained. He looked up at her. "Are you hurt?"

She nodded. "I think I broke my ribs, and I'm not sure about my arm."

He stood up, wobbling, before stepping over to her. He lifted her shirt, touching her ribs. Talla winced, drawing in a breath between her teeth. "You're not coughing blood?" he asked.

"No."

"Just cracked then, but they will hurt a lot. We'll make you willow bark tea." He took her arm, running his fingers along the skin, making the downy hairs stand on end. "Can you move your wrist?" he said.

She moved her hand up and down, gasping. "Yes, but it's sore."

"Where?" Talla pointed, halfway up her forearm on the outside. "I think that's broken too, but not bent out of shape. We need to put a splint on it soon."

She wrapped her left arm around him as her emotions caught up with her and tears flowed.

"Col, I don't want to do this any more. I want to stop fighting the spirits. I can't lose you."

He wrapped her in his arms as she burrowed her face into his neck, wary of squeezing too hard. The spirits of the elements were trying to break them.

"They didn't give us a choice, Talla," he whispered. "Albyn said we were the only ones who could fix this. The spirits said we had to fight each of them. We didn't choose to do this, we have to do it."

"Th–this was the wind... air?" she asked.

"Yes." Col stepped back, looking at the grubby, dishevelled figure. "I'm sorry you got hurt, Talla. I don't want to lose you either, you know, but we're still together, we still have each other."

Talla gazed into his eyes. Those deep brown eyes. She shivered as her mouth met his, then pulled away, a smile playing across her lips.

"I'll be ready when you are," she said.

"What?"

"You work it out for yourself."

* * *

It took half the day, but they found most of their clothing and their packs. The shelter was undamaged, too. Beside the river, they discovered the carcass of a deer, taken by the storm. Col stripped away the skin, cutting a piece to wrap around Talla's arm and binding it with a long strip. She smiled at his idea. The heat of her body would soon dry it, creating a hard shell of rawhide to support the damaged limb. He looped a piece of hide around her neck to hold the arm up and, for the first time since it happened, Talla was almost comfortable.

They made a camp beside the river, lighting a fire and heating water for willow bark tea before Col put up their shelter.

"We'd better stay here a while," he said. "To let your arm and ribs settle."

"Can we get meat from the deer carcass?" she asked.

"I think so. The storm must have killed it, it's fresh."

Col butchered the animal, and they roasted enough for a few days, then crawled into their bed. Talla tossed back and forth, but could only find comfort on her left side. Col lay beside her and put his arm around her as she laid her head on his chest.

"Better?" he asked.

"Yes, but you..." she began.

"I'll be fine," he smiled. "Sleep."

* * *

It was a restless night; the pain keeping her awake for long periods before exhaustion took her. When she woke again, Col was climbing into the shelter, soaking wet with a platter of food.

"Thank you," she said. He returned a moment later with his own food.

"Get your wet things off and come and get warm," Talla said. He snuggled in beside her as they ate their meal. "Col, I haven't seen Raf since the storm," she said, worried for her little spirit animal.

"No. There's no sign of Kark either. I hope they're all right."

"He was in the pouch on my waist," she said. "Afterwards, I couldn't find him."

"If he's alive," Col said, "He'll find you."

Chapter 9

Col and Talla idled away the day while the rain drummed on the shelter.

"Meadowsweet," Col said.

"It's for the swelling-joint disease. It helps the digestion and burning in the stomach," said Talla. "Valerian."

Col smiled at her. "Pain, especially headaches. It helps to bring sleep too."

When they'd exhausted remedies and treatments, Col taught Talla the ceremony to send the dead across the river to be with the ancestors. She recited the five-line chant over and over until Col gripped her arm.

"You were slipping into the lower world," he said, "That's dangerous without a drum to carry you home."

Talla smiled. "If it's pulling me down, I must have it right though."

Before dark, Col served food, then helped Talla to climb out and relieve herself.

They were preparing to sleep when there was a rustling in the heather beside the shelter. Talla turned just as a small, brown, pointed nose wormed its way onto their bed.

"Raf!" she said, scooping him up in her hand, running her fingers over his soft fur. He scurried up her arm, wrapping himself around her neck.

"That's one," Col said. "I wonder where that lazy bird has got to?"

"Kark. Kark." came a voice. Col peered out of the shelter.

"I swear that bird can read my mind. Come on then," he called. Kark glided down to the opening of the shelter, strutting inside and hopping onto Col's arm. He bobbed his head, giving a deep purring sound in his throat, greeting them.

"Yes, I'm pleased to see you too," Col said, stroking his feathers.

* * *

They stayed three days at the camp by the river. The cold and wet discouraged them from moving on, but they knew they had no choice. When the fourth day dawned dry, Col packed up their shelter. Talla couldn't carry the weight she had before, so Col put more stuff into his pack. He cut a stout staff from a hazel tree.

"What's that for?" Talla asked.

"It's to help you balance," he said, smoothing the end.

Talla kissed his cheek. "Thank you," she said.

It rained and rained. The wind was icy, and they felt chilled every day. It was at night they warmed up, only to venture forth again the next morning.

After two days, they found a settlement; a busy little community of about thirty people. The spirit messenger made them welcome, and they slept in a house for the first time in half a moon. The clan's crops were drowned in the fields, and they were surviving on meat and wild greens. Berry fruits were just ripening, but the yield was low. They shared what they had, though, and Col and Talla left two days later with meat and cheese.

They were travelling through a thick forest now. Col peered about him, unused to having his field of vision so restricted. Tracks through the woodlands led them to villages, though many were less than pleased to have extra mouths to feed. Still, they headed south, and another moon passed before they knew it.

They checked the villages as they found them, trying to see if they had food to spare. Col got good at trapping the inquisitive crows and the greedy magpies to supplement their diet, and there were soon berries and nuts on the forest edges too.

"It's time to take the splint off your arm," Col said after they'd made camp on the edge of woodland, overlooking a grassy plain. Talla had been using the hand more, and it was not as sore. Col cut through the strapping with a blade and unwrapped the arm. He peeled off the rawhide sheath to show the crinkled pale skin. Talla flexed her wrist and curled her arm, wincing at the discomfort and stiffness. Col made her sit and got her to stretch her arm out, palm upwards. He put a large pebble in her hand.

"Now grip the stone and curl your arm until it touches your shoulder," he said. She followed his instructions, unable to bend it as far as he wanted.

"Show me," Talla said.

Col took her wrist, levering her arm up a little at a time. When Col's face was just a hand's breadth from hers, she smiled and pecked him on the cheek.

Col blushed, "Keep doing that every morning and night," he said. "It'll help the muscles get stronger again."

Talla giggled. "The kiss?"

The blush deepened. "No, the exercise."

* * *

They started across the plain the next day, moving faster in the open grassland. On the afternoon of the third day, they spotted it in the distance; a ring of stones with a huge ditch and bank around it.

"Do you think that's the place they told us about?" Talla asked.

"It looks like it," he smiled. "Come on."

Talla was back to taking her share of the load now and carrying the staff in her right hand to help it strengthen. As they neared the massive construction, they skirted the outside, unsure if they should venture nearer for fear of causing offence. As they got halfway around, they saw a group of three people. The bank had hidden them, but they turned at once to meet Col and Talla as they approached.

"Why are you here?" called the tall woman, dressed, like the others, in a white linen cloak. "This is a sacred place."

"We are travellers," said Col. "We wish no disrespect to you or your circle."

The trio walked closer to them until the woman stopped, staring at them. "Are you protected-of-spirit?"

"Apprentices, yes," Talla said.

"Your colour... your hair," the woman said.

One man stepped forward. "I have seen this before, Yalta," he said. He turned to Talla. "Is this how you were born?" he asked.

"Yes, I have always had pale skin and white hair."

"I saw a man, the same when I was an apprentice," the man said.

"We forget our manners," said the woman, holding out her hands. "I am Yalta, Spirit Master of the Guardians of the Circle of Stanna, Plant Master, Lore Master, Fire Keeper, and Healer."

"I am Tooev, Spirit Master of the Guardians of the Circle of Stanna," said the older man, "Lore Master and Fire Keeper."

The younger man stepped forward. He was a similar age to Col and Talla. "I am Gren, Spirit Apprentice of the Guardians of the Circle of Stanna. Plant Keeper, Lore Keeper, and Fire Apprentice," he said.

Col and Talla bowed their heads. "You first," Col whispered.

They each gave their status, and Yalta, Tooev, and Gren bowed.

Yalta smiled at them for the first time, beckoning them closer. She looked at Col's tattoos, then Talla's. "Your tattoos are similar, yet different," she said. "I recognise your status from them, though."

Talla glanced at Yalta's eye. "May I see, Spirit Master?" she asked.

Yalta laughed. "I am a server of the spirits, as are you. We do not think so much of ourselves that one of our own may not look at us," she said.

"Thank you, Yalta. We have travelled a great distance, customs change from place to place. With our own master, we sat to show respect for his greater status."

"Interesting," said Yalta. "I do not know of your Tribe or Clan. Where do you live?"

"Far, far to the north, on the Long Islands to the west," said Col. "Our master is Albyn, spirit messenger of our Clan and guardian of the sacred stones of Classac."

"They are real?" Tooev gasped. "The Long Islands? The stones?"

"Yes," Col said.

"Walk with us," said Yalta, "Come and stay at the village. We have much to discuss."

They walked along a broad track-way, Col holding Talla's hand. Yalta noticed and smiled. "We have a legend," she began. "The ancient ancestors who built our circle are supposed to have built circles in the islands you speak of, and on the northern isles. We never knew if this was true, or a fable."

"Our master travelled, like us, as a young man," said Col. "He went to the islands to the north, he has seen the great circles of stone there."

"Is there lore about your stone circle?" Yalta asked.

"Yes, a whole story; I know it well," Col said.

"Then you shall tell it to us tonight," said Yalta. "Gren, run ahead and make sure Shola prepares a meal for our guests." The young man set off at a trot.

"You honour us," said Col, smiling at Yalta.

"It's not every day we get visitors from a place of legend," she said.

* * *

The village was huge. They strode in behind Yalta and Tooev, gazing at the rows of houses. "Where are all the people?" Talla asked.

Tooev laughed. "This is a ceremonial place. There are fifteen of us. We use the village just twice a year, at the solstices. Then there will be too many people to count."

"So just the guardians live here?" Col said.

"Yes," said Yalta, "Tooev and me, Gren, two younger girls and enough others to work the ground and care for the livestock. Ah, here's Shola, our housekeeper."

A small, broad woman hobbled out of the largest house, shooing a young pig before her.

"Out! Out of the house, you stupid creature," she shouted. "Oh. Sorry, Spirit Master. When I catch that idle swineherd, I'll wring his neck."

Yalta grinned. "Shola, this is Talla, and Col. They are visiting apprentices, they are the protected-of-spirit."

"Yes, Yalta." Shola held out her hands. "Greetings, Talla, Col."

Talla and Col greeted the woman.

"Yalta, Tooev," Col said, "We may not know all your customs and do not wish to be disrespectful. Please tell us if we embarrass ourselves so we can learn."

Tooev wrapped an arm around Col's shoulder. "You two are the most respectful visitors we have had in many a moon," he said, grinning. "I will tell you stories later that will make your sides ache. Now come in and get warm. Shola, may we have tea?"

"Please, have one of the young ones serve you, Tooev," she said, "I need to find that unfortunate swineherd."

They trooped into the house, rectangular and larger than they were used to, and were given seats at the hearth. Two identical girls of, perhaps, seven summers pulled stones from the fire to heat water.

"What shall we make for you, Spirit Master?" said one girl.

"Mint and Nettle. Col? Talla?"

"Oh, the same please," Col said.

"Do you have willow bark?" Talla asked.

The girl looked doubtful. Talla rummaged in her pack, pulling out a small bag and passing it to her. She smiled and bowed.

"Are you in pain?" Yalta asked.

"I had a broken arm and ribs. They are still a little sore," Talla said.

She raised her eyebrows, but said nothing, turning to one twin. "Talla and Col are Plant Keepers and Lore Keepers. You may learn from them, Arva," she said.

"Thank you, Spirit Master, but I am Atta."

Yalta smiled. "Sorry Atta, I still can't always tell you apart, even after three years."

The other girl approached. "Talla, can you tell me how to make the willow infusion please."

"Of course, Arva," she smiled. Talla explained to her how the bark was harvested and dried, then showed her how much to use. Arva passed Talla the cup.

"Taste it," Talla said. The small girl sipped the liquid, wrinkling her nose. "Bitter!" she gasped.

"Atta," Talla said, passing her the cup. She took a drink.

"This is for pain?" she asked.

"Yes, do you have willow trees here?" Atta looked at Yalta.

"We do," Yalta said. "Will you take the twins tomorrow and show them? There are willows by the river."

"We'd be honoured, Yalta," Talla said, retrieving her tea and taking a drink.

They fell into easy conversation, discussing their journey and the things they'd seen. Yalta and Tooev were interested in the purpose of their quest, vowing to help all they could. Col told the story of the cave and their battle with the earth spirit. Talla told of the twisting wind and their struggle with the air spirit.

"Do you have Spirit Animals?" Tooev asked.

"Yes," said Col, "Talla?" She gave a soft whistle, and Raf crawled out of her hood, perching on her shoulder, surveying his audience.

"A stoat!" Yalta said, clapping her hands.

"Arva, open the door, please," Talla said.

The girl smiled and ran to the door.

"Was that a guess?" asked Yalta.

"No, she carries her left shoulder lower and raises her left eyebrow when you talk to her. Her sister is the opposite," Talla said.

"You are very observant," Tooev smiled.

"I learned to be... at an early age," she said.

Col cupped his hands to his mouth and called. "Kark! Kark!"

There was a raucous cry, and the raven swooped in through the door, scrabbling at Col's shoulder before settling himself. He gave a soft warble, then stretched his neck.

"Kark," the raven said. "Lazy bird, lazy bird."

"You have taught him to speak?" Yalta asked.

"He learned it himself," Col said, smiling. "I say that to him a lot, he just imitates me."

"They have both followed you on your journey?" Yalta asked.

"Yes. I lost Raf for a day after the twisting wind, though," Talla said.

Col grinned. "I see Kark at least once a day," he said, "when he's hungry!"

They all laughed, then Yalta whistled, and a tiny wren fluttered to her shoulder. "Oh. The same as our master, Albyn," Talla said.

Tooev whistled, and a mouse scurried up his arm and sat on his shoulder, twitching its whiskers.

"And Gren?" Col said. The young man blushed but shook his head.

"His spirit animal is the white owl," Yalta said. "He will take one next spring when they are fledged."

"What about you two?" Talla said, kneeling beside the twins.

"We don't know yet," said Arva.

"Will you find their animals for them, while you're here?" Tooev asked.

"We'll try," Col said, grinning at the girls.

Talla and Col told stories after dinner, the other workers joining them around the fire to hear the tales. Flickering yellow danced on the rapt faces as Talla gave their version of the creation story. Col smiled as the small group clapped at the end of her tale. He stood and paced across the floor.

"In ancient times, when giants still roamed the land, Yorvyn, the greatest of the giant race, fell in love with Geena, a human spirit master," he began. He strode back and forth, hands expressing what his voice could not, as he spun the tale of the building of the stone circle of Classac. When he reached the end of his story, Tooev stood, thanking the visitors.

"Perhaps tomorrow I will tell of the building of the great ditch, here at Stanna," he said. "I think that your giant Yorvyn, and our giant Yorev, maybe one and the same.

Later, they prepared for bed, Yalta offering them a sleeping platform in the big house.

"Are you bonded?" Yalta whispered.

"Not yet," Talla smiled.

"Do you want separate beds?"

"No, I can't sleep without him now," she giggled, squeezing Col's hand.

"Ah, young love," Yalta said, heading for their own house. Col glanced at Talla, a small smile crossing his lips.

The large house was a communal space, Shola's kitchen, and a dormitory for Gren and the twins. Now it was Col and Talla's temporary home too. Talla crawled into the comfortable bed, and Col joined her, wrapping his arm around her shoulders. Since the broken arm, Talla had got used to sleeping with her head on his chest. She saw no reason to stop.

* * *

Yalta followed Tooev into their home, closing the door. Shola had lit a small fire for them, and it gave enough light to undress and climb into bed. Once she was settled in Tooev's arms, she voiced her thoughts.

"We will push those two hard, Tooev," she said. "They are so close to spirit messenger status, but they'll need all the knowledge we can give them to survive their ordeals."

"I agree," Tooev said. "They only just survived the battles with Air and Earth, Water and Fire are far stronger opponents. How shall we work with them?"

Yalta thought for a moment. "You take Talla. Teach her all you can. I'll take Col. We'll get them to mentor the twins, it'll push them to teach others, and it will give those girls a great learning opportunity. We'll work on their ceremonial knowledge in the evenings."

"Yes," said Tooev. "We need to get them to stay with us this winter. Soon it will be too hard to travel, anyway."

"The apprentices will arrive after the next full moon," Yalta said, "Let's give them their spirit messenger status now, and get them teaching. It will strengthen them, or it will break them."

Chapter 10

Shola had porridge ready for them when they woke the next morning, and they ate with Gren and the twins. Talla and Col liked the two girls, Atta and Arva. The youngsters were never still, rocking from leg to leg, playing with their hair, always in motion. They had charming smiles, with deep dimples in both cheeks.

"Good morning," said Yalta, stepping into the house. They bowed their heads to her, then to Tooev as he followed her. Shola served them porridge, and they sat on the bench by the fire.

"Join us, Col, Talla," Tooev said. Yalta smiled at Col and patted the seat beside her. Tooev sat Talla next to him.

"We want to help you," Yalta said. "Your challenge is great, to fight and beat the spirits of water and fire. Stay with us for the winter, learn all that we can teach you before you travel onwards."

Talla looked at Col. "It would be nice to settle for a few moons," she said, "And I want to learn everything I can."

"We will be very grateful for anything you can teach us, Spirit Master," Col said, bowing.

"Don't thank me too soon," Yalta said. "We will make you work very hard. You three are now responsible for training these two scamps," she said, pointing to the twins. "They must be ready for their apprentice tattoos by the winter solstice. You will all get your messenger tattoos today."

"Spirit Master, we're not ready!" Gren said.

"Listen," she said, "You will behave as messengers; if you do as well as we think you will, you'll get your status at the solstice. Now, the apprentices arrive at the full moon, I want you to be ready."

"Apprentices, Spirit Master?" Talla said.

She smiled. "Each year, two moons before the solstices, we take all those who wish to progress to the next level. We spend the time teaching and testing them. Tooev and I will take those who wish to be spirit masters, you three will take those that wish to be messengers."

Gren looked terrified. "What if we fail?" he asked.

"We won't fail," said Talla, "We won't let each other fail."

"What about us?" Arva said.

Yalta smiled. "Ah, yes. Each year a few children come, chosen by the spirits to serve them. You will learn enough from your teachers here to give them a taste of being one of the protected-of-spirit." The two girls giggled and hugged each other.

"Atta, Arva," Talla said, "Where are your manners?"

The girls bowed to Yalta. "Thank you, Spirit Master."

Yalta grinned. "You are welcome. Make us all proud, girls."

* * *

"How many will come, Gren?" Col asked as they walked. The young man was becoming a friend of the two travellers.

"Last winter there were twenty-five," he said, turning towards the river. "Are you not frightened that we'll make fools of ourselves trying to teach them, Col?"

"We will make fools of ourselves, Gren," Col smiled, "But they will learn, and so will we. The three of us must become a team and show a united front."

Gren nodded. "Ah, willow trees," he said, pointing to the river bank.

Talla and Col showed the twins how to strip the bark from the trees without killing them, then explained how to scrape away the inner part to dry for the healing tea. Atta and Arva observed, then each took the polished axe, cutting their own strips from the smooth green trunks.

"Like this?" Arva asked, holding up a length of bark. Col smiled and nodded.

That afternoon, Col showed them how to make frames for hand-drums, then Talla worked with them to make rawhide to cover them. Gren promised that the following day they'd each make their own drum, ready for the solstice.

* * *

Tooev brought out a pouch of tools: flint blades, soft leathers, and lamp-black for tattooing. Sinew and awls for wound sewing.

"I want you each to work on your own tool pouch in the coming days," he said, "I will expect you to tattoo the successful messengers after the solstice. Now, Col, you will finish Talla's messenger tattoo, Talla will do Gren's, and Gren will do yours. We will watch you."

Col sat in front of Talla and inspected her current tattoo. The change would be filling in the shapes, plus adding a scroll to the end. Holding his hands over the tools, he spoke a quick incantation.

"Spirits, sharpen my blade and my eye, steady my hand and my heart for this work."

He noticed Yalta turn to Tooev and nod her approval. Talla closed her eyes while Col cut the new designs into her pale skin. She winced when he rubbed on the black dye, then smiled.

"Thank you, Col," she said.

Col looked into her eyes. "Beautiful," he whispered.

"The marks?"

His face reddened. "Yes, yes, the marks," he said.

Col watched while she tattooed Gren's new marks. Her steady hand cut line after fine line, her tongue poking from the corner of her mouth as she dabbed at the blood with a soft cloth. Gren pulled back when she added the lamp-black, but she was soon finished.

Col sat for Gren as he worked on the messenger tattoo, used to the stinging pain now. Gren was shaking, and Col hoped it didn't show in his work.

"Well done," Yalta said. "Now, food is ready, then we will start on your formal lessons.

They ate a tasty stew with plenty of wild vegetables. Shola was an excellent cook and was teaching the twins to help her. The meal finished, they sat around the fire talking.

"Gren, fetch three drums," Tooev said. The young man clambered up into the roof timbers, reappearing with the frame drums and beaters. He handed one to Col and one to Talla.

"Col, take us to the river to converse with the ancestors," Yalta said, sitting back and folding her arms.

Col looked at Talla and Gren. "Heartbeat to start, then follow me," he said, staring the slow rhythm.

He whispered an invocation, then built up the speed to a steady beat, feeling Talla with him. His mind searched about for Gren, finding his energy and pulling him in.

* * *

They were near the river. The dim light and muted greys of the landscape made seeing difficult. Col walked forward, standing close to the water's edge. Vague shapes were forming on the far bank as he held out his hands in greeting.

"Ancestors that love us, come and speak to us," he called.

The shapes moved and solidified, one came to the front.

"Col, you have made me proud," he said.

A woman formed beside him, arms outstretched. "You wear a messenger's tattoo, my heart is full, Col."

Col stared at the beautiful woman beside his father. "Mother?"

"Yes, my handsome son. I have watched you grow, though I couldn't be with you."

Pictures of what could have been rushed into Col's mind. He imagined a childhood filled with this woman, being held and loved by her. His vision blurred, and he felt an arm around his shoulders. He turned, looking into Talla's concerned eyes.

"Speak with them, Col," she said, her thumb brushing tears from his cheek.

He stood tall, feeling Talla release him. A deep breath quieted the sobs, and he smiled through the tears.

"Mother, Father, thank you. How can we teach others when we still have so much to learn?"

"Become as one, the three of you," said his father. "Your masters and your students will test you, do not weaken."

"Your ancestors love you, come to us for advice often. We will give it," said his mother.

Gratitude shone through his reddened eyes. "Thank you. I will see you again. I love you both." He turned to Gren, his throat too tight to say any more.

Gren stepped forward, jaw set, eyes wide. "Ancestors that love us, come speak to us," he said.

An enormous bear of a man appeared on the opposite bank. "Gren?"

"Th... that is my name," he stuttered.

"Then stand tall, for you are Gren, son of Tarn, a warrior of the Ammen Tribe."

"Father?"

"Yes," the great man said. "the spirits have chosen you to serve them, but you may still be a warrior. Stand tall, Gren, and be proud of your heritage."

"Thank you, Father," he whispered.

"Talla?" Col said, turning to her. She stepped forward, facing a pretty, slim woman.

"Hello, mother," she said.

"Hello, child. Remember, my death was not your fault," the woman said.

"He thinks it was."

"Your father was wrong, the spirits wanted me back, I had to go. You bear no blame, Talla."

Talla bowed. "Thank you, Mother. I love you."

The shadow of the woman faded from the far bank of the river.

"Back," Col said, "follow the drums home."

It was strange, riding on the beat of the drum when he knew it was his own hand that was beating it. He felt himself rising.

* * *

Col slowed the beat to a stop, laying down the beater, then the drum.

"Thank you, Col. You did well," Yalta said, a broad grin on her face. "Gren, you hesitated. Why?"

"I was frightened," Gren said.

"Trust your friends," Tooev said, "Your life may depend on them." Gren nodded.

"Col, you pulled him in," Yalta said.

"Yes, Spirit Master."

"Do it with the apprentices if needed. Never do it in a test, they must be capable of it themselves."

"Thank you, Spirit Master," he said.

She smiled. "When we are working together, I am Yalta, my mate is Tooev. Save the titles for the apprentices. They will call each of you, Spirit Messenger. Insist on it. You will call them Spirit Apprentice, followed by their name. Understood?"

"Yes, Yalta!" they chorused.

* * *

Col lifted his arm to let Talla's head lie on his chest. She grinned up at him and kissed his cheek, snuggling down in the bed next to him. Col pulled the furs over them.

"Thank you for letting us stay," she said.

"Thank you for suggesting we did," Col smiled.

"Goodnight, Spirit Messenger," she said giggling.

"Goodnight, Spirit Messenger," he replied, pulling her close.

* * *

The twins, Atta and Arva, were the best of students, soaking up each lesson Col and Talla gave them. They played games with them but instructed them through the play. The twins learned to be observant, sitting while something happened, then answering Col and Talla's questions. They sang songs and discovered essential herbs for teas and medicines.

Talla and Col became close to the small girls over the next half a moon, often sitting with them on their laps as they fell asleep, weary from their busy days.

Col laid Arva in the bed the twins shared, Talla putting Atta beside her.

"They are good kids," Talla said.

"The best," Col said, taking her hand.

They returned to the fire, picking up the drums lying there. Gren joined them.

"Gren, take us to the lower world. We wish to speak to the spirits of the elements," said Tooev.

Gren turned to Talla and Col. "Fast beat, straight in," he said. His confidence had increased now, since his meeting with his father. He'd never known him in life but now devoted himself to making him proud. The drums started pulling them down, dropping them into the grey dusk of the lower world.

* * *

They stood in a line. Gren and Talla, Yalta, Tooev and Col. The four spirits of the elements materialised before them.

"You have bested two of us," said the Spirit of Fire. "Water and I will not be so lenient. You must all best us to continue."

"All?" said Yalta.

"These three, and the other," the spirit said.

"Who is the other?" Col asked.

"You will know her. Four will leave, two will return," the spirit said.

"Two will die?" Talla asked.

"Four will leave, two will return," he said, his shape fading as they watched.

"Back!" said Yalta.

* * *

"What does that mean?" Talla said as soon they were back in their own reality.

"I don't know. The spirit of fire is a trickster," Yalta said.

"And a fourth?" Col asked.

"Yes. I don't know who that is."

"Sleep," said Tooev, "Maybe our dreams will tell us."

"Yes, bed," said Yalta, "It's late."

* * *

The next day, the first apprentices arrived. Most were the same age as Talla and Col, around seventeen, others were older, a few younger. They waited until the third day of the full moon to begin.

Towards evening, Yalta stood at the front of the group of seated people. She smiled, a predatory smile the three young messengers had never seen.

"Spirit Apprentices, I am Yalta, Spirit Master of the Guardians of the Circle of Stanna, this is Tooev, also a Spirit Master here." Her hands swept towards Gren, Talla and Col. "These are your teachers. Each wears the tattoo of a spirit messenger, each has great knowledge and training. Do *not* let their ages fool you, they will know most of what you need to know. If they do not, they will come to us. Do you understand?"

There was a shout of, "Yes, Spirit Master."

"Stand, one at a time," said Tooev, "State your name, your tribe and your status. The first will go to Col." Col raised his hand. "The second to Gren, the third to Talla, and so on. These will be your mentors. You will take most of your learning from them, but there will be changes and group activities too. They will take you to your roundhouse. You will cook and clean for yourselves." There was a general groan. "You will be awake and ready to learn every morning. Do not expect this to be easy, if it were, everyone would be a spirit messenger. Learn, work hard, make your mentor proud of you. Not all of you will pass, it has never happened. If you fail, learn from it and return in the summer. I took three attempts to become a messenger. Begin."

The apprentices stood one at a time, reeling off their status, then crossing to one of the three messengers. They ended up with eight each. Col took his group to their roundhouse, showing them where to find everything, then told them to be ready the next morning.

Back at the meeting house, Talla and Gren had returned.

"Well?" Col said.

"Alright," said Gren. "I've got one lad that will challenge everything I say, though."

"You know more than him," said Talla.

"Do I?"

"Yes!" they both said.

"Talla?" Col said.

"Most are fine. One who already asked if I was bonded."

"Oh?" he smiled.

Talla grinned. "I said I was promised, and if that was where his mind was, he would fail."

"Come on," Col said, "bed, we've got an early start."

* * *

"Promised?" Col asked as they climbed into bed.

"Well, sort of," Talla said.

"To who?"

Talla blushed. "Um, you?"

He looked into her eyes. "Talla, we've been the only company for each other for more than half a year. That's not a good way to choose a mate."

She glared at him. "Why not?"

"You've had no choice. It wouldn't be fair to you."

"Hmmph!" she said, turning her back to him.

Chapter 11

Talla was gone the next morning. Gren said she'd eaten half a bowl of porridge and stormed out. Col rounded up his apprentices and asked if any had drums. None did, so they devoted the morning to making drum frames.

There were five boys and three girls in Col's group, and so far, there had been no challenges to his status. One girl stood out. Her skin was darker than any suntan Col had ever seen, and her black hair curled like moss. She had a ready smile. Her name was Zoola.

The apprentices had formed a semi-circle around the hearth, each curving and binding the hazel frames of their new instruments.

"Spirit Apprentice Zoola," Col said, squatting beside her. "How is the frame coming along?"

"Well, thank you, Spirit Messenger," she said. She passed him the frame. "Are the bindings tight enough?"

"Yes, as the rawhide shrinks, they will tighten more," he said. "Where are your tribe from? I am a visitor here. I know little about your people."

"About three days' walk west of here. We are the Danna. Kaden is Danna too." She touched his arm, then pointed out a tall lad who Col remembered had a limp.

"Bal is our close neighbour, from the Yofa tribe." Bal waved.

"I will get to know you all over the next two moons," Col said, smiling. He noticed Zoola's large, brown eyes never left him as he spoke. "Now, finish up and get food, Spirit Master Yalta wants us all at the meeting house after you've eaten."

* * *

Yalta stood, and the assembled apprentices quietened. "Spirit Messenger Talla will take us to the lower world," she said. "She will explain what will happen and drum us on our journey. Follow the drum."

Yalta came to where the three spirit messengers sat.

"Just drum, don't direct them," Yalta whispered. "If any need help, let Tooev and I handle it this time." They all nodded.

Talla talked about the power of the drum, its ability to take them to the world below to meet ancestors or spirits. She drummed, increasing the volume and speed. Soon the beat pulled them into the lower world. Col spotted Bal, hesitating on the edges, then Yalta hooked him in with her mind.

* * *

The apprentices appeared throughout the dark landscape at random. They found their bearings and congregated around Talla. She led them to the river, where they observed the shapes of the ancestors across the water. Since they'd called no one, there was no conversation, just being in the space. Col glanced around, unable to see Bal.

"Let's return," said Yalta, as Talla drummed the call back.

* * *

Yalta was smiling, looking from face to face. "One by one, tell us what you experienced," she said.

Col glanced across to the apprentices, finding Bal still sitting, eyes closed, head slumped. He jumped up and went to him, lifting his chin and patting his cheek. "Talla, drum me back down, please," he said, sitting beside her.

* * *

They appeared in the lower world. "Help me find Bal," Col said.

"Why? He's one of yours," she said.

"Talla, he's younger than the rest. I won't put him at risk because we have fallen out. That's between you and me."

She looked contrite. "Sorry, Col. You go left; I'll go right." He'd only gone a short way when Talla shouted. "Here Col!" He ran back, finding her wading into the river. Bal's body floated more than halfway across. He rushed to join her, pulling the limp body to the shore. "You should have let me do it," she said. "You could have died doing that."

"We're a team, remember?" Col said. *He laid Bal face down and pressed on his back, trying to revive him. There was a cough, and he vomited. Col rolled him onto his back as he gasped for breath. "Bal, can you hear me?" he said.*

"Sit him up," Talla said, helping to lift him.

"My mother," Bal said.

"She's dead?" Col asked him as his eyes opened.

He nodded. "I wanted to see her."

"If you'd got across, you would not have been able to return, Bal. That's the river of death," said Talla.

"Maybe I didn't want to come back," he whispered.

"Come on, back," Col said. *"Follow Talla's drum."*

* * *

"Well spotted Col," said Tooev, "He could have become trapped."

"Yes. I'll speak to you later." Col said. Tooev nodded, looking puzzled.

Yalta finished their discussion of the journey, then dismissed the apprentices to gather herbs.

"What happened, Col, Talla?" she asked when they'd all gone.

"I found Bal face down in the death river, more than halfway across," Talla said.

"How did you get him back?" she asked.

"Waded in to fetch him," she said.

"You could have died," said Gren.

"Talla has crossed the river before," Col said. "I'm afraid I didn't think of the consequences, I acted."

"Talla, is this true?" Yalta asked. Talla nodded. "How?"

"I don't know. The first time Albyn took me on a journey, I saw my mother. She died when I was born. I crossed and hugged her, then came back."

"That should not be possible," Yalta said. "Crossing to their land should make you one of them. Touching an ancestor spirit should anchor you in their world for good. Yet you came back?"

"I think it's one reason the spirits told Albyn that we were the only ones who could take this journey," Col said.

"You two are special, I realised it when I saw how you worked with the spirits and the ancestors," Yalta said. "You have the skills of messengers much older than yourselves, and Gren is benefiting from working with you."

"We will think on this," Tooev said, "Test your apprentices on their plant knowledge now."

As Talla and Gren left, Col took Tooev aside. "Bal was not so keen to return with us," he said. "He was happy to stay with his mother."

"He wanted to die?" Tooev asked.

"I think that was his intention. Perhaps one of us should find out his story."

"Will you try?" Tooev asked.

"Zoola and Kaden come from a neighbouring tribe. I'll see if they know anything," he said.

* * *

Talla and Gren were with the apprentices when he got outside. "Apologies," he said, "I had to speak to Tooev."

"Why, is there something you don't know, Spirit Messenger?" said an older lad in Talla's group.

"There are many things I don't know," Col said, glaring.

"So I believe," he said.

"Spirit Apprentice Janric," said Talla, "Go back to your house and make up the fire. You can prepare the evening meal for the group."

"Why, Talla?" he said.

"You address me as Spirit Messenger Talla, and with your attitude, it is unlikely that you will learn anything else today. Go!"

He turned, smirking at Talla and glancing back at Col before strolling off to his roundhouse.

"Watch that one," Col said to Talla as they turned back to the apprentices.

"Oh, I intend to," she said.

They worked on plant knowledge for the rest of the afternoon. Some apprentices were excellent with plants and medicines; others might poison themselves before the solstice.

* * *

Col had already got into bed when Talla came in. She stripped and climbed over him, settling on the inside of the bed.

"Are you talking to me, Talla?" he asked.

"Yes."

"I'm sorry if I upset you yesterday."

"I've been thinking about what you said." She chewed her lip. "I'll wait for one moon."

"I don't understand," he said.

"You want us to wait because you think we're too close or something. Is that right?"

"Well, yes," Col said.

"Right, we both have one moon. If we haven't found someone else by then, I'll be expecting a proposal to be bonded," she said.

"From me?"

"No, from Raf! Of course, from you. Do you agree?"

"I agree."

"Good, now in the meantime, I still want my cuddles," she said, lifting his arm and burrowing into his chest. Col held her close; sure he would never understand women.

* * *

The days passed, and they worked the apprentices hard. They made drums, learned chants and invocations, took drum journeys, and made medicines. They stocked up the supplies of herbs and treatments, ready for the influx of people at the winter solstice.

Col noticed Zoola seemed to sit and speak with him each day, touching him often. He assumed touching must be more common in her tribe, and he guessed she must be a little lonely.

Janric's offhand attitude still worried Talla. He continued to undermine her and niggle at Gren and Col when he had the chance. Tooev had noticed and was prepared to step in, but the three messengers agreed to give it a little longer.

Col spent time, one evening, with Zoola who knew Bal's family. She told him that Bal's mother had died from an infected wound. Their spirit messenger was old and forgetful and had not given her the right treatment. Bal had become quiet and sad, trying to drown himself in the local river twice before his father talked him into apprenticing himself to spirit.

"Do you think he'd still rather cross the river to be with his mother?" Col asked her.

"On some days, yes; on other's he's almost himself," she said.

"Thank you for your help," he said. "I feel responsible for him while he's with me."

She stroked his face. "You're a good man, Col. If there's anything else I can help you with, let me know."

Col blushed. "Umm, thanks, I will."

Zoola kissed his cheek. "See you in the morning," she said. Col passed the story on to Talla and Gren, and they both agreed to monitor Bal.

* * *

They were gathering firewood with the apprentices one afternoon. Yalta wanted them all to have at least the basics of fire magic. Col had taught the entire group the incantations to the fire spirits that morning, and they would put it into practice that evening once they had enough wood.

"As dry as possible," Col shouted, "The stuff on the ground it too wet. Break dead branches off the trees if you can."

"Can you help us, Spirit Messenger?" said Kaden, "A little more weight on this and it will break."

Col jumped up, catching the end of the branch, four of them now hanging off the length of deadwood. It broke with a sudden snap, flinging them all to the ground. They lay laughing for a moment before they got up and dragged the branch onto the pile. Col stopped, hearing something in the distance. A muffled scream and shouting. He walked towards the noise. Over a ridge was a bank of bushes. The voice came again.

"No, stop. Get off. Janric, STOP!"

Col ran over, pulling the foliage aside just as Janric's open hand met with Talla's face. She screamed. Her shirt lay torn open, and her leggings were ripped. Janric was on top of her struggling form. He was twice her size.

"Shut up, you stupid sow," he said, grabbing her breast.

"Get off her and stand up," Col said.

"Go away," Janric shouted, "This is nothing to do with you."

"I said, get off."

A small, brown shape scurried from Talla's discarded cloak, leaping at Janric. Raf locked his jaws on the apprentice's hand drawing a scream of rage from Janric.

"Get off me, damned rat," Janric said, flinging the tiny creature aside.

While he was distracted, Col charged, taking him by surprise. His foot came up under Janric's chin, snapping his head back, and he rolled off Talla.

"Talla, run," Col said.

"No," she said, pulling her leggings into place.

"Run. Now!" he shouted.

Col watched her run back to the apprentices as a fist caught his chin. He flew back, landing in the soft leaves. Janric was on him in a moment.

"I'll kill you, you interfering fool," he shouted. "She's mine."

His fist hit Col's face again. Col struggled, rolling to the side, pushing him away. He regained his feet, crouching and waiting to see what Janric did next. Janric lunged. It was when Col put up his arm to defend himself, that he saw the flint blade in his hand. The sharp edge sliced into Col's arm and he stepped back. Janric came again, plunging the knife towards him. Col was smaller than him but quicker, and he sidestepped at the last moment. Col kicked at his leg as he passed, knocking him over. He jumped on Janric before he could rise, pinning his arms with his knees as he punched his face.

Col felt strong arms grab him. He struggled, trying to escape, but Tooev's voice in his ear stopped him.

"I'm here. We're here, Col. It's alright, Talla told us what happened," he said, pushing Col to a sitting position on the woodland floor. Col looked for Janric, but a group of apprentices were holding him.

"Tie his hands and feet," said Yalta, striding over to him and glaring at the bloodied apprentice.

"That lunatic attacked me," Janric spluttered through split lips.

"That's not what they told me," said Yalta. "They say you tried to rape a spirit messenger."

"The girl wanted it," he said. "I did nothing wrong."

"Take him. Watch him." Yalta said. "We'll listen to both sides later." She turned to Col. "Are you hurt?" she asked.

"Not too bad."

"You are wounded," she said, lifting his arm to look.

"Good practice for the apprentices," Col said, holding the gaping wound closed.

"Idiot," she said, punching his shoulder. "Can you walk?"

Col stood. "Yes, and thank you. You too, Tooev."

"Come on," Tooev said, heading for the village.

They got back to the meeting house, and Yalta got Col settled. The apprentices were waiting.

"Right," Col said, "You have a live patient. Gren, can you get dried sinew and an awl for them?"

"You're going to let them practise on you?" he asked.

"Yes, they've got to do it sometime."

They warmed water and washed the wound. Zoola took over the sewing, saying she'd done it once before. Col watched her pounding dried sinew to extract the fibres, then winced as she made the tiny holes in his skin to tie the wound shut. She fed the threads through and knotted them.

Gren explained how one of the best treatments for cuts was honey, as it stopped the bad spirits. He poured some onto Col's arm, rubbing it into the injury. Zoola applied fresh moss and bound the arm.

"There," said Zoola, giving Col a peck on the cheek. "You'll live."

"I hope so," he said, "I've still got to train all of you."

* * *

They seated Janric on the floor of the house, his back against a support pole. His hands and feet tied.

"Talla, what happened?" said Yalta.

Talla stroked the quivering form of Raf in her lap.

"We were gathering wood, and *he* asked me to help him with a big branch. I followed him, and he dragged me into the bushes, trying to get my clothes off. I fought him, but he's so much bigger than me. Col must have heard my shouts, he rescued me, and I got away to raise the alarm."

"Col?" Yalta said.

"I heard the shouts. I went to find out what the noise was and found Janric holding Talla down. He had torn her clothes and, as I got there, he hit her across the face."

Yalta looked at Talla's mouth, the lip split and bruised. "Go on."

"I kicked at him to get him off Talla. She got away, and we fought. He had a blade," Col said, holding up the injured arm.

"Janric?" Tooev said.

"They're lying. She wanted to have sex with me; I mean, who wouldn't. This fool came along and got the wrong idea."

"So she asked you to tear her clothes and to hit her?" Tooev asked.

"What? No. You know what, forget it, just let me go, and I'll return to my village."

"You admit it?" Yalta asked.

"Yes, so what? Send me home. I don't want to be a spirit messenger," he said.

"You also injured a spirit animal."

"The rat?" Janric sneered. "It bit me."

"Gren, get my tools," Yalta said.

Gren passed over the small decorated tool bundle, and Yalta opened it, laying out her blades and lamp-black.

"What are you doing?" Janric said, squirming in his bonds.

"Hold his head," said Yalta, taking the blade between her finger and thumb.

Gren and Tooev gripped his head as Yalta moved towards his eye.

"Wait, you can't. I'm the Clan leader's son. You can't do this!" Janric screamed.

Yalta cut line after line under his right eye, rubbing in the black dye, covering his apprentice tattoo with a solid bar of black.

"No, no, no," he sobbed. "You can't. They'll kill me if I go back like this."

"You can't go back," said Gren, his mouth a hand's breadth from Janric's ear. "You can never go home, never live in a village, never have a mate. You are an outlaw, an outcast."

"No!" Janric cried.

"Release him in the morning," Yalta said, wiping the blood from her hands, "He gets one skin of water, no food. If any of you see him again, kill him." She stood and left the house.

Tooev tied Janric to the post, and his head dropped forward, blood-tinged tears dripping onto his chest.

* * *

Talla was lying, illuminated by the flickering light from the fire, as Col climbed into their bed.

"Is it alright to sleep here – with you?" he asked.

She turned towards him, her cheeks wet. "Where else would you sleep? You saved me, Col."

"I wasn't sure. It must have been horrible, to be forced like that. I wondered if you wanted to be alone."

"No," she said, wriggling closer. Col lifted his arm, and her head was on his chest at once. He pulled her closer.

"How is Raf?" Col asked.

"Sleeping," she said. "I think he'll be alright." She ran her fingers over his chest.

"Thank you, Col."

"I..."

"Shh," she said. "Thank you."

* * *

Zoola unbound the wound, discarding the moss and inspecting the stitches. The edges of the wound were red, but not hot. Col was lucky that the cut had been clean. She rubbed on more honey and bound fresh moss to the arm.

"You were brave to tackle Janric," she said, finishing the dressing.

"He is a bully. I worry he will join an outlaw band somewhere, the little knowledge he has of spirit will be dangerous."

"A brave man like you would be a good catch as a mate for someone," she said, kissing his cheek.

"A mate?" he said.

"Mmm-hmm. A girl might expect a proposal to be joined if she made her attraction obvious enough."

"A proposal? I..."

Zoola pressed a finger to his lips. "You think about it for a few days, Col. Otherwise a girl might have to break with tradition and do the asking."

Chapter 12

A draught made Talla shiver as Col lifted the blanket. She opened her eyes as he tried to slip out of bed.

"Where're you going?" She winced from the bruised lip.

"Time to get up," he said.

"Just a moment more," she said, pulling his warm body closer.

"Come on," he said, escaping her arms, "Spirit animals today, with the apprentices. You and I have the only ones apart from Yalta and Tooev."

Talla grumbled as she slipped on leggings and tunic. The weather had turned colder, and snow was on the ground again. A whistle brought Raf from amongst the blankets. The little stoat was never far away, and now seemed none the worse for his adventure. He climbed up her arm and into the hood of her cloak. They prodded Gren into action and left, promising Shola they'd return for breakfast.

They packed the apprentices into one house for the brief talk. Col explained how important it was to have a physical manifestation of your spirit animal, then told how he captured his raven. Right on cue, Talla opened the door as he called, "Kark! Kark!" The raven glided to a halt in the doorway, strutting up to Col. He scooped him up, setting him on his arm.

Talla talked of finding Raf, giving a whistle to bring him from her hood to sit on her shoulder.

Gren told them of his white owl, and how he would track and catch a chick in the spring.

They sent them off in pairs to drum for each other, seeking their own animal spirits.

The three messengers were heading back for breakfast when Arva popped out of a house. They'd set the twins up with the younger children, who were considering apprenticing. They had six students from seven to ten summers. The two girls were natural teachers, passing on songs and stories, playing games that taught awareness and making basic teas.

"Spirit Messenger Talla," she said, grinning as she used the full title. "Can you come into the house?"

"Yes, but why? What do you want me to do?"

"We're doing observation, so it doesn't matter what you do. Atta and I want to see how much they notice."

Talla grinned and waited until Arva had gone back inside. She knocked and entered while Gren and Col waited. A short while later, Talla came back out, smiling. She put her finger to her lips, and they stood, listening, as Atta spoke. "Who just came in?" she said.

"Spirit Messenger Talla," said a girl.

"What is her status?" Arva asked.

"Um, spirit messenger."

"And?" said Arva.

Talla knew she was finding out if they had noticed her tattoos, telling them her other skills. There was silence.

"Spirit Messenger Talla!" Atta called.

She walked back into the house, standing in the doorway, her left eye visible to the youngsters. She crouched to Atta's level as she pointed to the status tattoos. "This one?" she asked.

"Plant keeper?" said a young lad with a hunched back.

"That's right, now, this one?"

"Fire... apprentice?" said an older girl.

"It's fire..." Arva hinted.

"Keeper!" said the girl, "It's the spiral, isn't it?"

"That's it!" Atta said. They finished the last tattoos, and Talla joined the boys for breakfast.

* * *

They were drinking their tea when the apprentices returned. Each one knew their own animals now.

"Zoola, what is yours?" Col asked as she entered. She wandered over and sat on his lap, kissing his cheek. Talla glowered at her, and she stood again.

"Sparrow, Spirit Messenger," she said, losing herself at the back of the group. The apprentices could lead drum journeys for each other now, so the messengers sent them off in pairs to speak to the ancestors about their animals.

"Gren," Talla said, "Will you work with Bal, please?" She wanted him with someone experienced in case he got any more ideas to join his mother in the land of the dead. "Right, what's going on with Zoola?" she asked.

"I... I just... um..." Col stuttered.

"She likes you," Talla said, "Are you going to join with her, be her mate?"

"She thinks I'm going to ask her," he said.

"Are you?"

"No."

"Does she know that?"

Col stared at the floor, kicking at the crushed straw with his toes. "No, not yet."

"She'd make a suitable mate," Talla said. "She's strong, pretty, she'll be a capable spirit messenger."

Col muttered something she didn't hear. "What?"

"She's not you," he mumbled.

"You want to bond with me?" Talla asked. "After all the delaying, you want me?"

"Yes."

"And when did you decide this?"

Col blushed. "When we fire walked together."

Talla stood open-mouthed. He'd decided moons ago but put her through this torture.

"You Pig! You gave me all this talk about waiting. For what?"

"I needed you to be sure it was me you wanted. I never wanted you to regret it if you bond with me," he said, meeting her gaze. Talla threw her arms around his neck, pulling him into a kiss. Col lifted her off her feet.

The door opened. "Sorry, I forgot my drum... Oh!" said Zoola, standing in the doorway, mouth gaping.

"Just carry on and get it, Spirit Apprentice Zoola," Talla said.

"Um, oh, yes," she said, dashing into the room and picking up her drum and beater. "Sorry."

"That was unfortunate," Col said.

"Yes, now go after her," Talla said, pushing him towards the door.

"After her?"

"Yes, you have some explaining to do."

She stood in the doorway as Col ran out, calling after Zoola. The dark girl turned, flustered, drum in hand. Talla saw him take her hand, talking as she nodded. Zoola looked over towards Talla, glancing back to Col as he finished speaking. She dropped the drum, her arms wrapping around Col's neck as he hugged her. Then she pulled away, taking his hand and leading him back to Talla.

"I believe this man is yours," she said, giving her Col's hand. "Talla, I'm so sorry, I didn't know, I thought you were friends, travelling companions."

"That too," Talla said. She looked at Col. "He hasn't asked me, yet, if I'll bond with him," she said.

Col looked mortified. He took back his hand, stood tall, then bowed his head. "Talla, Spirit Messenger of the Hill Clan of the Tribe of the West, Plant Keeper, Lore Keeper, Fire Keeper, Healer, will you do me the honour of becoming my mate?"

"Yes, Col. Spirit Messenger of the Hill Clan of the Tribe of the West, Plant keeper, Lore Keeper, Fire Keeper, Healer, I will."

Zoola squealed as Col's arms enfolded Talla. She leapt on them, wrapping herself around them both. "That was so beautiful," she said. "I've never seen anyone propose a bonding."

"You'll find one of your own, Zoola," Talla said. "Someone who's looking for a clever, strong and pretty spirit messenger."

"If I pass," she said, the smile slipping from her lips.

"You'll pass," said Col.

"Gren is single," Talla said, giggling and leading Col back inside the house.

"Um, yes. I'll make this drum journey then," Zoola said, turning away.

Talla pulled Col to their bed. "Tell me about our bonding ceremony," she said, kissing him.

* * *

Zoola became more of a friend after that, spending time with them in the evenings and over meals. She and Gren soon noticed each other, often sitting close.

"Is this proper?" asked Yalta, one evening as Zoola and Gren were cuddling and giggling beside the fire.

"I think so," Talla said. "There is something important about Zoola, and Gren likes her."

"I'll trust your judgement, Talla," she said.

The solstice was approaching, and tribes from the surrounding area arrived over the following few days. Shola, the cook, got them all housed with no fuss. Gren and Zoola got much closer, with Gren having a companion in his bed once or twice. Col and Talla complained about the giggling but were pleased for them.

Talla was dressing on the first morning of the celebrations when Yalta strode into the house.

"Right! Everyone up and ready, please," she called, "Lots to do."

There was a chorus of, "Yes, Spirit Master," from Col and Talla, from Gren and the twins.

"That includes you, Spirit Apprentice Zoola," Yalta said, staring at the pile of furs on Gren's bed.

"Damn!" said a voice from the bedding. "Yes, Spirit Master," she said. Zoola crawled out of bed once Yalta had gone. "Sorry, Gren," she said, kissing him, "I hope you won't get into trouble."

"You're worth it," he said.

* * *

Preparations took all day, lugging load after load to the circle. As night fell, the assembled spirit messengers and masters gathered. Col, Gren and Talla were just leaving the house with what they hoped was the last load, when Yalta appeared.

"Where's Zoola?" she asked.

"In her group's house," Col said, "They're preparing for the ceremony for new messengers tomorrow."

"Fetch her," Yalta said, pacing back and forth. Col disappeared, soon returning with a guilty-looking Zoola.

"Spirit Apprentice Zoola," Yalta said, "I have brought you here because I have something to tell you."

"I'm sorry, Spirit Master, I know I messed up," Zoola said, "Fail me, if you must, but don't punish Gren for my behaviour."

Yalta looked confused, then smiled. "Your love life is no concern of mine, Zoola. I wanted to ask you if you were ready to become a spirit messenger."

"Me? I passed?" Zoola gasped.

"Yes, but there's another matter," Yalta said, pacing again. "Is your relationship with Gren serious?"

"Yes, Spirit Master."

"Gren?" she asked.

"Yes, Spirit Master," he said, stepping close to Zoola and taking her hand.

"What is this about, Yalta?" Talla asked.

"Come inside," she said. They all found seats around the hearth, Tooev joining them. "We have spoken to the ancestors tonight," said Yalta, "The spirits too. Zoola is the fourth."

"Zoola?" Talla said, "But, she doesn't know."

"Exactly," Yalta said, turning to the dark-skinned girl. "Zoola, Col and Talla are on a journey to find the cause of the spirits' displeasure with the tribes of man. Soon they will move on from here. Gren will go with them. The spirits have told us that there will be a fourth person in their group. That person is you."

"If Gren goes, I will go," she said. "I have no family left to stop me."

"There is a prophecy from the spirits," Tooev said. "The spirit of fire told us that four will leave, but two will return. The fire spirit is a trickster, but maybe some of you, even all of you, may die. Will you accept that risk?"

Zoola looked into Gren's eyes, a smile crossing her lips. "Yes."

"Get dressed then," said Yalta. "We will conduct the messenger ceremony for the four of you tonight, a day before the others."

"But Talla and Col... Gren too... they're already spirit messengers, You introduced them as that when we arrived," Zoola said.

"I believe I said they wore the tattoos of spirit messengers," Yalta grinned. "Just as we have tested you, teaching the apprentices was their last test. Prepare, we'll leave soon."

* * *

They stood inside the impressive ring of stones, together yet apart. Talla in the east, her pale skin representing the element of air in their circle. Opposite her, far on the other side of the central fire, Gren stood in the place of water, his face dyed blue with woad. Zoola, her dark skin representing the element of earth, was in the north. To the south, in the place of fire, stood Col, face painted with red ochre.

Yalta raised her arms, beginning a chant. The drums of the assembled Messengers and Masters joined in, then their voices. Some followed a tune, some sang a low drone note, others wove their voices in and out of the melody, creating a magical sound. Tooev walked to the fire, raising his arms. The singing and drumming stopped.

Yalta went to Zoola, her palm on the girl's forehead, reciting an incantation. She took black paint, fingers drawing lines, lost on the dark skin of Zoola's cheeks. "I dedicate you to the service of the spirits and the ancestors," she called to the sky. "Your path is not an easy one; follow it with courage."

She moved around the circle, sun-wise, stopping in front of Talla. The palm on her forehead felt hot. "I dedicate you to the service of the spirits and the ancestors," she said. "Your path is not an easy one; follow it with the power of the mind." She marked Talla's cheeks, the paint cold on her hot skin.

She moved on to Col. "I dedicate you to the service of the spirits and the ancestors," she said. "Your path is not an easy one; follow it with passion."

Finally, she stood before Gren. "I dedicate you to the service of the spirits and the ancestors," she proclaimed. "Your path is not an easy one; follow it with all your heart."

Yalta walked to the centre of the circle, beside the fire. She raised her arms as the crowd of those in the service of spirit watched.

"These are our newest messengers," she shouted. "Their purpose is a journey on behalf of us all. Hold them in your hearts, ask for their success, whenever you work with spirits or ancestors."

She beckoned the four to her. "Go now, the spirit master ceremony is not for your eyes. Finish your sister Zoola's tattoo."

They walked towards the gate of the circle, a gap opening in the assembled people to allow them through. Someone passed them a torch, and they followed the well-worn path back towards the village, followed by the remaining messengers.

* * *

"Who do you want to finish your tattoo, Zoola?" Talla asked.

Zoola's brow creased. "Can you each do part, I don't want to choose one of you," she said.

Talla smiled, taking her tool pouch from the shelf and sitting in front of Zoola. She turned her left eye towards the fire. Her tattoos were just a darker shade on her skin, not the stark statement they made on Talla's pale complexion. Talla cut the spiral on the end of the apprentice tattoo, rubbing in the black dye. Col took her place, filling in the outlines of the tattooed eye on her cheek. Then Gren finished the final flourish of the design, making her a messenger. Gren reached in and kissed her.

"Well done, Zoola," he said, dabbing at the blood on her face with a soft cloth.

"Well done to us all," she said, claiming another kiss. "Now, tell me where we're going on this adventure."

"We don't know," said Col, "All we know is that we have to head south until we find the reason for the spirits' anger."

"Across the water?" Zoola asked.

"Water?" Talla said.

"South of here is the sea," she said, "To go further, you must cross to the land beyond."

Chapter 13

Atta and Arva were sitting between the bed Col shared with Talla, and the one Gren was sharing with Zoola.

"Good morning, Spirit Messenger Zoola," they said together, finishing with a fit of giggles.

"Good morning Atta, good morning Arva," Zoola mumbled, smiling at them through a tangle of tight curls.

"Tomorrow, you must call us by our titles," said Arva, moving to the hearth to start the tea infusing.

"You will apprentice?" Talla said, propping herself up on one elbow.

"Of course," Atta grinned.

"And the others?" Col said, "How many of them wish to apprentice?"

"All six," said Arva, her little chest swelling with pride. "They all want to be protected-of-spirit."

Gren tumbled out of bed, heading for the door to relieve himself. He ruffled the twins' hair as he passed. "Well done, girls, I'm proud of you."

"We all are," Col said, sitting up. Arva abandoned the tea and ran to him, jumping into his lap for a cuddle. Not to be outdone, Atta dived under the furs to get her hug from Talla.

"Is the tea ready?" Yalta said, coming in through the door. Atta and Arva looked guilty.

"No, Spirit Master," said Atta.

"We needed a cuddle," said Arva.

"Oh, well, if it's something that important," she grinned, sitting close to the fire, "I can wait."

The dimpled twins prised themselves away from Talla and Col, getting back to their tasks.

"So, how does it feel this morning?" Yalta asked, turning to Zoola.

Zoola's fingers traced the fresh scars under her left eye. "I feel very honoured to have your trust, Spirit Master Yalta," she said, pulling on her clothes.

"Just call me Yalta now, except in ceremony," she said, smiling at the new messenger. "I want you four to take your roles as the spirits of the elements again tonight when the other apprentices become messengers. You will conduct the ceremony between you."

"What will we have to do?" Col asked.

Yalta's predatory smile was back. "That's up to the four of you," she said. "Adapt from your own ceremony, ask the ancestors, it's up to you."

Col bowed his head. "Thank you, Spirit Master, we'll do our best," he said.

The corners of her mouth curled. "I know you will."

* * *

The four young messengers huddled to one side of the house, going over the plan for the ceremony together. Zoola led her first drum journey to consult the ancestors. The twins sat with them, taking their first journey to the lower world.

Col found Yalta and Tooev with the new spirit masters and waited for his chance to speak to them. They both nodded as he explained the ceremony to them.

"That will be perfect," said Tooev.

"We want to involve the twins," Col said.

"You can't, they're not apprenticed yet," Yalta said.

"They will be tomorrow," he smiled.

Yalta sighed and closed her eyes for a moment. When she opened them, her gaze locked onto Col. He knew not to break the eye contact.

"I have given you and your companions many freedoms," she said. "Everything you have done is unusual. You had tattoos before you earned them, taught apprentices before you were messengers. I made you messengers in a closed ceremony. None of you has disappointed me.

"You will find the twins and have them take their apprentice vows. You and Talla will tattoo them before tonight. Then, and only then, may they help in your ceremony."

Col bowed, unable to keep the grin from his face. "Thank you, Spirit Master," he said, turning to leave.

"Col," Tooev called.

"Yes?"

"Those girls are precious to us," he said, catching up with Col and resting a hand on his shoulder. "They are the children that Yalta and I cannot have. They came to us as orphans; little more than babies. Take special care of them."

Col knew he shouldn't, but he pulled Tooev into a hug. "They're precious to us, too," Col said. "They'll make you proud tonight."

* * *

"Atta, Arva, are your chores done?" Col called, stepping into the house with Talla.

"Yes, Col," said Arva, running to him.

"Come and sit," said Talla, moving to a bench by the fire. "You asked to help with the ceremony tonight," she said, "Yalta will not allow it as you are not apprenticed."

Both their little faces fell at the news. Talla winked at Col. "Now, if you were apprenticed, you could take part," Col said.

"But we won't be, until tomorrow," said Arva.

"Any spirit messenger can apprentice you," Talla said.

"Do you know any spirit messengers who might do that?" Col asked.

"You?" Atta gasped. "You'd do that for us? Today?"

"If you will take your apprentice vows, and let us tattoo you now, yes," he said. "This is serious, girls, and the tattoos will be sore. Be sure."

The twins held hands and looked into each other's eyes, communicating. "Yes," they said in unison, "Do it."

Talla fetched the cleansing herbs, lighting them from the fire. She wafted the smoke over Col and herself, then the twins. "I cleanse you with the spirit of air," she said.

Col took red ochre paste, dipping his fingers and drawing two lines on each cheek. "I ground you with the element of earth," he said.

Talla brought a cup of water, giving a drink to each child. "I quench you with the spirit of water."

Col stood before Arva, placing his palm on her forehead. "I give you the passion of fire," he said. "Do you dedicate yourself to the service of the ancestors and the spirits from this day onwards?"

"I do, Spirit Messenger Col," she said in a small voice.

Talla placed her hand on Atta's head. "I give you the passion of fire," she said. "Do you dedicate yourself to the service of the ancestors and the spirits from this day onwards?"

"I do, Spirit Messenger Talla," Atta said.

"Spirit Apprentice Arva, Spirit Apprentice Atta, you are now the protected-of-spirit," Col smiled, hugging Arva to him. Talla cuddled Atta, then they sat them on the bench in the fire's light.

"Ready?" Col asked, taking out his tool pouch. Both girls nodded. Col took the small blade, cutting into the thin, smooth skin of the child before him. Arva winced at the cut but held still for him to continue. He incised the outlines of the eye on her left cheek, rubbing the lamp-black into the fresh wounds. Tears were streaming down her face now, and she was sniffling quietly.

"We can do the others later," Col said. "You need not have the plant, lore and fire apprentice marks now."

Arva turned to her twin, their eyes locking. Nothing was spoken, again. "Finish them," she sniffed, holding her head high and tilting it back for him, "We may not be this brave again."

Col glanced over as Talla began the zigzags of the Plant and Lore marks. He did the same for Arva, rubbing in the dye. He moved on to the fire scroll outside her left eye, finishing with a flourish. "Done!" Col said. He dabbed at the blood seeping from the fresh cuts, passing the cloth to Arva.

The twins turned to each other, hugging, and he heard Atta whisper, "We can do anything together, sister." They each turned to hug Talla and Col, just as Tooev arrived.

"Spirit Apprentice Arva, Spirit Apprentice Atta, I believe you are working on the messenger ceremony tonight," he said grinning.

"Yes, Spirit Master," they chorused.

"Make Yalta and me proud," he said, wiping a tear from the corner of his eye.

The twins could hold it in no longer and ran to the only father figure they'd ever known, giggling and hugging him.

Tooev turned to Talla and Col as he stroked the twins' hair. "Thank you, both," he whispered.

* * *

Just a few torches eased the pitch black of the chilly night. In the distance, beyond the silent crowds, the frosted blue-stones around the circle glinted. Atta and Arva stood beside the unlit fire, torches in their hands, warm breath clouding their faces. The grins were gone tonight, and they stood still. They knew this was serious. This was the spirit work they'd dedicated themselves to that afternoon.

Gren and Zoola had coached them in building a fire to be quick, fierce and long-lasting. Col nodded to the two small apprentices, and each plunged their torch into the kindling. As the blaze flared, Col spread his arms wide, raising them above his head. The assembled spirit masters and messengers began a chant as drummers stepped forward around the circle. A gap opened in the crowd and the spirit apprentices filed in. Twenty had advanced to become Messengers, including Zoola, the other three would pass in the summer, Yalta was sure.

Col looked at his companions; each nodded. Talla was dressed in white, her face pale in the firelight. Zoola wore black, her face shining like obsidian. Gren was dressed in a costume of blue ribbons, his face dyed with woad. Col's own face was stained with red ochre, heavy black lines around his eyes. Kark, his raven, sat on his left shoulder, surveying the crowds. He glanced at the twins, the ochre stripes still stark on their cheeks, getting a nod from each.

Col raised his arms. The chanting and drumming stopped. He paused for a moment, letting the tension rise, then stepped forward, facing the apprentices.

"Greetings Spirit Apprentices," he called. "You have each met the standards set by your spirit masters. You are about to become messengers. Step forward one at a time to meet the spirits of the elements."

The first lad walked up to the polished blue-stone trilithon, standing just outside, his eyes wide, glancing back and forth. Zoola stepped up to him, her face hard, like the stone itself. She dipped two fingers into the ochre paste and drew lines down each side of his sweating face. "I dedicate you to the service of the spirits and the ancestors," she said, "I align you with the spirit of earth to bring you grounding and courage."

Zoola stepped back, Talla taking her place. She lifted the bowl of smouldering herbs, wafting the fragrant smoke over the apprentice with a feather fan. "I align you with the spirit of air to cleanse you and bring you clarity of mind."

Gren stepped forward next, Atta at his side. She scooped a cup of water from her pail, handing it to Gren. He lifted it to the lips of the apprentice. "I align you with the spirit of water," he said. "May it quench you, but never your thirst for knowledge."

As Gren stepped back, Col approached the first apprentice. His hand came from behind his back, and he placed the palm on the apprentice's forehead. The lad flinched at the heat coming from it as Arva began a slow heartbeat on her drum. "I align you with the spirit of fire," Col said, "May it bring you the passion for striving to be more tomorrow than you are today."

Col held his hand steady as Arva's drum heartbeat got faster and faster. There was sweat running from the lad's face and a look of terror in his eyes. As the drumbeat reached a crescendo, Col pulled his hand away, and Arva stopped her drumming. They both bowed their heads.

"We honour you, Spirit Messenger Kaden," Col said, addressing him for the first time. "Welcome."

On shaking legs, he stepped through the portal and walked off to the side where Yalta and Tooev waited. The next apprentice stepped up to the ceremonial arch.

They carried on, dedicating each to the service of the spirits. Arva fetched a new hot stone from the fire after each fourth apprentice, popping it into the pouch on the back of Col's belt. She winked at him as she picked up her drum, and he slipped his hand onto the stone to heat it again.

Finally, the last one turned from Col and walked to Yalta. Col raised his arms again. "Spirit Masters, Spirit Messengers, people of the many assembled tribes. I present to you, your new spirit messengers."

There was a roar from the crowd as drummers played and people danced.

"Take them back to the camp," Yalta said, appearing beside Col. "This will be one big party now, but the new Messengers need their tattoos before dawn tomorrow."

They rounded everyone up and set off back to the village. Arva and Atta made it halfway home before they were falling asleep standing. Gren and Col carried them home and put them into their bed.

Zoola watched Col do the first two tattoos before gathering the courage to do them herself. Soon the four of them were busy converting the apprentice tattoos to messenger marks.

As the last new messenger thanked them and left, Col stepped outside into the crisp air. He could still hear the drumming and shouting from the circle in the distance as the red-orange of dawn crept over the horizon. A warm hand slipped into his, and he turned to see Talla's weary smile.

"Come to bed," she said, tugging him inside and kicking the door shut. She stripped off her clothes and crawled under the furs.

"I still have ochre on my face," he said, touching his skin.

"Morning..." Talla mumbled, patting the bed. Col smiled and pulled off his clothing, climbing in beside her. Her head settled on his chest, and she was asleep. Col lay for a few moments, thinking how their lives had changed over the past moons. Then sleep took him.

* * *

The following day was half done when they crawled out of bed, glad of the hot nettle tea the twins had made. Arva grinned at Col as she handed him his cup.

"Thank you, Spirit Apprentice Arva," he smiled.

"Thank you," she said, moving close for a hug, "For trusting us to work with you last night."

"You were both amazing," Col said. "You were so professional and not a single giggle." The twins giggled at that, Atta getting her hug from Talla beside him.

"Can we get fires built, for the feast tomorrow?" Yalta asked, stepping into the house.

"You want us to do it?" Col asked, pointing to Talla, Gren and Zoola.

"You and Talla take the twins, pick a few new messengers to help," she said, "I have another task for Gren and Zoola." She took them aside, whispering to them before they all left.

"What was that about?" Talla asked. Col shrugged his shoulders, taking a bowl of barley porridge from Shola.

The twins worked hard, remembering the incantations to the fire spirits as they piled the dry wood in the outdoor hearths. They had set two enormous fires, with spits for roasting, by the end of the day.

Col and Talla saw Gren and Zoola often through the day, but they were always busy. They spent a while with the twins later, teaching them the creation story, then ate with them before bed. Zoola and Gren came in late after Talla had fallen asleep.

* * *

Yalta whisked Talla away before lunch the next day and left Col to teach the twins herb lore for the afternoon. They seemed unable to retain information, getting the uses of the herbs wrong, so he had to go over and over the same work. He was aware of the fires being lit for the last feast that night, and of preparation work going on outside, but the twins kept him busy. He was just about to finish and let the two girls get ready for the feast when Gren arrived.

"Col, could you come with me to the stone circle later? I need help with a ceremony," he said.

"What kind of ceremony?" Col asked.

"Oh, nothing complicated. Just a simple, last moment thing," he said, turning to leave, "Meet me there at dusk."

Col looked around for Arva and Atta, but they'd disappeared too. He sighed and made himself a cup of rose-hip tea, sitting by the fire, wondering what on earth was happening.

He spent a while sewing new swan's feathers to his best cloak, the whole upper back and shoulders now covered. As the sun approached the horizon, Col washed and dressed, then set off for the circle.

Chapter 14

Col met no one as he walked down the broad avenue to the great earthwork. For a last moment ceremony, many people had gathered. Four fires blazed within the circle, and the excited crowd chattered in groups as he approached.

As he crossed into the circle, Gren appeared at his elbow, taking his arm.

"What's going on?" Col asked as Gren led him towards the centre.

"Just wait, and you'll see," he said, peering over his shoulder. They arrived at the centre where Zoola was standing smiling at him.

"Zoola, please tell me what's happening," Col said.

She chuckled. "Turn around, Col," she said, looking behind him. Col turned to see a group of girls and women entering the circle. The new female spirit messengers, the new apprentice girls, including Arva and Atta, and at their centre, a tall figure in a pure white linen robe. The long garment reached the ground, and she appeared to float across the grass towards him, her face hidden deep in the cowl. She stepped up beside Col as her companions formed a semi-circle around them. Gren and Zoola stood facing them. Col turned to the cloaked figure as one pale hand moved up and pulled back her hood.

He smiled at her. The white hair, the pale complexion, her brows and lashes sprinklings of frost above her impossibly violet eyes. A soft smile curled her lips.

"What are you doing here, Talla," he said.

"Oh, I've come to bond with the man I love," she said.

"You've... the man... you..."

Talla took his hand, her thumb stroking the back. "You're having trouble with words today," she said, smiling, "Why not let Zoola and Gren do the talking for a while?"

Col turned to their friends, catching the grins on their faces.

Gren stepped forward a pace. "Col, Spirit Messenger of the Hill Clan of the Tribe of the West. Do you choose this woman to be your mate?"

"Mate? Um… yes, yes I do."

"Good answer!" he whispered. Zoola stepped towards Talla.

"Talla, Spirit Messenger of the Hill Clan of the Tribe of the West. Do you choose this man to be your mate?"

Talla smiled at Col. "Yes, I do."

"Will you honour each other as companions, friends and lovers through the years to come?" Zoola asked.

"Yes," Col said.

"I will," said Talla.

Zoola lifted their clasped hands as Gren tied a ribbon around their wrists, joining them together. "You are now bonded, each as mate to the other. The assembled tribes, the ancestors and the spirits have witnessed this," she proclaimed.

The crowd cheered as Talla pulled Col into a hug, her soft mouth finding his.

"You knew?" Col said.

Her lips, beside his ear, breathed warmth onto his neck. "Only today, when they came and took me away," she said. "Are you angry?"

He pulled back, looking into her glistening eyes. "No, I asked you to be my mate, and now you are. Thank you."

"Thank them," Talla said, turning to Zoola and Gren, "It was their idea."

Yalta and Tooev appeared, each hugging the newly bonded couple. "Congratulations to you both. You make a lovely couple," said Tooev.

"It surprised me when I learned you weren't bonded," Yalta said, "You looked like a couple that day you arrived."

"Well," Col said, "perhaps we were, but didn't know it yet." Talla squeezed his hand. He turned to see a single tear roll across her cheek.

"Yes," she said, "Maybe we were."

Atta and Arva ran up carrying a bundle. Yalta smiled and took it, opening it to reveal a beautiful woven blanket. She draped it around their shoulders.

"A gift from us all," she said, smiling.

"A bonding blanket?" Talla gasped. "It's lovely!"

"Thank you," Col said, looking around at their friends, a tear creeping from his own eye this time.

They chatted for a while, then he took Talla back to the village at the head of a huge procession.

The feasting continued into the night. Talla and Col danced to the rhythmic drumming, then ate their fill of roasted meats and bread. Congratulations came from every side, and as the evening drew on Col saw Gren and Zoola raking the embers from the cooking fires into a row. He smiled at Talla.

"Look," he said, "They're building a firewalk."

Talla smiled. "Was that when you knew you wanted me for a mate?" she asked.

"Yes. When did you know?"

"When you set my broken arm," she said, grasping his hand. "Come on, let's see if they'll let us walk the fire together."

Yalta was standing by the glowing coals when they got there. She raised her hands.

"Quiet! Quiet!" she called. "As both our newly bonded couple are Fire Keepers, they will be the first to walk the coals tonight."

The crowd cheered as Col and Talla walked to the end of the fire. Hand in hand they stepped onto the embers; heads held high, strolling at a steady pace over the coals until they reached the end. They turned as Yalta and Tooev followed them onto the fire, then other spirit keepers and masters took their turns, singly or as couples. Gren and Zoola were lingering at the end of the firewalk when they got back.

"Are you going to do it?" Talla asked.

Zoola looked at Gren, then grasped his hand. He nodded, and they turned to the fire.

"Two Fire Apprentices will make the walk!" Col shouted above the din. The people nearest quietened as their companions stepped onto the embers. They walked over the coals, helping each other to balance until they stepped onto the grass at the far end. A cheer came from the crowd as Gren and Zoola bowed.

Col and Talla went to congratulate them, hugging both as they celebrated.

There was a sudden quiet, then a gasp from the crowd. Col turned to see two tiny figures walk to the fire, their hands clasped.

"Arva, Atta. No!" he shouted, running to them. Talla caught up with him as he reached them.

"Girls, you can't do this," Col said.

"It's too dangerous," said Talla.

Arva looked into his eyes. "We can do it. We know we can," she said.

"We can do anything together," added Atta.

Col glanced at Talla, but she shrugged. He took Arva's hand, Talla took Atta's. They walked the twins to the fire.

"Go slowly, feet flat," Col explained. "One shout from either of you and Talla and I will pull you clear. Understand?"

The twins nodded, their hands clasped, eyes fixed on the far end of the fire. Talla and Col walked either side, holding them as they stepped onto the embers.

One step. Col tightened his grip on Arva's hand. Two steps. He glanced at Talla. She smiled. Three steps. Col realised that these two small girls could do this. They paced on, their gaze never leaving their goal; the end of the fire.

Finally, they stepped onto the scorched grass. Loosing hands, they fell into each other's arms as a roar went up from the crowd.

"What do you think you are doing?" yelled Yalta, running up to the girls. She dropped to her knees, lifting Arva's feet, checking for burns. She pulled Atta to her, inspecting her too.

"Are you mad? You let children firewalk!" she shouted at Col.

"They knew they could do it," he said. "We would have pulled them off at the first shout."

"They're children!" she screamed.

Col took Yalta's shoulder, pulling her away from the crowd between two houses. He turned to look at her.

"They are fire apprentices," he said. "The *problem* is that they are *your* children."

"They're orphans," she said, "I can never have children."

Col looked at her as she glared into his eyes. Tears spilt down her cheeks as she threw herself into his arms.

"I love them so," she said, sobbing, "They are the closest thing to our own Tooev, and I will ever have. I would die for those girls."

Col held her as she cried. "So would I," he whispered into her ear.

Finally, she pulled away, rubbing the back of a grimy hand across her eyes. She gave a sad half-smile.

"You really love them too, don't you?" she said.

"Yes, we all do. They're special, but they will grow up Yalta. Those are two very mature young people, despite the giggling. I'm sure they will cause you many more tears before they are adults."

"We had better get back," she said. "Thank you, Col, I over-reacted."

Col took her hand, leading her back towards the fire. "Just talk to the twins," he said, "I expect they think you're mad at them, or at me, or both."

Arva and Atta were standing holding hands with Talla when they got back. Yalta whispered in Talla's ear, then took the twins' hands, leading them away from the fire.

"Are we in trouble?" Talla asked.

"No."

"I thought she would kill you."

Col smiled. "Just a mother bear protecting her cubs."

"What did she say?"

"She's admitted, to herself, that she looks on the twins as her own children," he said. "Perhaps that will make their relationship easier, perhaps not, but it's out in the open."

Talla took his hand. "Clever man," she said, "Come to bed."

* * *

They devoted the next day to clearing the village. Teams of people scoured the sites, gathering anything that had been discarded and piling it onto the midden. Talla, Gren and Col spent most of the day with the new messengers, doing final tests on plants, lore and healing. They finished tattoos, Zoola's and their own included.

They waved off many friends after lunch and, by evening, it was just back to the few caretakers. They sat around the hearth in the main house, each of them quiet with their own thoughts. Shola bustled in and made tea for everyone, stirring life into the fire and settling herself on a nearby seat.

She smiled at the twins, sandwiched between Talla and Zoola on a bench.

"Your apprentice tattoos look very fetching," she said.

"Thank you, Shola," they said grinning.

"You did well in the ceremony for the messengers," Col said, "We were proud of you."

The twins blushed and giggled, whispering to each other.

"Col," Yalta said, "I want to say something to you, but in front of all our friends. You have treated these two girls with respect and made them take responsibilities beyond their years. I shouted at you when I thought you'd let them walk the fire. I was wrong, and you were right; they are fire apprentices, and it is their right to decide when they are ready for each step in their learning."

"The girls and I talked after you and I had spoken, and we decided things had to change. They will no longer call Tooev and me by our names. Will you, girls?"

"No," said Arva, "We'll call you mother..."

".. and you father," said Atta, grinning at Tooev.

Talla pulled Col closer, burrowing her head into his chest as she wiped her hand across her cheeks. Col looked over at Yalta, her own eyes glistening in the firelight.

"All of us have grown to love Arva and Atta," he said. "I'm glad you've adopted them, they'll need strong, wise parents as role models in their lives."

"I expect them to be fire keepers before they have ten summers," Yalta said, "And they may yet be the youngest spirit messengers the tribes have ever seen."

Arva jumped off her seat, followed by her sister. She climbed into Col's lap, hugging him, as Atta did the same to Talla. They ran to Yalta, kissing her.

"Goodnight, Mother," they chorused, then ran to Tooev's open arms, hugging him.

"Goodnight, Father. Goodnight, everyone," they said, toddling off to their bed.

* * *

Over the next two moons, Yalta and Tooev tried to instil as much knowledge as possible into the four messengers.

They worked on healing, travelling to nearby villages to learn from other plant masters. They learned the traditional stories by heart, telling them in the evenings, around the fire. Yalta pushed them to take longer and more complex drum journeys, starting their spirit master's training.

They knew the time was coming when they'd leave and head south again. Tooev gave them directions to a coastal tribe that sailed the seas, telling them that the Danna could get them over the water to the land beyond the sea.

Then the day came. They each packed their belongings and tools, then stood, wondering how to say goodbye after becoming part of a family like this.

The twins were sobbing. Clinging to each of them as they shouldered their packs and hugged Yalta, Tooev and Shola. They wished each other luck, and the four messengers set off on the path southwards.

* * *

They'd taken two new hide shelters with them, one for Talla and Col, one for Zoola and Gren. The first night was comfortable, if cold, and by the evening of the second night, they'd reached Zoola's home.

People smiled and greeted her as they walked into the village. A few stopped to hug her. She led her friends to a central house, larger than the rest. An old man with fading blue tattoos on his right eye smiled as he hobbled out of the doorway.

"Zoola. You came to see us," he said, pulling her into a hug. Kaden, her friend who'd been at the solstice with her, hugged her next then greeted the others.

The old man smiled at them and stood tall. "I am Beren, Spirit Master of the River Clan of the Danna Tribe. Plant Master, Lore Master, Fire Keeper and Healer," he said.

Col smiled at the ritual greeting and bowed his head. "I am Col, Spirit Messenger of the Hill Clan of the Tribe of the West, Plant Master, Lore Master, Fire Keeper and Healer," he recited, adding his new plant and lore status.

Talla stepped forward. "I am Talla, Spirit Messenger of the Hill Clan of the Tribe of the West, Plant Master, Lore Master, Fire Keeper and Healer," she said, smiling.

Gren smiled. "I am Gren, Spirit Messenger of the Guardians of the Circle of Stanna, Plant Master, Lore Keeper, Fire Keeper and Healer," he said.

Col knew it was not their custom, but he felt compelled to sit in the presence of the elderly master. He dropped to the ground, legs crossed, head bowed. Talla sat beside him. Col glanced at Gren, who looked confused, but sat beside Talla.

"Your actions speak of customs long forgotten," Beren said. "I believe you are from far to the north."

"We are," Col said. "Our mentor, our messenger, taught us these ways. They seemed proper for a spirit master of your standing."

He stared at Talla for a second. "You are the spirit of air?" he asked.

Talla chuckled. "That was my role, in the messenger ceremony," she said.

"A role, you say? Perhaps... perhaps." He turned, "Come in, come in."

They found seats in the large roundhouse as a boy of about eight summers set about making tea. Kaden brought food for them, and they chatted as they ate.

"You'll stay for a few days?" Beren asked.

"If it's no inconvenience, thank you, Spirit Master," Col said.

"Beren, Beren," he chuckled, "enough formality."

"You have three apprentices?" Talla asked.

He smiled, sipping his tea, "Two of them are Messengers now, and you have stolen away one of those to run errands for the spirits. Var has not yet taken apprentice vows."

"I'm sorry, Spir... Beren," Zoola corrected, "they gave me no choice in being the fourth in this group."

"Hah! Go, go, young people don't travel enough these days. It was the making of me in my youth." He pushed away his platter, and the young lad at once collected them from all the visitors.

"Kaden, fetch a drum," he said.

Kaden returned with a frame drum, passing it to the old man.

Beren looked at him. "You're a spirit messenger now," he said, "Take us to the lower world."

Kaden smiled and seated himself with the drum.

"Var. Sit with us," Beren called to the young lad.

"A journey, Spirit Master?" he gasped, sitting behind Kaden.

"Yes, it's about time, and you couldn't be safer with a master and five messengers. Begin," he said.

Kaden began a slow beat, escalating the rhythm as they slipped into the lower world.

* * *

The watery light filtered into the dusty grey landscape. Beren strode towards the river, his crippled leg healed in this reality.

Four dark shapes materialised before them, blocking their path. The spirit of fire came to the fore, his face magnified, shimmering like a heat haze.

He bowed his head. "Master Beren," he said.

Col glanced at Talla. She had noticed it too. The first time they'd seen the spirits show deference to a human.

"Fire Spirit," he nodded, his voice sharp. "You feel the need to challenge mortals again?"

"I must test them, find them courageous enough for their ultimate task," the spirit said.

"You plan to kill them?"

"I must test them," the spirit repeated.

"Bah! Smoke and flames," he shouted, "Can't see through either."

"Be careful, old man," growled the spirit.

Beren raised his hand, pointing across the river. "Soon, I'll be over there," he said, "Beyond all your trickery, then it won't matter a damn. Tell me."

The visage of the spirit floated nearer, close to the old man's shoulder, whispering to him. Beren's head spun towards him.

"Is this what the spirits have become?" he asked, "Where is your honour?"

"Four will go, two will return," the fire spirit repeated, his shape becoming less distinct as the four spirits dissolved into the shadows.

"Back," said Beren, turning.

* * *

The old man's face was pale when they opened their eyes. Zoola rushed to his side. "What is it, Beren? What did he say?"

He waved her away. "I'm fine, sit, sit!"

"What can you tell us?" Gren asked.

"They will test you," Beren said, "You may die, but that is not their aim. When you reach your ultimate challenge, one of you will have to make a hard choice."

"That's all he would tell you?" Talla said.

"That's all I can tell you," he said, sighing.

"But who? What choice?" Talla asked.

"I can't say."

"Why, Beren?" Col asked.

The old man turned, fear in his eyes. "You are important—all of you. But you are a threat to the spirits, too. He will let me tell you no more."

"Why?" Col asked again.

"The honour of the spirits is corrupted," he said, his hand dragging over his face, "He threatened Var."

Beren reached out and ruffled the lad's hair. "Make up the fire, then you may go to bed," he said.

"Thank you, Spirit Master," Var said, attending to his task.

"Corrupted," Beren whispered.

Chapter 15

"Corrupted," Beren whispered.

"What do you mean?" Talla asked.

He turned to her. "Talla, tell me about your encounters with the spirits of earth and air." She recounted the tales, Col filling in details here and there. The old man sat, silent for a moment. "There was a time, a time I remember, when the spirits of the elements were benign to humans. Over time, their mood has changed. You have seen it in the crops they have destroyed, the cold, the wet that threatens human survival. You have seen it first hand in their attempts to destroy you and Col. They are like cornered wolves, fighting for life. Somehow you threaten them. Be very careful, Talla. You and your companions must overcome them. You must!"

Beren struggled to his feet, Kaden jumping to his aid. "I must go to my bed," he said, turning towards the back of the house. "Kaden, organise beds for our guests, I will see you in the morning."

* * *

Var, Beren's young helper, brought Col and Talla barley porridge, then served Zoola and Gren. Kaden came in, shutting the door against the rising gale.

"Weather's bad again," he said, shaking the rain from his cloak. Var ran over to him, a look of adoration in his eyes.

"Breakfast, Messenger?" he asked.

Kaden smiled at the eager lad. "Your excellent porridge, please, Var," he said.

"Is Beren up and out?" Talla asked.

Kaden glanced towards the rear of the house. "No, he sleeps later each day. He claims to have over sixty summers, though I've never heard of anyone so old."

"Shall I wake him?" she said.

"Yes, he'll be grumpy whenever he gets up," Kaden said, grinning.

"I'll come with you," Zoola said.

They went back to the darkest part of the large roundhouse, finding Beren's bed. "Beren, wake up," said Zoola.

Talla shook his shoulder. She knew something was wrong. His body felt odd. She touched his forehead. Cold. Ice cold. She reached for his arm, pulling it free of his blanket, searching with her fingers for the pulse of his blood. She put her ear to his chest, more in hope than expectation.

"What is it, Talla?" Zoola asked, "What's wrong?"

Talla placed her hands on his head and his heart, muttering the incantation for the dead they'd learned. "He's dead, Zoola," she said, turning to hug her.

"Dead? He can't be. He was fine. How can he be dead?"

"He's cold, there's no heartbeat," Talla said, "He's gone."

Zoola pulled back from Talla's arms, eyes glaring. "It's them," she shouted. "They threatened Var... threatened Beren. He said they were corrupted, that they had no morals. They did this."

"We don't know that," Talla said, pulling Zoola into her arms again.

Col, Gren and Kaden came running. Col looked at Beren's body, then at Talla. She shook her head. "Beren was my friend," Zoola sobbed. "He took me in when my mother died, cared for me, let me live with him and be protected-of-spirit. They killed him."

"Kaden," Talla said, "Tell the Clan leader, we need to arrange a funeral."

* * *

They stood with Kaden as he conducted the ceremony to send his master across the death river, then watched the men carry the body out of the village to the prepared platform. Kaden and Var followed the procession as they lifted Beren's body onto the tall structure, laying it out for the carrion birds to strip bare.

The older women wailed the ritual songs for the dead, at the foot of the sky burial platform, until the daylight faded. Zoola said many had travelled from neighbouring villages for his funeral; he was well-liked.

Later, they sat around the hearth in the big roundhouse; the four companions, Kaden and Var. "Journey with me," Kaden said. "I'm not sure I want to do this alone."

Talla smiled at him. "We'll all do the last journey for him," she said. Zoola and Kaden took drums and set a steady beat as they closed their eyes.

* * *

They walked to the river, gazing across the turbulent waters. It was the only life there. No wind blew, no sun shone, no plants grew—dead grey light in a dead grey land.

"Ancestors that love us, come," called Kaden, raising his arms. Dark shapes materialised across the water, one gaining in substance as it stepped forward. Beren looked younger somehow. His hair had a hint of colour to it, the wrinkles were less pronounced. He walked upright.

"I am safe with the ancestors," he called, "Thank you for your kind thoughts on my death."

He turned to Kaden, who stood clutching the hand of Var. "Take care of our clan, our tribe," he said. "Look after the boy."

"Yes, Spirit Master," Kaden said.

"Will I ever see you again?" Var asked, sniffling.

"When you are grown, when you are trained, like Kaden," Beren said. "I will come to you, do not fear." He turned to the companions. "You four. Travel well, but take care. You must succeed."

"They did this, didn't they?" Zoola shouted.

"I don't know, Zoola, I only know that I am here," Beren said, his form fading.

"Let's go back," Talla said, turning from the water. As they walked away, a shape materialised in the distance, far to their right. The face shimmered red.

"You did this," Zoola shouted, pointing a trembling finger at the spirit. *"Come over here, coward."*

The visage shifted as a grating, dry laugh echoed through the murk. It faded, receding into the distance.

"Coward!" Zoola screamed.

Gren grabbed her arm to stop her running after the indistinct shape. He held her tight until she calmed a little. "Back," Talla said.

* * *

Zoola was in tears, both sadness and rage, as they opened their eyes.

"I thought I was being taken along on your journey, just an addition," she said, "But now it's personal." She looked over at Kaden. "Will you be alright? Do you need me to stay?"

Kaden walked to her, pulling her to her feet and hugging her. "You have an important task, Zoola, Var and I will be fine. I have to be the Messenger they trained me to be."

Talla turned to the lad. Tears still streaked the dirt on his cheeks. "Will you apprentice?" she asked him.

"Yes, Spirit Messenger Talla, I will." He looked at Kaden. "One day, you will be the master, and I will be the messenger," he said, trying to smile. "Make me your apprentice."

"We'll do it tomorrow, Var," Kaden promised.

"No, now," the boy said, his eyes fixed on him.

Kaden glanced at his friends and saw Col nod.

"Very well, fetch my tools," he said.

Kaden dedicated the boy to the service of the spirits and the ancestors, then sat him close to the fire as he cut the apprentice marks into his skin. The boy trembled, and tears flowed, but he uttered not a sound.

"You were brave, Spirit Apprentice Var," Talla smiled, as he dabbed blood from his cheek and grinned for the first time.

"Thank you, Messenger. I will try to be as brave as our master was," he said.

Kaden seemed to get something in his eye and turned from the fire.

* * *

The four travellers left the following morning, promising to visit if they returned that way. A trader from the Danna Tribe guided them to the coast in exchange for them carrying trade goods for him and, two days later, they saw the sea for the first time in many moons.

Their guide made the introductions to the Bay Clan of the Danna Tribe. Talla was sure he said something of their mission, as no one mentioned it, and they were never asked for any payment. Two days of the tribe's hospitality later, they sailed.

The boat was like nothing they'd ever seen, a vast wooden canoe, four times the size of the one that carried Col and Talla from their island so long ago. Two wooden spars ran across the hull of the boat, connecting to a smaller canoe strapped a few paces from the main one. A tall mast rose from the centre of the craft, with a crossbeam that supported a furled sail.

Three powerful men paddled the boat out of the bay and into the fresh breeze. They raised the sail, and it billowed like a pregnant belly. Talla glanced at Col as the sudden spurt of speed threw them back, then the sturdy boat scudded across the white-flecked waves. Gren clambered towards the rear, chatting to the man steering the vessel with a large board hung from the side of the boat. He returned to his companions, sitting to talk, his hand trailing over the side, splashing through the small waves.

"I'm going to see how they handle the sail," Gren called above the crack of the linen and the splash of waves on the hull. Zoola kissed his cheek, and he grasped a rope as he climbed forward.

"He's fascinated by this," Zoola grinned as they watched him take a rope from one of the crew, following his instructions as the boat turned and rolled hard to the right. He almost lost his footing, and the crewman laughed as he hauled Gren upright again.

"What are they carrying for trade?" Col asked.

"Grain," said Zoola, "Pottery, wooden bowls, flint, and stone for axes."

"What will they bring back?"

Zoola shrugged, "Whatever they need, or the other tribe has to spare."

A bag at their feet squirmed, soft grunting noise coming from it. Talla turned to the lead trader, Bern, standing at the steering board. "Pigs?" she said, pointing to the bag.

"Yes," he shouted, "They have good milking cattle, if I can get a calf from one, I'd trade them for it."

"He seems to know what he wants," she said to Zoola, smiling.

"He's their best trader. Fair but good at getting what the tribe needs. They say he goes on every journey."

"How often do you cross the water?" Talla called to Bern.

"Once each moon," he said, "Twice if there's fit weather."

Talla sat, watching birds flying around them, diving into the water; surfacing with small silver fish in their beaks. The motion of the boat was soothing. Kaden had told her of an illness of sailing, but Talla just felt sleepy. She laid her head against Col and heard him chuckle as his arm encircled her shoulders. She nuzzled her head into his chest, breathing a long, satisfied sigh.

* * *

When Talla opened her eyes, Col was twisting in his seat towards Bern at the rear of the boat.

"Hmm?" she mumbled.

"Oh, you're awake," he said, taking his arm from her back. The warm place on her skin was cold without his body heat. She pulled up her hood.

"There," Bern shouted, pointing forward, "The lands of the Frass Tribe."

Talla lifted her hand to shield her eyes against the glare of the bright day. There, in the distance, was a bank of cloud, and, between the sky and sea, a dark strip. Talla felt the boat lurch as the waves seemed to tremble. She grasped the side of the hull and reached for Col.

"What's that?" she asked, as the shaking sensation continued. Col turned to Bern.

"It's a shaking of the earth," he said. "I've felt them on land, but never while at sea."

Talla grasped Col's hand tighter. She'd experienced a shaking of the earth once in her life when she had perhaps six summers. She remembered the terror as the houses shuddered and two collapsed. An old man had died, crushed in his home.

"Shh," said Col, pulling her close, "I remember it from when I was a child too, but we're at sea, nothing can fall on us here."

The shuddering stopped, and the little ship sailed on as if nothing had happened. The coast grew closer, a beach coming into view, a few people scurrying about on it. As they got closer, they could see them shouting and pointing. Talla turned to Bern, but he shrugged. Then they all turned and ran up the beach towards the dunes.

"Bern, look," called one of the crew, pointing back.

Talla turned, and her mouth gaped. An immense wave, perhaps as tall as four or five men, was rolling towards them far faster than their craft could sail. She heard the sucking roar as the water beneath them was drawn away. The boat crashed onto the shingle, lurching to a halt and throwing her forward, landing on Zoola's back. She'd just tried to sit up, when a wall of water hit her from behind, driving her on top of Zoola. It forced the breath from her body, then pulled her up and away in a swirling maelstrom of water.

Then it was quiet, as water filled Talla's ears. She opened her eyes to countless tiny bubbles floating in the stinging saltwater. She tried to breathe, then closed her throat as her mouth filled with water.

Talla felt herself being lifted, a sucking sensation in her belly. Her lungs were hot, fit to burst, as she tried not to inhale the cold brine. Then the sea dashed her onto the sand, and the wave rolled off her body, leaving her lying face down on the weed-strewn beach.

She lay for a moment, gasping good cold air into her aching lungs, then fear struck her again as she remembered waves came one after another. Scrabbling on hands and knees up the steep bank of wet, clinging sand, she fell flat and rolled to check behind her. She gasped as she saw the receding wave, not at her feet, but thirty or forty paces away, the foam settling as she watched.

Talla took in the upturned boat; the mast snapped, the outrigger floating in the shallow water beside it. Strewn across the beach were trade goods, pots and bowls. A linen bag wriggled and struggled, then the fastening burst open and six tiny pigs scrambled out. One stationary shape lay unmoving in the wet sack.

She sat up. Where was Col? Where were Zoola and Gren?

Chapter 16

Talla stood on shaking legs, not thinking to check for injuries until she saw the blood running down her chest. Inspecting her shoulder, she found a small flap of skin torn back, maybe a fingertip wide. She checked at the rest of her body, seeing nothing else wrong, except she was left wearing just her tunic, torn open. The sea had stripped her cloak and leggings.

Shading her eyes, she scanned the beach. A body was lying in the sand and, beyond it, another. She ran across the steep bank, her feet slipping under her.

"Zoola!" she yelled, recognising the shock of black hair and the dark skin of her face and hands. "Zoola." She rolled her onto her back as she coughed, spitting water.

"Are you all right?"

"Think so," she said.

Talla pulled her up, so she was sitting. "Stay there, I can see Col," she said, rushing over to her mate. "Col, speak to me," she said as she lifted his head. His eyes blinked open, and he smiled.

"Thank the ancestors, you're alive!" he said, pulling Talla into a tight hug.

"Are you hurt?" she asked.

He rubbed at his leg. "Bruises. Help me stand."

She pulled him to his feet as Zoola arrived. "Where's Gren?" she said, her voice trembling.

"I haven't seen him," Talla said, "Come on, we'll find him."

"You two go that way," Col said, "I'll go this way."

Zoola and Talla hobbled off, each bruised by the sea's battering. They walked a short distance, finding Bern sitting on the beach looking dazed. One of the other crew waved to them from the top of the beach. He was holding his leg but didn't look in distress. Zoola spotted Gren first, running to the figure lying in a tangle of seaweed. Talla shouted for Col and ran to the prone body. He lay on his back, his face pale, eyes closed. "No. No, he can't be!" Zoola said, lifting her hands to her face.

Talla knelt beside him, inspecting him for damage. "He's bleeding," she said, noting the blood soaking into the wet sand beside his head.

"Is he dead?" Zoola asked, her body shaking.

"If he's bleeding, his heart's beating, Zoola," Talla said. "Calm yourself and help me."

"Sorry," she said, kneeling opposite Talla. They rolled Gren onto his belly, turning his head, so the wound was uppermost. Talla ripped off what remained of her tunic, pressing it to the gaping head wound, staunching the flow of blood. Zoola checked his arms and legs, then felt over his ribs and shoulders. "I can't find anything else," she said, lifting the cloth from his head. "This needs sewing." She felt for her tool pouch at her belt, but it was gone.

Col ran up, dropping to his knees beside their friend. "How is he?" he said, catching his breath.

"He's unconscious. There's a head wound," Talla said, lifting the cloth.

Col laid his ear to Gren's back, listening. "His heart is strong, but his breathing is quick, shallow," he said. "Sit him up. He may have breathed in water." They pulled him into a sitting position, as Zoola knelt behind him, cradling his head against her chest.

"Is he hurt?" Bern said, hobbling towards them.

"Yes, his head," Talla said. "Do you know where to get help?"

"Yes, I know these people," he said, turning for the dunes at the top of the beach. "Wait here, I'll bring someone."

A short while later, two men came down the beach with Bern. They were carrying a skin stretched between two poles. The men stopped, staring at Talla. She glared at them, pointing to Gren.

"He's hurt," she said. One of them smiled, jabbering quick words to his companion. Talla heard the mangled words for 'pretty' and 'naked', then the word 'white'. She looked down, realising that she had wrapped the last of her clothing around Gren's head. Their speech was fast and almost unintelligible, but there were words she understood through the strange accent.

"Cloak?" Talla said.

One looked at the other, then a third man joined them. She smiled when she saw the tattoos of a spirit messenger around his right eye.

"Apologies," he said in a thick accent. "I am Spirit Messenger Carg of the Beach Clan of the Frass Tribe." Talla stood straight to recite her status, but he raised his hand. "Later, you are naked, and your friend is hurt." He turned to the men, saying a few words of which Talla recognised 'help' and 'cloak', though the emphasis was different. A hooded linen cape appeared, and Zoola wrapped it around Talla's shoulders. She pulled it tight around her body and limped up the beach as the men lifted Gren onto the carrying device.

Col's arm supported her as they walked into a sizeable village, smoke issuing from the roof of a large house in the centre. The men carried Gren inside and lifted him onto a bed near to the hearth.

They led Talla to a seat by the fire, her teeth chattering now, though whether from cold or shock she didn't know. Zoola went to Gren's side, lifting the cloth from his wound. "I need an awl and sinew to sew this," she said to Carg. The older man peered at her tattoos.

"These marks are new," he said, "I can do this."

"No," she said, "He is with me."

"Your mate?" Carg asked.

"Promised," Zoola said. "Col, come here, please." Col walked over, and Zoola lifted his right arm, showing the long wound on the underside. "I sewed this," she said, "It has healed well."

The messenger inspected the scar on Col's arm, prodding at the tiny holes where she had removed the knotted sinew.

"Your work is skilful. Ivarra, bring tools," he said. A small girl of perhaps seven summers ran up with a decorated leather pouch. Carg placed it beside Zoola.

"I'll see to your friend," he said, moving over to Talla. He pulled down the cloak to look at the torn skin on her shoulder. He glanced at her eye, taking in the status marks.

"Would you like us to sew it?" he asked, deferring to her own knowledge.

She smiled at him. "I am Talla," she said, holding out her hands, "And you have read my status already."

"Welcome Talla," he said, "I wish it could have been in happier circumstances. Shall we sew this?"

"Please," she said, recognising, now, the different pronunciation of familiar words.

"Ivarra, bring your own tools," he said.

The small girl disappeared, returning holding a pouch with a crude child's drawing of a bear on the top. She opened it, laying the contents out on the bench beside her. Talla looked at her and gasped. Her eyes were blue, her skin fair. The apprentice tattoo was recent but healed. As Talla stared, the girl smiled and reached up to pull a dark woollen cap from her head. A curtain of barley straw hair fell over the speedwell eyes.

"Yes, Ivarra, someone else different, like you. Now we must sew the wound," Carg said.

"These are your tools?" Talla said. Ivarra nodded. "Will you sew the wound? Are you trained in healing?"

The girl froze and looked up at Carg. "If you trust her, Talla, she has seen and helped me with wounds many times. Everyone has to start sometime." He looked down at Ivarra. "Will you do it?"

"Yes," she whispered, looking at the wound and lifting the flap of skin.

Talla looked up at Carg, raising her eyebrows. He nodded his permission for her to instruct the girl. "Three stitches, Ivarra," she said. "Start with one in the centre, then one each side. Get your bone awl and begin." Talla watched her lift the thin, sharp tool and press it to the damaged skin. Talla flinched as it pierced her, and Ivarra jumped back.

"People will always jump when you poke holes in them," Talla said, grinning, "You must learn to ignore it." The girl smiled, pushing the tool through the skin once more, then taking the fibrous, pounded sinew and threading it through the hole. She tied a neat double knot and proceeded to the next stitch. Soon she'd completed the job and stood upright to inspect the work. "Excellent," Talla said, "What will you do now?"

"Honey," she said, turning to a shelf behind her and lifting down a small pot. She smeared it on the wound, then looked to Carg.

"A linen bandage," he said, smiling at her. He looked to Talla. "Would you use something else?"

"Damp moss," she said.

"Yes, I know of this. We do not have it here. We steep the linen in boiling water though, and dry in the sun."

Ivarra wrapped the wound and Carg went to Zoola to see how she was doing.

"Do you need help?" he asked.

"Thank you, yes," Zoola said, smiling at last. "Can you hold the skin while I sew it?"

Carg looked, seeing she'd shaved the hair from Gren's head around the wound and pricked the holes for the stitches. As Carg pulled the skin together, she threaded and knotted the sinew. He pointed out the delicate stitches to Ivarra as Zoola spread honey on the wound and bandaged it. She made Gren comfortable, pulling his remaining wet clothing off and covering him with furs, then came to the hearth.

"Are we all comfortable?" Carg asked, standing beside the blaze. They each nodded or answered yes. He extended his hands, empty palms up. Standing tall, he addressed them. "I am Spirit Messenger Carg of the Beach Clan of the Frass Tribe. Plant Master, Lore Master, Fire Keeper and Healer."

They each bowed, as Col stood to face him. "I am Col, Spirit Messenger of the Hill Clan of the Tribe of the West, Plant Master, Lore Master, Fire Keeper and Healer," he said. Carg nodded.

They each stood, reciting their status until it left only Ivarra. She pulled herself upright, head high, hands held out in greeting. "I am Ivarra, Spirit Apprentice of the Beach Clan of the Frass Tribe, Plant Keeper, Lore Apprentice, Fire Apprentice and Healing Apprentice," she said.

"How old are you, Ivarra," Talla said, bowing her head.

"Eight summers this year, Messenger."

"You are very accomplished for one so young."

"Thank you, Messenger," Ivarra said, her cheeks reddening.

There was a knock at the door, and Bern stepped in, scanning the assembled group. "Greetings, Messengers, Apprentice," he said, holding out his hands.

"Come in, Bern," said Carg, smiling at the trader.

"Is everyone alright?" Talla asked.

"Ged and I have bruises," he said. "Valco is dead. Drowned."

Zoola leapt to her feet. "Where is his body?" she asked.

"Outside, Messenger."

She turned to Carg. "He is of my Tribe, my kin. I must attend to him," she said.

Carg got to his feet. "Ivarra, clear space. Bern, have him brought inside please."

Bern and Ged carried their crew-mate into the house, laying him on the bed the girl had cleared. Zoola rushed to his side, kneeling. She placed one palm on his forehead, one over his heart, as she recited the call to the ancestors for him.

"Col, Talla, will you do us the honour of building the burial platform with us?" Carg asked.

"We will," Col said.

Carg turned to Zoola. "Will you perform his funeral rites?"

"Yes," she said, standing from her dead kinsman, "But I will stay with Gren until then."

Carg nodded. He sent Ivarra to fetch clothes for Talla, then led them out of the house. The people of the village brought the wood, and Carg, Col and Talla, assisted by Ivarra, built the tall structure. Prayers going into each piece before they lashed it in place.

"Where are you from, Ivarra?" Talla asked as they were laying the platform for the body.

"Far north of here, I'm told. I have no memory of it."

"Your parents?"

"I don't remember a father," she said, the piece of wood she was holding frozen in mid-air. "They sold my mother. I don't know where she is."

"You were a slave?" Talla asked.

She nodded. Talla took her piece of wood, placing it on the platform and hugging her. "Me too," she said.

* * *

It was evening when a knock came to the door. Ivarra opened it and let in a young lad her own age.

He bowed. "Spirit Apprentice, I found this on the shore today." He held up a wriggling cloth bag.

"What is it?" Ivarra asked.

"A stoat, but it has no fear of humans. I wondered if it was magical."

Talla overheard the conversation and came to the door. "A stoat?" she asked, "May I see it?" The lad opened the bag, and Raf's face appeared. He spotted Talla and leapt at her, scurrying up her arm to her shoulder, where he surveyed his new environment. "He's mine," Talla said, stroking the small animal, "Thank you for bringing him back."

"You're welcome..." he glanced at Talla's left eye, ".. Spirit Messenger. There's a raven on the roof too."

Talla smiled, "That will be Col's spirit animal. Thank you again." They had returned her pouch to her earlier, and she took out a flint knife and handed it to the boy. "A present," she said, "for your kindness."

"Th... thank you, Messenger," he said, eyes wide, as he bowed and ran from the house.

* * *

The next morning, they carried Valco's body to the village centre. Talla sat with Gren while Zoola conducted the funeral rites. She could hear the ritual wailing from her seat beside their unconscious friend.

Later that evening, they had Carg bring in the village leader while they explained their journey and their mission. Carg blew out a long breath when they'd finished their story.

"This was the test of the water spirit?" he asked.

"Yes, and they have taken another life," Talla replied.

The elderly village leader struggled to his feet, leaning on his staff. "I will leave you with our messenger," he said, "But anything we can do to help, we will do."

"We lost everything in the wreck," Talla said.

"My people have scoured the shore," he said. "They have rescued many of the trade goods, we even caught the pigs! They will bring the rest of your personal things to you tomorrow." He bowed and left.

"I am worried about Gren," Col said. "He should have woken up by now."

"We need to journey to the lower world for him," Talla said.

Carg looked at Zoola. She nodded. "Ivarra, fetch drums for us, please," he called to his apprentice. There was clattering in the roof space a moment later, then the small girl appeared in the timbers above them, grinning as she passed them three drums.

"Zoola?" Talla said, pointing to the drums.

"Can you do it, Talla, I want to stay with Gren," she said, stroking her lover's head.

"I will journey with you," said Carg, sitting cross-legged beside the fire.

"And Ivarra?" Col asked.

"This is not the time," he said. "Ivarra, go to my sister and help her prepare food for our guests." The small girl nodded, disappointment on her face, as she left the house. Col lifted the drum and beater, glancing at Carg and Talla before closing his eyes and starting a steady rhythm.

* * *

Talla stood behind Col, Carg at her side. The dull, grey landscape never changed. She heard Col gasp as a figure materialised just paces in front of him. The distorted red visage of the fire spirit loomed out of the dusk-light.

"So, three of you survive," his harsh voice grated.

"Gren lives," Col said, glaring at the spirit.

"Oh?" his gravelly chuckle conveyed anything but humour. "For how long, bearer of the fire beads?" He spat the title at Col as if it were an insult.

"Gren lives," Talla said, "and we will take him back."

"He has passed over the river, pale one. Who will bring him back from there?" the spirit asked.

"His body is alive," she said, stepping towards the apparition.

"His spirit is gone. It cannot return, Daughter of the Winds."

His shape became less substantial, then drifted away on a non-existent breeze. Col took Talla's hand, dragging her towards the river as Carg trailed in their wake. At the water's edge, Col stopped and raised his arms. "Ancestors who love us. We ask for your help to find our companion. Come to us."

Vague shapes gathered on the far bank, coming in and out of focus, then one form solidified. The prone body of Gren, half on the grey sand, half in the water of the death river – motionless.

Chapter 17

Zoola sat beside Gren, running her fingers through his hair. They'd only been together one moon; she couldn't lose him now. She felt, rather than heard, a presence next to her.

"You are the one they call Zoola?" a brittle voice asked. Zoola turned, finding the tanned, wrinkled face of an old woman. Her eyes were deep-set, and her long hair was white. Her tattoos... Zoola snatched her hand back from Gren's head, standing and bowing.

"S... sorry, Spirit Master," she said, "I did not recognise your status."

She rested her hand on Zoola's shoulder. "Sit girl, my status is of no importance at the moment." She turned Zoola's face towards the firelight, taking in her tattoo. "Mmm-hmm," she said. She nodded toward the three drummers, sitting, eyes closed, steady beat continuing. "They journey for him?"

Zoola nodded. "His name is Gren," she said.

"Your mate?"

"We... we are... promised."

The old woman chuckled. "Does he know?"

Zoola glanced at nervous fingers, shaking her head. "Not yet."

The old woman sat beside her, a hand returning to her shoulder. "Don't you think you ought to tell him?" Zoola looked at her, eyes questioning. "Do it! Don't you think he needs to know of your intent wherever he is now?"

The hand pushed her towards Gren. Zoola stooped, bringing her mouth to his ear.

"Gren, wherever you are, know that I love you," she whispered. She turned to the old woman, who smiled and nodded her encouragement. "If... When you come back, I want us to be bonded. I want to be your mate." Zoola sat up, wiping a tear from her eye.

"There, he knows," the old woman said. "Now I must sleep, Nuru will sit and talk to you."

Zoola looked up, wondering who she was talking about when a movement on the next bed showed another figure. Nothing but a shadow. It stood, kissed the old woman's cheek, then sat in her place beside Zoola. In the fire's glow, the features emerged. Her face was black, darker even than Zoola's skin, black like her mother's skin.

"I am Nuru," she said, her wide smile revealing rows of perfect teeth. "I am Spirit Master Dirva's apprentice. You will have met my sister, Ivarra."

"Your sister?" Zoola asked.

Nuru grinned again. "Sister in spirit. We come from different ends of the lands."

"She has, what, eight summers?" Zoola asked.

"Seven," Nuru said, smiling, "She likes to pretend she's older."

"And you?"

"I have fourteen summers, I will try for messenger status at the solstice."

Zoola turned as Gren gave a soft gasp. He rolled his head to the side, mouth moving, though he made no sound.

"Gren, my love. I'm here," Zoola said, "Come back."

"Water," he mumbled. "Water, water, water."

"You're safe now, you're out of the water," she whispered, stroking his face.

"Fire! Fire is here. What do you want of me?" Zoola glanced at Nuru. She shook her head. "Fire... no, I must go back."

"Yes, come back to us. We love you, Gren, come back," Zoola said.

"No, no, no," he whispered, despair in his voice.

"Yes," she said, "Come back and be my mate. Stay with me forever, Gren."

"Z... Zoola?" His eyes flicked open, unfocused. "Zoola?"

"I'm here, my love," she said.

His hand reached up to his bandaged head. "So sore," he said.

Nuru looked at her. "Willow bark?" she asked, making for the fire. Zoola nodded.

* * *

"Col, we must help him!" Talla said, gripping his arm. He put out his hand to stop her.

"Wait," he said, "Can you still cross the river, unharmed?"

"Yes, nothing has changed."

Col raised his arms again. "Ancestors of our brother, Gren. Come to us," he called. The spirit of Gren's father materialised, looking at his son's body.

"Gren? No! How has this happened?" he asked.

"The meddling of the spirits of the elements again," Col said, "Tarn, can you enter the water?"

"Only so far," he said, bending to lift his son.

Talla and Col waded into the black waters. "He is alive, breathing still in our world," Col said, "We want to take him back."

Tarn strode into the river, reaching the half-way mark and stopping. "I can go no further," he said.

Talla and Col reached him, and Col pulled Gren from his father's arms. Talla's hand never left him, protecting him perhaps, yet there was a tingle as he touched Tarn's spirit. He wondered if he had joined the dead; wondered if he'd be able to return.

"Thank you, Tarn," said Talla, turning towards the river bank.

Col stepped from the water, sure now he was still alive. Carg and Col each wrapped an arm around Gren, supporting him. "Take us home, Talla," Col said.

* * *

As soon as he was back in his body, Col put down the drum and turned to Zoola and Gren. She was fussing over him while a girl, blacker even than Zoola, raked stones from the fire to heat water.

"Zoola?" Col said, drawing her attention.

"Col, thank you. Talla and Carg too, thank you. He's back," she said.

The sharp smell of willow bark tea turned him back to the fire. The black girl smiled.

"I am Nuru," she said. "Wait while I give Gren his tea." She handed the wooden bowl to Zoola, then turned. "I am Nuru, Spirit Apprentice of the Beach Clan of the Frass Tribe. Plant Keeper, Lore Keeper, and Fire Keeper," she said.

Talla and Col made their introductions, then Zoola stood giving her status, then Gren's. Gren waved from the bed, propped up on one elbow now. The door opened, and Ivarra walked in with two steaming bowls of food. A plump woman followed her in with a tray bearing more dishes. A young lad in her wake, carrying two loaves.

"Beef stew," she announced, "And wheat bread."

"Thank you, sister, will you join us?" Carg asked.

"I have a mate and children to feed, Carg," she said. She smiled and bowed her head. "Brother, Messengers, Apprentices," she said, turning for the door, chivvying the lad before her.

Nuru ran to Ivarra, kissing her cheek and whispering to her, before taking the bowls and serving Carg and Col. Ivarra made sure everyone else had food, then sat beside Nuru with her own bowl. They circulated the bread, each tearing a piece.

"Your sister is a wonderful cook," Col said, devouring the broth soaked bread.

"The best," Carg said, taking another mouthful.

After the meal, the apprentices cleared the bowls and went to wash them. Gren struggled to the edge of the bed and sat with Zoola's arm around him. "What happened?" he asked.

"The spirit of water happened," Col said. "Do you remember the enormous wave?"

"Yes, but nothing after that."

"Your head was split open," he said, "Zoola sewed it, with Carg's help."

Gren squeezed Zoola's leg and bowed his head to Carg. "Do I remember seeing my father?" he asked.

"He carried you back from the land of the dead, half-way across the river," Col said. "Talla and I brought you home."

Gren turned to Zoola, his hand going to his bandaged head. "Why do I remember we are to be bonded, yet I don't remember asking you?" he said. "Perhaps it was the knock to my head."

Zoola giggled. "I told you I wanted to mate you while you were unconscious. How can you remember?"

"If you asked me to bond with you, how could I forget," Gren smiled, kissing Zoola.

"Do you have room for us here, Carg?" Col asked. "We lost our shelters in the wreck."

"You may stay as long as you wish, Col," he said, "At least until Gren is well again. The girls will prepare a bed for Talla and yourself."

Carg seemed to gather his thoughts for a moment.

"What you did – what Gren did, it should not be possible," he said. "Had I not witnessed it, I would say that you are all spirits of the dead now."

"Talla has crossed before, and I have ventured half-way to save an apprentice. It seems we have gifts to help us in our quest."

"Quest?" Carg said.

Col stood and paced, his preferred method of storytelling.

"We have been charged with healing the rift between humankind and nature," he said, telling their story once more.

* * *

They spent the following days salvaging as much equipment as possible. Carg made sure they had new tool pouches and replenished their travelling supplies of medicines and herbs. He gave them hides to replace their shelters, and they helped with healing tasks in the village.

They often saw Dirva, the old spirit master, sitting outside the house, watching. The day before they left, she took the four of them aside.

"Be wary, Children of Men, for your last opponent is fire," she said.

"We are not children, Spirit Master," Col said.

She waved her hand at him. "This body will have seventy summers this solstice, you are all children. Now listen. Trust nothing that trickster says. He will lie to you, try to fool you, and worse."

Col stared into the ancient master's eyes. "Perhaps it's time to admit defeat, Spirit Master Dirva. Valco is dead, and Beren may have been taken by the spirit of fire too. Are two lives not enough?"

Dirva held his gaze. "Two men have died for your cause?" she asked. Col nodded. "Do you wish their sacrifice to be in vain? If you do not best the fire spirit, all the tribes of men will suffer. Many more will die."

Col's shoulders slumped as he realised he had no choice. He and his companions had to prevail.

Dirva pointed at the amber necklace around Col's throat. "These fire-stones. They hold his power, his essence. He will try to use them against you, but you must use them against him. You must have them or destroy them. If they fall into the wrong hands, you will not beat him."

"How can we destroy them, Spirit Master?" Talla asked.

"You will find a way if it becomes necessary," she said, easing to her feet. "Now, I must prepare, I leave tomorrow for the north."

They stood and bowed their heads as she shuffled into the house.

* * *

"Do we have everything?" Talla asked.

Col glanced at the bulging packs at their side. "I hope so, we can only just carry this."

Talla grabbed his arm, feeling the muscles.

"You're strong enough to carry it all," she said.

"No, you can carry your own," he smiled. Gone was the skinny girl that had fled Classac with him so many moons ago. Her long legs were well-muscled, her arms strong, her shoulders broad. "Is Dirva coming to say goodbye?" he asked Carg.

"She left at first light, Col. I thought you knew."

"We knew she was going north today, but not when," he said.

"She went without me?" Nuru asked, looking offended.

"Yes, she wants you to study with me until summer," Carg said.

"I suppose she was your teacher, Carg," Gren said.

"No, she only appeared here two summers ago. I remember the day she came from the south, bringing Nuru with her. It was the day I bought Ivarra from the traders. I couldn't bear to see a child that young becoming a slave."

"So where is she from?" Zoola asked.

Carg paused. "I don't know. She calls herself Frass, but I've met no one in the tribe who knew her before she arrived here."

"Where did she bring you from, Nuru?" Col said, turning to the black girl.

"Oh, south... a long way south."

"And your parents?" he asked.

"They... they..." she looked at him, brow wrinkled in confusion. "I don't remember," she said, staring at Col.

"You don't remember your parents?"

"No. I don't think I had any. I never think of it, but I've no memory of them." She sat on a bench. "I don't have a picture in my head of where I came from either," she whispered, resting her head in her hands.

"Ivarra, you remember your mother, don't you?" Col asked.

"Yes... well, no. The spirit master told me of her. She was tall and pretty. She had sky-blue eyes and yellow hair."

"Dirva knew your mother?" Carg said, "But she arrived here from the south, the same day the traders came from the north."

Talla squeezed Col's hand. "What's going on?" she asked.

"We must ask Dirva when she returns," Carg said.

"Carg," Col said, "I don't think you'll be seeing Dirva again."

"But who is she?"

"Do you remember what she called us last night?" said Zoola.

"Children," chuckled Gren.

"No, you're right, Zoola," Col said, "She called us 'children of men'. Why use that term, unless you were not 'of men' yourself?"

* * *

Soon after that, their goodbyes said and no nearer solving the puzzle of Spirit Master Dirva, they left. The weather was still cold, a thick blanket of cloud covered the sun each day and showers of rain, and sleet were frequent. They were welcomed in many villages along the way, only using their shelters a few times. The language changed, but they learned as they travelled, unfamiliar words, new pronunciations, and different emphases.

They'd been travelling half a moon when they noticed black, gritty dust covering everything. It was on the leaves of the trees, on their shelters when they broke camp, everywhere, until the next shower of rain.

One evening, they came upon a massive mound of earth, covered in grass, in a flat landscape. There was an entrance to one side. This was a place for the ancestor spirits, so they moved on a respectful distance before making camp. They lit a small fire and heated stones for hot drinks, feasting on dried meat and bread from their last hosts. Talla and Col bid Zoola and Gren goodnight and crawled into their shelter, snuggling together for warmth.

Talla's scream woke Col as someone grabbed his ankles, pulling him from the shelter. He tried to focus through the grey dawn as he felt his hands being bound behind his back.

Chapter 18

Talla turned over in their cosy shelter, snuggling up to Col's warm back, wrapping an arm around his waist. She closed her eyes again; it was still dark. She felt hands grip her ankles, dragging her from the hide shelter. She screamed, flailing, trying to grab onto something. The movement stopped, and she looked up as a flaming torch appeared, illuminating four men standing over them, a spear-point at her chest.

"Stand up," one yelled. Talla glanced over to find Gren and Zoola being herded away. She struggled to her feet, feeling the flint tip of a spear nick her arm.

One of their captors bound her hands, "That way, move," he said.

"We are spirit messengers on a journey. We mean no harm to you," Col said.

A fist hit his face, and he staggered back nose bleeding. "I said, move!" the man shouted.

They were pushed and prodded by spear butts as dawn broke around them. Just as the sun cleared the horizon, they came to a village.

"Fetch Brag," their captor called to a woman. She disappeared inside, emerging a few moments later followed by a wild-haired man. He looked at them, and a sickening smile spread across his face.

"What have we here?" he said, parading around them, his wide-eyed gaze devouring Zoola and Talla. "An earth spirit, and an air spirit! The spirits honour Brag by their presence."

"We are spirit messengers," Talla said, "Why have you captured us?"

"These are my lands, Spirit of Air," he said. "Those who pass here must pay me homage."

"We are protected-of-spirit," said Zoola, "You have no right to hold us."

"Our own spirit messenger was protected-of-spirit too," he said.

"You have a spirit messenger? Can we talk to him?" Col asked.

"He talked too much," Brag said, swaggering back and forth in front of them. "I had to silence him."

He pointed to a space between two houses where a man hung by a cord around his neck. His swollen, black tongue protruded from his mouth, a faded blue tattoo around his right eye. Talla opened her mouth to speak, glancing at Col. He shook his head.

"Take the men and tie them up," Brag said, "Put the spirit women in the Messenger's house and guard them."

They grabbed Col and Gren by their arms, dragging them away, then prodded Zoola and Talla towards a central house. They shoved them inside, slamming the door. Talla looked at their surroundings. If this had been a messenger's house, they had stripped it. There were bare shelves, bare bed platforms—none of the paraphernalia of a healer.

"Who are these people?" Zoola said, sitting. "Why do they want us?"

Talla sighed, sitting beside her. "I don't know. That Brag, did you see his eyes? There's something wrong there."

"Does he really think we're spirits, Talla?"

Talla frowned. "Maybe, we don't have to dress up for the part."

She walked to the door, peering through the gaps in the boards. Two men were sheltering in the doorway. Guards. Talla could hear a commotion from somewhere nearby; shouting, two men's voices, one was Col.

"Tell me how you control the spirits."

"I don't control them," Col shouted, "They're humans, not spirits."

"Tell me!"

"I don't control them."

There was a bang, a door slamming. Talla put her arm around Zoola's shoulders. "I'm frightened, Talla. He won't hurt Col and Gren, will he?"

"I hope not," she said.

* * *

Talla had woken stiff and chilled. The guards had brought dry bread and water late the previous night, and a thin fur for sleeping. She and Zoola had huddled together on the same bed for warmth. Their guards came in, pulling Zoola and Talla to their feet and binding their wrists with a cord.

"What are you doing?" Talla asked.

"Brag wants to see you," one said, leading them from the house.

"Well! It's the earth spirit and the air spirit," Brag said, as the guards pushed them into his house.

"We are not spirits," Zoola said.

"Well, now, you would say that. Now, I have decided that you two will be my mates. To be bonded to a spirit would give me great power. To be bonded to two…"

"I am bonded," Talla said.

"And I am promised," said Zoola.

"Promised is nothing, you can still be bonded to me," he told Zoola. "Who are you bonded to?" he asked Talla.

"To Col."

"The shorter man?" he asked. She nodded. "Well, we'll see about that. Take them back to the house," he said. The guards pulled them to the messenger's house, freed their hands, and slammed the door.

"What are we going to do, Talla?" Zoola said, slumping onto the bed.

"We need to get away," Talla said.

They heard shouting again that night, Brag trying to get Col, and Gren, to give up control of the spirits. The next day they never went out. The guards brought bread and water, but they saw no one else. On the third day, the guards tied their hands and dragged them outside again. In the centre of the village they had built a funeral pyre; a body wrapped in linen lay on the platform.

"I wonder who has died?" Zoola said. Talla turned to answer, then gasped as they dragged Gren to the altar by a cord around his wrists. He stood glaring at Brag, his face swollen, his right eye blackened and closed. There were bruises on his arms and legs.

"You," said Brag, sauntering up to Gren, "Conduct the funeral."

"Who has died? I need a name and a Clan, a Tribe," he said as they untied his hands.

The wild-eyed leader laughed. "His name was Col. You know the rest."

It took a moment for the information to settle in Talla's mind. Then she screamed. She ran towards Brag, hurling herself at him, beating him with her tied hands. "You pig! You evil pig! What have you done to my mate?"

Strong arms grabbed her, pulling her back, holding her. "He refused to tell me what I wanted to know," Brag said. "Now you are no longer bonded, you are free to bond with me, Spirit of Air."

Talla spat at him. "Never. I'll die first," she said.

He walked away, laughing. "Begin the ceremony," he said to Gren.

Talla watched through her tears, as Gren stepped up to the covered body, laying one hand on the forehead, one on the heart. She couldn't look, and turned, burying her face in Zoola's shoulder, sobbing for her wonderful lover. Their guards took them back to the house as the pyre was set alight, a strange practice they'd never seen before.

Talla lay on the bed, staring at the ceiling. What would she do without him? She wanted them to be together forever, to go back to their island, have a family. Now, none of that could happen. Zoola lay beside her that night, holding her. Talla stared up into the roof. She was so lost, so alone.

"We have to get out, Talla," Zoola said.

"He's killed Col," Talla said, "Without him, I don't know what to do."

"Do you want to be bonded to that pig?" she asked.

"I'd die first."

"Then help me get away."

She sat Talla down and whispered her plan. Talla nodded, boosting her friend up into the roof timbers, then passing a hearthstone up to her. She went to the door.

"Help. Zoola is sick, help me," she shouted.

The door opened, and a guard entered. "What's wrong with her?" he asked.

"She won't get up," Talla said, walking to the back of the house. She pointed to the bed where they'd piled their cloaks and furs. He lifted the bedding.

"She's not here," he said, standing. As he turned to Talla, a rock hit him on the head and he fell to the floor.

"Quick, pass it back up and lie on the bed," Zoola whispered. Talla passed her the rock and lay down, pulling the furs over her just as the other guard appeared.

"Dar? Where are you?" he stepped closer, looking at his friend's body. He stood to raise the alarm, but he never got the chance. Zoola dropped the heavy stone onto his head, and he too collapsed.

Zoola sprang from the roof timbers, grabbing her cloak and a fur. "Come on," she whispered. They crept out of the house into the darkness. The next building was open, a torch burning in a holder. They peered inside, and a tear came to Talla's eye as she spotted Col's swan's feather cloak hanging from a peg. She lifted it down, pulling it around her shoulders, then followed Zoola outside again.

There was a guard outside the next house, twisting a spear in his hands. Zoola picked up a small stone and threw it across the doorway. It clattered off the wall.

"Who's there?" called the man, going to investigate. Zoola beckoned Talla, and they hurried into the house. Gren was tied to a post, sitting on the dirt floor.

"Zoola! Talla!"

Zoola shushed him, whispering in his ear, then climbed into the roof timbers. Talla passed a good-sized stone up to her from the cold hearth and hid.

"Who's been in here?" the guard said.

"No one."

"The door's open."

"Must be the wind," Gren said.

As the guard turned to go back outside, there was a clunk, and he fell to the floor. "Take his spear," Zoola said, rushing to untie Gren's hands. They got him to his feet and dashed out of the house.

"Which way?" Talla asked.

Gren looked at the sky, taking in the moon's position. "This way," he said, leading them out of the village.

* * *

They walked that night and the next day, stopping only to drink from streams along the way. Talla was empty. Without Col, what was the point?

They smelled wood-smoke the second night but, unsure if they may be the same people as Brag's tribe, they walked around the village and kept going. Late the following afternoon, they walked into a settlement. They were wary but tired and hungry. A woman grinding grain outside a house spotted them and stood.

Gren held out his hands in greeting. "We are spirit messengers on a journey. Is there a messenger or master here?"

Her eyes narrowed as she took in their appearance. "Are you Bragga?" she asked.

"No, we have travelled from far across the water. Is there someone we can speak to?" Gren said.

"Wait here," she said, running to a nearby house. A small woman came out, greeting them, hands outstretched.

"I am Regga, Spirit Master of the Alv Tribe. Plant Master, Lore Master, Fire Keeper and Healer." she recited. Gren, Zoola and Talla each recited their status. Regga looked at Gren's battered face. "You are hurt, come into the house," she said. They told their story of being held by Brag, of Col's murder and their escape. Regga paused in her cleaning of Gren's wounds. "He has gone too far, we will have to act against him," she said. "When did you last eat?"

"Two days ago," Talla said.

"Longer," said Gren, "they only gave me water."

"Fetch food for our guests," Regga called to an apprentice. "Meat, cheese, bread and beer."

Once they had eaten, they told Regga of their mission. She talked about how poor their crops were with the cold, wet weather. The three messengers asked about the black dust, but Regga said it had been falling there for a year.

"Will you travel south?" she asked.

"Yes," said Gren.

"Far to the south is the coast of a great sea, almost contained by land," Regga said. "I travelled there as a messenger, earned my master status with the keepers of a great stone monument there. Perhaps what you seek is there."

"We have nothing," Talla said, stroking Raf, her constant companion. "Brag and his tribe took everything we had."

"We will help you," Regga said. "Let me talk to our leader tonight. We can give you a shelter and food to travel with at least."

Regga was as good as her word and found a shelter, clothing and tools for them. They left the next day fed and provisioned.

They continued south, though Talla often found that Gren and Zoola had got far ahead of her. Her mind wouldn't settle. Had they killed Col because he'd been bonded to her? Did her curse still follow her? If she'd agreed to bond with Brag, would he be alive? She looked up to find her companions sitting on a rock, waiting for her. Gren took one of Talla's hands, Zoola the other.

"Walk with us, Talla. Talk to us," he said, leading her along the path.

"I don't want to be here any more, Gren," she said. "What is the point, without Col?"

Chapter 19

Col sat shivering in the hut, his hands tied back to a post. His right eye was swollen shut and there were bruises on his ribs and arms.

The tribe leader, Brag, had decided that Talla and Zoola were spirits and that Gren and Col controlled them. He'd shouted at Col the first night, demanding to know the secrets of their control. The second night the beatings started. Col doubted he could have fought him, even in a fair fight, but tied to a pole he was soon battered and bleeding.

This was the third day and, apart from water, they had given Col no sustenance. There was a commotion outside, screaming. It sounded like Talla. He struggled with his bonds, cords cutting his swollen wrists, as women wailed the ritual chants of a funeral. Who had died?

Brag returned that night, but the beating didn't come at once. Instead, he gloated over the fact that he was going to be bonded to Talla and Zoola. Talla had finished with Col; impressed by Brag's power, she'd agreed to be his. Col told him he didn't believe him, and his fists flew again, knocking Col senseless. When he came to, Brag had gone. Col sat up, easing the pressure on his bindings. He moved his arms, feeling torn skin and the slick stickiness of blood. With his head leant back against the pole, Col drew deep breaths, trying to find peace. He was sure now that, barring a miracle, Brag would kill him. He was not strong enough to tackle the guards alone. Closing his good eye, he tried to sleep.

A spear butt in his stomach woke him. "Up, up," the guard said. Col realised they had freed his wrists. He struggled to his feet, and they tied his hands together again.

"Where are we going?" he mumbled through split lips.

"Brag wants you," the second guard said, dropping his torch into a holder.

They dragged him from the house, and he only just kept his balance as his stiff legs failed him.

"Ah. The spirit messenger!" Brag roared as they shoved him through the door.

"What do you want now?" Col asked.

"Tomorrow I will join with the spirits," he said, "It's your last chance. You will tell me how to control them."

Col noticed his string of amber beads tied around the big man's neck. "Not a chance," Col said.

"You'd rather be dead?"

"I'd rather die than see either of my friends joined with you."

"Take him back to the house," Brag raged. "Fetch the other one."

They dragged Col back to his prison. The door slammed, and he lay back. They'd left the torch and not tied him to the pole this time, and he looked around for a means of escape. His eyes came back to the support post beside him. His swan cloak had been hanging there when he left. Someone had taken it. He shuffled around, looking for a way out, hearing shouting from outside the house.

Col sat on the earth floor, wondering what the commotion was, then spotted a sharper edge on one hearthstone. Bringing his wrists to the jagged rock, he sawed his arms back and forth, wearing away the cord. Blood soaked his hands now, but he was almost there. With a final tug, his wrists separated. He inspected the rope cuts to his skin, untying the remaining knot and grabbing the torch from its holder. He ran to the door, peering through the gaps, finding the guard still there.

Col went to the back of the house, spotting a patch of wall where the dried mud had crumbled from the woven hazel rods. He jammed the torch into the dried wood, and it caught like kindling. Dipping the hem of his tunic into the last dregs of water in his bowl, he pulled the material over his mouth as the flames consumed the wall, creeping into the roof.

He waited, watching the dry sticks burning away. Smoke filled the house, and he knew he had to get out. He held his breath and ran at the low wall, rolling onto his side at the last moment as his body crashed through the charred lath. He breathed in fresh, cold air, coughing the bitter smoke from his lungs.

Running to the next house, Col looked inside, searching for his companions. On the floor were two bodies. Brag's men, dead or unconscious, he no longer cared as he thrust the torch into the edge of the thatched roof, watching the flames catch the straw. He ran to the next building, finding another body on the floor, a piece of bloodied cord lying beside one of the support poles. Had this been where they held Gren? If so, where was he now?

He ran out of the house, straight into the guard with the spear. The man lunged at him, and he stepped to the side, swinging the burning torch at his head. Col parried a spear thrust then, as the man drew back to strike again, kicked between his legs. The guard gasped and dropped to his knees, and Col swung the torch at his head, knocking him to the ground. He turned to find Brag coming out of a burning house.

"Messenger," he screamed. "Where are they?"

"Who?" Col said, holding the torch in front of him, waving it back and forth.

"The spirit women, and the other man. Where are they?"

Col grinned as much as his battered lips would allow. "They've escaped?" he asked.

"I'll kill you," Brag shouted, charging at him. Col brought the torch up, catching Brag on the side of his head. The leader screamed as Col smelled the reek of burning hair. He ran at Col again, grappling him to the ground. Col grasped at Brag's throat as he rolled away. He got to his feet at the same moment as Brag.

Something black flashed past Col, then broad wings were thrashing at Brag's face. Kark gave a triumphant caw as Brag screamed. The big man batted the bird away but, as it fled, Col saw the gaping black hole where the leader's left eye had been. Taking his advantage, he ran at the disoriented man, shoving him in the chest with the torch. Brag toppled backwards, through the open door of the burning building, falling flat on his back. He snarled, then Col saw his eyes widen as the roof of the house gave a dying creak and collapsed onto Brag's writhing body.

An agonised scream was followed by violent coughing, then nothing. He turned, expecting another onslaught from the guards, but none came. The fire had spread, at least six houses now aflame, and the villagers were panicking as they ran around beating at the flames.

Col hobbled away from the carnage, heading for the edge of the settlement. He staggered clear of the houses, finding his way into a small copse, then collapsed.

* * *

When Col awakened, it was daylight. He peered out of his thicket, seeing that most of the village was now smoking ruins; two houses remaining standing. He watched the people scavenging for belongings; bodies being pulled clear and laid out. A huge black raven pecked at the eyes of one of the corpses, croaking "Lazy bird," before swallowing the morsel.

Col felt something grasped in his fingers. He opened his hand to find the string of amber beads ripped from Brag's throat in the struggle. He watched the village for a long time, wondering if the fire spirit had influenced him to burn the settlement to the ground. No, it was his own revenge for the torture he and Gren had endured, he decided, drifting at last into an exhausted sleep.

When he opened his eyes again, it was dusk. Col stood, watching a full moon drift up over the trees. He turned, keeping the moon to his left, then walked away from the stench of smoke and death. He walked all night, rested for a while the following day, then set off again, heading south. Towards evening, he found himself on the edge of a village. His strength was almost gone as he stumbled along a track, aware of people staring at him as he fell to his knees, then blacked out.

* * *

"You're awake, Spirit Messenger," said a woman as he opened his eyes. Col tried to focus. One eye was still swollen and closed. "Drink this," the voice said.

She held a cup to his lips and raised his head. He tasted the bitter flavour of willow bark but drank it from thirst.

"Where am I?" Col asked, levering himself to a sitting position.

"Rest, Messenger," the woman said. "We call our tribe the Alv. I am their spirit master, Regga. I can only imagine that the Bragga caused your injuries."

"The Bragga are in disarray, I set fire to their village when I escaped," Col said. Regga gave him another drink of the healing tea.

"What of Brag himself?" she asked.

"Dead," said Col, closing his eyes again.

Col drifted in and out of consciousness, once feeling his face being washed, another time being given more to drink. When he opened his eyes with a sense of who he was, a small boy was sitting on his bed.

"Hello," Col said through cracked lips. The boy jumped, eyes wide, and ran towards the door. He returned moments later with Spirit Master Regga.

"Greetings," she smiled, holding out her hands. "I am Spirit Master Regga of the Alv. Plant Master, Lore Master, Fire Keeper and Healer." Col struggled to get up to recite his status. "From the bed will suffice," Regga said, "You are not healed yet."

Col bowed his head. "I am Col, Spirit Messenger of the Hill Clan of the Tribe of the West. Plant Master, Lore Master, Fire Keeper and Healer," he said. "Thank you for taking care of me, Spirit Master."

"Call me Regga," she said, "We serve the same spirits, the same ancestors. Your name is Col?" He nodded. "Were you in the company of another man and two beautiful women, one black and one pale?"

"You've seen them?" Col asked, sitting up, then groaning and laying down again.

"They were here a few days ago," Regga said, "But they think you are dead; murdered by Brag."

"Dead? How can they think that?"

"Gren said they made him conduct your funeral. Talla is your mate, isn't she?" Regga asked.

"Yes." Col thought for a moment. "I heard a funeral, the wailing. They thought it was me?"

"Brag told them it was you," she said.

"I need to follow them," Col said. He struggled to sit up, turning to set his feet on the floor.

Regga stood in front of him. "No, Col. They inflicted your wounds over many days. When you arrived, the bad spirits had got into them. You've been ill, and I can't let you travel until I'm sure you are healed."

"But Talla…" Col began.

"Is with friends," Regga said. "They're heading south, you'll catch them up if you wait until you're fit to travel."

Col swung his legs back onto the bed, wincing at the pain. "How bad is it?" he asked, glancing down at his battered body.

"Bruises," she said, "but I had to sew your face, here." She pointed to his right eye, still swollen, though he could see a little through it now. Col traced a finger along the line of sharp knots from his eye to the centre of his cheek. "This one had the bad spirits in the wound," Regga said, as she unwound a bandage from his upper arm. "I couldn't sew it, but it will heal in time. The rest are minor cuts."

Col looked at his bruised wrists. A ring of scabs encircled each one now, itching. "How long have I been here?" he asked.

"Three days. Now rest, I'll have Quin bring you tea."

"The boy?" Col asked, remembering waking the first time. "Is he your apprentice?"

"No, though he may make a healer, of sorts. He can't speak, never could since birth," she said.

Soon, the boy arrived with a hot drink. He thanked the child who smiled and bowed, running his finger under his right eye to show he recognised Col as a spirit messenger.

There was a raucous cawing from outside. Quin looked up, then drew himself a beak with his fingers and flapped his arms.

"A raven?" Col asked. The boy nodded. "He's mine. He will cause no harm."

* * *

The next few days were torture for Col. He needed to catch up with his friends, to let Talla know he lived. Regga thanked him for his information on the Bragga. The Alv leader had taken a party up to their village. His son and a spirit messenger had remained there to keep order in case any of them thought they could continue Brag's reign of terror. Regga reported that since the fire, they were broken people and most unlikely to misbehave. Many wanted to become Alv and enjoy the protection of a larger tribe.

At last, Regga said he could travel. The Alv gave him a shelter and furs, and Regga gave him tools and medicines for his journey. It was with a grateful sadness that he said his goodbyes.

* * *

Col continued south, never stopping longer than one night. He had been travelling almost a moon since leaving the Alv, finding that his companions had passed along the same route. He reached a tiny village with only five buildings. They had no spirit messenger, so the leader offered space in his own house for Col.

"Thank you for your hospitality," Col said. "Have you seen three people pass through here?"

"Yes," said the leader, "two days ago. One woman is black, the other pale. You know them?"

Col smiled. "The beautiful pale girl is my mate," he said.

"Well, you'll catch them soon," the leader said, "They're heading for the coast, it's just over a day's walk south of here."

* * *

Col was up early the next morning, refusing breakfast and striding off to the south as fast as the terrain would allow. Before nightfall he was heading downhill towards a sparkling blue sea, a large community clustered along its shore.

Chapter 20

Talla lay awake, staring up at the cloudy sky, the moon peeking through once in a while. Her thoughts were with Col, wherever his spirit was now. The slightest thing made her cry these days. She'd left Zoola and Gren to the shelter this evening, tears falling as she'd listened to them making love. That should have been her and Col, loving, living life together. Now it was just her.

"Come inside, Talla!" Zoola called.

"It's alright; you can have the shelter," she said.

"Talla, we've done what we were going to do," she said, chuckling. "It's going to rain; come inside." Talla pulled herself to her feet, walking to the open end of the ox-hide shelter. Zoola rolled to the middle, and Talla crawled in beside her, pulling her furs over her chilled body. "That's better," Zoola said. "Now cuddle up and sleep."

* * *

It had been a moon since they'd left the Alv village behind, and they were pleased to see the ocean as they reached the top of a hill. The blue sea lay before them with five or six boats sailing nearby. A large village spread along the shore, smoke rising from the houses.

They worked their way down the slope, and it was almost evening when they reached the edge of the settlement. Gren led them in, surprised when no one challenged them or asked who they were. They found a central area with a larger roundhouse, spotting a young woman tying bunches of herbs. They got closer and saw the tattoo surrounding her left eye. An apprentice.

"Good evening, Spirit Apprentice," Gren said, holding his hands out in welcome. She looked up and gasped.

"Sorry, I am Chirra, Spirit Apprentice of the Boat Clan of the L- Locan Tribe. P- Plant Apprentice, Lore apprentice, and F- Fire apprentice," she stuttered. "I'll fetch the Master." She dropped her bunch of herbs and ran into the house.

Soon, an older man, perhaps forty summers, came out, Chirra just behind him. He smiled and held out his hands. "Greetings, I am Gordo, Spirit Master of the Locan Tribe. Plant Master, Lore Master, Fire Keeper, and Healer," he said. The three companions each gave their status as Gordo nodded and studied their tattoos. "You must have travelled far," he said, "Your tattoos are recognisable but different from our own. Come in, come in."

They entered and were soon seated by the hearth, sipping tea. Chirra set about preparing food as they talked to Gordo. They told of their mission and losing their friend Col.

"No one challenged us when we arrived here, Gordo," Zoola said.

He laughed. "This is a trading port. We see many strangers. It becomes a waste of time to ask who everyone is. It's a good job you spotted Chirra." The girl smiled, passing platters of cold meats, cheese, and bread to each of them. She glanced at Gordo from under her lashes. He smiled. "Come sit with us, Chirra," he said, patting the bench.

"You are a recent apprentice?" Gren asked.

"Y-yes," she said.

"A few days," said Gordo, placing a hand on the girl's shoulder. She flinched. "Chirra is nervous. She was bonded to a man when she was young. He beat her. His family released her from the bonding when they found out what he was doing. She ended up here, looking for a home."

Chirra smiled as her finger traced the raised scars of the apprentice tattoo under her eye. "Master Gordo has been good to me," she said before bowing her head again.

They finished their food, passing the platters to Chirra.

"What were you doing when we arrived, Chirra," Talla asked.

"Drying herbs," she said.

"Will you show me?" Talla asked, glancing at Gordo.

"An excellent idea," he said, smiling, "You can tell Talla of the plants she does not know." Talla took the girl's hand and led her outside, chatting. "A friend will be good for Chirra," Gordo said, "And I think Talla has taken her mate's death hard."

"Very hard," Gren said. "She cries a lot. We find her staring into the distance, but seeing nothing."

"Then a friend will be good for her too."

"Gordo, what do you know of the black dust that falls?" Zoola asked.

"Ah, the fire mountain," he said.

Zoola frowned. "Fire mountain?"

"Far across this sea is a mountain that spits fire and rock into the air. It did so when my grandfather was a child and does so again now."

Zoola looked across at Gren. He nodded. "Then that is where we must go," he said.

"But why? It is dangerous," Gordo said.

"We have one last trial," Gren said, "We have to face the challenge of the spirit of fire. The fire mountain is where he will confront us; I can feel it."

"I will have to arrange a ship for you, to travel by land will take many moons," Gordo explained.

"And by ship?" Zoola asked.

"Perhaps five days," he said.

"May we stay here until we sail there?" Gren asked.

"You will be our guests," Gordo replied.

* * *

"What do you use this plant for?" Talla asked, binding another bunch of leaves for drying.

"Pain, but you must be careful not to use too much," Chirra said, smiling.

Talla looked at the leaf. "I think we have a similar plant with a smaller leaf, more rounded," she said.

"Your mate. You loved him very much, didn't you?" Chirra asked.

"Yes, but I lost him."

"I have never loved," the girl whispered. "My mate beat me." She lifted her linen shirt, displaying white stripes across her tanned skin. Talla looked at her marked flesh, then lifted her tunic. Chirra gasped at the crisscrossed mess of lines on her new friend's back.

"Your mate did this?"

"NO!" Talla said. "Sorry. No, I was a slave for nine years. One of my masters beat me."

Chirra dropped her bundle of herbs and pulled Talla into a hug. "Gordo has promised never to beat me," she whispered into Talla's ear.

"You like him, don't you?" said Talla, pulling back from the embrace.

"Yes," the girl whispered, wide eyes glinting.

"A lot?" Talla asked.

"Yes. Is it wrong?"

"No, but he's much older than you, Chirra."

"I don't care," the girl said.

Talla smiled and wondered whether Gordo knew of his new apprentice's infatuation with an older man.

* * *

They sat around the fire later, talking about the fire mountain and their plan to travel there.

"Did you hear me, Talla?" Gren asked. She'd been staring at the wall, tears in her eyes, fingers clasped in her lap.

"Something about a fire mountain," she said.

"Yes," Gren said. "We must travel there."

"Just the three of us?" Talla asked.

"There are only three now."

"What about the testing; the hard decision they prophesied? What if that was for Col?" she asked. Gren slipped onto the bench beside her, holding her.

"We have to try Talla; you know it."

"I want him back!" she squeaked, her face screwing up as tears came again.

Later, Chirra showed them to their beds. Zoola sat on the edge of one, her arm around Talla. She looked up at Gren.

"I'll sleep over here," he said, pointing to the spare platform, "You comfort Talla."

* * *

The following day, Gordo went to the dock to speak to the boat masters, hoping to find passage for the young messengers. Gren and Zoola left to explore the village, while Talla sat with Chirra, crumbling the dried leaves of peppermint.

"I'm frightened," Chirra said.

"Of what?" Talla asked.

"Gordo."

"He won't beat you; he's promised."

Chirra swallowed. "If I tell him how I feel, he'll think I'm too young."

"How old are you?" Talla asked.

"Seventeen, eighteen at midsummer."

"And Gordo?" Talla said.

"Almost forty," she whispered, "He'll say I'm a child."

Talla took in the girl's generous breasts and full hips. "You're not a child. You're a woman."

"I could ruin everything," she said, wiping a tear from her face.

"Let me talk to him," Talla said. "I'll find out without embarrassing you."

Chirra hugged her. "Thank you," she said.

Talla looked up at a figure crossing the yard in front of the house. She gasped and toppled sideways, her head landing in Chirra's lap.

"Talla!" the girl shrieked, lifting her head. Her eyes were closed, her body limp. Then a man was beside her, stroking Talla's face. Chirra looked at his dark eyes, noting the Messenger tattoo, an angry red scar running straight through its centre.

"Talla. Talla." Col said, his hand caressing her soft cheek.

"You know her?" Chirra asked.

"I'm her mate," Col said.

Chirra pulled away, her hands coming to her mouth. "I can't touch an ancestor spirit," she gasped, "I'll die!"

"I'm not dead," Col said, "Close, but not yet."

Zoola and Gren arrived just as Gordo was returning from the dock. Zoola screamed, her hands forming the warding sign, palms out, wrists crossed.

"You are dead," she screamed. "Get away from her. Go back across the river and leave us alone!"

Kark came gliding across the square, perching on Col's shoulder.

"If he were dead," Gordo said, "the raven would peck at his bones, not sit on his shoulder. Can I assume you are Col?"

"I am," he said.

"I conducted your funeral," Gren said, "Brag burned your body."

"I'm sure it was a very nice funeral," Col said, smiling, "But I wasn't there. Now, is there somewhere to take Talla? She's fainted."

The friends carried Talla into the house and laid her on a bed while Chirra fetched water to bathe her brow. Talla sighed and opened her eyes.

"I thought I saw Col," she whispered when Chirra stooped over her.

"You did, Talla, he's not dead. Look."

She stepped back, allowing Col to sit, his hand going to Talla's face. She grabbed it, kissing it repeatedly.

"Col? Is it you? I'm not dreaming?"

"No, my love. It's me."

"But how?" Talla asked, "I saw your body burn."

Col recounted the story of his captivity, the beatings, and how he'd set fire to the house where he'd been held. "We searched the houses when we escaped," Zoola said. "The place he kept you was empty."

Col smiled at her. "You took my cloak," he said.

"I have it," Talla said, pointing to the next bed.

"What about Brag?" Gren asked.

"Burned to death," Col said. "I was hurt, beaten. I made it to the Alv Tribe."

"Regga?" Talla asked.

"Yes, she healed me, gave me supplies, then I followed you here."

Talla hugged him to her, kissing him over and over.

"I love you," she whispered.

* * *

The two couples settled in with Gordo, happy to help until a ship became available to them. Col was convinced, like Gren, that their last trial would be at the fire mountain.

Talla took Gordo aside one evening, leading him out of the house.

"What's wrong, Talla?" he asked when the door closed behind them.

"Sit with me," she said. They sat on a bench, watching the moonlight on the sea.

"Were you ever bonded?" she asked.

"Yes. My mate died four years ago."

"I'm sorry," Talla said. "Do you ever think of taking another mate?"

"Hah! Women my age are bonded, or there's a good reason why not."

"What about a younger mate?"

Gordo looked at her. "You have a mate," he said.

"Not me. There's a young apprentice whose eye you've caught. She's too embarrassed to talk to you, frightened you'll send her away if you don't want her."

"Chirra?"

"Shh. Yes, Chirra. Would you consider a younger woman?"

"She's a child."

"She said you'd say that," Talla said. "If you don't want her to make any further mention of it, I'll speak to her, and you can pretend you know nothing."

"No... No, I..."

"You're thinking about it, aren't you," Talla said, grinning. "She's beautiful."

"I'm over twenty summers older," he said.

"She knows. Shall I leave it to you to tell her you've noticed her?"

"Yes. Yes, and thank you, Talla," he said, standing and walking back to the house.

* * *

Talla climbed into bed, Col sliding in beside her. She pulled him to her, planting her lips on his, wrapping her arms and legs around him.

"Make love to me," she said.

"We're not alone," he whispered.

"Don't care," she said, "You came back when I thought you were dead."

"I'm not."

"No, I can see that," she said grinning.

* * *

Talla lay, content, with her head on Col's chest. His arm held her close as he kissed her hair. She watched Chirra tidying and banking up the fire. Gordo wandered over and sat on the bench, patting the seat beside him. His head dropped to her ear, whispering. Chirra looked into his eyes and nodded.

Talla nudged Col and pointed towards the fire as Gordo stood, took Chirra's hand, and led her to the back of the house.

"Are they...?" Col said.

"Mmm-hmm."

"She's young."

"And he's older. They look well together," Talla said.

"They do. I hope he makes her happy."

There was a squeal from the back of the house. "I think he's doing just that!" Talla said.

* * *

Col opened his eyes to find Chirra standing over their bed.

"Your raven is on the roof," she said.

"Ah, he's hungry then," Col said, rolling out from under the furs to a dissatisfied grumble from Talla.

"Kark! Kark!" he called. There was a flutter of wings, then the sleek bird settled in the doorway, strutting to Col.

"Come on then," Col said, lowering his arm. The bird jumped on, and Col lifted him, stroking his breast. "Hungry?" The bird warbled. "Thought so," he said.

"What does he eat?" Chirra asked.

"He seems to be fond of eyeballs," Col said, grinning.

"What?" Chirra gasped.

"Never mind, is there any leftover meat?"

"Yes, a little."

"Can you bring it for him?"

"Raf will share it," Talla said, whistling. Soon the two animals were sharing the remnants of the last evening's meal while Chirra stood transfixed.

"Do you know your spirit animal?" Talla asked. Chirra shook her head. "Well, we'll find out for you," she said, stretching. "After breakfast."

Once the friends had finished their porridge, they conducted a drum journey for Chirra. They all agreed her spirit animal was the firecrest.

"That's such a tiny, shy bird," Chirra said.

"Yes, but when provoked, as brave as a bear," Gren smiled. "Gordo will tell you how to find one of your own, I'm sure."

Gordo looked over from the burn he was treating. "Yes. Look out for a nest on your plant hunting forays," he said, "You may yet find one nesting, they often have a second brood."

Chirra went out gathering later, and Talla followed her out of the house.

"How was it?" Talla asked.

"What?" the apprentice said.

"Last night."

Chirra stopped and turned to Talla. "I never knew," she said, eyes glowing, "It was so beautiful, thank you."

"You make a wonderful couple," Talla said.

"Despite the age gap?" Chirra asked.

"Despite everything."

* * *

Two days later, a swarthy, muscular man knocked at the roundhouse door. Chirra opened it, and he bowed.

"Spirit Apprentice," he said in a thick accent, "Is the master at home?"

Chirra nodded, stepping back. "Come in, Ship Master Tollo, come in!" Gordo said. The two men talked before Gordo called to the four companions. "Tollo is sailing for the large islands tomorrow," he said. "He will take you most of the way to your destination, and then he will try to find you a ship going to the far coast."

"Thank you, Spirit Master Gordo," Col said, "But how will we pay for our passage?"

"All taken care of," Gordo said. "Just pack and be at the dock by dawn."

Chapter 21

The four friends carried their belongings to the dock as the sun peeked above the horizon, loading them into one side of Tollo's double-hulled boat. It was the biggest sailing vessel they'd seen.

"Travel well," Chirra said, hugging each of them.

"Come and see us when you return," Gordo said as he bid each one farewell. He took Talla aside, hugging her. "Thank you, you have made me happy. I think Chirra and I will be good together."

Talla kissed him on the cheek. "Look after her," she said, stepping into the boat.

One of Tollo's crew cast off the last line, and the laden ship eased out of the dock and into the bay.

* * *

Gren was fascinated by the ship, talking with Tollo and turning in to help the crew sail it. The wind held good for the whole of the first day, dropping as night fell, and they lowered the sails while they slept.

They were away at first light, tacking back and forth as the wind turned. Gren loved to stand in the bow hand on the ropes, face into the spray of the sea, as the boat carried them across the ocean.

"The wind is getting too strong," Tollo called, "We must take down some sail."

"We're making good headway," Gren shouted. "Let's keep going."

The boat appeared to skip over the waves now, skimming the higher peaks of the foam-flecked surface.

"We'll go too far north, Gren," Tollo yelled above the wind and spray.

"Talla. Help me," Gren called back to her. Talla made her way to the bow, climbing up beside Gren. "Turn the wind with me, Talla," he said.

"Turn... How?"

"We can do this," Gren said. "I'm keeping us out of the troughs in the waves, I just have to close my eyes and think it. Try to think the wind round towards the sun more."

Talla gripped her friend's hand, the other holding a rope, as she closed her eyes. The spray wet her clothes as she tried to feel the wind. Somehow, she could see what Gren was doing with the water, teasing it into a smooth passage for the speeding ship. She felt herself blowing the vessel along, billowing the sails. She turned her face to the sun, turning her body next, then the wind.

"That's it," Gren said, "A little more." Talla turned again, sensing the wind at her back as Tollo turned the vessel into the sun. "How's that, Ship Master?" Gren shouted.

"I don't believe it," the old sailor said. "I've seen nothing like this!"

Gren climbed back to his seat beside Zoola, smiling at Col. "She has the measure of the wind now," he said.

Col shook his head and grinned at his friend. "How did you know?" he asked.

"As we conquer the spirits of the elements, we gain their powers," he said. "It came in a dream. Today I proved it was real."

* * *

By the third morning, the hills of the islands were growing closer. Tollo steered the ship to a gap between the two landmasses, sailing up to a wooden dock on the north island. The crew tied the boat up, leaping ashore to unload the goods. Tollo greeted a dark-skinned man with a hug, talking loud and fast in a language none of the friends could understand. Eventually, they reached a deal, and the two men hugged again. Tollo yelled instructions to the crew, selecting the goods to go ashore, then waiting while they brought the exchange goods. He inspected delicate pots and skins, woodenware and flints before having them loaded.

"Cast off the lines," he called, once they completed the trades. The ship drifted out into the bay, and they set the sail.

"We're not staying?" Zoola asked.

"No," Tollo said, "We have to visit the south island." He steered a course along the strait, glancing back every so often.

"Clear," he shouted to the crew as they lost sight of the port. Tollo turned the vessel towards the far coast.

"What's that about?" Gren asked.

"The north island and the south island are different tribes, they're always at war," he said. "They don't know we're going south, and the south islanders must not know we went there."

Gren shook his head. "You are a scoundrel, Tollo."

The old sailor showed a row of gapped yellow teeth as he laughed. "Just an honest trader," he said.

The welcome on the south island was much friendlier, and two women with children came to the dock to greet the crew.

"Family," Tollo said, nodding towards the happy crewmen.

"Do you live here?" Col asked.

"When we're unable to sail, we stay where we land. I have a mate here," he said winking.

"A mate?" Talla said. "You have another?"

He chuckled, "Two, one in Gordo's village and another further north at the next trading port."

"Do they know about each other?" Talla asked.

Tollo looked at her sternly. "Do I look stupid, Spirit Messenger?" he said, his lined face cracking into a grin once more.

They left the trading for the following day and Tollo stationed a young sailor on board to guard the goods. The friends followed the rest of the crew up to a village overlooking the sea.

"Greetings, Tollo," boomed a deep voice, "Greetings, Spirit Messengers!" Gren turned to see Tollo hugging an enormous man, not just tall, but fat. Gren had never seen a man so large.

"Indalo, you old dog," the sailor laughed as he tried to get his arms around the giant.

The big man pulled himself from Tollo's grasp and held out his hands.

"I am Indalo, Spirit Master of the Benno Tribe. Plant Master, Lore Master, Fire Keeper and Healer," he recited. The friends each gave their names and status, Indalo bowing to each one. "Come in. We must find room for you. I'm not sure we have space," he said.

"We are bonded couples," said Col. "Well, Talla and I are, and Gren and Zoola are promised."

"That makes life easier," he said, "Erra, fetch drinks for our guests and make beds." A thin, tanned girl with black hair and dark eyes bowed and set about heating water.

They gathered around the hearth. The tradition amongst all the peoples they'd met dictated that hosts received their guests at the fireplace. They talked about their journey and the need to reach the fire mountain.

"It is a dangerous place," Indalo said, "Come."

He led them out of the house and to the top of the small hill behind it. Col gasped as he saw the bank of cloud on the distant horizon; rising from it a massive plume of black smoke that stained the sky far towards the north.

"So this is where the black dust comes from," he said, his eyes following the thick smear across the sky.

"Yes, it falls on the island," Indalo said. "When there is a big explosion, small rocks fall, even here."

"I can get you a passage there if you still wish," Tollo said, his hands on Col and Gren's shoulders as he stood between them.

"If you can, Tollo, please do," Col said.

They ate well with the big spirit master, and Tollo returned before they retired to bed.

"Two days from now," he said, "My neighbour will sail to the port nearest the fire mountain. You will be welcome aboard his ship."

"Thank you, Tollo, we'll be there," Col said.

They climbed into bed exhausted that night, Talla resting her head on Col's chest. "So, we reach the end of our journey," she said.

"Yes, I hope so," Col said, stroking her hair. "Though spirit knows what we'll find when we get there."

"The fire spirit's challenge," Talla whispered.

"Yes," he said, pulling her close.

* * *

The friends spent a day with Indalo's apprentice, Erra, seeing the sights of their island. She showed them stone working and farming, which was familiar to them, yet different. The beautiful pottery they made, and the way they worked their leather and cloth impressed Zoola.

Col and Gren wandered down to the dock at dusk to meet with their new ship-master. Reddo was young, perhaps twenty summers. His long hair was sun-bleached, and his skin weathered dark. He smiled a lopsided grin at them.

"You are my passengers for the morning?" he asked.

"We are. When will you leave?" Gren said.

"Come at dawn, we'll sail soon after," Reddo replied.

"You have a crew?" Gren asked, eyeing the small boat with its single outrigger.

"Just my brother and me," Reddo smiled, "Though Tollo tells me you are a natural sailor yourself."

Gren grinned at him. "I'll help if I'm allowed," he said.

* * *

Zoola and Talla, Col and Gren, were at the dock just as the sun broached the eastern horizon. Indalo saw them off, and Tollo was already loading his ship for a return journey.

"The wind is well set!" Reddo called to the old ship-master.

Tollo wrapped an arm around Talla's shoulder. "There's no such thing as an ill wind with this one," he said.

The friends made their farewells and jumped aboard, as Reddo's brother cast off the lines. The journey took all that day, and the wind stayed at their back the whole way. It was early evening when they sailed into a busy dock on the estuary of a great river. Reddo pulled alongside one of the smaller quays, tying up the boat.

"There we go, Messengers," he said, jumping ashore. "The land of the Vessa. They name themselves for the fire mountain. You'll find their spirit master at the largest house." He pointed to a cluster of buildings spread across the flat land by the harbour.

"Thank you, Reddo," Col said. "We are in your debt."

They made their way through the busy town, largely ignored, until a lad of about ten summers joined them.

"Looking for the spirit master's house?" he asked. Talla glanced at him, taking in the sharp, black tattoo around his right eye.

"Thank you, Spirit Apprentice. Will you lead us?"

"Follow me," the boy said.

Soon they stood outside a large house. Herbs hung drying around the eaves of the roof, and a young man was cutting wood with a stone axe beside the door.

"Come in," the boy said. "Visitors, Spirit Master," he called. A shape moved from the rear of the house as their eyes became accustomed to the lack of light. A woman of perhaps thirty summers, dark-skinned like Zoola, stepped into view, her hands extended in welcome.

"Greetings, Spirit Messengers," she said. "I am Garla, Spirit Master of the Harbour Clan of the Vessa Tribe. Plant Master, Lore Master, Fire Keeper and Healer."

The friends introduced themselves, bowing to Garla. "You have many apprentices," Talla said.

Garla looked at Talla, taking in her colouring and dress. She smiled. "We have much work here. I have two Messengers and four apprentices. What brings you to the lands of the Vessa?"

"We have to go to the fire mountain, Spirit Master," Col said. "We have a challenge to meet from the spirit of fire."

Garla's jaw dropped before she recovered herself. "Then I will have Horda lead you there tomorrow," she said, pulling their young guide forward. "The mountain Clan are his people, they will be glad of a visit from him."

* * *

The friends ate well and given comfortable beds, then at first light, they were off on their travels once more.

Horda was a talkative lad, telling them about the people and the landscape as they trudged, ever uphill, towards the mountain village. They camped overnight, needing no shelters in the spring air, and were travelling again as the sun rose.

It was noon when they entered a small village, set between green fields and black rocks, at the foot of the fire mountain. The plume of black smoke looked much more threatening now as the dark peak loomed above them. Horda took them to a central house where an older spirit master greeted them.

"Greetings, Spirit Messengers," he said, his arms extended. "I am Arlo, Spirit Master of the Mountain Clan of the Vessa Tribe. Plant Master, Lore Master, Fire Master and Healer."

The companions introduced themselves, then Col peered at Arlo's tattoos. "You are a Fire Master?" he asked.

"I am. Since I reached that status, I have been the only one. My master sacrificed himself the day I was qualified."

"Sacrificed?" Zoola asked.

"The mountain requires human sacrifice," he said, "Each time there is an eruption, a volunteer comes forward to be our offering to the mountain."

"They volunteer?" Talla asked, shuddering.

"Of course," Arlo said, "It's a great honour to become one with our sacred mountain. But come in, we can talk inside."

He led the way into the house, offering them seats around the fireplace, while a small woman made tea and gave them platters of bread and meat.

"My mate, Jessa," Arlo said as the woman bowed to the messengers.

"You are not protected-of-spirit?" Zoola asked.

"No," she grinned, "I leave that to Arlo."

"It is unusual for us to find a master whose mate does not serve the spirits," Gren said.

"She has no wish to serve," Arlo said, pulling Jessa close.

They discussed their journey, and it surprised Arlo the distances they had travelled. He knew of their own lands, though he had never gone further than the shores of the inland sea. People of Zoola's colour were more common in these lands, two being part of the Mountain Clan. Arlo said they came from the south of the inland sea. Talla's colouring fascinated him, though. His gaze wandered to her often until he asked her of her origins.

"I think I am unique," she said. "There are none like me in my tribe, nor anywhere on our islands."

"You have an affinity with the winds?" Arlo asked.

"So it seems," Talla smiled.

"And you, Zoola. You are of the earth?"

"It may be so, Master," she said.

"Gren, you are water?" Gren nodded. Arlo turned to Col. "Then you are the one who will challenge the spirit of fire."

"Perhaps me, perhaps all of us. We don't know," he said.

"Well, I should train you in the skills of a fire master," Arlo said.

They housed them in the large roundhouse, along with Arlo's joint spirit master, Batta, an old woman with a wicked smile. There was an apprentice too, called Jowa. She was a young girl of maybe twelve summers, with an atrophied left arm that hung limp at her side. She seemed to cope well, using her chin or her feet to hold things, or wedging things under the paralysed limb.

They soon settled into life with the Vessa, Col working with Arlo, while Talla and Gren began spirit master training with Batta. Zoola had Horda, their guide, take her to the nearby caves where she worked with the energies of earth.

Zoola split her time between Arlo and Batta when she wasn't at 'her' caves. The back of the cavern where the floor met the roof was her special place. She would wedge her muscular body right into the narrow crevice, coarse black rock pressed to her shoulder blades and her breasts, to her buttocks and her belly. Her soles flat on the stone and knees braced against the roof, at one with her element.

She meditated, feeling her way into the surrounding stone, finding the heat of the molten earth, glowing red in the depths. Her mind harked back to the darkness in her childhood, but now she could put it behind her. Earth was her element.

"Master Arlo, can I borrow Jowa tomorrow to come to the caves and drum for me?" she asked one evening.

"Yes, it will be good practice for her," Arlo said.

The next day they set out together, Jowa excited to be taking part in a ceremony for once. With two masters in the village, they seldom involved her with the deeper workings of the clan's spiritual life.

Zoola drummed with Jowa for a while, getting the girl used to the cadence. "Keep going, whatever happens," Zoola said, "I will rely on you to bring me back." Jowa nodded and continued to drum as she watched Zoola press herself into the crevice at the back of the cave.

* * *

The grey landscape stretched before them—dim light illuminating three figures. Jowa glanced at Zoola, eyes questioning, but Zoola just shook her head. The first figure turned, her pale face shining in the grey light. Talla.

"Why have you brought me here, Zoola?" she asked.

"I didn't," Zoola said. "I wanted to consult the spirits."

The second figure turned, Gren's features showed through the blue dye on his skin. "Zoola, Talla! What has happened?" he asked.

"I don't know, Gren," Zoola said.

The third figure turned, and all of them gasped. The shimmering red features of the fire spirit glared at them with molten eyes.

"So, mortals, the secret is out. Soon we will be united in the service of the greater powers."

"Where is Col?" Talla asked.

"He has a different destiny to you three," the spirit said. "He fulfils a separate role in our game."

The spirit's features softened and dispersed to a grating, dry cackle. "We four shall be one!" the disembodied voice crowed as his shadow drifted away.

"Back," said Zoola. "Back now!"

* * *

Zoola and Jowa hurried back to the village, finding Batta teaching Talla and Gren. The two friends smiled at her but said nothing. Zoola wondered if they'd been there at all, or if it was all her imagination. She went to find Jessa, helping the spirit master's mate prepare food for the evening, but her mind was elsewhere.

Talla and Gren sat long into the night, discussing the work they'd been doing on using plants and mushrooms to travel beyond the realms of the spirits and ancestors. Zoola grew tired and, eventually, lay down on the edge of Talla's bed beside Col.

* * *

Col felt the warm body beside him and wrapped his arm around her. His fingers traced the soft belly, slipping up towards the swelling breasts, the long rigid nipple. He snatched his hand back as if burned. These breasts were bigger than his mate's, the nipple far from the little pink tips of Talla's breasts.

"Gren? What's wrong?" mumbled the bush of curled hair beside him. Zoola turned and looked straight into Col's wide eyes.

"Oh, it's you," she said, grinning, "Sorry."

"Zoola, why are you in my bed?" Col asked.

Chapter 22

Zoola giggled and kissed Col on the forehead, rolling her warm body out of his bed. She glanced over to the next sleeping platform and smiled.

"Look, Col," she whispered.

Col sat up, rubbing his eyes. There was Talla, still dressed, cuddled up to Gren. They had talked until they fell asleep where they sat.

"I'm sorry about..." he began.

Zoola stroked his face. "I didn't complain, did I?"

"Um, no," Col said.

"So, it's alright then." She stood, pulling on her discarded clothing, and walked to the hearth to revive the fire. Not long after, Talla slumped onto the bench beside Col, a grin on her face.

"Sorry," she said. "We were so caught up in the new teachings we talked until we fell asleep."

"It's alright," Col said, "Zoola slept in our bed."

Talla cocked her head, "With you?"

"Well, there was no room in her own bed, was there?"

"No," Talla said, taking the drink Gren offered her. "No, I suppose not."

It upset Col that his mate had slept with Gren, no matter how innocent it had been, but was more discomfited by his own touching of Zoola. She, though, seemed unworried by it, so he decided not to mention it again.

"I had strange dreams last night," Talla said, her fingers running through her long hair as if trying to grasp the memories. "I was in the lower world; Zoola and Gren were there, as the spirits."

"I dreamt the same thing," said Gren, "But the fire spirit was there."

"That's right!" Talla said, "He said something about Col's destiny being different to ours."

"You dreamt that last night?" Zoola asked. They nodded. "It happened yesterday. Jowa was drumming for me at the cave when I made the journey. You remembered it much later, yet you were still there in my experience too. What do you think it means?"

* * *

Col's lessons with Arlo were long and complicated. He had to learn complex incantations to the fire spirit, remember the plants that could help him gain a deeper understanding of the nature of fire. He would meditate for hours with his eyes, and mind concentrated on the flames.

Arlo admired the fire beads, Albyn's amber stones that still adorned Col's throat. He asked to see them often, but Col wasn't happy to let them out of his sight after the dire warnings he'd received from the mysterious old woman, Dirva. There was avarice in the Fire Master's eyes when he saw the gems, and that worried Col. He wondered if he was being controlled by the amber stones, or if they gave him power over the fire spirit.

Two nights later, as Talla and Gren sat talking late again, Zoola surprised him by stripping and crawling into bed with him.

"Hey! That one's mine," Talla called, a wide grin on her face.

"He's cold, you're busy, and I want a cuddle," Zoola said, snuggling up to Col. "Come and throw me out later."

Talla nodded, then returned to her conversation with Gren.

"This is better than sleeping alone," Zoola whispered.

"We shouldn't, Zoola, I'm bonded," Col replied.

"Me too, more or less," she said.

Her head snuggled into him, an arm wrapping around his waist. Col sighed, happy that Zoola understood.

* * *

Col wakened as a leg slid over his hips and a warm female body settled on him. He opened his eyes, gasping as he realised it wasn't Talla, but Zoola. She smiled in the last glimmers of the firelight, lowering herself onto him.

"Zoola, NO!" Col squeaked, pushing at her rolling hips.

"Shh!" she giggled, "You'll wake the others."

"We... we can't," he whispered as Zoola's hips continued rocking.

"We are," she grinned, "And it's nice." Her face descended in the near dark, her lips finding his.

"Zoola..."

"Mmm-hmm," she groaned.

"Zoola!"

"Yes!" she whispered as her body shuddered, her teeth sinking into his lower lip. Col tasted blood, his own blood, as he failed to hold back his own climax.

Zoola rolled off him, snuggling into his chest once more.

"Thank you," she whispered.

"Zoola... we..."

"Shh, goodnight," she said.

Col lay awake for a long time. He heard Zoola's breathing settle to a steady cadence. Batta turned in her sleep, muttering. He was just dropping off to sleep himself when soft giggles from the next bed roused him: Whispers... his name... wet kissing sounds, then a gasp. Soon, the unmistakable sounds of coupling drifted to his ears, and he pulled the furs over his head, tears filling his eyes.

* * *

Col kept his distance from everyone the next day. He meditated, though his mind was racing, and he achieved nothing. He revised the chants and incantations in his head, forgetting the order of the verses repeatedly. He went to Arlo, hoping for something to take his mind from the sounds of the previous night; from his own actions with Zoola.

"Col," Arlo said as he entered the house. "It's time we found out what the spirit of fire has in mind as your challenge."

"A drum journey?" Col asked.

"Yes, get the four of you together," he said.

Col looked for his companions, finding them together with Batta, working with drum rhythms.

"Arlo wants us to journey together," he announced, turning to return to the house. Talla caught up with him.

"Col, I've hardly seen you today," she said, taking his arm.

"No."

"What's wrong?" she asked.

"I know."

"Know what?"

"You... and Gren... I heard. I wasn't asleep."

"Oh, Col," Talla gasped, wrapping him in her arms. Col stood, his arms useless at his sides as he decided what to do with them. Then he held her as she sobbed.

"I'm sorry, we've been getting so close, it just happened," Talla cried.

Col pulled back, causing Talla to look up at him, reluctant to let him go. "It's worse than that, Talla. I slept with Zoola."

"I know."

"No, I slept... made love, to Zoola. She started it, but I didn't stop her. I'm sorry."

Talla gazed into her mate's eyes, tears falling, though she was no longer sure which revelation caused them to sting so much.

"Are we over?" she asked, "Finished already?"

"I don't want that," Col said, pulling her close again. Talla's arms crushed him.

"Neither do I," she whispered, "Neither do I."

* * *

The drumbeat began. Col closed his eyes, dropping into the lower world.

He opened his eyes in the alternate reality, finding Arlo and Batta at his side. Gren, Talla and Zoola were not beside him. He looked up to see the spirits of the elements lined up opposite. One pulled off her hood, and Col gasped as Zoola faced him. There was Talla, then Gren, his face dyed blue. The last figure too was familiar to him — the shimmering visage of the fire spirit.

Then it made sense. They had bested three of the elements now. His companions had replaced each one as they were defeated. The final one was fire.

"What is your challenge, Fire Spirit?" Arlo asked.

"A sacrifice," the spirit said, his grating laugh echoing.

"Another? You have had many sacrifices."

"Another," the spirit rasped.

"Who?"

"I wish the sacrifice of a Fire Master," the red figure gloated. His gaze settling on Col.

"A Fire Master?" Arlo asked.

"That is my challenge. Do this, and I will make the fire mountain cease its eruptions."

"But..."

"These are my conditions, there will be no bargaining," the spirit said. *He gave a humourless smile as his face and body dissolved into the air, cackling.*

"Back!" called Batta, taking Arlo by the arm.

* * *

Col stayed silent as the three companions and the two spirit masters jabbered and argued over the fire spirit's message. His mind worked over how he could save his relationships with Talla, Gren and Zoola.

"What do you think, Col?" Arlo said.

"I'll do it," Col said, turning to the spirit master. "How far am I from being a fire master?"

"Half a moon, if you apply yourself."

"Train me, I'll be the sacrifice."

"No!" screamed Talla. "No, I won't lose you again. Col you can't, you mustn't."

Col gazed into his mate's eyes. "If we are to survive, our tribes, our clans, we must meet his challenge," he said.

"There must be another way."

"No bargaining," Col reminded her. "He said, no bargaining."

Zoola took Talla outside, her arm around her friend. Gren followed.

"I will work hard," Col said to Arlo. "We will meet his challenge."

Arlo nodded, then his gaze settled on the amber necklace. "I must have the beads," he said, "Before the sacrifice. You will become a fire master at the mountain, I'll finish your tattoo then."

"I'll no longer have a use for them, Arlo," Col said.

Col wandered outside to find Talla. He walked over to where Zoola and Gren were comforting her. Col heard Gren shout in dismay as he approached. Then Gren turned, his fist slamming into Col's face.

"You slept with Zoola."

Col shook his head, wiping the blood from his nose as he focussed on Gren. "Yes."

"You evil pig!" Gren screamed as he hit Col a second time. Col knew he should defend himself, but Gren was right, he'd made love to Zoola.

"You made love to my mate. My Talla," he said, spitting blood from his mouth, smearing it across his face with the back of his hand.

"What?" Zoola said. "You never told me that. You made love to Talla? Then you hit Col for being with me? You hypocrite!"

"I'm…" Gren began.

"Damn you," Zoola shouted, storming off. Talla ran after her, trying to slow her retreat, to get her to talk.

Col looked at Gren, his eyes unblinking as Gren broke the gaze and lowered his head. Col turned and walked away.

He felt Talla slip into bed that night, her head resting on his chest, like always. His arm wrapped around her as he felt warm tears drip onto his chest. He wanted to say something, but he had no words. Gren and Zoola had moved to another bed, far across the roundhouse, beside Batta. At some point, his staring eyes closed and sleep came.

* * *

Col mastered everything he could over the next days. Arlo's final instruction was in the eating and breathing of fire. Col learned that there was a substance, called Spirits of Beer, that Arlo made. A stick, soaked in this and set afire, could be extinguished in the mouth without pain. The same potion, held in the mouth and sprayed over a burning torch, enabled the Fire Master to appear to breathe flame.

Col sat with Talla the day before his last trial. He held her hand, unable to meet her gaze.

"Don't do it, Col," she said.

"I must."

"It's the beads," Talla said. "They are making you agree to this."

Col reached for the amber necklace, pulling it from his throat. He rolled the yellow stones in his hand before giving them to Talla. "I don't think so, but hold them for me until the sacrifice," he said.

Talla gazed into the distance as she squeezed Col's hand. "I don't want to be alone again," she said.

"You have Zoola and Gren."

"Gren is a fool," she said, pulling her hand from his. "He had no right to hit you. He is as guilty as you. We all are."

Col met Talla's gaze, staring deep into her violet eyes. "This is my last day, Talla. I have no room for hate now. I love you, and Zoola, and Gren. What is done is done. I know we are all to blame, so we can each forgive."

Talla clutched him as if she'd never let him go. She stayed at his side through their meal that evening and crawled into bed with him that night. She straddled his waist, leaning in to kiss him before making love with her mate for the last time.

Chapter 23

Talla took the string of fire beads from her throat. Col was the sacrifice. The fire spirit had demanded it, and only he could save the tribes of man. There were no words to say, nothing to do but hold him. He pulled back from her grasp, at last, looking into her eyes.

"I love you, Talla. I always will," he said.

Her body shuddered. "I love you too," she said, as he turned and walked towards Arlo. "I'll see you soon," she whispered.

Zoola rushed to him, burying her face in his chest, before turning and running into the house. Gren stood and glared until Col met his gaze, then turned away, following Zoola.

* * *

The walk to the fire mountain took half of the morning, Col trudging behind Arlo up the steep path. They turned a corner and came upon the precipice of the crater. Col gazed out across the vast lake of boiling rock; a dip on the far side emptying the sulphurous magma towards the sea.

Arlo placed his pack on a rock, opening a bundle of flint tools and a small cup of lamp-black. He lifted out a covered pot and passed it to Col.

"Drink," he said, "This will align you with the spirits and make your journey, to the realm of fire, easier."

Col took the vessel and drank, gulping the cool liquid. He paused, tasting the earthy tang of forest mushrooms. Which ones he was unsure, but he could guess. He supposed the draught was to quieten him if he changed his mind. He wondered how many sacrifices Arlo had drugged before their final plunge into the mountain. Col set the pot beside him, pouring the rest of the liquid into a crack in the hot rock at his side.

"Have you drunk it all?" Arlo asked, smiling.

"Yes, Fire Master," Col said, struggling to his feet. He watched Arlo setting out his tools, his vision blurring as he stumbled forward.

"Wait! Not yet," Arlo said, catching Col's arm. "We have to complete your tattoo."

Col reached to his throat, unfastening the string of fire beads. "You must have these," he slurred, trying to pass the glowing amber necklace to the old Fire Master. Arlo took his hand and grasped the beads, fastening them around his own throat. He took the tiny flint blade and leant toward Col, bringing the sharp edge to the side of his eye. Col flinched and stepped back. The face before him was no longer Arlo's. The shimmering red visage was a far more sinister thing, his opponent, the fire spirit. He jerked his arm up, knocking the hand, holding the blade, away.

"Keep still!" Arlo's voice said as the face changed again. "You must have the tattoo before the sacrifice."

Col felt the bite of the blade on his flesh, the trickle of blood on his cheek, then the burning sting of the lamp-black. Arlo stepped back, admiring the new marks. He placed his hands on Col's shoulders, beginning the incantation for a new Fire Master.

Col closed his eyes as his lips followed the words of the prayer, but in his mind, he saw Talla. She stood by a lake, a baby in her arms, two small children at her feet. He saw Zoola and Gren; saw how the four of them formed a perfect balance of the powers of the elements.

Col looked up as the chant ended, staring into Arlo's eyes.

The mountain seemed to anticipate the sacrifice, as molten rock flew high in the air. Col pushed Arlo away as a man-sized lump of magma splashed onto the ledge. His befuddled mind watched, horrified, as the lava grew arms and legs. The figure levered itself to its feet as the visage he knew well, formed atop it. The face twisted into a vicious sneer as the spirit spoke.

"You are mine now, Fire Master Col. Step forward. Come. Come to your death." The spirit had him by the shoulders, walking him towards the edge. "One step and they will be mine," the spirit gloated. "The two women, earth and air, and the man, water. I shall rule them as puppets. The elements will answer only to me."

Col struggled from the spirit's grasp, turning to face him. "No! They have a future, a destiny," he said, lunging at the glowing red face.

"None but that which I choose for them," the fire spirit said, grappling with Col once more. They fell to the scorching rock, fingers scratching, legs kicking. Col saw Arlo, clutching the fire beads, watching Col's battle from a safe distance. He must possess the beads or destroy them. He had to prevail.

Col struggled to his feet. The mountain seemed to tilt, and his arms flailed for balance. The spirit came at him again, grabbing his arm and forcing him into the rush of hot air rising from the mountain's yellow core. Col felt the ground beneath him crumble, and he tumbled to the searing rock. His opponent crashed on top of him, and he kicked out.

Col's strength was waning as he gained his feet, and his enemy charged him once more. Arlo came towards them, reaching for Col's arm. For a moment Col thought the Fire Master might help him, then he saw the murderous yellow orbs of his eyes.

Col grabbed the fire spirit, swinging him around until he slammed into Arlo's body. The force of the collision unbalanced them both, and Arlo clutched the spirit as the two of them toppled from the ledge, plummeting into the lake of fire.

A scream pierced the roar of the mountain as Col clawed his way to the back of the ledge.

* * *

Col came to, sitting with his back to the rock. His vision was still blurred, and his head ached. He spotted Arlo's cloak fluttering in the hot wind, but of the man, or the spirit, there was no sign. Col hauled himself upright and staggered towards the mountain path; away from the searing yellow heat.

* * *

Dusk was falling when he stumbled back into the village. Zoola spotted him first, struggling to hold him up as he staggered and fell. She fetched water, giving him small sips as Gren and Talla ran to his side.

"Col, my love," Talla said, stroking his blistered face, "Are you alone?"

"Arlo became the sacrifice," he croaked, reaching for more water.

"Thank the Spirits," Talla said, pulling him to her and kissing his cracked lips.

* * *

Batta took charge, informing Arlo's widow of his death, and arranging a funeral for the following day. Talla helped the exhausted Col undress and slipped into bed beside him.

"When did you know the sacrifice didn't have to be you?" she asked, tracing her finger along his jaw.

"I think I realised this morning. Without the necklace, I could think clearly. Then when you handed it back, it all seemed to make sense. I wanted to be the sacrifice. Then I gave the beads to Arlo, and the fire spirit lost his control over me."

"I would have followed you across the river, Col," Talla said. "If you hadn't returned, I would have taken foxglove."

"Then I'm glad I got back," Col said, smiling. The grin melted after a moment, and he looked into Talla's eyes. "If you had crossed the river and left me, I'd have followed," he whispered.

* * *

Gren and Batta conducted the funeral for Arlo the next day, speaking of his dedication to fire and his work with the mountain clan. Without a body, the ceremony was nothing but a memorial.

The four companions gathered around the hearth that evening, though an uneasy truce hung between Col and Gren. "We need to make a drum journey," Col said. The others nodded, they needed to face the Spirit of Fire one last time for him to acknowledge their success; Col's victory over the final element. Batta and Jowa sat in as they drummed themselves to the lower world for their confrontation.

* * *

The four friends found themselves close to the river, the dark waters splashing over submerged rocks, flecks of white foam floating to the banks. Col looked around, hoping for closure with the last spirit. He turned to Talla, her face pale in the grey light. Her robe was white, like the one she'd worn for their bonding ceremony. Her eyebrows and lashes sparkled over her violet eyes.

Zoola was dressed in a black cloak, her skin like polished jet, her head held high, a look of vague amusement on her face.

Gren stood in his blue ribboned cloak, his hair tied back, face dyed with woad. Col looked down at himself. His robe was red, his skin was painted with ochre. He looked at his companions and raised his eyebrows.

"Is he not here?" Zoola asked. "As we have conquered them, we have replaced them. I am earth, Talla is air, Gren is water, and now you are fire. Perhaps he has gone."

"I don't know," Col said.

The grating laugh echoed around them, and the four companions looked around for the fire spirit.

The disembodied face appeared in front of Col. "Do you think you have won, Fire Master?"

"We have met the challenges from each of the spirits of the elements," Col said. "We survived the earth, the winds, and the sea. And I have beaten you, Spirit. Your tame fire master is dead, your fire beads have been destroyed. You lost our battle."

"You think fire can kill me?" the spirit said. "I AM FIRE!"

"Fight me, then."

The spirit sneered. "You are a weak human. Why should I bother?"

"Come. Manifest a body and fight me again," Col said. "Perhaps I am stronger than you think."

The air below the floating head shimmered, but nothing appeared. Col smiled.

"You can't do it!"

"I am the spirit of fire. I do not concede our battle."

"Your power is gone," Col said. "Take form and fight me, or begone."

The glowing face seemed to flicker, fading away until nothing but a faint glow remained.

Batta stepped forward, Jowa at her shoulder. She raised her arms, summoning.

"Spirits of the elements," she called, "We honour you, and ask for your blessings on the tribes of men. We ask that earth be bountiful, air be gentle, and that water is quenching to our plants and our people. Spirit of Fire, we ask you to calm our mountain, and abide within our hearths. We ask that your sun shines on all we do."

Zoola bowed, then Talla, then Gren. Col looked at Batta, then glanced at Gren.

"Bow and smile, you're a spirit now," Gren whispered. Col smiled at Batta and bowed his head.

"Col, I owe you an apology," Gren said, turning away from the others. "I had no right to hit you."

"It's alright," Col said.

"No, I am as guilty as you. You never even defended yourself."

"Maybe I thought I deserved it," Col said.

"Can we be friends again?" Gren asked.

Col pulled his companion to him, embracing him. "Of course," he said.

Batta smiled at the two young men. "Let us return," she said.

* * *

Zoola opened her eyes and set down her drum. She looked over at Batta, who smiled.

"I wasn't sure if we were coming back," Zoola said.

"Yes, for now, I think," Batta replied, "You are half-spirit, half-human. You will live this life out before you are confined to their realm."

"What happens now?" Talla asked.

"We need to train another Fire Master, then you can make your way home," Batta said.

"I thought there could be only one?" Col said.

"That was Arlo's restriction, not the spirits," Batta replied.

"Four will go, two will return," Zoola reminded them.

Talla smiled. "Well, it looks like the prophecy was wrong."

"No, Gren and I will stay here for a while."

"But why?" Col asked.

"Because I'm pregnant," Zoola said, "And I'm not giving birth in a ship, or travelling across the length of the lands with a new child."

Talla grabbed her friend, hugging her tight as she congratulated her on her news. Col stood and pulled Gren into an embrace too. "It will be strange travelling without you two," he said. "Will you follow us when your child is old enough?"

"Nothing could stop us," Gren smiled, "we have a shared destiny."

* * *

The death of Arlo left a void at the mountain clan. He'd been the leader and spirit master for many years, and there was no successor. Batta took over in the meantime. Col needed to find someone to train as the next fire master, but there was no one at the mountain clan ready to learn the advanced fire teachings.

Col found Jowa, the spirit apprentice, eating breakfast the next morning.

"Jowa, how would you like to work towards becoming a spirit messenger?" he asked.

"I would love to, but there has been so little opportunity," she said.

"Would you travel to a new village?"

"I would, what do you have in mind?" she asked.

Col explained his idea of swapping Jowa with one of the spirit messengers from the harbour clan; someone he could train to be a Fire Master. Jowa squealed with delight and packed.

"Jowa and I will leave in the morning for the harbour," Col said. "I should be back in three days."

"I'll get my stuff packed then," said Talla.

"You're coming too?" Col asked.

She stepped up to him, wrapping her arms around his neck. "I'm not letting you out of my sight, Spirit Messenger Col," she said, pecking him on the lips.

They left at dawn, Zoola and Gren waving them off, then heading inside to make tea.

"Will you be happy staying here," Gren asked Zoola.

"Yes, I want our child to be born here. We can travel again when it's older; a summer or two."

"Do you want us to find Talla and Col then?" Gren asked.

"Yes, but I want to go back to my village first, and spend time with Yalta and Tooev at the circle of Stanna." Gren hugged his mate, their lips meeting in a soft kiss.

A cough from behind them heralded the arrival on Batta. She grinned at the young lovers. "When am I going to get to celebrate your bonding?" she asked.

Zoola looked at Gren. "Soon?" she asked.

"When Col and Talla get back," he said, kissing her again.

* * *

It was three days later when Col and Talla appeared on the mountain path, followed by two others. They dropped their packs in the roundhouse and introduced their new messenger.

"This is Jolo," Col said. "Garla, of the harbour clan, has two messengers, but the other is bonded with a child. Jolo wanted the challenge of coming here to be a fire master."

"Welcome, Jolo," Batta said, reciting her full status. Jolo smiled and gave his in return. Batta noticed the boy by the door.

"Horda?" she said, recognising the lad who'd guided the friends to the mountain clan when they first arrived. "You have returned."

The boy bowed and smiled. "Col said you had no apprentice here. I thought I would volunteer to go with Jolo. We are used to working together."

"Well, you are welcome too," the old woman said.

They sat and talked, eating together and swapping stories until Col noticed Talla falling asleep where she sat.

"Come on, bed," he said, taking his mate's hand.

* * *

Two days later, Batta stood before the assembled clan. She raised her hands, and the murmur of chatter stopped.

"We are gathered to witness the bonding of two people as mates," she said. "Zoola, Gren, step forward." The young couple stepped up to the old spirit master, holding hands. Batta looked from one to the other. "Gren, Spirit Messenger of the Guardians of the Stones of Stanna, Plant Master, Lore Master, Fire Keeper, Healer, do you take this woman to be your mate?"

Gren bowed his head. "I do."

"Zoola, Spirit Messenger of the River Clan of the Danna Tribe, Plant Master, Lore Master, Fire Keeper, Healer, do you take this man to be your mate?"

"Yes, I do," she said, smiling.

Batta lifted their wrists binding a cord around them, joining them together.

"Will you honour each other as companions, friends, and lovers through the years to come?" Batta asked.

"Yes," said Gren.

"I will," said Zoola.

"You are now bonded, each as mate to the other. The ancestors, this clan, and your companions have witnessed this," she said. She leant forward, kissing each one on the cheek. "I wish you both happiness."

The villagers wished them well, then danced and feasted into the night.

* * *

Jolo was progressing well with his fire master training, and Col left him to learn the incantations while he went outside for some fresh air. Zoola and Talla were sitting in the sunshine, talking. Zoola's hand stroked her rounded belly.

"It's moving!" she gasped, eyes wide as her hands hugged the tiny life inside her. She lifted her shirt and Talla pressed on the distended skin.

"I feel it too," she grinned. "Col, come and feel the baby."

Col smiled and stepped over to Zoola's side, running his hand over the bump. His fingers felt the tiny kicks through his friend's skin, and he smiled.

"He's a strong one," he laughed.

"He?" Zoola said. "How do you know?"

Col thought for a moment. "I don't know," he said, "When I touched you, I saw a beautiful little boy with skin and hair like his mother. Maybe it's the ancestors' way of letting us know."

Zoola stood and hugged him. "That's beautiful, Col, thank you."

* * *

The next full moon saw Col and his friends back at the top of the fire mountain, as Col gave Jolo his Fire Master's tattoo. The crater was still hot, smoke belching from cracks in the hardened, black lava. Its anger was spent, though, for now.

"Jolo, Spirit Messenger of the Harbour Clan of the Vessa Tribe, I align you with the spirit of fire. Serve the fire well!" Col took the flint blade from Horda, cutting the triangular shape around the fire keeper mark, making Jolo the second fire master. He chanted the incantation as he worked.

"Thank you for the opportunity, Col," Jolo said. "I will continue the teaching here when you leave."

Col smiled. "You'll stay here?" he asked.

"Yes. Batta has asked me to be the co-leader with her, and Juda has agreed to be my mate," he said. "I think I can make my life here on the mountain I serve."

Col patted the young man on the back, and they turned towards the village.

* * *

The days that followed were awkward. Col and Talla were leaving behind Zoola and Gren. After everything they'd been through together, it seemed wrong. The friends talked and made promises to find each other once Zoola was ready to travel with her child.

It was their last night, and Col and Talla stood facing Gren and Zoola. Friends wasn't a strong enough word for their relationship. They were closer, like siblings, or battle-hardened warriors. They knew each other's stories; each other's hopes and fears. Col hugged Gren as Talla wrapped herself around Zoola. They changed, Col now holding Zoola as Gren embraced Talla. The black girl leant in and pressed her lips to Col's. The kiss lasted longer than he'd expected, her arms pulling him close. Col glanced at Gren, hoping Zoola's display of affection did not upset him, but Gren was busy kissing Talla. Finally, they separated, Zoola's breathing fast and shallow. Col looked over at Talla and caught her winking at Zoola.

"Time for bed," Talla declared.

"Yes," said Zoola, leading Col to the nearest sleeping platform.

"Zoola... what..?" Col began.

"Talla. What are you doing?" Gren asked.

The two women grinned at each other, then turned to their men.

"This happened before. We talked about it, and we accepted it," Zoola said.

"So," Talla said, "Unless one of you objects, it's happening again."

"Our last night together for... I don't know how long," Col said to Gren.

"I'm alright with this if you are, Col," Gren said, glancing at the two women.

"Will you four make a damned decision and get to bed," shouted Batta from the back of the house, "Some of us are trying to sleep."

Chapter 24

Col felt an arm slip around his waist. He peered down to see Zoola's black fingers against his pale belly. He smiled, turning over to face her.

"Good morning," she said, her grin lighting up her face.

"Good morning," Col said. He wanted to pull Zoola close again but stopped himself.

As if reading his mind, Talla giggled and called from the next bed, "No guilt, Col, remember?" Col turned to find Talla grinning at him, her head on Gren's chest, his arm around her. Col knew he should be jealous, but he wasn't. He loved these friends, the closest, most important people in his life.

Zoola's hand snaked up and grabbed the hair at the nape of his neck, pulling him to her for a kiss. Col surrendered.

* * *

All awkwardness had gone by the time they rolled out of bed and dressed.

"That was nice," Zoola said, "A nice goodbye."

"You know, our pairs make sense when you think about it," Talla said.

"What do you mean?" Col asked.

"Well, you and I, Fire and Air. Wind makes the fire burn brighter, but the sun calms the strongest winds. Same with Gren and Zoola, Earth and Water nourish everything that grows."

"So what about last night?" Gren said, smiling.

"Water and Wind," Talla said, "Like a storm at sea."

"And Earth and Fire," Zoola said, "Like the fire mountain."

Col sat between the two women, his arms going around their shoulders. "You are both crazy," he said. He kissed each one on the cheek, "But I love you both."

Gren pulled Col to his feet, hugging him. "I love you too, Col, don't forget it."

"The feeling's mutual," Col said, "But I'm not sleeping with you."

"Ugh, no. Fire and Water? Never works."

* * *

They had packed their belongings, and they had said it all. Col and Talla hugged their friends one more time and hoisted their packs to their shoulders. With a last goodbye, they turned and headed down the track towards the sea.

"I'll miss them," Talla said.

"We'll see them again," Col replied.

"It'll be years from now, though."

Col took her hand. "I know."

* * *

They camped the first night, needing no shelter, and reached the village of the Harbour Clan by the following afternoon.

"Talla! Col!" came the girl's voice. Jowa ran to greet them, her good arm giving each a hug. "I love it here," she gushed, her cheeks glowing, "There're so many things to do, and I'm learning so much."

"Well, we're pleased to see you too, Spirit Apprentice," Col said, grinning.

"Sorry," Jowa said, holding out her arm. "Greetings, Spirit Messengers."

Col hugged her. "I'm only kidding, silly. It's good to see you happy." Talla wrapped an arm around the young girl as they walked to the spirit master's house.

"Spirit Master Garla, we have guests," Jowa called as they entered.

"Col, Talla, welcome," she said, holding out her hands in greeting. "You'll stay with us a while?"

"Until we can get a crossing by boat, yes," Col said.

"Jolo has made Fire Master, then?" Garla asked.

"Yes, and found a girl he wants to bond with," said Talla.

Garla grinned. "I've lost him then? Well, I'd better get this one trained to messenger status," she said, pulling Jowa to her side.

"If you think I can, Master Garla," Jowa said.

"Can? You will." She turned to Col and Talla, "Do you know this one treated a deep wound two days ago. Sewed the flesh with no need to call me? Know how she did it?" Talla glanced at Jowa's atrophied arm and shook her head. "Used her teeth," Garla grinned. "She's got mettle, this one." Jowa blushed and made tea as they fell into conversation.

* * *

Three days later, they spotted Reddo in the village. He smiled when he recognised them.

"Looking to sail back, Messengers?" he asked.

"If you've room, Reddo," Col said.

"Not much, but we'll squeeze you in," he said. "We sail the day after tomorrow, come at dawn."

* * *

Jowa accompanied Col and Talla to the dock two days later as they boarded Reddo's boat.

"Thank you for bringing me here," Jowa said as she hugged them goodbye. "I'll never see you again, will I?"

"Look for us in your ceremonies," Talla smiled.

"What do you mean?" the girl asked, puzzled.

"Wait. You'll see," Col chuckled as they pressed themselves into the tiny gaps between trade goods on the laden boat. They waved, as a fair wind carried them out of the bay and on towards the south island.

* * *

They spotted Boat Master Tollo as the little ship moored at the dock.

"Spirit Messengers," he called. His eyes scanned the boat. "Where are Gren and Zoola?"

"Safe," Col reassured him. "Zoola will have their first child soon, she didn't want to give birth while travelling."

"Thank the spirits," he said. He gestured to the distant coast. "You tamed the fire mountain then?"

"I met the fire spirit's challenge, and won," Col said. "Now we can go home."

"Well, I leave in two days, if the wind holds fair," he said, "Will you come?"

"We'd like that," Talla said.

"Messengers!" thundered a voice. Col turned to see the bulk of Spirit Master Indalo, waddling along the path towards them. "Where are Gren and Zoola?"

"Zoola's having a baby," Tollo explained.

"So, just two of you?" Indalo asked. Col nodded. "Well, come and tell me all your tales," he said.

* * *

They recounted their adventures around the hearth that night, Tollo joining them and bringing a skin of beer.

"Travelling has been hard for you," Indalo said, "But you have learned much. It would help all apprentices and messengers to travel. Information gets lost or forgotten when we isolate ourselves."

"We would welcome that too," Talla said. "Our own island, far to the north, preserves traditions forgotten elsewhere, yet they have lost the status of Fire Keeper."

Indalo glanced at Col's tattoo and gasped. "Col. You have the fire master's tattoo. Why did I not see it?" Col grinned and told the story of the battle with the fire spirit, and of the amber necklace that twisted the wearer's thoughts.

"So you are the one fire master now?" Indalo asked.

"No, another of Arlo's lies, to preserve his own power," Col explained. "I trained a new master who remains at the fire mountain. He will train others."

Indalo rubbed his finger along his lips for a moment. "Erra, come sit with us, will you?" The slim, black-haired girl walked to the fire, eyes fixed on the floor. She sat next to Indalo, not meeting anyone's gaze. "This girl will, one day, be an excellent messenger. Eh, Erra?" he said.

"Yes, Master," she whispered.

"Yes, if I can ever get her to look at people and talk to them."

Talla slipped over beside the girl, taking her hand. "Do you enjoy working with the spirits and the ancestors?" she asked.

Erra's eyes flicked up, taking in Talla's tattoo, then dipping back to her feet. "Yes, Spirit Messenger."

"My name is Talla," she said.

"Yes, Spirit Messenger Talla."

"Do you enjoy healing work? Plants? Remedies?" Talla asked.

Erra looked up for the first time, a shy smile gracing her lips. "Oh yes, Messenger Talla. I love it."

"Have you thought of letting Erra travel?" Talla said to Indalo.

"Yes, but she's so shy. How would she cope?" Indalo said.

"Would you like to travel with us, Erra? Col and I are both Plant Masters and Healers; you could learn a great deal."

Erra looked up at Indalo, eyes wide. "May I, Master Indalo?" she asked.

"If you wish, you are free to go, Erra. Perhaps you'll return as a messenger." Despite her tanned skin, the girl blushed.

"If it would please you, Master Indalo, I will," she said.

Talla glanced at Col. "Shall we take her? Meeting more people will help her shyness too, no doubt." The matter settled, they retired for the night, Talla cuddling up to Col in their warm bed.

* * *

Two days later they boarded Tollo's boat for the trip across the inland sea. The ship was piled with beautiful pottery, grain and salt meat; Col, Talla and Erra wedged in the middle. The fresh breeze blew the laden vessel across the blue waters, spray splashing from the bow. Talla stood, feet braced, hand on the ropes. She grinned back at Tollo.

"We're set fair, Messenger Talla," he smiled, "This wind is perfect." Talla nodded and turned forward, closing her eyes. Her mind sought the wind, feeling its force hitting the small sail. She sensed movement beside her.

"Messenger Col said I could come to stand with you," Erra said, grabbing for a rope. Talla grasped her waist, showing her how to spread her feet to balance better as the boat rolled. "Are you the air spirit?" Erra asked.

Talla thought for a moment. "Half spirit, maybe," she said. "I am human, like you, but beating the spirits of the elements has given each of us responsibilities. Neither of us is sure what those are yet." Talla took Erra's hand. "Close your eyes," she said. "Now listen to the wind. Hear only the wind. Feel the gusts in your mind. Now travel with them."

"I can feel it!" the girl cried, "I am the wind!" Her hand let go of the rope, stretching out like a bird's wing as she balanced on the balls of her feet beside Talla. She opened her eyes and blinked. "It's gone," she said, her face dropping.

"Yes," Talla said, "But now you know how to do it."

* * *

They slept, crammed together in their small space that night, Col in the middle with Talla and Erra on either side. Erra looked at Col as Talla snuggled to his chest. Col smiled at the shy girl and lifted his other arm. "Come on, Erra, sleep."

"But you are half spirit, Messenger," she said.

"I promise to keep the spirit half on Talla's side," he replied. Talla giggled. Erra gave a soft smile and laid her head on Col's chest. He put his arm around her, and she breathed a sigh, glad he felt no different to any other man.

* * *

"We are making a quick journey, Talla," said Tollo, as their destination came into view on the horizon.

"The winds favour us," she said.

"Perhaps they know better than to disrupt your journey, Messenger," the old sailor said, as a grin split his weathered face.

As the day wore on, they could see a bank of cloud at the far shore, blacker now as they drew close. "It looks like smoke," Col said.

"Perhaps they're celebrating the summer solstice," Talla replied.

"That's not yet though," Col said, frowning.

It was past noon when they got close enough to see details of the little trading village. "There are houses on fire," Tollo shouted. "More than one. I can see three... no four."

"Get the ship tied up and follow us," said Col, as the boat approached the village.

One of the crew sprang ashore, tying off the rope as Col and Talla jumped onto the dock, Col turned to catch Erra as she too, jumped. They ran towards the houses, the acrid wood smoke burning their throats.

"To Gordo's house," Col shouted. People were milling about, many with wounds. They rushed into the big roundhouse. "Gordo. What has happened?" Col said as they entered.

"Over here," said a voice from the back of the house. Talla and Erra made their way back as Col took in the wrecked interior of the house.

"Chirra, what happened," Talla asked.

"Outlaws. They attacked us. They took everything they could carry and destroyed what they left," she said.

Talla looked at the bed where Chirra was sitting. There, lying stretched, with a bloody cloth across his head, was Gordo, the spirit master. Talla dropped to her knees, inspecting the wound. There was a split in the skin under his hair. It was bleeding, but a quick examination showed no damage to his skull.

"We need to help," Talla said, "People are hurt. Do you have healing skills yet, Chirra?"

The young woman shook her head. "I am not long apprenticed, there's been no time," she said.

"Right!" Talla shouted. "Col, get someone to keep this fire going. Chirra, Gordo is in little danger, I want you to heat water and get bandages." The girl nodded.

Tollo came in with his two crew at that point.

"Tollo, work with Erra. She is a healer but may need help to lift people or to fetch supplies. You others, get outside and find the wounded. Bring them here so Erra and I can help them. Col will go to those that we can't move."

The little group went into action, Erra setting up outside the door, instructing Tollo to bring the most seriously injured to her first. Talla set up in the house, preparing sinew and awls for sewing wounds. Col ran across the yard outside the roundhouse, one of the crew calling him.

"Messenger Col. Here."

Col ran over, finding a man with a spear gash in his forearm. Blood was pumping from the wound. Col wrapped a cord around the arm, slowing the blood loss, then sewed the wound shut. The stitches were coarse and quick but held the skin together. He bound it up, tying the strip of linen off, then checking for other wounds.

"Go to the spirit master's house," he said. "Get a healer to check this later."

"Thank you, Messenger," the man said, heading for the big roundhouse.

"Messenger Col, help me," called the second crewman. Col ran to him and saw the woman he was holding. She lay in his arms, in a pool of blood; her belly split open, entrails spilling out. Col swallowed and reached into his pouch for a flint blade. He spoke a prayer to the ancestors, then pressed the knife into the sobbing woman's wrist, cutting between the arm bones. Blood spurted up, and Col turned the wound so that the life ran from the agonised woman onto the earth. He waited until her eyes fluttered closed, then placed a hand on her head and one over her heart.

"Ancestor Spirits, take this sister back to you," he whispered. "Her time here is over, she wishes to be with those that love her again."

Col looked up, finding a man standing over them. "She is your family?" he asked.

"My mate," said the man.

"I'm sorry, she has gone to be with her ancestors, I can do no more," Col said.

* * *

Talla was treating burns on a child when she heard shouting from outside the house. "Bandages, Tollo," called Erra.

"There are none left," the sailor said.

"Get more."

"Where from?" he asked.

"I don't care, ask Chirra but get me something. Do it now!"

Talla smiled. She wondered where the shy young woman had gone.

"Bandages?" he asked, running into the house.

"There's clothing on the bed there," Chirra said, heating more water, "Tear it into strips. Then come back for more hot water."

"Yes, Spirit Apprentice," he called, running out with the clothing.

They worked on treating burns, sewing wounds, bandaging and dressing. As darkness fell, able-bodied villagers appeared, holding torches so the healers could continue to work. At last, the stream of injured slowed and stopped. Col returned to the house, his face dirt-streaked, his hands bloody. Talla patted a young man on the back and sent him home, and Erra stood and stretched her back after stitching her last wound.

"Water, please," said Col, to anyone listening, as he slumped to sit on the ground. Once the villagers realised the healers had done what they could, they brought food and water. A tall white-haired man walked over, one Talla recognised she'd treated earlier.

"Spirit Messengers, Spirit Apprentices, thank you," he said. He held out his hands in formal greeting. "I am Yarro, leader of the Boat Clan of the Locan Tribe. We offer our thanks for your work here. The attack was unexpected and brutal."

"How many dead?" Col asked.

"Perhaps twenty," Yarro said. Col knew that he'd helped two to travel to the ancestors, their wounds untreatable. A glance to the side revealed another covered body he suspected Erra had helped to meet those that loved him.

Col stood, raising his arms for silence. "Once we have eaten, those of you with sewn wounds, come to us again so we can check you," he said.

Chirra smiled at the lad who'd been keeping the fire, curled up and sleeping on the floor. She lifted him onto a bed, covering him with furs. She stepped out of the house; her face streaked with soot from the fire, her shirt soaked in sweat. Col put an arm around her.

"Thank you, Chirra, you kept us supplied with all we needed," he said. "How is Gordo?"

"He's conscious and sitting up. Talla sewed his wound once we'd treated the worst injuries. He's asking for you."

"Col. Welcome, and thank you," the spirit master said as Col walked over to his bed.

"How are you, Master Gordo?" Col asked, bowing.

"Dispense with the titles, Col," he said, smiling. "I'm dizzy. My head took a nasty knock."

"Chirra said these were outlaws," Col said.

"Yes, a band of them lived in the hills a few years back. The local tribes hunted them down, we thought the last of them had gone."

"It seems not," said Col.

Two men came in the door, dragging a struggling body between them.

"What's going on?" Col asked. He recognised the captive, a man with a leg wound he'd treated earlier. "You should not move this man," he said, "The wound could open."

"He's not a villager," said one of his captors, "He's an outlaw."

The village leader, Yarro, rushed to the man. He grabbed the outlaw by the hair, yanking his head up, glaring into his eyes. "Where is the outlaw camp?" he shouted.

"I'll tell you nothing," the man said.

Yarro's fist plunged into the captive's belly, expelling the air from his lungs.

"Where is the camp?" The man spat in Yarro's face. Yarro held out a hand. "Blade," he commanded. One captor handed him a glinting flint flake. He clutched it and rested it on the outlaw's skin, just under the brow ridge.

"I'll take one eye, to begin," Yarro hissed through his teeth. "If you don't tell me then, I'll take the other."

"No!" the man screamed, pulling away. Yarro pressed it into the soft flesh, and blood spilt over the man's cheek.

"In the hills. Follow the stream from the village. At the falls, turn right and walk over the ridge," he said.

Yarro pressed the blade harder. "How many?"

"Aargh! Twenty, maybe a few women and children."

Yarro lifted the blade, held it to the man's throat and slit it wide open. Blood spurted from the gash, soaking Yarro's tunic, though he never flinched. The captive gurgled as blood filled his airways, thrashing in his captors' arms.

"Take him to the edge of the village, leave his body for the wild animals. There will be no funeral rites," he ordered, as terror filled the man's eyes.

"No funeral rites?" Erra whispered to Col. "But that means..."

"He will never cross the river to the ancestors," Col said, "His spirit will roam the lands here forever. Trapped."

Erra's hand clasped her throat, and she swallowed. "And Yarro told him before he died," she said as the outlaw's body sagged, and they dragged it from the house.

"Yes, perhaps that's worse than death itself," Col said.

"Messenger, I'm sorry for the mess," Yarro said, walking towards Col. "That had to be done, and I would ask no one else to do it."

"It was unfortunate, but there was no honour in their attack, they deserved no mercy. You should apologise to the spirit master, though, it's his house," Col said, stepping back.

"Gordo!" Yarro said. "I thought you were dead."

"No," Gordo laughed, "Just a bump to the head and some sewing. Now Yarro, look at Col's status tattoos."

The leader turned back to the young messenger, then his hand went to his mouth, and he bowed his head. "Fire Master. You honour us. I apologise for not noticing earlier," the old man said.

"There are but two of us, Yarro, and you are a leader, do not bow."

Yarro looked up. "Thank you, Master Col."

Col laughed. "Just Col, please. Now can we eat?"

Yarro smiled and joined the protected-of-spirit as they ate. The two men who'd brought the captive returned, cleaning up the blood from the floor and strewing fresh straw over it. Yarro nodded his thanks as they left.

"We will hunt them down," Yarro said. "Tomorrow I'll send word to the surrounding villages. We'll kill them for this attack."

"If we can be of help, Yarro," Col said, "Let us know."

Chapter 25

The band of warriors crept over the dry ground. Yarro held up his hand.

"Col, Talla, follow me," he said beckoning. They stooped, making for the skyline, smelling wood smoke before they reached the top. They crawled to the ridge, peering into the gully. There was a cave in the cliff wall and two ramshackle shelters beside it. A dozen people were visible.

"How can we trap them?" Yarro asked.

"The gully is blind to the north, and there's the cliff to the east," Col said. "If we could block their escape to the south, they'd have to come this way."

"Fire," said Talla. "The grass is dry. If you set a fire at the base of the gully, the wind will blow it towards the camp."

Yarro shook his head, "The wind direction is wrong for that."

"Set the fire," Talla said, "Let me handle the wind."

Col ran back to the group of warriors. He pulled out his fire bow and kindling.

"Fetch dry wood, and someone make me a torch," he said, sitting with the fire starting kit between his legs. Col wrapped the cord around the pointed stick, placed the tip in a hole in the board and sawed at the bow. Smoke drifted up from the tiny coal formed by the friction. He piled dry moss onto it, fanning it to a small flame. A man ran up with dry sticks, and Col soon had a tiny fire blazing. He fed in the dry branch they had brought him, waiting for the flame to catch, then looked up towards the ridge.

Talla stood, arms outstretched, her back to the breeze. As she turned, Col saw the concentration on her face. The wind shifted to the south, the gusts becoming stronger as Talla raised her arms and flung them forward.

The torch flamed now, and Col ran around the knoll to the south. Out of sight of the outlaw camp, he walked across the gully, dragging the torch through the dry vegetation. He reached the far side, looking back as the blaze leapt northwards towards the cave. He dropped the torch and ran back.

"Stay this side of the ridge and spread out," Yarro ordered. "As they come over, pick them off."

"Yarro, there may be women and children," Talla said.

"They showed no mercy when they attacked our village," Yarro replied.

"The women wouldn't have joined this band by choice, Yarro, and the children are innocents," she said, holding his gaze. Yarro broke the eye contact first.

"Take the women and children and tie them up," he shouted. "Do not harm them."

Talla nodded to him in thanks, though Yarro scowled.

Soon they could hear shouting from the gully. Women screamed, and men yelled, then two men appeared over the hilltop. Their eyes widened in fear as spears tore into them. Three more men followed, meeting a hail of arrows and dropping beside their confederates.

The next wave of people fleeing was bigger, and the village warriors ran to engage them one-on-one, thrusting with spears at the smoke blinded men. A woman carrying a small child, and dragging another by the hand, came running towards the armed men. Talla shouted, "Bring them here." Two men pulled the woman and the screaming children to her, and she bound the woman hand and foot. They brought another two women and a child to her. Then everything went quiet. Talla looked up to see twenty or more bodies strewn about. Yarro walked amongst them, slitting the throats of any still breathing.

"Check the camp," he shouted. He glanced at Talla. "Spare the women and children."

Half of the men ran over the ridge, through the smouldering grasses towards the cave. They returned with a woman; her hands bound. One man carried a tiny baby.

"Take them to Talla," Yarro said, "Were there more?"

"An old man with an outlaw mark. He is dead," came the reply.

"Strip the corpses," Yarro said, "Take everything of value from the camp, then destroy it. Leave the bodies, there will be no funeral rites." He glanced towards Col, receiving a nod of acquiescence. It was a fitting punishment that their spirits never find rest.

When the work of salvaging any food and goods was complete, they set off back towards the village. Talla carried the baby while Col took the smallest child. The other two walked until the younger one, a girl of perhaps six summers, stumbled and fell. It surprised Col and Talla when Yarro scooped the child up and set her on his shoulder, keeping pace beside them.

"Thank you, Talla," he said. "I was angry and would not have acted as you suggested. You were right, these children bear no blame, nor the women either. None of them wears an outlaw tattoo."

Talla smiled. "I will ask Gordo to question each woman when we return," she said, "He is an excellent judge of character."

"A good solution," Yarro said.

* * *

The village soon returned to normal. They held funerals; Col and Talla officiating at the ceremonies, while Gordo recovered his strength. The day of the raid on the outlaw camp had been the summer solstice, but no one had felt like celebrating.

A few days later, Gordo, Col and Talla journeyed to speak to the ancestors on the tribe's behalf. They foretold a time of peace and abundance for the Locan Tribe.

Gordo was back on his feet, and busy with the aftercare of the injured as Col, Talla and Erra packed their belongings once more.

"Thank you, all of you," Gordo said. "Without your help, more would have died."

Chirra came to his side, her arm slipping around his waist. "I have learned a lot from you three," she said. "I am determined to become a good healer."

They said their farewells, Gordo pressing a small pouch into Col's hand as they left. Outside, they met Yarro, the village leader, and ship-master Tollo.

"Thank you, Messengers, Apprentice," Yarro said, bowing. He handed each a linen bag. "Salt," he said, "It may be of use for trade on your journey."

Tollo stepped forward. "This village is important to my trade route," he said, "You three have helped to save it." He gave each of them an exquisite inlaid pottery beaker. "A gift, to keep or trade," he smiled. "I don't suppose I'll ever see you again, travel well."

"We hope our friends, Gren and Zoola, will follow us one day," Talla said. She pointed to Erra, "and this one may return with news of us when she goes home."

They had interacted with every family at the Locan port, and many people came out to wish them well, as they walked through the village and up the track towards the hills.

* * *

They travelled from village to village, heading north, often receiving the hospitality of the clan messenger or master. The older protected-of-spirit recognised Col's fire master tattoo, resulting in a recounting of the story of their travels. Erra became more talkative as they walked, and she told the legends of her tribe and people.

As they entered a village one evening, Col spotted a small boy, smiling as he ran toward them.

"Quin!" Col shouted.

The boy stopped, bowing to Col, then ran his finger under his right eye. He turned to Talla, then Erra, repeating his action on his left eye.

"What's he doing?" Erra asked.

"Greeting you as protected-of-spirit. He cannot talk, so he shows his recognition of your status tattoo with his finger." Col looked at the boy again, spotting a new zigzag tattoo above his right eye. Col held out his hands in welcome.

"Greetings, Plant Apprentice Quin," he smiled, running his own finger above his right eye. The boy's face split into a wide grin at the recognition.

"Col!" came a voice from a doorway, "I see Quin has greeted you."

Col and Talla stepped forward, hugging Regga, the spirit master who had healed Col. Erra made her formal introduction, which Regga returned in the traditional fashion.

"Come in," Regga smiled, "Stay awhile. Where are your companions?"

Col and Talla found seats at Regga's hearth, Erra joining them, as they recounted their stories. Talla got Erra to repeat their adventures at the fire mountain. Apprentices had to remember every legend and tale from their tribe's history, and this was good practice for the girl.

Regga fed them well and gave the latest news from the reformed Bragga tribe, now a satellite village of her own tribe. As they settled in their beds that night, Erra called over to Col and Talla.

"Thank you, both. This journey is an amazing opportunity for me to learn. I am grateful."

"It is an honour to have you with us, Erra," Talla said, snuggling up to her mate. "What's this?" she said, finding a pottery disc hanging on a cord around Col's neck.

"It was a gift from Gordo," he said. "It has a ship on one side, and a man's head on the other."

"What does it do?" she said.

Col shrugged. "Maybe, we'll find out."

* * *

They left Regga's village, and the Alv tribe, two days later, and aimed for the coast to their west. Regga had said traders of the Karna tribe worked that coast; perhaps they'd be able to take a ship from there. They settled into their travelling routine, telling stories, singing songs and teaching Erra any healing plants they found on their travels.

A little after noon on the fourth day, they saw the sea and, soon after, the village of the Harbour Clan of the Karna. The travellers made their way down towards the sea, a cluster of good-sized boats tied up at a dock. They found it was like the village of the Locan tribe; there were many strangers, and no one looked twice at them. They found their way to the dock and looked for boat masters.

"I'm a boat master, what do you seek?" Col turned to find the creased face of an old man, his features tanned by sun and salt.

"Passage to the Great Island to the north," Col said.

"The lands of the Danna and the Yofa?" the old man asked.

"You know of it?"

"I trade there. Who wishes to travel?"

"The three of us," Col said.

The wrinkled mariner sucked in a breath through gapped teeth. "Can you pay?"

Col bent to open his pack, lifting out a linen bag. "Salt," he said, "You'll take it in trade?"

The sailor took the bag, hefting it in his hand. "Scarcely enough to take one of you," he said.

"Then it's as well we have one each," Col said.

The old man smiled. "What else do you have?" His gaze alighted on the ceramic disc hung from Col's neck. "Where did you get that?" he gasped, lifting it to inspect it.

"A gift from a friend. Do you like it?"

There was reverence in his voice, now. "It's a charm, a talisman from Manno, the spirit of the sea." His fingers dropped the disc. "They come from the coast of the inland sea. A spirit master there has power over Manno. He makes these discs with a binding spell, to protect the wearer."

"It is genuine, then, for that is where I got it. Our friend Gordo..."

"That's the name!" the sailor gasped. "This... I'll take you to the Danna in exchange for this," he said, never taking his eyes off the pendant.

"When we land on the Great Island, it's yours," Col said.

"Ah, well, I'd need to have it first..."

"The moment we land," said Col.

"A deal," the old man said, holding out his hands.

Col grasped them. "A deal," he said, grinning, "But we keep the salt."

"Ah, now, I'll need that too..."

"Look," said Talla, "A boat loading almost the same trade goods, let's see where they're sailing."

"A deal," muttered the old sailor, extending his hands again. "Name's Jonev, be here at dawn."

* * *

The three friends found the spirit master's house, where they were made comfortable, but little more. The food was excellent, as was the bed. Next morning, with the three travellers crammed in amongst trade goods, Jonev's ship set sail. They made good headway the first day. They lowered the sails at night to allow them to sleep, then they were away at dawn again. Their destination was just in view when the wind dropped, and they heard Jonev cursing from the back of the boat.

"Half a day and we'd be there. Why do you stop now?" he shouted at the sky.

"Does the wind desert you, Jonev?" Col called, climbing back towards the boat master.

"Damn it! Just half a day," he said.

"Well, I have the talisman of Manno. Shall I use it?" Col asked.

"Will it work?"

"Let's see," Col said, winking at Talla. He closed his eyes, holding the disc in his right hand. Behind him, Talla clutched Erra's hand and closed her own eyes.

They waited a few moments. "It's not working," the old man said.

"Wait," Col said. Just a few heartbeats later, a soft breeze breathed into the sail from the south-west. It strengthened as Col continued to squeeze the disc in his hand. He smiled and turned towards the sailor.

"Enough, Boat Master?" he asked.

"Y... yes. How? That's..." he said, his eyes wide.

"Let's try to make port by dusk," Col said, as he stepped back to his seat. "Thank you," he whispered to Talla. She grinned.

* * *

As deep pink streaked the western sky, the ship pulled in to the Danna port. Jonev's crew tied the boat at the dock, and Col reached back to unfasten the talisman.

"This is yours now, Jonev," he smiled, dropping it into the old man's palm. "May the spirit of the sea serve you well."

Jonev bowed his head, the first sign of deference he'd shown to the protected-of-spirit since they'd met. "Thank you, Messenger. Thank you, all of you. I shall treasure this," he said, ushering them ashore.

Col handed him a bag of salt. "A little extra for your trouble, Jonev. Thank you."

The Bay Clan of the Danna Tribe welcomed them into the messenger's house for the night, but early next morning they were on their way once again, heading for Zoola's home village.

Chapter 26

Talla spotted Kaden first, calling to him as they approached the messenger's house.

"Talla, Col!" he gasped, dropping the cord he was weaving. He glanced behind them, his face darkening. "Where is Zoola... Gren...?"

"Safe, Kaden," said Talla, hugging their friend. Col embraced him too, then stood back so Erra could give her status. Kaden bowed, then recited his own accomplishments.

"Your accent is strange, are you from across the water?" Kaden asked Erra. The confused girl looked to Talla to explain.

"Erra is from far to the south," Talla said. "Across the land beyond, then over another sea. She is travelling to improve her skills. Her language is not so different, she will understand what you say soon."

"Well, come inside," Kaden said. "Var, where are you?" he called.

"Here messenger," the young apprentice shouted, staggering towards the house laden with firewood. He dropped it beside the door, running over to the guests.

"Messenger Col, Messenger Talla!" he said, nodding to them. He turned to Erra, who bowed, then gave her status. Var replied with his own, then offered Erra his hand.

"Come, help me with the tea," he grinned. "These three will talk all day." Erra smiled and looked uncertain. "Tea," Var said, mimicking drinking. "They'll talk all day." He pointed east, then drew his finger across the sky to the west. Erra smiled and followed him into the house.

Once they were seated and had drinks, Col and Talla recounted their journey.

"So Zoola and Gren are bonded?" Kaden asked.

"Yes, and Zoola is expecting their baby," Talla said. "Once the child is bigger, they plan to come home, you'll see them in a year or two."

"I look forward to it," Kaden said.

Erra sat listening. The cadence and tone of her mentors' speech were familiar, and she soon picked up the words and pronunciations she had misunderstood. She joined in their conversation, telling her own story, then the tale of the outlaw attack at the Locan port.

"You will have learned much, Erra," Var said when she'd finished.

"I've learned more in the last two moons than in the previous year," she said.

"Will you teach at the great circle at Stanna again this winter?" Kaden asked Col.

"We haven't thought," Col said, looking to Talla. "We will visit, though. Were you at the summer solstice there?"

"Yes, I took Var. This winter, he will learn towards his messenger status."

"Will you pass, Var?" Talla said, turning to the boy.

He grinned and shook his head. "No, but next summer, I may."

"Think about it," Kaden said, "You are both excellent teachers."

"You are a good teacher too, Kaden," Talla said, "Perhaps you should volunteer."

Var grinned to see his teacher squirm at Talla's praise.

"Perhaps," Kaden admitted.

They talked until Var served a meal, then again well into the night, until Var showed them to the guest beds.

* * *

They spent the next day around the village. The River Clan thought well of Kaden, as he was an accomplished healer.

In the morning they set off for the great circle of Stanna, camping the first night and making good time. They pushed on to arrive at the guardian's village at dusk. They made their way to the biggest house, seeing the firelight glinting through gaps in the door and at the eaves. Col knocked on the door frame and waited. He heard muffled voices from within, then the door swung open.

"Col!" screamed the small girl, running at him and leaping into his arms.

"Well, hello, Spirit Apprentice Arva," Col chuckled, hugging the child. Another small shape flew past them, landing in Talla's embrace.

Talla grinned, "Hello, Atta."

"Change," shouted Arva, wriggling out of Col's grasp and replacing her sister in Talla's arms. Erra stood back, amused by the giggling, squealing twins.

"Let us in," Col said, "We have introductions to make."

"Mother, Father, it's Col and Talla," Arva said, leading them into the house.

"I gathered that," Yalta said, rising from her seat by the fire and walking to welcome her two friends.

"Where are Gren and Zoola?" said Atta, looking behind them.

"Don't panic," Talla reassured them, "They are safe, but they are not with us."

Tooev stepped forward to greet the new arrivals, his gaze settling on Erra. She lifted her head and stood tall, extending her arms in the universal greeting.

"I am Erra," she said, changing her accent to the language of her hosts. "I am a Spirit Apprentice of the Benno Tribe. Plant Master, Lore Keeper, and Fire Apprentice. I am training to be a healer."

Yalta and Tooev bowed, each giving their own status, followed by the twins. Yalta beckoned a lad forward. "This is Faran," she said, "Our new apprentice." The boy bowed, listing his accomplishments. Despite having perhaps twelve summers, he was not long apprenticed. Yalta glanced at Col's face, noticing his tattoos for the first time. "Faran, can you tell me what this tattoo means?" she said, pointing to Col's right eye.

"Umm, it's fire, but I've never seen it before," he said blushing.

"No," Yalta said, "I've never seen it either, but I know it." She rounded on Col. "When were you going to mention that to us?"

Col grinned. "When you noticed." He turned to Faran. "This is the Fire Master's tattoo," he said, running his finger alongside his eye.

The boy's eyes went wide as Yalta turned to him. "Tell Shola, three more for supper," she said. "So, where are Gren and Zoola?"

"Bonded," said Col, "And expecting their first child. Zoola didn't want to give birth while travelling. She may have had the baby by now."

"I'm so glad for them," Yalta said, "Will they come home?"

"Yes, when the baby's grown," Talla said.

They talked long into the night, Arva crawling into Col's lap, and Atta into Talla's as they grew tired. "So, you two are, what, eight summers?" Col asked.

"Nine," said Arva.

"They are small for their age," Yalta said, looking at the girls with pride.

"Mmm-hmm. Half the size, twice the trouble," Tooev added.

"Father!" Atta squealed.

Faran made beds for them as the fire died. They said their good-nights, and soon Talla snuggled up to Col under the warm furs.

"Do you want to stay?" she asked.

"They haven't asked us," Col replied.

"If we leave soon, we may make it to our island before winter sets in," Talla said, "But if the snow comes early, we may be stuck."

"You want to stay, don't you?"

Talla nodded into his chest. "Yes," she said.

* * *

The twins, crawling into their bed, wakened Col and Talla. Arva snuggled up to Col.

"I missed you," she giggled.

"Missed you too," Col mumbled, smiling.

"Mint and Rosehip?" she asked.

"Hmm? Oh, tea, yes, thank you."

"Come on, lazy-bones," Arva called to her sister, "We have to make tea."

"And porridge," said Atta, clambering over the two messengers.

"I'd forgotten how active those two are," Talla said.

"Still want to stay?" Col asked.

"Yes."

* * *

Yalta and Tooev joined them for breakfast, sitting around the fire.

"Yalta, do you have room for us to stay over winter here? Our time is short for reaching home before the storms come," Col said.

"Well..." she said, a pensive look on her face, "That means you'd be here at the solstice."

"Yes."

"Well... I suppose we could use your skills if you must stay." Talla suppressed a giggle as she noticed Yalta trying to keep from smiling. Yalta burst into laughter, Tooev and the twins joining her. "Of course you can stay, you idiots. I intend to work you to the bone again, then make you spirit masters before you leave."

Erra sat beside Yalta. "Spirit Master," she said, bowing, "Will you train me as a messenger?"

Yalta turned to the girl. "Erra. Before you leave here, I want you to be a messenger, a Lore Master, a Fire Keeper and a full healer." Erra protested, but Yalta held up her hand. "You can do this. I have listened to the stories of your journey, but there will be a cost."

Erra looked up at Yalta, her eyes wide. "Whatever you demand, Master Yalta."

"First, we will push you hard for the next moon. You will get your healer's tattoo before the apprentices arrive. You will teach healing to them this winter." Erra opened her mouth, only for Yalta to silence her again. "Second, I want you working with the messengers during the apprentice teaching, not as a student, but as an assistant. Talla will explain how we taught them as messengers, I will push you as hard as I did them. Third, I am Yalta, my mate is Tooev, and I'm sure you use Col and Talla's names. No titles in private."

"Yes, Spirit... Yes, Yalta," Erra said, breaking into a smile.

Yalta put an arm around her. "Is your own master so strict with you?"

"No, Yalta, he is the size of a mountain, but soft as a puppy. He works me hard, but is always fair."

"Well, you'll find you fit in here just fine then," Yalta said.

"Will there be other teachers for the apprentices?" Col asked.

"Maybe, we'll see who arrives. Did you have someone in mind?"

"Kaden would make a good teacher."

"You're right," Yalta said. "He is the messenger of his own village now and has his own apprentice. I'll send word before the full moon."

* * *

Over the next moon, they worked the three visitors hard. Col and Talla spent days with Erra teaching healing techniques. They never questioned her wound stitching, and she set two broken bones in the first half of the moon. She worked on local herbs, complimenting her knowledge of the plants native to her own island. Days before the full moon, Yalta sent a runner off to Kaden's village to invite him to teach at the solstice apprentice camp.

They were gathered around the fire after a good meal. Shola, the cook, sitting, chatting with the protected-of-spirit.

"Erra," Tooev said, "You are ready. You have earned your healer's tattoo. Who do you want to do it?"

Erra looked at the assembled company, her eyes settling on Yalta. "You please, Spirit Master," she said.

"Fetch my tool pouch, girls," she called to the twins. "It will be an honour," she said.

Erra sat, still as a stone, while Yalta cut the intricate design, though she hissed in pain when Yalta rubbed the lamp-black into the cuts.

"Now Erra," said Yalta, "Tell us about Fire Master Col's exploits at the fire mountain, then recount the tale of the attack on the outlaw camp."

Erra looked towards Col. He nodded. This was a proper test of her skill, of remembering and re-telling a story. She'd been present at neither event, so had to rely on the mental picture she had from hearing the story told herself.

"Spirit Messenger Col arrived at the fire mountain by ship. He had sailed from the south island with his three companions..."

Erra wove the story, her hands and facial expressions telling as much as her words. These new tales entranced Faran and the twins. Once Erra had finished, she turned to Col.

"Well done," he smiled. "Told to perfection, I applaud your memory and story-telling skills." Erra blushed. "Now, maybe it's time the twins told us the creation legend," he said.

The two girls at once became calm. Though they spent their lives giggling, always in motion, with their apprentice work they were solemn. Arva began, turning to her sister when she wanted her to take over the story. They recounted the tale of the first warrior, their hands working to explain the movements, the emotions. There was a brief silence as they finished, then cheers from everyone.

"A wonderful story to end a good evening," Tooev said, stretching his arms above his head. "and now it's time for bed."

He and Yalta departed for their own house while Shola gathered the last platters from supper. The twins said their goodnights before trundling off to their own bed.

"Do you ever think of Albyn?" Talla asked, her head laid on Col's chest as always.

"I wonder if he still lives," Col said. "Without him giving us apprentice marks and sending us on this journey, we would be dead. Sacrificed."

"He lives," Talla said with conviction. "He will welcome us home one day."

"I hope you're right," Col said, closing his eyes.

* * *

Kaden arrived on the first day of the full moon, Var trailing behind him. He greeted the protected-of-spirit before sending his apprentice to one of the lodging houses with the other arrivals.

"I'm glad you could come, Kaden," Talla said, "Come and choose a bed."

The young messenger settled himself in the great house and took a seat at the fire. "We shall have three teaching groups," Yalta said. "Col and Talla will take a group each, Kaden will take the third. Erra will help each of you but will teach healing to the apprentices. Faran, along with the twins, will work with those deciding if they wish to apprentice. Tooev and I will teach the masters. That includes you, Col, Kaden and Talla, once you have done your duties for the day."

Talla sat with Kaden after their meeting, perching beside him on his bed. "You were staring at Erra," she said grinning.

Kaden blushed, "She's beautiful. I'm not good at talking to pretty girls."

Talla pouted. "So, I'm not pretty, then?"

"No... Yes! I mean... I know you so I can talk to you, even though you're pretty," he said.

"Well, get to know Erra, then you'll be able to talk to her too," Talla said, bidding him a good night and heading for bed.

Chapter 27

The three messengers, along with Erra, were in charge of the apprentices, Yalta and Tooev only appearing to introduce themselves. There were three groups of ten, and the friends soon got them into a routine. Erra joined one group or another after lunch to teach them healing skills.

"Why are we being taught by an apprentice?" one girl asked.

"Because Erra is an accomplished healer, regardless of her spirit status," Talla said. "Erra, how many people did you treat after the outlaw attack at the Locan port?"

"Over thirty, Messenger Talla," she said.

"And the injuries?"

"More than half had a wound that needed sewing, others had many wounds. I treated three broken bones and many burns." She looked at her feet. "I could not treat one man, they broke his skull, and even though he still lived, I had to send him to join his ancestors."

Talla looked towards the girl who'd asked the question. "This was after noon on one day," she said. "Col and I treated a similar number. Are you happy to learn from an apprentice now?"

The girl looked embarrassed. "Yes, Messenger Talla, I apologise," she said, bowing her head.

Erra smiled. "Healing is my passion," she said. "Now, who has seen a wound sewn?" Talla patted Erra's shoulder as she left her to teach the group.

* * *

They spent their days teaching, and soon the three messenger's evenings were taken up with the master's lessons. Col and Talla had assumed that the higher level would be more advanced, but they did not realise how much the spirit masters kept secret.

"Each of you has a spirit animal," Yalta said, "You will know your animal can help you, and perhaps advise you."

Each of the trainee masters nodded; there were eight, the three friends plus five more. "You will not know that a human spirit guides you too. We call them walking spirits, and they can cross the death river, in spirit form, to aid you." Col nodded, and Yalta turned to him. "You have heard of this, Col?" she asked.

"No, Master Yalta, but I am not surprised. We go to the river to ask for advice from the spirits. It makes sense one may take a personal interest in us."

"Well thought out, Col," she said. "These walking spirits may be a close ancestor, someone in your recent history, or maybe unrelated. They have chosen you for a reason. They may have similar ideas to you, similar goals, the same personality. Today we will start our search for these helpers."

Tooev took a small cloth bag, tipping out a crumbled brown substance onto his hand. "These are spirit mushrooms," he said, "You have all heard of them. You think them to be poisonous, the name telling us they will send you to the spirit world should you eat them. This is not the whole truth, though too many will make you sick. Their correct use is to allow the initiated to contact the spirits with greater ease. An infusion, a tea, made with these dried fungi will alter your thinking, allowing you to access the upper world, the home of the walking spirits."

"Will we be using these mushrooms in our training?" Talla asked.

"Yes, now," Tooev said, "Kaden, heat water for us, please."

Kaden soon made the infusion, then strained it into a bowl. Tooev explained he would not partake, staying in this reality to watch over their physical state during the journey. They passed around the pot, each drinking the earthy flavoured tea. Yalta explained how to access the upper world, then Tooev drummed.

Col took Talla's hand as his head started spinning. He closed his eyes and felt his spirit lifting through the roof, up into the night sky, to a place of light above the clouds. Talla gripped Col's hand tighter as they felt themself being pulled upwards, emerging in a bright landscape still holding hands.

* * *

They glanced at each other and blinked in the white glare. Their previous journeys had been to the lower world, a place of darkness and gloom.

"Son of fire," said a male voice behind them.

"Daughter of the winds," called a woman. Col and Talla turned. There stood an ancient couple, holding hands like themselves. The man wore a flowing cloak of brown linen. His hair and beard were long and white. The woman had grey hair and was short in stature. Her crooked smile showed a sense of fun, amusement. Talla stared at the master's tattoo around her left eye; she looked familiar.

"I am Galvac, your walking spirit, Col," the man said, holding out his hands in greeting.

"I am Dirva, your guide," said the woman, reaching her hands towards Talla. Talla gasped. Dirva, the old woman from the Frass tribe, stood before her in spirit form. "I see you recognise me, Spirit Messenger," she said.

"Have you died and crossed the river, Dirva?" Col asked.

The old woman smiled. "I have been in the spirit world for many generations, young Messenger."

"But... we knew you... in life," he said, his brow wrinkling.

"I came to you, and to the apprentices, Nuru and Ivarra. I brought a warning to you and your companions. One day the two girls will be great spirit workers, and I will be their walking spirit too."

"Are you our ancestors, then?" Talla asked.

The old man gave a toothless grin. "We are not blood, Spirit of Air, but once took a role, it is your destiny to inherit. We were a couple, bonded in life. As your guides, either of you may consult either of us. It is our task to help you fulfil your destiny, Children of the Elements."

"Our friends, Gren and Zoola, do they have walking spirits?" Col asked.

"They have not sought their helpers yet," said Dirva.

"Then they are well?" Talla asked.

Dirva smiled. "They are well and happy, as is their son."

"A boy? Col, a boy. They have a baby now!"

Col squeezed her hand and grinned, then turned towards their walking spirits. "You call us 'Son of Fire, Daughter of the Winds'. Are we spirits, then?"

Dirva glanced at Galvac. He nodded. "You are both human and spirit," Dirva said. "You will one day be of our world, but you have much to achieve in your human form first. Seek us when you need help. We will always be at your sides, even if you cannot sense us." The old couple became indistinct then, their shapes blurring as they dissolved into the air.

* * *

Col and Talla opened their eyes as the drumming stopped. Their hands were still clasped as Talla tried to focus. Her vision was distorted, things moved like dripping honey, voices were deep and unintelligible. Tooev's face appeared a hand's breadth from hers. He was speaking, yet she didn't understand. Her hand was being pulled, and she staggered to her feet. Col was beside her, leading her to their bed. He helped her off with her clothes, laying her on the platform.

An age later, he slipped in beside her, strong arms holding her. Talla grabbed her mate, frightened she could be so out of control. Screwing her eyes shut, she waited for sleep to take her.

* * *

Col wished the drumming inside his head would stop. He tried opening his eyes, but the sun streaming in through the smoke-hole and the door blinded him, setting the insistent pounding off again.

He opened his eyes a fraction and turned to Talla. She lay sprawled on the bed, furs kicked off, snoring.

"Talla," he said, stroking her shoulder.

"Mmmh?"

"Talla, are you all right?"

"Mmm? No," she mumbled. "Sore head... my mouth feels like it has fur in it."

"Me too."

"Col. Talla. You're awake," Arva said, jumping onto the bed.

Col gasped, grabbing his head. "Shh."

"You had spirit mushrooms, didn't you?" Atta said, joining her twin. Col stared at her, mouth open. "We're not supposed to know, are we? We're not even messengers yet. Wait there, we'll make you tea."

The twins ran back to the fire, giggling. Col heard them arguing in whispers, then Arva saying, "Right, willow bark, mint, rose-hip and nettle."

"Yes," said Atta.

Col must have dozed off, as moments later the girls were back with two steaming cups. "Drink it while it's hot," Arva instructed, smiling as she took her sister's hand and they returned to their chores.

At last, Col and Talla surfaced. A glance out of the door told Col it was midway between dawn and noon. Late. Yalta came in smiling.

"You're up," she said, sitting at the fire and accepting a cup of tea from Atta.

"It's late," Col muttered.

"You're the first to wake," she said. "These journeys have a long recovery time."

"Do we have to use the mushrooms every time we need to speak to our walking spirits?" Talla asked.

"At first. Then you'll become more in tune with them and be able to hear them, even see them, without the mushrooms." Talla sipped her second cup of tea, amazed at how it was easing her head. Yalta took the cup, sniffing it before handing it back.

"The twins?" she asked. Talla nodded. Yalta closed her eyes and shook her head. "They shouldn't know how to treat the after-effects of spirit mushrooms," she said.

"They're inquisitive, and they live with two spirit masters who teach. Are you surprised?" Talla asked.

"No," Yalta sighed. "Don't tell them that I know. They're good kids."

Talla smiled and nodded.

* * *

"You won't try taking spirit mushrooms, will you?" Talla asked the twins later.

"What and end up like a three-day-old corpse?" Atta said.

"No chance!" said Arva, "We'll wait 'til we're really old like you and Col."

* * *

Tooev and Erra taught the apprentices that morning while the messengers recovered. Col and Talla found Kaden at lunch, still nursing a sore head, with a cup of the twins' tea.

"Teaching, later?" Col asked, smiling.

"Maybe," their friend mumbled, attempting a smile.

Tooev came in, glancing at Kaden and shaking his head. "Did you at least find a walking spirit?" he asked.

"Yes," Kaden said, finishing his drink. "Her name is..."

Tooev's hand shot out, pressing over Kaden's mouth. "Never share that name!" he said, "We should have told you. The spirit has influence over you, someone knowing their name could use that against you. Never repeat it." Kaden nodded.

Col looked uncomfortable, looking up at Tooev. "Talla and I know each other's walking spirit's names," he said.

"You shared them?" Tooev asked.

"No, we held hands, travelled as a couple. Our helpers are also a couple."

"You are bonded. It should not be a problem. I must talk to Yalta though," he said, rising from his seat, "I have never heard of this."

* * *

They made Erra a messenger a day before the larger group, allowing her to take part in the messenger ceremony in the north, representing earth. Kaden took the role of the water spirit.

The tribes had arrived now, filling the village, and the spirit masters gathered for those who had achieved master status. Yalta and Tooev marked their new rank with an elaboration of their messenger tattoos. Talla and Col, relieved to have passed, left the ceremony once it had become nothing more than a party, returning to the village to sleep. Col stirred once during the night as Kaden climbed into his own bed, a laughing Erra slipping in beside him.

* * *

Col woke to the sound of the twins lighting the fire. As always, it involved giggling. He rolled over, glancing towards the next bed. Erra smiled at him.

"Good morning, Messenger Erra," he said.

"Good morning, Master Col," the girl said, bowing her head. "I was just... I mean, Kaden and I..."

"Erra, it's none of my business," Col said. "You have sixteen summers, you may sleep where you wish." Erra blushed as Kaden sat up, disturbed by the conversation. He smiled at Col, wrapping an arm around the young woman. She made a token protest before he pulled her back under the furs.

* * *

The tribes were packing up to leave after the celebrations when Kaden found Erra stuffing her few belongings into a bag.

"Are you leaving?" he asked.

"Yes, soon."

"I wanted to ask you if you would like to come to my village with me," Kaden said.

"That would be nice. I could stay for a few days," Erra smiled. She liked the tall spirit messenger.

"Oh, only a few days? I thought you may stay for longer. Even for good."

Erra looked up, eyes wide. She reached for Kaden, pulling him into a hug. "Kaden, no. I have a life, a clan, a tribe. I am expected to return to my master on the island."

"I wanted to propose you join with me. Be my mate. I'm sorry... You and me, we..." Kaden stuttered.

"It was nice, Kaden," she said, holding his face in her palms. "If things were different, I'd be honoured. You'll make a wonderful mate, but I have to leave."

"Can I come with you?" he asked.

"You must care for your village. They need you, Kaden," Erra said.

"In a few years Var will be a messenger," Kaden said. "Once he is ready, I could follow you, come to your island."

Erra grinned, hugging him. "I'd like that. Do you mean it?" Kaden nodded and received a long kiss from Erra. "Well, I'd better come and stay with you for a while before I go then," she said, grinning and reaching for his hand.

Soon there were only the Guardians of the Circle of Stanna, plus Col and Talla left. Kaden and Erra departed amid many tears, though the twins promised to find Erra's island when they were older.

* * *

Col coached the twins to Fire Keeper, and Talla spent many days with Faran, teaching him plant knowledge. Two moons after the solstice, the weather warmed, and Talla and Col made their own departure from Stanna.

"Will we see you again?" Yalta asked, hugging each of them.

"You never know," Col said. "We don't know what is in our future. We plan to make our own stone circle at Classac into a teaching centre like yours."

"I think we'll meet again," said Tooev, hugging them both. The twins clutched Col and Talla. There were no tears, though both were in a sombre mood. They were growing up, Col thought.

"We'll visit," Arva said.

"Together," Atta added.

Talla smiled. "I thought you were going to Erra's island?"

"We'll do both," they chorused.

Col lifted his pack, taking Talla's hand as they waved to their friends and mentors, and headed north.

Chapter 28

Col and Talla travelled north, stopping at many villages. The people welcomed them now that the seasons had returned to normal. Crops were being sown early, and winter feedstuffs had been plentiful. As they travelled, they taught plant knowledge and fire magic, telling the legends of the clans along the way. They often offered their healing skills too, as they made progress towards their home.

A moon and a half into their journey, they came upon the Uru tribe again. Garav, the messenger who had taught them their first fire teachings, met them with a smile.

"Col, Talla!" he said, holding out his hands in welcome. As Talla and Col stepped closer, he glanced at their tattoos. "My apologies, Spirit Masters. You have learned much since I last saw you."

"We have," said Col, "But we are happy to see you again, Master Garav."

Garav inspected Col's eye again. "A new fire tattoo?" he asked.

"Yes, I am a Fire Master," Col said. "We have travelled across two seas to confront the fire spirit, but our weather has returned to normal, at last."

"We are glad," Garav said. "You have mastery of each discipline now, Col. And you Talla?"

Talla smiled. "All but fire, Master Garav. Air is my element, the spirits call me Daughter of the Winds."

Garav grinned, "A suitable title. Now, will you stay a few days and allow us to hear the stories of your quest?"

Talla smiled. "Yes."

* * *

They feasted that night, followed by the telling of the couple's passage to the inland sea. They slept late the following day, before helping with healing work and medicines.

That evening they told of the confrontation at the fire mountain, of Col's brush with death, and his triumph over the spirit of fire. The third night, they told of their trek home, including the attack by the outlaws.

"We have driven off the bandits, to the north," Garav said. "After you left, a group of our men went to their camp and confronted them. They put up a fight, but we beat them."

"That's good," said Col, "We'll pass that way soon."

Two days later, Col and Talla left the Uru tribe and walked up into the hills. They travelled fast, their strength replenished by their stay. Talla stopped as they crested the brow of a hill on their second day.

"Col, look, that's the cave of the outlaws," she said, pointing across the valley. A small fire burned outside.

"Garav said they'd gone," Col said. He sat in the heather, watching the cave for a while, before turning to Talla. "There's only one person," he said, "Maybe it's Vinna, their slave."

"I'll go to see," Talla said.

"It could be dangerous, Talla. Maybe I should go."

"No, you wait. I'll call you if it's safe. If not, come and get me."

Talla made her way down the hillside, calling out as she approached. "Hello, the cave!"

"We are unarmed," came a voice, "A woman and a child, we have nothing."

"Vinna?" Talla said, approaching the cave mouth.

"You're the spirit apprentice the outlaws sold as a slave. I'd know your hair and eyes anywhere."

"Yes, we are returning home. Why are you still here?" Talla asked.

"They killed most of the outlaws. Those that survived went further east. I hid myself and my children until it was safe."

Talla turned and beckoned. "Col. It's safe."

"Your friend?" Vinna asked.

"My mate now, and we are spirit masters," Talla said. Vinna bowed her head, apologising. "You weren't to know," Talla said.

Col arrived, smiling at the bony woman in the ragged shift. "It's Vinna, isn't it?" he asked. She nodded.

"Vinna hid with her children when the outlaws left," Talla explained.

"Are your children safe?" Col asked.

"Verra, my daughter, died," Vinna said, wiping a tear from her eye. "My son, Lorev, is in the cave, but very weak."

"May we see him?" Talla asked, "We are healers."

Vinna led the couple into the cave where she'd laid the boy on a makeshift bed. He was pale and skeletal.

"Have you no food?" Col asked.

"What little I can catch," Vinna said. "We have eaten earthworms and frogs often, but it is never enough."

Talla got their travelling food from their packs, feeding the boy and his mother small quantities at a time. Col made an invigorating tea and sweetened it with honey, which the boy guzzled. "We'll stay a day or two," said Talla, "Then take you back to your tribe."

Vinna shook her head. "They won't accept us. Lorev's father was an outlaw; I've no idea which one, they all used me. They say it taints his blood. I may return, but only without my son."

"We'll deal with that later," Col said, "First we have to get you fit and well."

Over the next days, Col set snares for the mountain hares and caught fish in the stream. Talla gathered what she could. Vinna looked healthier, and after six or seven days, Lorev could move around a little.

"We'll leave after the full moon," Talla said. "We'll go to your tribe and argue your case for you."

Vinna sighed. "I have begged them, Talla. They will not accept him; I may as well be an outlaw myself."

* * *

The journey to the Forest clan of the Poan people was uneventful if slow. Lorev walked when he could, but Col carried the boy on the steeper hills. He was small, stunted, no doubt by a poor diet over his eight summers.

The Poan messenger greeted them and welcomed them into his house. "Spirit Masters," he said, bowing, "I have stood against our leader on this matter, but he will not budge. The outlaws slaughtered his own child in a raid two years ago. He is still angry and afraid."

"I will speak to him," Col said.

The leader was an impressive man, taller and broader than Col by far. A fading scar crossed his right cheek, twisting his mouth into a grotesque half-smile.

"I will not allow it!" Torvan, the leader, snapped at Col.

"You'll allow a blameless child to die?"

"My son died at their hands," Torvan said.

"And this boy was responsible for that? He had six summers when your son died. Do you think he did it?"

"I am no fool, Spirit Master. The outlaws taint his blood. He will not live in my village."

"His mother cannot support him alone in the mountains. You sentence him to starve to death, then?"

Torvan moved closer to Col, hoping to intimidate him. Instead, Col stepped up to the leader, their noses a hand's breadth apart. "If you are so keen to save him, you take him. Vinna is welcome to return, but not the boy," Torvan said.

Col stepped back a little, waving Torvan towards the door. "Leave, we will discuss this," he said.

"I am the village leader! You do not give me orders!" Torvan blustered.

"This is the house of spirit, *Leader Torvan,*" Col said, "if one of the protected-of-spirit asks you to leave it, you will go." The big man turned, his face reddening, as he stormed out. Col and Talla walked to the back of the house. There was a brief conversation before they returned.

"Vinna, will you consent to us taking Lorev with us?" Talla said.

"You'd care for him? He would be free, not a slave?" she asked.

"We will adopt him as our own," Col said, his hand on Vinna's shoulder. "As our son, perhaps he may even become protected-of-spirit one day."

"Lorev, will you go with Col and Talla?" Vinna asked. "You know you can never live here with me. We would have to go back to the cave."

The boy thought for a moment. He'd become fond of the spirit masters over the last moon, and he knew his mother's efforts at the cave could never be enough. His fate would be the same as his little sister.

Lorev nodded. "I love you, Mother, but I will go with Talla and Col."

"They will care for you, Lorev," Vinna said, weeping now.

"I will return one day, when I am older," Lorev said, brushing away his own tears. "I will never forget you."

* * *

Col had conducted an ancestor ceremony adopting the boy and, two days later, there was a tearful goodbye. Lorev hugged his mother, then took Talla's hand as they left the village.

"You are leaving for good?" Torvan said, stepping into their path.

"We are not welcome here, Leader Torvan," Col replied.

"You know it's not you who are unwelcome," the leader said, glancing towards Lorev.

"If our son is not welcome, then we are not welcome," Talla said.

"Son?" the leader asked.

"We adopted him into the family of the protected-of-spirit," Col said. "Let us see what the spirits make of this slight against them."

"I meant no disrespect of the spirits," the leader said, "I didn't know..."

"Nor did you care," Col said, dismissing him. "Goodbye, Torvan."

* * *

They were walking most of each day, and Lorev's strength soon returned. Col and Talla made sure they fed the boy well, giving him meat and wild vegetables at each meal. After a while, he stopped bolting his food as if it was his last meal, savouring the flavours for the first time in his life. He was an inquisitive child and, after another moon of travelling, he could recognise many of the healing plants and give their uses.

At last, the three travellers made it to the coast where Col and Talla first arrived from their own island. It seemed like a lifetime ago. They wandered into the coastal village, Lorev between them, clutching their hands. A few people stared, and a young girl ran off when she spotted them, charging into a large roundhouse. As they approached, a young man, a little older than their eighteen summers, came out, smiling.

"Col, Talla?" he said. "We wondered if we'd ever see you again." A woman followed him from the house, beaming at them.

"Solla!" Talla gasped, "Are you and Gan joined now?"

"Yes, and Gan is the leader." Her face fell, "A fever took his father last summer."

"We are sorry," Col said. "May we pay our respects to Tarna and Genna before we visit with you?"

"Genna, yes, but Tarna died after the winter solstice. She had close to fifty summers." Solla spotted the girl again and called her. "Yella, do you remember Col and Talla?"

"Yes, Solla, they were there when I apprenticed," the girl said.

"Well, take them to Messenger Genna, please," she said.

Yella led them to the messenger's roundhouse. "Messenger Genna. Visitors," she called.

"Well, well," the spirit messenger said, hugging the two travellers. "You have been busy." She looked at their intricate tattoos, deciphering the information there. She gave up with a shrug.

"I am Genna, Spirit Messenger of the Shore Clan of the Atay Tribe. Plant master, Lore master and healer," she said, hands outstretched.

Col smiled, realising she needed to hear each of them recite their status. "I am Col. Spirit Master of the Hill Clan of the Tribe of the West. Plant Master, Lore Master, Fire Master and Healer," he said.

"I am Talla, Spirit Master of the Hill Clan of the Tribe of the West. Plant Master, Lore Master, Fire Keeper and Healer."

Genna gave a deep bow, smiling to herself. "I knew you two would go far," she said. "Now, who is this young man?"

"This is our son, Lorev," Talla said, smiling at the lad. Lorev remembered his manners and bowed his head.

"Greetings Messenger Genna," he said.

Genna grinned. "Son? You have achieved much, Spirit Masters, but a son of, what, seven summers?"

"Lorev has eight summers. His mother is Poan, but could not keep him," Talla said.

"His father?" Genna asked.

"Is dead," Col replied.

They sat, discussing the Atay tribe's newfound links with the Tribe of the South across the water, after the bonding of Gan and Solla. Talla told a little of their journey.

"Will you stay a few days?" Genna asked. "I'm sure all our people would love to hear the telling of your journey around a fire one night."

They settled in at Genna's roundhouse, though they spent as much time with Gan and Solla. The entire clan turned out for the telling of their journey the following night, and there were many congratulations given on the enthralling tale. Lorev sat transfixed throughout, unaware of what celebrated heroes his new parents were.

They'd been at the Shore Clan for six days when there was a shout of excitement from the beach one afternoon. A small boat appeared from across the water, sailed by Bek, Solla's brother, on a trading trip.

"Bek!" Solla yelled, running down to the water's edge as the small craft ploughed into the sand. He jumped ashore, hugging his sister.

"Solla. Being bonded agrees with you," he said, patting her expanding belly.

"That's your niece or nephew, silly," she said, taking his hand.

"A baby?"

"That's the result of being pregnant," she said.

Talla saw Col's smile and wondered when to tell him her own news.

"It will delight mother, when I tell her," Bek said.

"I'll tell her, I'm coming with you this time," she said, "And look who I've found."

"Col? Talla? You made it back. How far did your journey take you?" he asked.

"Well, you missed the telling of it last night," Talla grinned, "so how about we tell you on our journey across the water. That's if you will take us."

"I wouldn't miss it for the world," he said.

Chapter 29

The little boat pulled away from the beach the next morning, loaded with stone tools and pottery, grain and salt meat. Talla and Col sat with Lorev and Solla while Bek and his friend sailed the vessel across the calm seas.

"The wind is against us," Bek said, "It will be a long crossing."

Talla smiled and climbed from her seat, pulling herself to the front of the craft and standing, swaying, in the bow. She closed her eyes, feeling the breeze, becoming the wind, filling the little sail. Turning her face towards the distant island, she threw her free hand forward while the other clutched the rigging. The wind shifted, chasing the small ship over the foam-tipped waves.

"Is that better Ship Master?" she called to Bek. He stood open-mouthed, staring at the bellied sail.

"You did that?"

"Yes, Ship Master."

"What is a ship master?" he asked.

"If you were of the people to the south, the navigator of a boat, you would be."

"Well," Bek said, "With this wind, we'll be home in no time. Save the telling of your story until we're home. The Boat Clan will want to hear it too."

* * *

Sarn, the leader of the Boat Clan, met them at the shore. He waved to Bek, then called out, "Welcome back, Col!"

The little ship grounded on the beach and Bek stepped ashore, hugging his father. Solla followed, embracing the leader too.

"How did you know it was me?" Col asked as he stepped out of the boat.

Sarn grinned. "Your damned raven got here a while ago, sitting on the roof, squawking and scaring the children. No one else has a bird as tame, to my knowledge." He hugged Col, then Talla. Standing back, he eyed their tattoos and bowed. "It is many years since I saw one, but I assume that is a spirit master's tattoo you wear?"

"It is, but we are friends, Sarn. No need for ceremony," Col said.

"Come and meet our new spirit messenger," Sarn said, turning for the village.

The girl that stepped from the messenger's house looked terrified. She stood with arms outstretched, hands shaking, as she raised her head to look at Col.

"I am Rolva, Spirit Messenger of the Boat Clan of the Tribe of the South. Plant Master, Lore Keeper and Healer," she whispered.

Col smiled and gave his status, followed by Talla.

The girl dropped to the ground, sitting at their feet.

"Stand, Rolva," Col said, offering his hand. She took it, standing with head bowed.

"This is our son, Lorev," Talla said, "Why don't we have tea?"

"Yes, yes, tea," Rolva said blushing.

They entered the house, and Rolva fussed over the fire. "Lorev, why don't you make the tea for us while Rolva sits and talks to us?" Col said.

"Yes, Father," the boy said, seeing how Col was putting the nervous messenger at ease.

"How long have you been here?" Talla asked.

"Half a moon," Rolva said.

"And how long a messenger?" said Col.

"Half a moon," she whispered. "Spirit Masters, I'm not sure if I can do this. I went from being an apprentice to being responsible for the health and spiritual well-being of these people in three days."

"How many summers do you have?" Talla asked.

"Sixteen, in less than a moon," she said. It was almost solstice.

"Do you have a mate, an apprentice?" Col asked.

"Neither, Master."

"Our names are Col and Talla unless we are in a formal setting." Col smiled, "An apprentice is easier to come by than a mate. Make it a priority to find one, old enough to be of use to you, eight or ten summers. It will give you some company and make your job easier. The village is prosperous, it can afford the keep of an apprentice."

"Yes, Spir... Col," she said, meeting his gaze. "Thank you for having faith in me."

"We are going home, to the great stone circle at Classac. If you need us, send a runner, one of us will come," Talla said, taking the girl's hand.

"Thank you, Talla," Rolva said.

Sarn organised a feast that night, gathering the clan together around a massive fire. They roasted meat, and baked bread as the people of the Boat Clan welcomed the spirit masters and their son.

"People of the Boat Clan!" Sarn called, raising his arms. "The weather has improved. This year our crops are strong, and the harvest will feed us well. There is a tale to tell tonight, of how two travellers crossed the lands of many tribes to meet the challenges of the spirits. Col and Talla will tell it to you."

There was cheering as the couple stood and began their tale once again. The people gazed at the adventurers with open mouths as they described their travels. It was late in the evening when Col finished their story. Rolva, the young messenger, stood and produced a frame drum, leading the clan in a couple of well-known songs before they retired to bed.

"We are in your debt, Sarn," Talla said, "How may we repay you for our boat crossings?"

"The amber beads you offered me," he said, "They are the ones destroyed in your story?"

"Yes, we must find another way to pay you," Col said.

"When I touched them, two years ago, I knew there was something amiss with them," Sarn said. "They sent a shiver through me. After you left us, I thought about how important your journey was. Now you have brought back our summers, I've decided that the Boat Clan has a duty to carry the protected-of-spirit without debt."

Talla bowed. "Then the protected-of-spirit thank you, Leader Sarn."

"Have you had any news of Albyn?" Col asked as they made their way towards the messenger's house.

"A traveller from the far north of the island came through four or five moons ago," Sarn said, "She said he was old and grumpy. I told her that was normal."

Talla smiled. "He lives still, then."

"So they told me," Sarn said. "Goodnight."

They made their way to the roundhouse and, after bidding Rolva a good night, climbed into bed.

* * *

Talla woke with Col's hand, stroking her belly. He was always tactile, and she loved the way he made her feel valued. Loved.

"Are you ready to be a father, Col," she whispered.

"Lorev is a good boy, I'm glad we adopted him," Col said, kissing the back of her neck.

"What if we had a child of our own?" she asked, biting her lip.

"I'd be thrilled when it's time," Col said.

She clutched his hand to her distended waist. "It'll be time in about six months."

Col scrambled up, looking at his mate in the half-light of dawn.

"A baby?" he asked. She nodded. "At winter solstice?"

"About then," she said, glad he was happy. Their journey would soon be over, and Talla could relax a little back at Classac. Col's arms enfolded her, and his firm lips met hers.

"I love you, Talla," he said.

* * *

They stayed with the Boat Clan for a few days. Bek wanted to hear all about the larger boats they'd encountered on their journey, then asked how Talla controlled the winds.

"It is my gift, as fire is Col's," she said. "Our friends, from the story of our journey, represent the elements of water and earth."

"What happens when you get together?" Bek asked.

"One day, when it happens again, we'll find out," she said.

The next morning they made their way up the hill from the village, waving goodbye to their friends as they dipped out of sight. Col took Talla's hand, and Talla took Lorev's as they started the last leg of their journey. They spent two nights in their hide shelter, Lorev snuggled up to his adoptive parents, comfortable with them now. The afternoon of the third day, the great circle of Classac came into view on its hilltop, jagged points of stone against a blue sky.

"This is our home," Col said to Lorev, pointing out the vast monument in the distance. Kark squawked and flew up from Col's shoulder, flapping towards the distant village. Col smiled, "He knows we've arrived too," he said.

* * *

Albyn sat on a bench outside his roundhouse, Geth, the song keeper at his side.

"Raven," he commented as the bird alighted on the roof, squawking.

"It is," Geth said. "They seldom come so close."

"Unless they're tamed," Albyn said. He turned to Geth.

She smiled.

"You don't think..." he began.

"You're the spirit messenger, you tell me, you old fool."

"Fetch my swan cape!" he said, struggling to his feet and grasping his staff.

"What am I, your damned slave?" she muttered, shuffling into the house to retrieve the cloak.

* * *

The village sat at the base of the slope, below the hill with its great stone circle. Col took Talla's hand as they made their way into the settlement, each of them touching the sacred bull's skull hanging from the boundary post. Lorev stayed close beside them. People stopped and stared as the couple made their way towards the messenger's house. Many recognised the dark-haired boy, now a man, and his pale, white-haired companion.

"It's them," Geth whispered into Albyn's ear.

"Spirit Apprentice Col, Spirit Apprentice Talla, welcome!" Albyn called, hands held out in the universal gesture as they approached. Col stepped up to the old man; close enough to see that his eyes were not closed, as he'd thought. They were a mass of ragged scars.

Geth looked up, her eyes screwed half-closed as she focussed on the couples' tattoos. She smiled. "Perhaps you had better make this an official meeting, Albyn."

He pulled himself up to his full height. "I am Albyn, Spirit Messenger of the Hill Clan of the Tribe of the West. Guardian of the stones of Classac, Plant Master, Lore Master and Healer," he recited, bowing his head.

Albyn looked older if that were possible. Col felt tears at the corners of his eyes as he held out his hands.

"I am Col, Spirit Master of the Hill Clan of the Tribe of the West. Plant Master, Lore Master, Fire Master and Healer," Col said.

"I am Talla, Spirit Master of the Hill Clan of the Tribe of the West. Plant Master, Lore Master, Fire Keeper and Healer," Talla added.

Unable to contain herself any longer, Talla clasped the surprised old man in a tight hug. "We've missed you, Messenger," she whispered.

When she released him, his blind eyes looked about as if he could still see.

"Geth, where is Hessa?" he asked.

"I'm here, Messenger," a girl said, stepping out of the roundhouse. She bowed to the visitors.

"Make tea for us, girl," Albyn said, pulling his staff to his right hand for balance as he turned towards the door. "Come in, come in."

They sat around the hearth, a blaze burning despite the summer warmth. Hessa pulled stones from the fire to heat water.

"This is our son, Lorev," Talla said, introducing the boy.

"You are bonded?" Albyn asked.

"Your son?" Geth asked.

Talla laughed. "We adopted him. We have achieved much, but a son of eight summers is beyond our skills."

For the first time, Col and Talla saw the elderly messenger smile.

"You should use my given name; call me Albyn," he said. "Perhaps you will tell us of your journey?"

Col smiled. "We have told it many times," he said, "Perhaps the entire clan would like to hear it told tonight?"

Albyn's smile faded. "The Clan has changed in your absence," he said. "When the crops failed, Tan, the leader, became angry. When his plan to sacrifice Talla was foiled by your departure, he lost his reason. Instead of trying to grow crops, to raise animals, he turned to raiding. The Hill Clan has become the scourge of the other villages, near and far. We have become parasites."

"Where is Tan now?" Talla asked.

There was a banging on the door, then it flew open.

"Where is she?" shouted the leader, storming into the house, casting about for Talla.

"Good day, Leader Tan," said Albyn, standing.

"I want the slave girl!" he shouted.

"If you can't give a civil greeting, you'll get nothing," Albyn said, his voice quiet.

"You!" Tan said, pointing to Talla, "You were destined to die to appease the spirits. Outside now. I'll do it myself."

Col stepped in front of the rabid leader, fixing him with a glare. "Do you know this mark?" he said, pointing to the scarred symbol under his right eye.

"Spirit nonsense," Tan muttered, trying to push Col aside.

Col's voice was like ice. "It's the mark of a spirit master," he said, "Talla wears one too. Will you try to sacrifice one of the protected-of-spirit, one with the highest status?"

"I will do as I please, I am the leader here."

"Leader? You are a robber, a thief," said Col. "You steal from your neighbours. I saw crops being grown, coming into the village. Are you reconsidering?"

"They disobey me. I will destroy the crops, and I will punish them."

"No," said Col, "You will not. Now, we will gather at a fire tonight to tell the story of our journey, and of our battle with the spirits. You may wish to come, Leader Tan."

"Pah!" he spat, "Don't think I have forgotten this."

"You should not have provoked him," Albyn said, as Tan slammed the door behind him.

"A wise man once told me that the greedy are easily fooled," Col said, "Let's see if he was right."

* * *

The fire blazed as Col and Talla stood and walked forward. Yellow light danced across their faces, accentuating their intricate tattoos. Col raised his arms, silencing the chattering crowd. Albyn and Geth sat behind them with Lorev and Hessa, the old man's brow wrinkled with worry.

"We left here because Tan threatened our lives," Col began. "Messenger Albyn consulted the spirits. They told him that only we could solve the disconnection between the tribes and spirit. This is our story."

He began their well-practised tale, Talla taking over after a while, then Col finishing. The villagers sat transfixed. Tan and a half-dozen of his cohorts stood well back, listening. When Col finished, the people burst into shouts of appreciation, cheering the brave couple.

"A delightful story," said Tan, swaggering forward, "If it were true."

"Believe it or not, as you please," Talla said. "The weather has improved because of our battles with the elements; that you cannot deny."

"The weather changes all the time. Who says it was your efforts that changed it? Who says it won't change back tomorrow? You are liars and charlatans. I want you both gone by tomorrow." Tan turned to walk away, but Col stopped him.

"We are going nowhere, Tan. We have faced the spirits of the elements themselves and triumphed. What makes you think you can stop us? Are you man enough to challenge me?"

Tan sneered as he looked at Col's slim, wiry frame. The leader was a big man in both body and ego. "How could you hope to challenge me?"

"Oh, a simple test. May I set the rules?"

"I can best you at anything, spirit boy. Just tell me what I must do to rid myself of you," Tan said, turning to the crowd for approval. His face hardened as the villagers turned away, embarrassed.

Col walked to the fire and took two sticks. He pushed one into the ground at his feet, walked five or six paces, then pushed the other into the soft soil. "A simple game," Col said. "I stand by one stick, and you by the other. The first to reach the other's stick will win."

"A race?" the bigger man said, "I will beat you."

"No, you must get past me to get to my stick. I would have to get past you to get to yours. We must each go straight for our opponent's stick."

"Now?" sneered the leader.

"Tomorrow at sunset," Col said. "It will give you time to prepare your plan of attack."

Tan laughed, "I will swat you like an annoying fly," he said, turning to walk away.

"That was foolish, Col," said Albyn, walking up beside his former apprentice. "He is both stronger and faster than you."

"I agree, Albyn," Col said, "But is he cleverer than me?"

Chapter 30

Col wandered out of the roundhouse, a cup of nettle tea in his hand. He sat beside Albyn on the bench by the door.

"He has taken his friends and gone to raid another village," the old man said.

"Do the other clans not retaliate?" Col asked.

"They defend themselves, as best they can, but they have yet to attack us here."

Talla came out, joining Col and smiling at Albyn. "We missed you," she said.

"Missed my sparkling personality, eh?" he asked.

"Why did you never smile?" Col said.

"Because I feared for you. You were idle... I know why, but I had to push you beyond that if you were to be a messenger."

"Why was I idle, Albyn?" Col asked.

"Your father," he said, "He liked to help people; do things to improve the lives of the older ones. He died helping others; he'd have given all those gull's eggs away. Once you were healed, you only did what had to be done, no more. Now you return with tales of adventure and great bravery."

Col thought for a moment. "Those things I did, that we all did, they had to be done. We had to beat the elements, had to face the corrupt and the outlaws. I had to best the fire spirit at the mountain. Each time it was a choice of do or die. Perhaps I have not changed at all."

Albyn's hand found Col's shoulder, squeezing. "You have changed," he said.

"Tonight," Col said, glancing at Albyn and Talla, "Do not intervene. You will think me mad, but do not speak out."

"I will do as you ask," Albyn said.

Geth wandered over, squeezing in between Talla and Albyn. "Glad that your charges are back, old man?" she said, chuckling.

"Do you live in the house together?" Talla asked, "Are you bonded?"

Albyn laughed, a dry, hoarse sound the youngsters had never heard. "Bonded? I'm far too old for that nonsense. Geth is my sister."

"Sister? Why did we never know?" Col said.

"There was a time when everyone knew," Albyn said. "It was only recently that we realised those that knew are dead. When you left, Geth cared for me. When Hessa came, Geth stayed; it does the girl good to have a woman in the house."

"Cared for you? Why?" Talla asked.

"My eyes," he said. "I was in great pain, and bad spirits haunted me for over a moon."

Col laid his hand on Albyn's leg, and the old man turned to face him. "What happened to your eyes?" he asked.

"Tan gouged them out when he found you gone," he said.

"The scream," Talla said, "We heard it. But we heard his hounds. Why did he not catch us?"

Geth wrapped an arm around her brother. "Before he passed out, he told Tan you had gone east. Tan hunted you for over a moon, but you must have been far away by then."

Col clenched his jaw, his grip tightening on Albyn's leg. "Tonight, he dies," he whispered.

* * *

Hessa and Lorev helped Col and Talla to build a fire that afternoon, each youngster learning the invocations needed to bring strong fire spirits. Once they had finished, Col lit it, the flames consuming the stacked wood. The fire was just settling when a group of men dragged a lifeless body into the village.

"Quick, help him!" shouted one raider. "They were lying in wait for us. We should never have chanced a daylight raid on the River Clan." Talla ran over, checking the extensive wounds to the man's leg and torso. She felt for the beat of his blood, then lowered her ear to his chest. She stood and shook her head.

"He is dead," she said. "I think the belly wound cut a blood tube. He must have died soon after."

"You did this," Tan yelled. "You killed him, you told the River Clan we were coming. I should have sacrificed you when I had the chance."

"I say that the man who tried to raid a village in daylight was to blame," Col said.

Talla knelt beside the body, saying the verse to send the man across the river.

"Do you still have the courage to face me tonight, Tan, or did you learn your lesson from this?" Col asked.

"I will rend you limb from limb tonight," the leader said. He turned, beckoning the few remaining raiders. "Until dusk, when you die, along with your white spirit-woman."

* * *

As the sun sank at the western horizon, Col raked the embers of the fire out into a large rectangle. One of the marker sticks at each end. Tan walked up, spear in hand. "What trickery is this?" he asked.

"The fire?" Col asked. "That's for your benefit, to protect you from me. It'll make it harder for me to beat you."

"You hide behind it, spirit boy. You are a coward."

"On the contrary. I have to cross it to get to your stick, to win. Are you ready?"

Tan stood beside his stick, glaring at Col. "So, we stand here all night, until the fire goes out, then fight each other?"

"I don't think I'll wait," Col said, lifting his foot and stepping onto the glowing coals. There was a gasp from the assembled crowd as Col's other foot contacted the hot embers.

"Are you not joining me, Leader Tan?" Col taunted. "Afraid to do what I do? Frightened?"

"I'll kill you!" Tan screamed, waving his spear.

Col was halfway across the fire now, pacing with confidence. "I'll be able to reach your stick soon, Tan," he said, "Just a few more paces."

"I'll kill you then," the big man shouted.

"Once I've won? You'll kill me after I've won? Are you a man of no honour? Can you still sprint to my stick before I reach yours, coward? Run, and you may just beat me. I'm almost there now," he said, reaching forward.

Tan was red in the face as he watched Col move ever closer, unable to stop him unless he made a run for it; unless he used his superior speed. He glanced at Col once more, the confident step, the gloating grin. Tan leant forward, charging into the fire, his feet tearing into the searing coals. He felt nothing for a pace or two, then he screamed as his feet pressed through the surface of the fire, burying themselves in the scorching glow. He faltered as the pain became unbearable, losing his balance and falling forward, face-first into the red heat.

Col reached the end of his walk, pulling the stick from the ground before turning to watch Tan rolling back and forth in the embers, screaming like a child. He walked back beside the fire, pulling the writhing body from the coals. Tan's skin was blistered, his face and hands a mess of raw, scorched flesh. The stench of burned hair hung in the air.

"Water!" Col shouted. Talla grabbed a prepared pail, throwing the contents over the whimpering leader. Col knelt beside the almost unrecognisable body, leaning in, so his face was beside the remnants of Tan's ear.

"Never challenge the protected-of-spirit," he said, "Never play games with a fire master." Col stood, turning to the leader's few remaining friends. "Take him to the messenger's house," he ordered, walking away.

* * *

Col and Talla worked together on the leader. There wasn't a hands-breadth of skin unburned on the front of his body and, when Talla peeled back his eyelids, white, sightless orbs showed; his vision sacrificed to the fire.

"He cannot live," Albyn said, his hands exploring the weeping burns on Tan's chest and face. "Waste no more effort on him, he chose his own end."

Talla took a flint blade, passing it to Col. The spirit master closed his eyes, saying a silent prayer to the ancestors, then took Tan's wrist, cutting through the blistered flesh to the artery. He took the bowl Talla offered, turning the arm, so the blood drained from the agonised body. Soon Tan breathed his last, Talla placing a hand on his head and on his heart as she called his ancestors to take him.

Albyn conducted the funeral the following day, next to the spot where the leader had fallen. Afterwards, the old man stood to address the village. "Your leader is dead," he said. "The clan must choose a new leader. Until that time, our lore dictates the senior protected-of-spirit take the role. I am old, and I wish no part of this. Col has the highest status of any I know. He will lead you until we hold a vote."

The shout came from Art, Tan's son and Col's former tormentor.

"I will not allow it."

Col stepped forward, facing the angry man. He remembered the terror that Art used to strike into him when he was a child. Now he had met hostile spirits and outlaws, and the posturing man held no fear for him.

"No? Will you take up the challenge your father failed?" he asked. Art stepped back. "No braver than your father, then. But perhaps less foolish," Col said.

Art turned and stormed into his father's house, emerging moments later with a pack and a spear. He stopped beside a girl of about fourteen summers, his sister. "Look after our mother," he said, before stalking out of the village.

* * *

It was the summer solstice. Col and Talla rose early, climbing the hill to the sacred stones. There would be a celebration tonight, but now, they were alone. Col walked to the short row of stones to the south of the circle, following their line to the circle. Talla walked to the north end and, as the sun stretched its fingers above the horizon, began a steady walk up the avenue towards her mate. The red disc was half revealed when they met, arms enfolding, lips joining. Col laid his woman on the grass, dropping to his knees beside her. Talla smiled, opening her arms and, as a cuckoo called three times, welcomed her lover.

* * *

One man stood against Col for the Clan leadership. A former ally of Tan, who wanted to carry on with the pillaging of other villages. Col made it clear that, if he won, he would lead in partnership with Talla, as they'd seen Yalta and Tooev do at the circle of Stanna.

They gave each villager a pebble. One bowl represented Col and Talla, the other their adversary. When the voting was over, all the stones were in one bowl, and Col and Talla were clan leaders.

The solstice celebrations went ahead that evening, a fire blazing at the great circle as the villagers gathered for the ceremony. Albyn and Hessa sat with Col and Talla, drums in hand, as the spirit masters signalled a start and closed their eyes.

* * *

Talla found herself at the edge of the death river, its water only a trickle, reflecting the warm, dry summer in their own reality. She raised her hands, calling to the ancestors that loved them. As dark shapes formed on the far bank, Talla looked to her right, past her mate. There were two figures, like Talla and Col, standing at the water's edge. They, too, had their attendant drummers behind them. The closest was dressed in a costume of blue ribbons, his face dyed with woad. The second had dark skin and curled black hair.

Talla nudged Col and nodded to their right. Col smiled as the other couple turned and recognised them. They knew that this was not the time to meet, yet they were content to know that their friends were well and in ceremony on this solstice.

"Spirits who love us," Talla called, "We are the Hill Clan of the Tribe of the West. We have elected new leaders and have deserted our clan's thieving ways, returning to honest farming and hunting. We ask your guidance for the coming seasons."

A male figure stepped forward, pushing back a hood to reveal gaunt features. "You do well to change your ways. Your crops will be strong and plentiful, your animals healthy. Return your sacred stones to their proper use. Teach those who would serve the spirits, hold your ceremonies for all clans, all tribes. Travel to visit others and learn their ways, as you and your mate did. Make your ancestors proud, Daughter of the Winds. Always do what must be done, Son of Fire."

"Thank you, Ancestor," Talla said.

"You have work to do here before you return," the figure said, pointing a thin finger behind them. Talla turned to see people in small groups, standing, waiting. She took Col's hand and walked towards them, the lower-world bodies of Gren and Zoola joining them. They stood, answering petitions from tribes far and wide. 'How may we protect ourselves from the winds? May we dam the river? Why will our crops not thrive?' They dispensed their wisdom, as they could until all were answered.

"Back," said Talla, turning from the last petitioners.

* * *

They opened their eyes and took in the diminished fire, the apprehensive look on the faces of the villagers. Talla turned to Col.

"You speak to them," she said.

Col stood and raised his arms. "People of the Hill Clan. The ancestors foretell a time of abundance with good crops and healthy animals. They also ask us to make our circle, our village, into a place of teaching. We have seen this at the great circle of Stanna. It brings prestige for the guardians, and opportunities for the village.

"They ask us to reinstate travelling for our young people, especially the protected-of-spirit. This will help us to see how others live, to exchange ideas and to become more tolerant. We must reach out to our neighbours and make reparations. Tell them that Tan is dead and we are no longer thieves and robbers. Talla and I will lead you into this time of change. We will prosper." The crowd cheered, glad to have good news at last.

They brought the boards out, and they served food for the village. Col and Talla stood first, selecting the best of the food for themselves and their household; Albyn, Geth, Lorev and Hessa. Later there were stories and songs, Geth having composed a long ballad to the new Clan Leaders, telling of their travels. As the light faded, the moon long past its zenith, Talla and Col crawled into their bed. Col lifted his arm as Talla laid her head on his chest, smelling her unique scent through the smoke in her hair.

"Tell me our journey is over now," she whispered. "Tell me we'll stay here and raise our family."

"Yes, we'll stay here, but our journey, our learning, will never be done. We will still learn much from Albyn. People will come to visit with greater knowledge, but it will be many years before I'm ready for another adventure." He kissed the top of her head. "Sleep well, my love."

Chapter 31

Lorev watched as his little brother tottered across the roundhouse floor. His plump hand grasped at the support pole, and he gave Lorev his cheekiest grin.

"Vevev," he shouted, his best try at his brother's name yet. Glev was not quite two, and his big brother and their sister of six summers, Shilla, doted on him.

"What a clever boy," Talla said, coming into the house, baby Isla at her bared breast. "Are you showing off for Lorev?"

"Vevev," the toddler shouted, before making a dash to his brother's outstretched arms. He squealed as Lorev lifted him, throwing him into the air before catching him in strong hands.

Talla glanced at the apprentice tattoos around her son's eye. He'd waited until his twelfth summer before deciding on his path, but had worn the marks for three years now.

"Where's Shilla?" she asked.

"She took Albyn for a walk," Lorev said, "He promised her another story if she'd take him to the shore."

Shilla loved the old man. His sister, Geth, had died the previous winter, and Shilla was his constant companion. She would sit on his lap, and soaking up the tribe's lore, whenever Albyn had the energy to teach her. She had given a superb version of the creation story at the last solstice meeting. Lorev looked towards the door as Hessa entered. The girl had grown into a coltish young woman; a spirit messenger at sixteen summers. His gaze followed her across the room until his mother nudged him.

"Watching something, Lorev?" she asked, giggling at her adopted son, who reddened at once. Hessa turned and smiled at Lorev as she retrieved the herbs she needed and headed for the door.

"Tell her, Lorev," Talla whispered.

"Can't," he said, gazing at the floor, "She's a messenger, and has sixteen summers; I'm an apprentice and only fifteen." Talla ruffled his hair and pulled her shirt closed as Isla slept in the crook of her arm.

"Want me to talk to her?" she asked.

"NO!" he said, "I mean, no, I couldn't talk to her, anyway."

"You were such friends as children," Talla said.

"She's older now, we're not children any more."

"You're older, too, Lorev. There's only a summer between you," Talla told him. She despaired of the attraction between Lorev and the young messenger; they were both so shy, and neither had experienced a relationship.

A beaming six-year-old arrived, dragging Albyn through the door. "Shilla! Don't pull Messenger Albyn like that, he is old," Talla said.

"Leave the girl, Talla," the old man said, catching his breath. "She gives me my freedom, I must learn to keep up with her. Anyway, she's excited."

"Daddy's home," Shilla squealed, pressing Albyn's hand to the wear-polished support pole beside his bed. The girl jumped onto the bed beside her mentor, kissed his cheek, then ran out of the house.

"Daddy! Daddy!" she yelled, racing up the slope to meet him, leaping into his arms and squeaking as he hugged her.

"How's my big girl?" he chuckled, swinging her in a circle.

"Good, Daddy. Messenger Albyn told me a story about a big adventure, with spirits and everything in it. Was it you and mummy in the story?"

"If there was a fire mountain in the story, yes, it was us," he said, smiling.

"There was! There was!"

The shouting and hugging got too much for the glossy black raven perched on Col's shoulder, and it squawked as it flapped its way to the roundhouse roof.

"What are those birds, Daddy?" Shilla asked, pointing to the roof where Kark had perched.

"They're Magpies," he said, "But they don't belong. They are common across the water on the Great Island, but I've never seen them here."

"Come and see mummy and Isla," his daughter urged, "And Glev can walk now and everything," she chattered, dragging Col towards the house.

Col picked up Glev at the doorway, then found Talla and Isla. He embraced his mate as best he could, each carrying a child, but their lips sealed in a sincere greeting.

"I miss you when you go away," Talla said, resting her forehead on Col's.

"It was necessary. The wound was serious. I stayed an extra day to make sure the bad spirits didn't get into it."

A runner had come three days past, asking for a healer. A child in the next village had gashed an arm on flint, and their own messenger was away visiting.

"Greetings, Master Col," said Albyn, shuffling out of the shadow at the rear of the house. His arms were outstretched, halfway between a greeting and a means of avoiding the supports of the roundhouse.

"Greetings, Messenger Albyn," Col said, walking towards him and embracing him. Albyn had softened in his old age, showing his feelings and emotions more.

"Still filling my daughter's head with stories, old man?"

"She is a willing pupil, and she is my eyes. I am grateful to the spirits for her. Strangers are coming... visitors," Albyn said.

"Oh? Do the spirits tell you this?"

Albyn nodded. "I spend more and more time with the spirits and the ancestors these days, Col. One day soon, I'll join them."

"When you're ready, messenger. When you're ready," Col said.

* * *

Talla and Col had finished a meal of meat and bread and were sitting with tea when the commotion erupted.

"Col. Talla." said Hessa, running into the house, "We have visitors, protected-of-spirit. The two women are like reflections. I can't tell them apart."

Col smiled at his mate, Talla's eyes betraying a hope neither of them spoke. They abandoned their seats and rushed out of the house.

Two small women, clad in swan's feather cloaks, climbed the slope to the village, a tall man in their wake. The intricate tattoos around the left eye of each woman were visible. They drew closer, then a squeal emanated from them as they ran forward, flinging themselves at Col and Talla.

"Greetings Arva," Col laughed, squeezing the young woman.

"Change," Arva called, slipping from Col's grip and running to Talla.

"Greetings Atta," he smiled, hugging the other twin. He pushed her to arm's length, studying her beauty, her completed messenger tattoo, the designs showing mastery of all but fire. "You have high status now, Messenger," he smiled.

"We are messengers, and bonded too," Atta grinned. She turned as the tall young man behind them lowered his heavy load to the ground. "This is Arrat," she said.

"Your mate, or Arva's?" Col asked.

Atta hugged him again, her forehead reaching below his chin, snuggling into his chest. "We're twins, silly man, we share him."

Col looked at the tall, blushing man. His face was thinner than was common, and his skin darker. It was only when he spoke Col recognised the pronunciation and inflexions of the lands across the waters, far to the south.

"I am Arrat," he said, holding out his hands in welcome, "I am a farmer of the Guardians of the circle of Stanna."

"You are far from home, Arrat, and farther from the place of your birth," Col said.

Arrat smiled. "You and I have met before, Spirit Master." Col looked but didn't recognise his face. "It was you that saved my Clan, my village, with your mate and your friend. I was Arrat of the Boat Clan of the Locan tribe. The day you tended our wounded after the outlaw attack, I was the boy you instructed to bring firewood to Gordo's roundhouse so Chirra could heat water."

Col smiled, remembering the exhausted child who'd fallen asleep on the floor by the woodpile when the chaos ended that day. "Let us do proper introductions," Col said, "Only the twins and Talla and I know each other."

Col went first, reciting his status, followed by Talla. Albyn had hobbled to the doorway, and Shilla ran to retrieve him, dragging him to the group. He focussed on where he guessed most of the people were standing and gave his own achievements. Hessa and Lorev followed. Shilla stood tall, not wanting them to ignore her. "I am Shilla of the Guardians of the Stones of Classac," she said, "Daughter of the spirit masters, and pupil of Messenger Albyn. One day I will be a healer." The twins giggled at the tiny girl, then Arva stepped forward and whispered in her ear.

"Oh," Shilla said, "As I'm the biggest, this is my brother Glev, he can walk." She pointed to the baby. "And this is my sister Isla. She mostly sleeps and drinks mummy's milk."

Atta pulled Arrat forward, and he gave his status again, followed by the twins who gave their names, then listed their achievements with one voice.

"Come in!" Col said, stopping the chatter that had broken out, "Hessa, Lorev, prepare food for our guests." They crowded into the roundhouse, the twins gravitating towards Albyn, taking an arm each and leading him to the fire.

"Thank you, Messenger Arva, Messenger Atta," he said, bowing to each one. It didn't surprise Col that the old man could tell the young women apart, despite his blindness.

Hessa and Lorev served the food, sitting with the youngsters to help feed them. Talla watched the two shy teens dancing around each other, an occasional furtive glance, a smile, hands pulled away when they touched. If the spirits saw what she saw between them, one day they'd overcome their awkwardness.

"How are your parents?" Col asked the twins.

"They work too hard, but they love their work," Arva said. "They send their greetings to you both.

"You set out to visit us, then?" Talla asked.

"Of course," Atta said, "We never forgot you. We've come for the summer solstice celebrations with you."

"It's a special summer this time, too," said Hessa, wiping soup from Glev's grinning face.

"Yes, the low of the moon," Col added. "It is the first I remember, though there must have been one when I was a child."

"Eighteen years, seven moons and twenty-two days," said Albyn, from his perch between the twins. "That is the moon's cycle. You had just six summers when the last one happened."

They sat long into the evening, Hessa and Lorev getting the small ones to their beds as they fell asleep. Arrat told the story of a young messenger who'd come through their village, heading for the islands of the inland sea. He was well into his tale, and the twins' faces were split with wide grins before Col and Talla realised the story was about Kaden. Their friend had trained his replacement, then left to find Erra, the girl he'd fallen in love with years ago. His talk of the people who'd become legendary heroes in Locan tribe lore prompted Arrat to take his own journey north. He'd come, at last, to the circle of Stanna where he met the twins.

"They played games with me," he sighed, a smile pulling at his lips. "They made me guess who I was talking to, they never said their names. I asked one to be my mate; I think it was Atta."

The smiling girl nodded. "He'd slept with both of us, but I don't think he knew it."

Arrat shook his head. "I thought I had to make a choice, bond with one of them; then they sat me down and explained being identical twins. I took a few days to decide to take two mates and not go home."

Col grinned. "You're a brave man, Arrat. Do you ever regret it?"

The tall man smiled at Col, his arm slipping around Atta's waist. He reached to take Arva's hand. "Atta's fine," he chuckled, "Arva can be a handful."

"Ooh! I'll get you later," Arva squealed.

"I look forward to it," he said.

They opened the nearest of the guest houses for the twins and Arrat to occupy. Lorev and Hessa opted to join them, being of a similar age.

* * *

Four days before the summer solstice there was another commotion as a ship, much larger than any seen around the islands, appeared in the bay. The blue sail clattered to the deck as the boat drew up to the shore; it's bow stopped by the soft shingle of the beach.

They had called Col, and he ran to the beach just as the occupants jumped into the shallows and waded ashore. Col looked twice as he saw the two figures in the distance; one black, one white. Three children, somewhere between the two, crowded at the bow, calling and waving.

"By the spirits. It's you," Col gasped. "Zoola. Gren. Oh, it's good to see you."

"We said we'd come," Gren said, hugging his old friend. Zoola squeezed between them, wrapping herself around Col.

"Hello," she said.

"You both look so well," Col said, extricating himself from the melee, "And these three, are they yours?" he asked, pointing to the children.

"They are," Zoola said, lifting the smallest from the bow of the boat. "This is Orla, our youngest, then Jeeha and Gart."

"This is our son, Lorev," Col said as the young man appeared at the shore. "Run and fetch Arrat and a crew of men to haul the boat," he said, "while I take our guests to the village."

Lorev ran off as Gren hauled two bundles from the ship. "Your son?" he asked as Col took one of the heavy packs.

"Adopted," Col said, "No doubt you'll get the story from us around the hearth soon enough."

The small group moved towards the village, chatting until a chorus of squeals interrupted them. "Zoola. Gren," Talla shouted. She ran towards them, followed by the twins, who'd recognised them as soon as they saw them. They made their way towards the big roundhouse, gathering outside in the sun where there was room for everyone. They made introductions; both Zoola and Gren were now spirit masters and their eldest boy, Gart, wore the tattoos of an apprentice. A white owl skimmed past the group, settling on the village boundary post, peering down at the ancient bull's skull.

"She's mine," said Gren. "Her name is Skee."

They invited Albyn to the centre of their gathering to welcome the visitors, Shilla at his side, gripping his hand.

"We welcome you, Gren, Zoola and your family," the old man said. "We have heard about your exploits through the tales of your journey with Col and Talla. They are now the leaders and spirit masters of our Clan. We will make a roundhouse ready for you."

"Thank you, Messenger Albyn," Gren said, taking the old man's outstretched hands. "We have heard tales of you from our friends too." He passed a hand to Shilla, still at Albyn's side. The scarred skin covering the elderly messenger's eyes told its own story.

Talla looked to Col, giving a smile and a wink. "It will be easier to have the children together; they should get to know each other. Lorev, Hessa, can you take on that task?"

The two teens looked at each other. Hessa smiled. "Yes, Master Talla," she said, using the title for the benefit of the company, "I'd be glad to." She nudged Lorev.

"Hmm? Oh, yes, that's fine."

They gathered the children and shepherded them away. Hessa had left baby Isla and Grev with Talla, but Grev wailed, "Vevev, Vevev," until his big brother relented, and took him too.

They settled Grev and Orla in one bed, and Shilla and Jeeha in another. The two little girls chattered, soon overcoming their language differences. Gart, with seven summers, got the third bed.

"We'll... um... have to share this one then," Hessa said, dropping sleeping furs onto the final sleeping platform.

"I can sleep on the floor... or with Gart. You... you're a messenger, you'll want your own bed," Lorev stuttered.

"Oh," Hessa said, looking down.

"Um, it's alright. I mean... did you want to... um, share?"

"Not if you don't want to," she said, busying herself with the little ones. Lorev watched her lifting Glev, wiping mud from his face and then fussing with Orla's hair. Hessa was thin, as tall as himself, and a competent healer. Her face was half-covered by her long dark tresses. She struggled with Orla's hair, the tiny girl protesting, as Hessa attempted a plait. Her left hand was a hindrance, with only the thumb and two fingers remaining after a childhood accident.

"Let me," Lorev said, taking the fine dark hair in his hands; twisting and crossing the strands.

"You can plait hair?" Hessa asked.

"Shilla," he explained. "She'll let me do it, even when she won't let mother." They got the children organised, then took them to play in the sunshine.

* * *

"Is there a plan for the solstice?" Zoola asked as they sat around the hearth later that night. Her animal spirit, a sparrow, perched on her shoulder.

"There was, but now we're back together again, we should do something special," Talla said.

"We need to journey for the tribes," Col said, "let them know the ancestors' message for the season."

"We can each become our elements in the circle ceremony," Gren added, "Then we should consult our walking spirits later."

"That's a good plan," Col said. "We need to involve the younger ones too. Arva and Atta can lead the blessing of the circle with Hessa and Lorev, then Gart can go around with the water and burning herbs."

"Albyn," Talla said, drawing the old man into the talk, "Will you address the tribes from the rock?"

"If I may have my eyes," the messenger chuckled, referring to Shilla.

"It is not part of the ceremony," Col said, "It will not matter if she is not an apprentice."

Albyn smiled, staring at the fire, though Col knew he could see nothing.

"I think she will apprentice in her own time," he said, "She knows most of the legends; I only wish I could see enough to teach her plant lore."

"We appreciate your teaching of the old tales, Albyn," Col said, "She will be a skilled storyteller one day."

* * *

Gren stirred in his sleep as he felt his bed-mate move. Going to relieve herself, he thought, turning and drifting back to sleep. He woke again as light streamed in through the smoke hole of the roundhouse. A warm arm slipped around him, cuddling into his back.

"Morning," he mumbled. A cheek touched his, then lips kissed the skin.

"Good morning," a soft voice said. Gren opened his eyes, seeing the white hair, and turned.

"Talla?" he said. "You're..."

Talla nodded to the next bed, where a mass of tight black curls nestled on Col's chest.

"We didn't talk about this," Gren said.

"Did we need to?" Talla asked, pulling his arm back around her, "We're so close, we're interchangeable now."

"Do you want to..?" Gren said.

"If you want. A cuddle if not," she said. It was as if she had two mates, and Zoola did too. Getting their friends back, completing the circle again, it felt right. "We both love you. We both love Col. We're not changing mates, just sharing sometimes," Talla explained. She felt Gren's body relax, then a warm hand slid down her belly.

* * *

Orla ran into the roundhouse, spotting her mother's black curls and flinging herself on the bed. "Mama!" she shouted, pulling at Zoola's hand. She saw Col next to her in the bed, then looked over, seeing her father with Talla, then shrugged and cuddled between the two nearest adults.

Hessa ran in, glancing around for her small charge. She noticed the pairings and smiled. The tribes accepted sharing, though the only ones she knew who did, were the twins, who shared Arrat.

"Sorry, Zoola," she said, "I couldn't catch her."

Zoola smiled. "She always comes for a cuddle in the mornings, I've only just weaned her. Don't worry about it."

"Shall I take her, give you peace for a while?" Hessa asked.

"No, it's fine, we must dress. Big ceremony tonight."

Lorev wandered in, spotting his mother draped over Gren, and blushed. "Oh, I'll... um, just get Grev and Shilla up," he said, turning.

"Lorev," Talla called, sitting up and patting the bed. Lorev walked over, avoiding his mother's gaze.

"Sit," she said. Lorev perched on the edge of the platform. "This is how it is Lorev. This is how close we are," she explained. "Nothing is changing, just going back to what we've always had."

"You've done this before?" he managed, looking into Talla's eyes.

"Yes. Now, get your sister and brother up and let's get them fed," Talla said, finding acceptance in her son's eyes at last.

Chapter 32

Four fires burned around the great circle of stones at Classac as the sun dipped in the north-west. It fell to Lorev, in the north, to open the ceremony. He trembled as he raised his arms wide and high, hands open, and called to the powers.

"Ancestors of the north, element of earth, we call to you to come and bless this circle. We ask you to stand with us here and support our ceremony."

Gart stepped off around the circle, sun-wise, sprinkling water from a small bowl.

"Ancestors of the east, element of air, we call to you to come and bless this circle," Atta called as Gart passed her. Arva called to the south, then Hessa to the west as the water blessed the great stones.

Gart lit a bowl of dry herbs and, once they were smouldering, circled once more with a feather fan, wafting the smoke as he went.

"Ancestors of the north, element of earth, cleanse this circle of evil spirits," Lorev called. Again the plea for cleansing went around the circle.

Once Gart had completed his circuit, the four protected-of-spirit stepped to the centre. They circled once, sun-wise, then returned to their places. The four spirit masters approached them, taking the hands of their counterpart before the younger ceremonialists left.

Gren wore his suit of blue ribbons, his face dyed with woad. Col wore red ochre, black rings around his eyes. They faced outwards, arms outstretched, as they addressed the spirits.

Their prayers were for the assembled tribes, in the language of the masters; not for the ears of villagers. They turned as one, facing inwards to address the higher powers through their walking spirits, then moved to the centre, clasping hands, linking their minds.

They sat, as Albyn joined them, led in by the Hessa. The four younger ones returned with drums, taking stations around the circle again as the beat began. Slow at first, then faster, until the pounding rhythm carried them away.

* * *

Col shivered as his eyes opened in the alternate reality of the grey landscape. They stood, four abreast; the powers of the elements incarnate. Albyn was at their backs, standing tall, eyes bright in this world; the four drummers ranged behind him. Col gasped as he saw, for a moment, a reflection shimmering like a still lake. Four faces... then they were gone.

They approached the river, and Albyn stepped up beside Col as they addressed the ancestors. Each found a spirit, and they communicated with them before turning from the water. They formed a ring around Albyn, each imparting the wisdom of the ancestors to him as he nodded.

"Back!" called Col, as the drumbeat returned them to a world of light and life.

* * *

Col sat, eyes closed, for a little longer. He heard his daughter, Shilla, chattering as she collected Albyn from the edge of the circle, leading him off to the rocky outcrop to the south.

"What's wrong?" Talla asked, sitting beside him and taking his hand.

"Maybe it's nothing," he said, "For a moment, I saw a reflection of us, then it was gone."

Talla patted his hand as she stood. "Come and watch the moon bless the spirit of the earth," she smiled, pulling him to his feet.

They watched with wonder as the silver disc rose at the feet of the Earth Maiden, a range of hills that resembled a sleeping woman on the skyline. It travelled up her body, blessing her with its pale light, before rolling behind a ridge. The older tribespeople, those that had seen the spectacle before, turned their attention to the south where a huge rock stood proud of the surrounding land.

People gasped as the moon positioned itself above the rock, appearing to sit on its top. The silhouette of a man stepped out, a tiny figure at his side, clasping his hand. As the moon framed the old messenger, he raised his arms. Despite his age, his voice carried well on the still night air.

"People of the assembled tribes. It is the solstice, the full moon, and the lowest point of the moon's cycle. This is an auspicious night. The ancestors smile on our tribes. Food is abundant, crops and animals thrive. We are blessed!" Albyn wobbled, and a small hand reached up, taking one of his. "Thank you, Shilla," he whispered, then continued. "The spirits and the ancestors smile upon us. The tribes continue to honour them and live according to our given lore. We shall prosper."

A cheer came from the crowd as he told them what they wanted to hear. Albyn squeezed Shilla's hand, then raised his arms again. They quietened at once.

"We, the Protected-of-Spirit, will continue to expand our teachings and our ceremonies to appease the ancestors. We will continue to travel, to share knowledge between villages, between tribes." Albyn drew himself up to his full height, seeming to grow bigger in the shimmer of the yellowing disc. "We are blessed!" He cried to the shouts and cheers of the people. "Take me down, Shilla," he said, gasping for breath, "I need to rest."

Shilla led him from the high rock, taking him to the village. Young as she was, she knew her mentor had given everything in his one last performance. He would not attend the moon's blessing of the earth maiden again. Death was a fact of life in their society. None feared it. It was going home to the family that loves you. She knew that soon, her companion must leave for the river, never to return. It made her sad and happy at the same time. Shilla settled Albyn in his bed, pulling the warm furs up to his chin. She climbed onto the platform beside him, snuggling into him.

"Go," he whispered, "I'll be fine. There is more to see at the circle."

Shilla shook her head. "I'm tired too," she said. "Go to sleep, Messenger."

* * *

Gren pulled hot stones from the fire by the great circle as the tribes-people left for the feast. He dropped the rocks into a pot of water, steeping dried mushrooms in the hot liquid.

"Do we need a drummer?" Zoola asked.

"No, we'll be fine without one. We have no one at that level to drum for us," Col said.

Talla took the bowl of infusion Gren poured and walked to the circle. The others followed. They passed the bitter drink around, each taking a sip until they finished it. They selected their directions and lay down, feet to the centre, heads to the circle. Zoola felt a pull at her navel as if something was dragging her along by her umbilical cord. She shook her head as the world she knew, swam and dissolved before her eyes.

* * *

Zoola looked around, blinking in the bright sunlight, shading her eyes to take in the blue sky. A figure appeared, skin black as her own, tight curls cropped short, a curved bone ornament pierced through her nose in the custom of her birth tribe.

"Mother?"

"Hello, Daughter," the spirit said. She looked younger, not the diseased, skeletal woman she'd been at her death. Zoola stepped forward, hugging her mother.

* * *

Gren sat waiting, the sun warm on his back. He expected his walking spirit to appear at any moment.

"Son?" said a voice behind him. He turned, finding the warrior standing in his leather armour.

"Father? Why are you here?" he said.

"Are you not pleased to see me?" he asked.

Gren grinned, running to him. "Of course!" he said, attempting to fit his arms around the giant.

* * *

Talla watched as the beautiful woman emerged from the shade of a tree, her dark hair shining in the sun.

"My Daughter," she said, taking Talla's hand. "Come, walk with me and tell me about your life."

* * *

Col felt the being sitting on the soft grass beside him. He turned his head, finding not the walking spirit, but his father.

"Hello, Son," the smiling spirit said. "It is good to see you. I never imagined you would become such an important man in our clan."

"I do not do it alone," Col smiled. "There is my mate, and now my friends too. Each one of us is necessary for our power to endure."

"Is that so?" the spirit asked. "You need all four?"

"Yes, that is why we are so close, they are like the family I lost, like you and mother."

The spirit of his father took his hand. "Come, I'll take you where there is food and drink aplenty," he smiled.

Col marvelled at the feast spread before them. Roasted meats, vegetables, fruits and nuts. Cheese and barley bread, beer and clear water. He sat with his father, filling a platter, talking of his childhood, his mother.

He looked up, seeing Talla with her mother. Zoola arrived, joining the feast, a black woman holding her hand. He spotted Gren too, the giant that was his father at his side. He waved, acknowledging them, yet content to stay with his own kin. Time passed, unnoticed.

* * *

"Where are they?" Lorev asked, finding the roundhouse contained only a sleeping Albyn; Shilla curled up beside him.

"Perhaps they were up early," Hessa said, setting a struggling Orla on the floor.

"Mama!" she called, running from bed to bed.

"They haven't slept in the beds," Lorev said, inspecting the folded furs, just the way his mother left them the previous day.

"Can you watch them?" Hessa said, pointing to the children. "Take them to Bella, she had Isla for the night."

"Where are you going?" Lorev asked.

"To the stones."

* * *

Hessa gasped as she reached the edge of the circle. Sprawled on the damp grass were the forms of the four spirit masters. She ran to each, checking for a pulse, feeling the chest of each rise and fall. She ran back down the hill, searching for Arva and Atta, dragging them to the big roundhouse along with Arrat, their mate. Bella had kept the five youngest, though Gart insisted on being with the protected-of-spirit.

"What do we do?" Arva asked. "They're alive, but they won't wake."

"What has happened?" Albyn asked, feeling his way to the hearth.

"Col and Talla, Gren and Zoola, didn't come home last night," Hessa said. "I found them unconscious at the stones. We can't wake them."

"Was there a tea prepared? A bowl?" the old man asked.

Hessa passed him the pot they'd found, pressing his fingers to the surface until he grasped it. Albyn fumbled with the vessel, lifting it to his nose and sniffing. He nodded, then dipped a finger into the dregs of the infusion. His face wrinkled as he sucked the bitter liquid from it.

"They were performing a master's ceremony," he said, holding out the vessel for Hessa to take. "Dispose of the contents of the pot. Do not taste or drink it. Do you hear me?"

"Yes, Messenger, but what is it? You are a messenger like me, yet I know nothing of this," Hessa said.

"Long ago, in my youth, I trained as a master. I never finished my study, but I know things that, perhaps, I shouldn't. I cannot tell you more, except that they should have returned by now. You must bring them to this house and watch them. Something is wrong."

Lorev and Arrat constructed a litter out of poles, carrying the unconscious masters from the hill one by one. They made them comfortable on the beds, where Albyn sat with each, holding his palm on their foreheads for a few moments.

"They are far away," he said. "We must hope they can return. Their bodies need food and water to survive."

"Can we at least give them water?" Arva said, holding Col's hand in her own.

"Try," Albyn replied.

Arva took a small cup of water, supporting Col's head and putting it to his mouth, tipping the liquid between his parted lips. The water trickled into his mouth, filling it, then ran out over his chin. He didn't swallow.

"What do we do?" she asked.

"Wait," Albyn said.

* * *

Col stared at his father. "The leg is fine," he said, in answer to the question. His father rubbed the thigh of Col's right leg.

"You were lucky to survive," he said. "If the bone had pierced the skin, you could have died from bad spirits."

Col looked into the spirit's eyes. Something was wrong.

"Perhaps we shouldn't have tried to pick blueberries that day," he said.

"No," his father's spirit said, "But we were hungry."

Col looked towards Talla. She was chatting and laughing with her mother's spirit.

"Talla, can I speak with you for a moment?"

Talla looked annoyed at the interruption but left her mother. "What is it, Col?"

"Are you certain that is your mother's spirit?" he asked.

"Yes, she is the mother I lost at birth," she said, "Why do you ask?"

Col glanced at his father's spirit, who was beckoning for him to return. "Because something is wrong. Things he should know, he's getting wrong. He asked how my leg was but got the wrong leg. I said we'd been picking blueberries, and he said nothing."

"But you were collecting gulls' eggs, weren't you?" Talla said.

"Yes, and he said we were hungry. I was never hungry as a child. Our clan was prosperous."

"What do we do?" Talla asked as her mother's spirit tugged at her sleeve.

"Ask something, look for gaps in her knowledge," he said.

Talla returned to her mother's spirit. "Stay with me," the ghost said, "You don't need your mate now, you have your mother back."

"Perhaps not," Talla smiled. "It is nice to be with you. I cried when my father sold me as a slave at just five summers."

"He was wrong, Talla. I didn't get sick because of you," she said.

"What was it that took you from us?" Talla asked.

"An illness, bad spirits," she said. *"It wasn't your fault."*

Talla turned, walking back towards Col.

"Stay," her mother's spirit said, catching her sleeve. *"Don't you want to be with me? Don't you love me?"*

"I love my mother with all my heart," she said, reaching Col's side. *"You're right,"* she whispered to him. *"Something is not right. Father sold me at seven summers, and my mother bled to death after my birth."*

"We must warn the others," Col said. They walked towards Gren, who was standing laughing with his bear of a father. Col patted Gren's back. *"How are you getting on with your father?"* he asked.

"I am pleased to see him and talk like this. I'd love to stay here," Gren said.

"How old was Gren when you crossed the river of death?" Col asked the warrior.

"He was young... what, two summers? He doesn't remember me at all in life."

"Father?" Gren said, *"You died before I was born. How could you not know that?"*

"Because he's not your father, Gren," Col said, *"Just as this is not Talla's mother, nor this, my father's spirit. They have fooled us, enchanted us."*

Gren looked at the big man. "What colour were my mother's eyes?" he asked.

"Why, they were brown."

"So you never told her she had the prettiest green eyes you'd ever seen?" he said.

"These friends of yours, they are jealous of you, they don't wish you to return to your father's love," the spirit said. *"Come away from them, they lie to you. Come and stay with me."*

"You are not my father," Gren said, turning towards Col and Talla. *"We need to talk to Zoola."*

They found her sitting under a tree; an older, thinner version of herself knelt beside her, stroking her thick hair.

"Zoola, they have fooled us, these are not our ancestors, they are impostors," Gren said.

"No! It's my mother. I am of her blood." Zoola said, standing to face her mate.

"We each thought the same," Gren explained, "But there is history they get wrong. This is not your mother."

"Just because they have fooled you, you think they have fooled me too? This is my mother, my kin. Leave us alone, you are lying Gren. I don't want a mate that lies."

"Leave him," said the spirit. "Stay with me forever."

"We have children, Zoola. Gart, Jeeha and Orla. What will become of them if you stay here?" Gren said.

"The Clan will care for them. I want to be here now."

Col stepped forward. "If you don't return, we cannot either," he said, turning to the image of his father. "This spirit got that fact out of me."

"You will all be trapped here in an endless limbo," the spirit said, his heartless smile looking nothing like Col's father. Col thought fast and pulled the flint knife from his belt. Approaching the spirit of Zoola's mother, Col drew the razor-sharp blade across her throat. There should have been blood. Like the wounded, the ones screaming in pain at the end of their lives, when blood would gush from the severed tubes.

Instead, the knife sliced into cold, dead flesh; as if cutting into a butchered carcass. The body fell to the ground.

"Col. No!" Zoola said, running at him. "You've killed her... my beautiful mother... you evil pig," she screamed, tearing the blade from Col's hand and turning it on him.

"Look," Col said, holding his hands out in defence. "Look at the body."

"You've killed her, you never wanted me to be happy. You're jealous of my happiness."

"Look at her!" Col shouted. Zoola glanced down, then back to Col. Then the sight registered in her mind. The body on the ground was not her mother. She dropped the knife, falling to her knees and pulling the prone figure towards her. The face was male, the black was nothing but soot, streaked over white skin.

"What's happening?" she sobbed, clasping her hands to her eyes, trying to block out the sight, yet trying to make sense of what she saw. Gren knelt beside her, gathering her in his arms.

"They have fooled us, Zoola. We saw what we wanted to, but we were too clever. This was the last chance for the old spirits to take back power, and they have failed."

"It was her, Gren. I so wanted it to be her. I miss her so much. There were things I wanted to say to her," Zoola sobbed.

"Your mother is not here, Zoola. Think. She is with the ancestors, across the death river, not with the walking spirits."

Zoola hugged him, then looked at Talla and Col. "I'm sorry," she said, "They wanted us to stay, didn't they?"

"Yes," said Col, "Without our spirits, our bodies would have died, then we could not have returned... ever."

"Let's go home," Talla said. "Back."

Chapter 33

Arva gasped as Col's eyes snapped open, his body drawing a deep breath as he tried to focus.

"Col!" she said, leaning over him and waving a hand above his face. She smiled when his eyes followed the movement. The other youngsters ran over from the fire where they'd been whispering. Lorev ran to Talla, while Atta checked Gren.

"They're awake," Lorev said, hugging his mother.

Hessa sat Zoola up, holding her close as the dark woman sobbed in her arms. "What is it, Zoola?" she asked.

"I almost killed us all," she said shuddering.

Gren stood, walking over to his mate, taking her from Hessa and holding her close. "We're back now, we're safe," he said, running his hand up and down her back.

* * *

"Are we alone?" Albyn asked when the younger ones had gone to bed.

"Just us four and you, Albyn," Col said.

"I know what you were doing," Albyn said. "In my youth, I trained as a spirit master, I never completed it, but I have used spirit mushrooms. That told me where you had gone. I guessed something was wrong."

"It was the old spirits of the elements," Talla said. "They took the form of our ancestors, trying to isolate us and get us to stay with them. We had to make up the story for the younger ones, they cannot know of the power of the mushrooms until we have trained them."

"That is wise, the mushrooms can be dangerous," Albyn said. "Are you done with the spirits of the directions now?"

"I hope so, but we will check with our..." he stopped, looking towards Albyn.

"With your walking spirits, I know," he said. "Next time, I'll drum for you. Hold a presence here for your return. I am old now, but I may be of use."

"Thank you," said Gren. "We'll appreciate it."

* * *

"How long will you stay with us?" Talla asked Zoola the next day.

She grinned. "How long will you have us?"

"Forever!"

"All right," Zoola said.

"You'll stay?"

"We belong together. We will teach here and raise our children together." Zoola looked uncertain for a moment. "Talla, why was it so easy for the spirits to fool me?" she asked.

"We'll find out tonight, Zoola," Talla said.

* * *

The roundhouse was quiet, the young ones banished to their own houses while the spirit masters prepared the mushroom tea. They sat in a circle at the hearth, the cup passing from one to another. Albyn sat back, a frame drum in his lap.

"When you're ready, Messenger Albyn," Col said, lying on the straw of the floor. The drumbeat started becoming faster, louder, as the infusion worked its magic.

* * *

"Son of the fire! Daughter of the winds!" came the voices they recognised. "Son of the waters! Daughter of the earth!" they called.

The friends turned, finding the couple they trusted as their walking spirits. "Galvac, Dirva, greetings," Col said, holding out his hands. "Where are your Walking Spirits, Gren, Zoola?"

Gren smiled, realising what had happened. "These are our walking spirits," he grinned, "The four of us have just two mentors."

"This is true, Son of the waters," Galvac said. "It is unusual, perhaps it has never happened, but you are special. We knew of your destiny at Classac. Generations ago, when these stones were erected, Dirva and I were leaders and spirit masters here. We will guide your feet along the path if you allow it."

"We will be honoured, Master Galvac, Master Dirva," Gren said.

"I wish to ask a question, Masters," Zoola said.

Dirva smiled. "Then ask, Daughter of the Earth."

"When the old spirits tried to fool us, why was I more gullible that my friends, my mate?"

Galvac looked at Dirva, and she nodded. "You have not completed your tasks, daughter," he said.

"Not completed them? What did I not do, Master?"

Galvac rubbed the side of his finger along his lips. "Each of you faced the challenge of water, though it was for Gren. Each of you witnessed the challenge of fire, though it was for Col. Two of you were present at the challenge of air, though they sent it to try Talla. You, Daughter Zoola, have yet to face the challenge of the earth."

"You weren't with Col and Talla when they faced earth's challenge," Gren said, *"But neither was I."*

"Earth is not your element, Son of the waters," Galvac said. *"It is the element of your mate. She must endure a trial by earth."*

"What must I do?" Zoola asked.

"Only you can know that. It will be the thing you fear the most, your worst nightmare brought to life, but it will lay to rest the old spirits of the elements forever. Go now, and make preparations," Dirva said as their images faded.

"Back!" called Talla.

* * *

Albyn removed the evidence of the mushrooms from the fireside, then called Arva and Atta to help put the masters into their beds.

"Perhaps we shouldn't be here, Messenger Albyn," Arva said.

"You expect me to put them to bed myself? An old blind man?" He smiled then. The twins saw right through his terse pretence.

"We meant the ceremony," Atta said.

"Oh, the ceremony you two know nothing about?" Albyn asked.

"Yes, that one," Arva giggled.

"I am old, not a fool," Albyn said, struggling to contain his mirth. "Get Col into bed and then go, before you find out something you shouldn't."

The twins dragged Col to his bed, laying him beside his mate, then returned to the fire. Arva picked up a pouch from the hearth. "Shall I put the spirit mushrooms away, Messenger?" she asked, grinning at her sister.

"Give me that!" Albyn said, as Arva pressed the pouch into his hand. "Taking advantage of an old man who can't see..." he muttered, knowing they could still hear him.

"Goodnight, Messenger," the twins chorused.

"Goodnight girls," he replied, shuffling towards his bed.

* * *

Zoola opened her eyes... nothing. She felt around, her fingers digging into the damp, soft earth. She lifted a hand to her face, but it struck a solid surface, not a hand's-breadth from her nose. Panic rose from her belly to her chest, churning her stomach. Where was she?

She'd always been afraid of dark spaces, of being trapped. She'd got into one of her clan's tombs as a small child and had been there all night. Though she'd howled and screamed, the tomb was a long walk from their village. At daybreak, her mother had found her; cold and whimpering in the corner of the damp stone cyst.

Shaking fingers explored the surface above her; close-spaced boughs of trees. She pushed against them, but they refused to move. She hammered on the wood with her fists, shouting for attention. No one came. She was sweating now, yet shivering. Who could have done this to her? She heard movement above, voices, feet walking by.

"Help! Help! I'm trapped. Help!" she yelled. No one answered. Then there was a drumbeat... a voice.

"Oh great ancestors, spirits who love us, come and take back this member of your family. This is the body of Zoola, spirit master of the Guardians of the Stones of Classac, Plant Master, Lore Master, Fire Keeper and Healer."

"No, No, I'm not dead. I'm here," Zoola shouted. There was no response.

"We ask you to take her home to her ancestors. You who love her, carry her spirit across the river to the land of the dead." It was Col, calling to the ancestors. There was wailing now, the sad lament for the dead, sung by female voices.

"I'm not dead!" Zoola screamed. The drumbeat continued, the women's voices dirge-like, mourning her passing. "I love you all, Col. Gren and Talla and you. My children, and yours. I love Arva and Atta. How did I die? We went on a journey, to the walking spirits, to ask for their advice. Did the spirit mushrooms kill me? They said I had to face my worst fear to complete my challenge, I. …"

It hit her then—her worst fear. Shut away in the dark, dead and forgotten to those around her. Her children left with no mother. Tears welled in her eyes, not for herself but for those that remained. The drum continued, and, with her eyes closed, she felt herself being pulled to the river of the dead.

* * *

The river was low, only a trickle amongst the slick, black rocks. Zoola stood shivering on the bank, staring across the water. A shape formed on the far side, flowing and changing, before coalescing into her mother's image.

"Mother? Is it you?" Zoola said.

"Yes, my daughter, it's me."

"How did you die mother?" she asked, remembering the trickster that had fooled her.

"I died of the evil that consumes the breath, Zoola, but it was not your fault. You were not to blame," she said. "Don't you remember?"

"Yes, I remember now," she said. Zoola stepped into the water, paddling through the ankle-deep stream towards the far side.

"No!" her mother shouted, "Go back. If you cross, you will be trapped here forever, you will be dead."

"I am dead, mother," Zoola said, wading to the centre of the river. "My friends have called the ancestors for me. I lie in the ground, covered and alone. Though I hear them, though I shout to them, no one answers me."

"Zoola, no. You were to have a long life, with your mate and children. Go back."

Zoola stepped out of the flowing waters and reached a hand for her mother. The woman pulled back her arm.

"Do not touch me, Zoola. I am dead. Touch me, and it will anchor you here."

"I am here already," she said, wrapping her arms around the spirit of her mother, "and now I can stay with you forever."

* * *

Col turned to Gren, tears running down both their faces. Col kept the beat as Gren beckoned to the twins and Talla.

"It's almost dawn," he said, "I'm going to the lower world, she's been quiet too long."

Gren closed his eyes and flowed into the drumbeat. He felt himself sinking, pulled below to a different reality.

* * *

Gren snapped his eyes open, spotting Zoola on the other side of the river, clasped to her mother. "Zoola!" he called. "Zoola, talk to me."

"I tried to call to you, Gren," she said, weeping. "You could not hear me. I am dead to you, to my friends, to my children. I have touched a spirit, I am bound here now."

"No, Zoola, we had to have you face your darkest fear, your fear of the earth itself, of its confines, its darkness. You are not dead, you must return now," Gren said.

"No, Gren. It is too late. Tell my children stories of me. Tell them I love them, and will see them again someday."

"Zoola, come back. Please."

"No, I am sorry to leave you all, but it's done now. Goodbye, my mate, my lover."

Gren yelled in frustration. It had to be believable, it had to seem real for it to work. Now Zoola was committed to remaining in the land of the dead. He turned on his heel. "Back!" he shouted.

* * *

Gren opened his eyes and turned to Col. "She has accepted her death," he said incredulously. "She is with her mother and refuses to return. Can I not fetch her?"

"No," Col said. "Zoola is the only one of us never to cross the death river and return. She has to do it herself. She has to recognise that power in her."

"So how can we persuade her to return?" Gren asked.

"Do you trust me?" Col asked.

"Yes."

"Then fetch Orla."

Gren looked into Col's eyes and saw the truth. They had to use any means to get his mate back. He ran off towards the roundhouse.

Gren sat with a grumbling Orla on his lap as he tuned into the drum once more. He felt the pull on the tiny child in his arms as she started to cry.

* * *

"Zoola," he called, peering through the gloom to the far bank. It was empty. "Zoola, come to me," he commanded. He watched the darkness swirl and form as Zoola, and her mother appeared.

"I cannot come to you Gren, I am dead," Zoola said.

"You are not dead, you are a half-spirit. Cross to me."

Orla wailed at the sound of her mother's voice, at the shouting, at the dark, grey land. "Mama, Mama," she yelled, reaching her arms out across the water.

"Orla? Why have you brought my daughter to this place, Gren?" Zoola said, "She is of the living."

"As am I," Gren said, "As are you."

"Mama, Mama. Come here, I want you," Orla screamed.

"Orla, my baby. Mama can't come to you any more," Zoola explained.

"You can cross the river, Zoola, like Col and Talla and me. You're half-spirit. Come back to your family."

"It is not possible now. I am dead," she said. Gren clenched his jaw and clasped his daughter as he stepped into the water.

"No," Zoola screamed, "Gren, no, you can't bring her to me."

Gren stopped. "Then come to her," he said.

"If possible, go," Zoola's mother said, pushing her towards the water's edge. "I will always be here, waiting. Go."

Zoola stepped into the water, deeper now, swirling around her as she fought her way across towards her mate. At the half-way mark, it was up to her knees, the currents tugging and tearing at her faltering feet. Her foot hit a rock, slippery beneath the surface, and she fell, the river's waters covering her face for a moment.

She surfaced, coughing. "I can't do it."

"Get up," Gren called, clutching Orla, "You are past the middle."

Zoola struggled to her feet, pushing herself through the fast-flowing stream, reaching for the bank as she waded from the rising black torrent. Gren walked to her, pressing Orla into her arms. She hugged the child, planting kiss after kiss on her face, before passing her back to her father.

"*Back,*" *Gren called, as the dark, lower world, faded.*

* * *

As soon as Gren's eyes opened, he thrust the whimpering Orla into Talla's arms and ran to the makeshift grave. He pulled at the thick hides, rolling the heavy stones from the top and throwing aside the branches. He'd removed less than half when he reached into the shallow pit and pulled Zoola's quivering body out.

"I'm so sorry!" he said, holding her, as his tears mingled with hers. "I needed you to face your fears, but I never dreamed that you'd want to die."

Zoola calmed herself, her arms wrapped around Gren's shoulders. "It is over," she said. "I am alive, and I should have trusted you when you told me I could return. I have faced it now. Back in the lands of the Vessa, when I worked in my cave, I thought I'd beaten my fears, but I was never in darkness, never ignored, never left for dead. That was the challenge, to know that I am loved and that one day I will die; but also to know that I am a half-spirit, and I may return from the land of the dead at will."

Orla toddled over to the tear-streaked pair and squeezed between them. "Hug, Mama," she demanded, forgetting the drama of the night. "Hug."

Chapter 34

Col sat on a bench outside the roundhouse, Talla at his side. They'd spent the morning in the fields, pulling weeds from the barley crop. They had become involved in village life, rather than become aloof leaders and healers.

Gren sat on the grass nearby, Zoola snuggled into him, talking. The times of the solstices were busy for them, now they'd established Classac as a teaching centre once more. With four spirit masters, two messengers and two apprentices, there were plenty of hands at other times. The twins were planning their departure, hoping to head across to the Great Island before the next new moon.

"Happy?" Col asked his mate.

"Yes," she smiled, "This is what we're supposed to be doing, teaching, honouring the ancestors and the spirits, raising our families." Talla turned to Col, pressing her lips to his. "I love you, you know?"

Col grinned. "Yes, I know that. It seems so long ago now. When we left here, in the dead of night. I wondered if we'd even survive. Our journey was the making of us. We have good friends, beautiful children, and the service of the spirits to occupy us now. The thing I value most, though, is you." His hand stroked her face. "I love you, Talla."

A single tear rolled over Talla's cheek as she gazed at her partner. Col brushed it away with his thumb, smiling.

"Mummy! Daddy! Can I take Messenger Albyn to the shore please?" Shilla said, running up to them.

"Does he want to go?" Talla asked.

"Well, no, but I thought I'd ask him," the grinning girl said.

"Messenger Albyn is old, Shilla, you must wait for him to ask you. Do not press him."

The door of the big roundhouse creaked behind her, and Shilla beamed as Albyn shuffled out.

"I might like to go to the shore today," he said, smiling in Talla's general direction. "Maybe Shilla and Jeeha will take me."

Shilla ran to the old man, taking his hand. "Jeeha!" she yelled, "Come on. Messenger Albyn's going to teach us a story at the shore."

"Coming," called Gren and Zoola's middle child. At five summers, the girl had her mother's dark skin, yet her father's features.

"Do you assume that I'll tell you a story?" Albyn asked. "I may like to sleep in the sunshine today."

Shilla's face fell, but she tugged at his hand as Jeeha arrived. "That's all right, Messenger," she said, "We will take you, anyway."

"Well," he said, "While we're there, why don't you tell Jeeha and me the creation story?"

"Can I?" she gasped, "I'm sure I know it properly now. Perhaps Jeeha can tell it too, and you can tell us who's best at it." The excited girl's voice continued as they walked the path towards the water.

"That is a Lore Master in the making," Gren said, smiling at Col and Talla.

Talla grinned, "Hmm, perhaps two."

* * *

Lorev looked around the small roundhouse. There was a spirit messenger from the north of the island visiting, and his apprentice, a lad of ten summers, was bunking with Gart in Lorev's usual sleeping place. He looked at the floor beside the hearth, wondering if he could sleep on the hard surface.

"There's room here," Hessa called, smiling. She'd suggested it many times, but Lorev had never dared to share her bed. Though she was thin, coltish, Lorev thought the girl was the most perfect creature ever created. Far too perfect for him. She was a messenger to his apprentice, a plant master to his plant keeper, sixteen summers to his fifteen, beautiful, to his ordinary.

"Come on, I don't bite, the floor will be hard."

Lorev shrugged and walked to the bed, slipping off his clothes. Hessa threw back the furs, and Lorev averted his eyes from the flash of her perfect body. He blushed.

"Cuddle?" she asked.

"N... no. I'll just... give you space, you're used to your own bed."

"Oh," she said.

Lorev thought she sounded disappointed. He turned his back to her and pulled the furs to his chin. It was a long time before he slept.

* * *

Hessa wakened to the sound of little Orla, singing to herself nearby. She felt the warm body snuggled against her and grinned. Lorev. Her arm encircled his waist, pulling him back against her breasts and belly.

"Hmm?" he mumbled, stirring.

"Good morning, Lorev," she whispered.

"Hessa! I... I didn't... you just..."

"It's all right, Lorev," she said, struggling to keep contact with the agitated teen. "We're just cuddling."

"I'd better get up," he said, pulling himself from her arms, his face glowing red now. "I need to light the fire; feed the little ones."

"Lorev," Hessa said, sitting up in bed. The furs fell to her waist, and Lorev twisted away from the view of her small breasts. "It's mid-summer, I doubt we'll need a fire today. What's wrong?"

"N... nothing. I need to get going," he stuttered, pulling on leggings and a shirt. He stood and headed for the door.

Hessa fell back on the bed, pulling the warm furs over her head. "Why doesn't he even *like* me?" she whispered.

* * *

The summer sun set in the north-west as the four spirit masters made their way up the hill to the Stones of Classac. It was the third night of the full moon and, as the golden orb cleared the horizon, dark clouds crowded the western sky.

The four masters took up their positions around the circle, Col in the south, Gren in the west, Zoola in the north and Talla in the east.

"You're sure of this, Col?" Zoola asked, glancing at the black clouds.

"Yes, the walking spirits told me we could claim our power tonight, in the last light of this full moon. Each of us can command our own element now."

The fat moon heaved itself clear of the undulating hills and drifted south as Talla smiled and raised her arms. She closed her eyes, fingers outstretched as she sought the wind. Her mind linked with the air, moving in from the west. Strengthening gusts blew across the stone circle, dragging the lowering sky above their heads.

"I am the daughter of the winds," Talla called into the rising breeze, "Come to me, spirit of air." The freshening gusts wove in and out of the rough-hewn stones, ruffling the hair of the masters.

Gren stood, legs wide, arms reaching as he called his own element.

"I am the son of the waters, come rain and bless us."

The first drops of the approaching storm splattered onto skin as the young spirit master tilted his head back, welcoming the water of life.

"I am the son of fire," Col shouted, above the wailing of the wind, the hissing of the rain. "Come to me in the lightning, element of fire."

Col stood, body splayed before the storm as, moments later, the jagged fire of the heavens danced around the distant hilltops, blinding the four friends for a moment.

Zoola stood looking, open-mouthed, at her friends. Hers was the element of earth, slow, steady. Powering plants on their daily advancement towards the sun. What could she do to claim her power? She stood, feet wide, arms raised, "I am the daughter of earth," she called. "Come to me, spirit of earth!" She tensed, feet planted, straining her body to draw a sign from the ground beneath her. Nothing happened.

"Concentrate," said Talla, stepping up to her friend. Zoola clenched her fists, braced her sturdy legs, screwed her eyes shut. What was she hoping to do? How could she manifest such power as the others had?

Col came over, leaning in beside her ear, talking over the blustering gale. "Stop trying, Zoola, let go. Let go and just believe."

Zoola relaxed, her eyes opening in the deluge of water. She let go, allowing her body to move in the buffeting winds. She felt the earth beneath her feet and connected like a plant, sending nourishment-seeking roots into the black soil, piercing the dense grey rock.

"I am Zoola!" she shouted, confidence now powering her voice, "And I claim my right to the element of earth!" She dropped her hands to her sides, waiting. For a moment, nothing happened, then they felt it, a rumbling shudder of the land, the hill, the great stones. The earth heard her, shaking itself at her command. Zoola glanced at Col and Talla as Gren ran to her, hugging her.

"We did it," he shouted, rain glistening on his moonlit skin, "We claimed our powers." They formed a circle, clasping hands, dancing in the stinging droplets as the black clouds curtained the moon.

"Let's go home," Col said.

* * *

Arva and Atta hugged each of the protected-of-spirit, then all the children. Their mate, Arrat followed, now considered a member of the extended family.

"You are still going to the northern islands?" Col asked.

"Yes," said Atta, "A traveller came past the circle of Stanna last year who'd been there. He said it was a place of magic and beauty."

"I was there in my youth," said Albyn, "Those I met will have crossed the river by now, but it is a place of wonder."

"Will you return, on your way back?" Talla asked.

"Of course," Arva said. "Where's Lorev?"

Shilla ran to the roundhouse, returning with her big brother by the hand. "We're going, Lorev," said Atta, "We need a hug."

Lorev clasped each of the women to him, then Arrat.

"Travel well," he said as they lifted their packs and headed out of the village.

* * *

The moon was high when the door of the roundhouse creaked open, and a figure stepped out. He pulled a small pack to his shoulder, fastened his cape and walked towards the edge of the village. He almost left his skin when a voice came from the dark.

"What do I tell them, Lorev?" Albyn said. The old man stepped out of the shadows, Shilla clutching his hand. Lorev knew better than to try to fool the elderly messenger.

"Tell them I have to go, so I may become worthy," he said.

"Worthy of what?" Albyn asked.

"Worthy to ask for Hessa's promise of bonding," he said, stepping closer to the old man. He knelt before his small sister, taking her free hand. "I have to go," he said. Shilla nodded. "Look after mother and father; take care of Grev and Isla."

"Will you come back to us, Lorev?" Shilla asked, tears sliding down her cheeks.

"Yes, little one. As soon as I can." Lorev kissed her forehead, then stood to embrace the old man. "They won't understand," Lorev said.

"They may surprise you," Albyn replied. He felt for Lorev's hand and pressed a leather pouch into it. "These are talismans of power, they may be of use to you on your journey." The young apprentice looked askance at the old man then, realising he couldn't see, nodded and walked away into the night.

"The circle turns again," Albyn whispered, as Shilla led him back to his bed.

The end... for now.

Thank you for reading The Apprentice Tattoo. If you enjoyed this novel, please consider leaving a review at the site where you purchased it. As an independent author, I rely on your feedback on sites like Amazon, where your review will increase the visibility of this book.

Coming soon: **Children of the Spirits**: Guardians of the Circles: Book Two.

"Lorev!"

She was here again.

He pulled the warm furs from over his head. The child's dark-rimmed eyes glared. A few rags the only covering on her filthy, emaciated body.

"Why do you torment me, Verra?" he asked.

"Because you lived while I starved. You found parents, became protected-of-spirit, had siblings. I wander the earth, denied a place with my ancestors."

"I cannot help you, sister. I don't know where your bones lie."

Hessa mumbled in her sleep nearby, turning over. Lorev glanced back at her.

"She will never be yours unless you free me," Verra whispered. "Avenge my death, lay my bones to rest, or you will never be worthy of her."

"But..." Lorev began, as the ghost of his sister faded. "Wait, how can I..."

She was gone.

In **Children of the Spirits,** Lorev, haunted by the ghost of his sister, sets out to lay her to rest, but when powerful talismans he has been gifted prove to be stolen, Lorev must return them before Verra can join her ancestors.

Available 2021. Check www.apprenticetattoo.co.uk for more details.

Printed in Great Britain
by Amazon